The
BRIDGE
to
BELLE
ISLAND

The
BRIDGE
to
BELLE
ISLAND

JULIE
KLASSEN

BETHANYHOUSE

a division of Baker Publishing Group
Minneapolis, Minnesota

Published by Bethany House Publishers
11400 Hampshire Avenue South
Bloomington, Minnesota 55438
www.bethanyhouse.com

Bethany House Publishers is a division of
Baker Publishing Group, Grand Rapids, Michigan

Printed in the United States of America

Library of Congress Cataloging-in-Publication Data
Names: Klassen, Julie, author.
Title: The bridge to Belle Island / Julie Klassen.
Description: Minneapolis, Minnesota : Bethany House, a division of Baker Publishing Group, [2019]
Identifiers: LCCN 2019024670 | ISBN 9780764218194 (trade paperback) |
    ISBN 9780764218200 (cloth)) | ISBN 9780764236181 (large print) | ISBN
    9781493420308 (ebook)
Subjects: LCSH: Murder—Investigation—Fiction. | GSAFD: Mystery fiction.
Classification: LCC PS3611.L37 B76 2019 | DDC 813/.6—dc23

Unless otherwise indicated, Scripture quotations are from the King James Version of the Bible.

Scripture quotations labeled NIV are from the Holy Bible, New International Version®. NIV®. Copyright © 1973, 1978, 1984, 2011 by Biblica, Inc.™ Used by permission of Zondervan. All rights reserved worldwide. www.zondervan.com. The "NIV" and "New International Version" are trademarks registered in the United States Patent and Trademark Office by Biblica, Inc.™

Cover design by Jennifer Parker
Cover photography by Mike Habermann Photography, LLC
Map illustration by Bek Cruddace Cartography & Illustration

Author is represented by Books and Such Literary Agency.

19 20 21 22 23 24 25   7 6 5 4 3 2 1

To our sons, Aaron and Matthew.

We love you both so much.
And with deep gratitude to everyone
who has prayed for our family.
We appreciate your prayers more than you know.

All mankind is of one author, and is one volume. . . .
No man is an island, entire of itself.

—Poet John Donne

Let every man praise the bridge that carries him over.

—English Proverb

Therefore let all the faithful pray
to you while you may be found;
surely the rising of the mighty
waters will not reach them.

—Psalm 32:6 NIV

CHAPTER

one

APRIL 1819

Benjamin Booker sat in the Old Bailey, pulse pounding. His most important case to date had finally been called to trial—his chance to prove himself to the firm's partners.

The courtroom was the usual raucous scene: noisy spectators and newsmen in the gallery, milling witnesses awaiting their turn, and wigged barristers goading one another like boxers in the ring.

The grand chambers gleamed with polished, paneled wood, and a crowned cross adorned the wall above the elevated judgment seat, where a white-wigged judge sat resplendent in his robes. To his left, twelve male jurors congregated in their three-tiered box, listening to testimony.

As an attorney, Benjamin's work had all been preparatory and in the background. Now it was up to the barrister he'd retained to argue the case. Sitting off to the side, Benjamin breathed a prayer for success. With a shot of guilt, he realized he'd neglected prayer lately. He'd been so sure Susan Stark was telling the truth that he had wagered his career and reputation on the outcome of this trial.

And it was turning out to be a disaster.

The case was this: William Stark had married Susan Wettenhall, a breathtaking beauty without fortune. And now, having met a rich heiress with five thousand a year, he regretted that decision. Since divorce was nigh unto impossible to obtain, he'd decided to charge his current wife with bigamy in order to free himself, claiming he'd discovered she'd already been married.

But his wife had evidence on her side: letters between her husband and the heiress he wished to marry, witnesses who had seen the two meeting in clandestine fashion, even a newspaper advertisement Mr. Stark had placed, offering a reward for anyone named Jane Wilson—a very common name—who would testify in the case.

Benjamin himself had interviewed the vicar who'd married Mr. and Mrs. Stark the year before. All seemed in order. Even so, he'd had to use all his powers of persuasion to convince a noted barrister to defend the wronged wife in court. Mr. Sullivan had initially resisted, but after Ben assured him they would win, he'd accepted the brief.

Mr. Knowles, for the prosecution, had begun by calling the parish clerk of St. James's, Piccadilly, where Susan's first marriage had allegedly taken place.

The clerk produced a marriage register with an entry for an Enos Redknap and Sukey Hall. The bride's name was similar to Mrs. Stark's maiden name but not the same. The clerk admitted he had no memory of the persons involved, nor could he identify the defendant at the bar.

They had been off to a good start.

But then a second witness, a Mrs. Pruitt, formerly Jane Wilson, had identified the defendant as Sukey Hall, saying she had been present at the wedding.

Prepared for this possibility, Sullivan asked her, "Can anyone prove you are the Jane Wilson who signed the register?"

"My husband and sister could testify to my maiden name, of course." The witness tapped the register before her. "And that is my name in the book. I will swear to my handwriting."

The woman was quite convincing. Benjamin's chest tightened, and he began to feel dizzy. *Keep calm, Booker*, he admonished himself.

Sullivan displayed the advertisement Mr. Stark had placed and asked the witness if she'd received any remuneration for her testimony. She denied it, but Benjamin hoped doubt had been planted in the jurors' minds.

Next, a former lodging-house owner testified, and their case began to fully unravel. She too identified Mrs. Stark as the former Sukey Hall. She had not witnessed the wedding itself but had raised a glass to the couple afterward in her home, where Miss Hall had been lodging at the time.

Benjamin felt Sullivan's shocked and angry gaze on his profile but stared doggedly ahead, stomach churning. Had he misjudged this client? He doubted the partners would excuse such a blunder. Worse, if he lost his position, there would be no end to his father's I-told-you-so's.

From the dock, Mrs. Stark protested, "Are you getting a share of the five thousand as well, madam? You must be!"

"Unfortunately not, my dear," the old woman cheerfully replied. "I haven't a feather to fly with these days."

Sullivan asked the elderly witness a few questions, hoping to find fault with her memory, but the octogenarian was still very keen.

Finally, Mr. Stark himself entered the witness box.

"Look at the young woman at the bar," Knowles directed him. "Did you marry her?"

"Yes, on the sixth of April last."

"Was her first husband living at that time?"

"Yes—and living now. Though I only recently learned of his existence."

"How did you come by this knowledge, when it has so clearly evaded the defense counsel?" Knowles sent a sly look at Sullivan, who in turn glared again at Benjamin.

Mr. Stark explained, "My father was suspicious and engaged a Bow Street man to investigate his new daughter-in-law. It was he who discovered that I had unknowingly been taken in by a woman already married." Mr. Stark colored at the admission. "I was deceived in her."

Susan turned plaintive eyes to the judge. "I never asked Mr. Stark for a farthing, so help me God. And he worried me every day of my life to marry him. He knew what I was. It was no secret to him. And he married me anyway."

There it was. She had all but confessed. Ben felt sick, realizing the woman had lied right to his face, and he'd believed every conniving word.

Mr. Stark looked at her and said coldly, "If you think I would have knowingly entered into a bigamous marriage with a woman of easy virtue, you are grossly mistaken."

Bile rose in Benjamin's throat.

Sullivan made only a perfunctory cross-examination of Mr. Stark and called none of the witnesses they had waiting to testify. Benjamin knew it was over. His heart sank and his career with it. He had been taken in by a beautiful, lying woman just as Mr. Stark had been. He had failed utterly.

In the end, the defendant threw herself on the mercy of the court, and claiming poverty and distress, begged for leniency.

After consulting briefly together, the jury pronounced her guilty. The judge sentenced her to six months' imprisonment in the house of correction and a token fine of one shilling.

Clearly she would not be paying the barrister's fees herself. Having retained Sullivan, the firm would be liable for his fees. Benjamin determined to pay them from his own meager savings.

Sullivan was livid and humiliated at such a resounding defeat. He hissed under his breath that he would tell everyone Benjamin Booker had vouched for the woman's innocence and persuaded him to take the case against his better judgment.

Benjamin could not blame him. He was angry at himself and mortified as well, dreading Mr. Hardy's reaction when he learned of his colossal failure. Everyone would hear of it soon enough, thanks to the buzzing spectators, gloating adversaries, and scribbling newspapermen.

As the defendant was being led away, Benjamin forced himself to face her.

"I am sorry, Mr. Booker," she said. "I never thought they would find Jane—not after she married. And who would have guessed that old woman was still alive? They tore down her lodging house years ago. Well. Thank you for trying."

"I would not have done, had I known you were lying through your teeth."

"Ah . . ." she said sadly. "I miss the admiration I once saw in your eyes." She blinked back unexpected tears. "The truth is, Enos abandoned me six months after we wed to pursue some opera singer, leaving me to shift for myself. I learned too late how dangerous he is, so I changed my name to protect myself. When Mr. Stark began courting me, it seemed like a gift from heaven. I felt I had no choice but to marry again in order to survive."

Is any of it true? Benjamin wondered. He steeled himself

against her ploys—if only he had done so sooner—and walked out of the courtroom, head bowed and face burning. Catcalls followed him as he exited.

Benjamin retreated into the offices of Norris, Hardy, and Hunt. Mr. Hardy was out of the office meeting a client, so Ben would have to wait until that evening to talk to him. He dreaded the conversation to come even as he longed for it, hoping for absolution from his mentor, or at least understanding.

Benjamin tarried until it was almost dark before emerging from the office. The lamplighters had already lit the streetlamps when he crossed Lincoln Inn's Field and then trudged along Coventry Street to the Queen's Head. Mr. Hardy had long preferred this out-of-the-way public house to the much nearer Seven Stars, which was so crowded with members of the legal profession that every conversation was certain to be overheard by rivals.

Removing his hat, Benjamin entered the quiet establishment and surveyed the interior. The dark wood, warm fires, and cozy nooks and crannies usually promised comfort and pleasure. But not this time.

Mr. Hardy had arrived before him and sat smoking a cigar in their customary high-backed inglenook. The senior partner typically drank nothing stronger than the occasional half-pint. Tonight, a glass of whiskey sat before him.

Benjamin understood. He too longed for the relief of strong drink but refrained, knowing how temporary the relief would be and how painful the consequences. "I am sorry, sir. Deeply sorry. I was thoroughly convinced of her innocence."

The older man's thin, handsome face looked suddenly older than his fifty-five years. "I know you were. Staked your name on it . . . and Sullivan's."

Benjamin cringed. "And now I have irrevocably damaged

not only my own professional reputation but that of the entire firm."

Robert Hardy raised a hand. "No need to rehash it all again. Sullivan tracked me down and acquainted me with the particulars. He declares he will represent no more of our clients. And he is one of the best."

Benjamin sat down, enveloped in a haze of tobacco smoke—citrus and spice. "Again, sir, I am sorry. I—"

"Enough apologies," Hardy snapped. "Sorry will not address every problem. Sometimes action must be taken."

The sharp words were like a slap to Ben's face. Instantly, he was a boy again, cowering under his father's stern disapproval. Did Mr. Hardy intend to cut him loose? He could not blame him if he did.

His mentor studied him, and his gaze softened. "Well, I'll not pour more ashes on your head. You have already condemned yourself sufficiently for the both of us. I blame the blasted woman."

Benjamin nodded. "I truly believed her, sir. What an actress she is. And what a fool I am—a stupid, gullible fool."

The older man sighed. "You are not the first man to be taken in by a beautiful woman, nor will you be the last." Hardy swirled his drink. "It's over. You did what you thought had to be done. You risked a great deal to protect someone you esteemed, even if that regard turned out to be falsely placed. It is commendable, in a way. Though there will be a price to pay for it, make no mistake."

Again the senior partner sighed, eyes distant in memory. "What a trying few years this has been. My dear wife passing on. My daughter's disappointing marriage. Norris retiring. Capstone leaving the city to practice in some rustic hamlet of all things. A country solicitor! You won't do the same, I trust?"

"Never, sir. You know I am a Londoner, born and bred."

Hardy nodded. "And now this. . . . It is a blow, I can't deny."

Benjamin ducked his head, shame heating his ears.

Noticing, Hardy leaned across the table and gave Ben's shoulder a comforting squeeze. "Chin up. We'll soldier on somehow."

Hardy sat back and fiddled with his glass. It slipped from his fingers, spilling a few drops. Rarely had Ben seen the man so distracted.

Mr. Hardy glanced at his watch and rose abruptly. "I did not realize it had grown so late." He pulled on a pair of worn, stained gloves little better than Benjamin's own. He supposed that without a wife, the care of a man's garments suffered.

Hardy added, "Cordelia expected me an hour ago."

Benjamin rose as well, swallowed, and asked, "How is your daughter?"

"She is well. Big as a house. Expecting my first grandchild any day."

"Oh . . . Congratulations, sir. You might have said earlier."

"I did not wish to rub salt in the wound."

"Not at all, sir. I am happy for you both."

"Thank you."

Benjamin followed him outside, and they walked around the corner and started down Haymarket Street, the sour-sweet smells of the public house lingering on their clothes.

Knowing footpads often prowled after dark, Benjamin said, "I'll walk you home, sir."

"No need."

Benjamin remained by his side anyway. He had been at this man's side for years, and it seemed only right to walk beside him after such a difficult day.

As they neared St. James's Square, a shout rang out—a night

watchman raising the hue and cry. Following the sound, they turned toward the square.

A female voice wailed a loud lament. Exchanging looks of concern, the lawyers hurried past the statue of William III and across the central garden.

St. James's Square was fashionable and popular with the upper classes and aristocracy. However, the terraced houses on the more modest south side were occupied by artists, statesmen, and professionals.

As they approached these houses, Benjamin saw an elderly night watchman under the portico of number 23, its lamps lit.

Mr. Hardy drew in a jagged breath. "The Wilder residence . . ." He turned to Benjamin, mouth tense. "This is where Percival Norris lives."

Mr. Norris had all but retired from Norris, Hardy, and Hunt to focus his attentions on the Wilder estate, of which he was sole trustee. Benjamin had not seen the man in some time, but his name remained on their office door, stationery, and many old files.

Behind the watchman stood a middle-aged servant, weeping into her handkerchief.

Mr. Hardy addressed the watchman, "I know the gentleman who lives here. What's happened?"

"I'm afraid he's dead, sir."

At that, the servant wailed again.

The silver-headed watchman grimaced and hooked a thumb toward the house. "The parish constable just went in."

Benjamin looked at his mentor, heartsick for the man who had already lost so much. "I am sorry, sir."

The constable came out the front door a short while later. Benjamin recognized young Buxton from a few previous cases.

Noticing them, the constable said, "Oh, evening, Mr. Hardy. Mr. Booker. I suppose you heard. Your Mr. Norris has been killed."

"Killed?" Mr. Hardy echoed. "Heaven forbid. How? Are you certain?"

The constable nodded. "Looks that way. An intruder, I'm thinkin'. I'm off to notify Bow Street and the coroner."

Grim-faced, Hardy asked, "May I go in? He was an old friend of mine."

Constable Buxton hesitated, then shrugged. "Don't see why not. You lawyers know not to disturb anything. There's bound to be a coroner's inquest on this one." Instructing the night watchman to stand guard, he strode away to alert the appropriate authorities.

Benjamin offered, "I'll go in with you."

Hardy hesitated. "Thank you, Ben. But you go on home. You've had enough crises for one day."

"No, sir. It's the least I can do. You shouldn't be alone."

When the older man protested no further, Benjamin started up the steps, eyeing the door latch. "No sign of a break-in here. Is there a back door?"

"That's right," the watchman replied. "Unlocked and open when I arrived."

The servant wiped her nose. "I am the housekeeper here. I'll show you the way." She led them through the house to the garden door at the rear. Benjamin walked beside Hardy, the older man's face set in determined lines. How horrible to know you were about to see the body of a friend, especially one who'd apparently met with a violent end. Benjamin's throat tightened at the thought. He reminded himself that he had seen death before and was more accustomed to hearing details of people's demises than he would like.

At the rear door, they again looked for signs of damage but saw none.

"We don't always lock this door," the housekeeper apologized.

"Any windows broken?"

"Not that I've noticed." She pointed along the passage. "First door on the right. He'd taken over the morning room as his office." She, however, went no closer, quickly retreating the way they had come.

The door indicated was closed. Seeing Hardy hesitate, Benjamin reached over and pushed it open for him.

Inside, a lamp burned on a tall cabinet, illuminating the room. A grey-haired man lay facedown on the desk, one cheek pressed to its surface, hair over his brow, his exposed eye staring unseeing. His right arm lay outstretched across the desk, a pistol clutched in hand. The left hand lay fisted on the other side.

Mr. Hardy's gaze landed on the weapon. "I did not know he even owned a gun."

Benjamin looked from his stunned companion to the body once more. He remembered Percival Norris as stout and confident, full of swagger. All gone. Now only a pale shell of the man remained.

Benjamin surveyed the scene. "Easy to see why the constable believes he was killed by an intruder. Desk drawer open. Gun in hand. Perhaps he heard or saw a stranger and reached for his gun. Before he could shoot, the blackguard killed him."

Hardy looked around, face creased in disbelief. "How? With what?"

"I don't know." Benjamin saw no likely weapon either, except perhaps an empty decanter on the desk. Nor did he see blood or an obvious wound on the deceased.

Then he noticed a drinking glass lay shattered on the floor

across the room, a streak glistening down the wall. A glass thrown in anger, or self-defense?

The young constable returned, announcing, "The coroner should be here any minute." He stood near the door as sentry, rocking back and forth on his heels while he waited.

A few minutes later, a tall, dark-haired man of five and thirty entered, drawing up short to discover people in the room. Or at least, two particular people. He was young to have been appointed coroner to fill a Westminster vacancy. But he always had been ambitious.

The coroner frowned. "What are you doing in here? Is this a crime scene or a social club?"

Flinching, the constable said, "Sorry, sir. I know these two. Lawyers. Friends of the deceased."

The coroner's frown deepened into a scowl. "I know them as well, but that does not mean I would have let them in here."

"Sorry, sir. Won't happen again."

Benjamin greeted the man without warmth. "Evening, Reuben."

"Benjamin." The coroner dipped his chin, pinning him with a scathing look. "Don't you have more important things to do, especially now?"

Had word traveled so fast? Benjamin lifted his chin. "More important than a man's death?"

"That's my responsibility. Not yours."

"Better get to it, then."

Reuben humphed. He surveyed the room, the body of the deceased, and the gun.

Benjamin pointed out the broken glass.

Reuben turned to Mr. Hardy. "Was it Mr. Norris's habit to throw glasses against the wall?"

"No," Hardy replied. "Only to empty them, often and quickly."

"Meaning he was a heavy drinker?"

Hardy winced. "I'm afraid so. In fact, when I heard he died, my first thought was that he'd finally drunk himself to death." Mr. Hardy looked down as if embarrassed for his old friend.

This was news to Benjamin. Mr. Hardy had said nothing to him about Mr. Norris's drinking, probably hoping to protect the man's reputation.

Reuben nodded. "The empty decanter corroborates that." He pulled off the blue glass stopper and took a whiff. "Gin."

Then he extracted a narrow instrument from his inner pocket and pushed the hair off the deceased's temple, revealing a small gash, the blood congealed. Benjamin flinched in sympathy.

The coroner bent and studied the wound. "A minor contusion. He's been struck by something."

Mr. Hardy's eyes widened in shock. "Thunder and turf."

Benjamin murmured, "Perhaps when he fell to the desk?"

"I don't think so." Then Reuben leaned near the dead man's mouth and sniffed. "Not gin. Perhaps . . . oranges?"

Benjamin stepped to the wall, ran a finger through the sticky substance trailing down it, and sniffed. Amid the room's smells of leather, polish, and tobacco, he smelled oranges, both sour and sweet at once. "Orange wine, I believe."

Benjamin had been gifted with a keen sense of smell. A blessing or a curse, depending on his surroundings. He looked around the room again but saw no wine bottle or second decanter.

He moved nearer to the desk and studied Mr. Norris's face, several details catching his attention. Hearing his father's somber voice in his mind, he pointed them out. "See the spittle there? The foam? And how he's fisted his hand as though in pain? Might that suggest poisoning?"

Reuben frowned down at the body for a moment, then turned

to Benjamin. "Are you the coroner or am I? Always said you ought to go into medicine instead of the law. But you would not listen, so I will thank you to keep your uneducated opinions to yourself. The only poison I see is this." Reuben tapped the empty decanter again.

Then the arrogant man straightened and squared his shoulders. "Of course I shall do a thorough examination during the formal inquest. But for the present, I've seen enough to know we are not dealing with accidental death or natural causes." He nodded to the constable. "Summon a coroner's jury."

Reuben returned his annoyed gaze to Benjamin. "Now, if you and your *esteemed* Mr. Hardy would step out of the room . . . ?"

When they hesitated, the coroner raised his arms, shooing them out like an angry goose flapping its wings. "Out with you. No one must disturb the body until the inquest takes place."

As they stepped through the door, Mr. Hardy muttered under his breath, "I see your brother is as charming as ever."

"Yes," Benjamin agreed.

They followed the constable into a nearby parlour to await the Bow Street runner.

two

The officer from Bow Street arrived. With so many crimes in London and not enough runners to go around, not every death warranted an investigating officer, and many crimes went unanswered for—unless a victim or interested party hired a runner at their own expense. But Percival Norris was connected to both a wealthy family and a well-known law firm, so a magistrate had quickly assigned a man to the case.

The officer first spent time behind closed doors with the coroner and the deceased, then joined those waiting in the parlour.

"Officer Riley of Bow Street," Constable Buxton announced and gave the names of the assembled servants: Mrs. Kittleson, the housekeeper; Marvin, the manservant; and Mary Williams, the housemaid. He did not introduce Benjamin or Mr. Hardy.

Ben took the opportunity to study the officer, not having made his acquaintance before. He was in his midthirties with brown hair, ghostly white skin, prominent ears, and a long neck. Bow Street runners were reputedly skilled, well-trained, and cunning, but this small man did not seem to fit the image and, in fact, reminded him of a weasel.

Apparently noticing the constable's omission, the officer turned to Mr. Hardy and Benjamin and asked in a working-class accent, "And who are you gents?"

Hardy answered for them both. "Robert Hardy and Benjamin Booker, of Norris, Hardy, and Hunt."

The officer's eyebrows rose, and he barely concealed a smirk. "Ah . . . the bamboozled Booker, the benish Ben? I heard about you."

Benjamin clenched his jaw. Embarrassment heated his neck to be called such names in front of his superior, as well as several strangers. Though *benish* was slang for *foolish*, Ben had never had reason to dislike his given name. Until now.

The officer's hooded eyes twinkled. "The comely defendant threw dust in your eyes, did she?" He chuckled. "Told you a plumper, I'll wager, and you swallowed her faradiddles whole."

Benjamin fisted his hand. He felt Mr. Hardy's warning touch on his arm as he gently reminded the Bow Street runner, "A man has been killed, Officer Riley."

"Right. Just so." The officer turned a page in his small notebook, shaking his head, a smile still playing about his mouth. Then he sobered and asked, "And what brought you two here tonight?"

Benjamin explained, "We met at the Queen's Head, as we often do, and were walking home together when we heard the night watchman shout. So we hurried over to see if we might help."

The officer's thin lips quirked. "How civil of you. How selfless. No hope of sniffing out a wealthy new client or lucrative lawsuit?"

"None at all."

"Do you know the victim?"

Hardy nodded. "Percival Norris was a founding member of our law firm. He has mostly retired over the last few years, as his duties to the Wilder estate consumed too much of his time."

The housemaid rolled her eyes at this, but no one besides Benjamin seemed to notice.

Officer Riley turned to the trio of servants clustered near the hearth—the teary housekeeper, stoic elderly manservant, and sharp-faced housemaid.

He started with the housekeeper, who had discovered the body.

"Did you get on with your master?"

"He weren't my master—not really. Miss Rose Lawrence is my mistress now, and before her, her grandfather, Mr. Wilder. God rest his soul. Mr. Norris was only here as trustee and as Miss Rose's guardian."

"You didn't like him, I gather?"

"I did not." Mrs. Kittleson glanced at the manservant. "I think only Marvin liked him."

The elderly man answered in a raspy voice, "I liked him well enough. Shared a glass with me from time to time and paid my wages. Not my place to say anything against him."

The officer turned to the young housemaid, brows expectantly high and notebook open.

She supplied, "I have only been here about a year. I just do my work and keep my head down."

The manservant grunted. "Keep your ear to the door, more like."

The officer ignored this and asked, "No sign of forced entry—is that right?"

"That's right," the housekeeper replied. "I'm afraid we left the back door unlocked. It opens into the garden, you see, not onto a public street. We've done the same for years. I never thought—" Again tears filled her eyes, and she pressed a handkerchief to each in turn.

"Did you hear or see anyone enter?"

She shook her head. "You'll have to ask Mary. Marvin and I were not here. We left around four o'clock for a party at the Adairs', just up York Street. Mr. Norris gave us leave to go— the one kind gesture he ever made. Our own Miss Rose were celebrating her engagement, you see."

Incredulity twisted the officer's mouth. "You and Marvin were invited to a party in *this* neighborhood?"

"Not as guests. But I am acquainted with the cook there and offered to help her. She was thankful and invited us to join them belowstairs for a bit of supper. Even cake and champagne. We peeked in at the door and saw our girl in all her finery. She never looked prettier. And so like her departed mother, God rest her soul." Again the woman dabbed her eyes.

"I take it Miss Lawrence has yet to return?"

"That's right."

"Then I'll question her later."

The officer turned to the housemaid. "But first—were you here all evening, miss?"

"No."

"Where were you?"

The girl shrugged. "Out with my beau, if you must know. The old man gave us the evening off. I weren't about to waste it slavin' for some toffs."

The housekeeper frowned. "Mind your tongue, Mary. That's no way to speak of your betters."

"No better'n me. And in the old man's case, worse. He got what was coming to him, I say."

"What do you mean by that?" Riley asked.

Again the disrespectful shrug. "Only that it couldn't have happened to a more deservin' chap."

The young constable spoke up. "A thief, I'd say, taking advantage of the unlocked door. All was quiet so he slipped into the house, thinking to help himself to a few valuables, only to startle Mr. Norris into grabbing his gun. Several robberies in the area lately."

Riley considered, then asked, "Is anything missing from his office?"

The housekeeper shook her head. "Not that I noticed. Though I wouldn't know about his papers and such."

"And elsewhere in the house?"

"A few pieces of silver seem to be missing—a pitcher and two candelabras that I've discovered so far. I shall have to recount the inventories."

"Yes, please do," Riley said. "There is a broken glass on the office floor. Has Mr. Norris thrown glasses in the past? Perhaps when . . . foxed?"

"No, sir," Mrs. Kittleson replied.

The housemaid added, "Though he shouts and rails at us when he's vexed, sober or not. And now you mention it, I did hear a glass shatter on my way out, but I didn't wait around to be told to clean it up. I was dressed for a night on the town, and my beau was waitin'."

"I see. I will need the gentleman's name to verify your whereabouts."

Mary snorted. "Gentleman. Ha. That's a good one. I'll tell him you said so. What a laugh."

The officer frowned at that and wrote the man's name and direction in his notebook.

Benjamin spoke up. "I noticed the decanter on his desk was empty."

"We were out of Hollands," the manservant explained. "I had not yet, uh, bought more."

"The coroner smelled oranges on the deceased's person," Benjamin continued.

The housekeeper's face puckered in confusion. "I served him no oranges."

"No . . . orange wine?"

Marvin seemed to hesitate. "Well, there was wine in—"

"He preferred gin," the housekeeper cut in. "Though in a pinch, he might drink most anything. Is that not right, Marvin?"

Holding her gaze a moment, Marvin slowly nodded. "That's right." Again the old man hesitated. "Is there a . . . wine bottle in the room?"

"No."

"Ah. Well then . . ." He shrugged bony shoulders. "I must be mistaken."

Mistaken about what? Benjamin wondered, but the officer scribbled something in his notebook and moved on to another topic.

"An obvious question is who will benefit from Mr. Norris's death. Who is his heir?"

When the servants exchanged befuddled looks, Mr. Hardy said, "I believe Miss Lawrence's maiden aunt, Isabelle Wilder, was originally listed as heir, being his closest relative. Although Percival may have changed his will through a different attorney. I could look through his papers for you, if you like . . . ?"

The officer replied coolly, "I will search them myself, thank you."

Hardy said, "I understand. But you did ask."

Officer Riley scratched his ear, frowning with uncertainty. "They would probably be so much legal nonsense to me. I suppose it will do no harm—*after* the coroner is through in there. But you must let me know if you find anything related to his death."

"Of course. That is the point, after all."

The officer looked up, pencil poised. "And where is this Isabelle Wilder now?"

Mrs. Kittleson replied, "Belle Island. The Wilder family's country estate in Berkshire."

"Has she been here recently?"

"Bless me, no!" the housekeeper exclaimed. "Miss Isabelle hasn't come up to London in years. What a notion!"

The officer turned back to Mr. Hardy. "Any reason to suspect this Miss Wilder beyond the inheritance?"

Before Hardy could answer, the parlour door burst open, and a young woman in a formal evening gown swept into the room, pale silk swirling around her ankles, light brown hair arranged high atop her head. Startled to find a crowd inside, she took a step backward, colliding with the young man behind her. He reached out both hands to steady her, his concerned gaze lingering on her profile before sweeping over the rest of the room. After him, an older woman in black entered. Miss Lawrence's maid or governess, Benjamin guessed.

"What is going on here?" the gentleman asked. Dressed in dark evening attire, he was slight and freckled and nearly as pretty as his companion.

Ignoring him, Officer Riley asked, "Miss Lawrence?"

"Yes," the young woman replied. "And this is my intended, Mr. Adair. And Miss O'Toole." Noticing the senior partner, she said, "Oh, good evening, Mr. Hardy. I did not see you there. Come to visit Uncle Percy?"

"Not this time." He paused and added gently, "I am afraid he is dead, my dear."

Her gloved hand flew to her mouth. "Oh no. In his sleep?"

Hardy shook his head. "In his office."

The officer added, "He's been killed. By an intruder, perhaps."

"Killed?" Her dark eyes widened.

"While we were at the party," Mr. Adair said. "How tragic."

Tears filled the young woman's eyes. "Uncle Percy ought to have come with us. I told him he ought to come." Miss Lawrence shook her head. "To be attacked here in our own home. Did someone . . . shoot him or . . . ?"

"Bludgeoned," the officer replied.

Miss Lawrence winced, then asked, "Was he . . . inebriated?"

"We're not sure. Why?"

"I suppose I am hoping he died unaware. Without pain."

Mr. Adair said coolly, "In Mr. Norris's case, I think drunkenness is a fairly safe assumption."

The officer said, "The coroner smelled no gin on the man. Only oranges, though the housekeeper maintains she served him none of those."

Rose glanced over her shoulder at the young man. A look passed between them. She opened her mouth to speak, but he grasped her arm, forestalling her.

Scribbling in his notebook, the officer did not notice, but Benjamin and Mr. Hardy certainly did and shared a significant look of their own.

"Now, think back," the officer said. "Did any of you hear or see anything that might be helpful?"

The housemaid stepped forward. "I did hear him arguin' with some fellow before I left the house, but I didn't stand at the door and listen, contrary to what some might think of me." She jerked a thumb toward the manservant.

"Was this before or after you heard a glass shatter?"

"Just before."

"Do you know who he was arguing with?"

The maid's gaze darted across the room, then back again. "I . . . No, sir. I never heard him mention a name."

Had she glanced at Mr. Adair, or had Benjamin imagined it?

Unaware, the officer turned next to the dignified older woman in immaculate black. "Are you a maid here as well?"

The woman stiffened. "I am Miss Lawrence's former governess and present companion and chaperone."

"Ah. And had you anything against Percival Norris?"

"I did not like the way he treated my young mistress. But beyond that, no."

Officer Riley looked from person to person. "Do you know anyone who had reason to hurt Mr. Norris? To want to see him dead?"

Around the room, furtive looks were exchanged. Finally, Miss Lawrence spoke up. "Only me, I suppose."

"Rose . . ." Mr. Adair cautioned under his breath.

"Why not? The servants will tell all anyway. I'd rather he hear it from me."

She turned back to Officer Riley. "I was angry with him. That is no secret. He put obstacle after obstacle in my path. He didn't want me to accept Mr. Adair, limited my allowance, and demanded an unreasonable marriage settlement. So yes, I admit I had reason, but I did not hurt him. I could not have, even had I wanted to. I have been at the Adairs' since midafternoon. We have only just arrived home after the party."

Her matronly companion nodded. "It is true. I was there with her all the while."

"As was I," Mr. Adair added his assurance.

Miss O'Toole shot him a scandalized look. "Not *with* her, Mr. Adair. Take care. You give the men the wrong idea."

"Of course not *with her* while she dressed for the evening, but in the house, yes. I spent the time with my father and a nice bottle of Bordeaux, listening to his advice for a long and successful marriage." His fond gaze rested on Miss Lawrence, and he took her hand.

The officer asked, "Then, can you think of anyone else who held a grudge against Mr. Norris?"

"Goodness," Miss Lawrence replied, "I don't think many people liked him. Pray forgive me, Mr. Hardy. I know he was your friend and law partner. But I can't think of anyone who'd actually harm him either. Except . . ."

"Except?"

Her brow furrowed. "A man of business came here recently. The door was closed, so I didn't see him, but I heard him. He was clearly angry and raised his voice."

"What was he angry about?"

"He wanted Uncle Percy to invest in some scheme or other. I only listened at all because he mentioned Belle Island."

"Do you know this man's name?"

"I don't."

"Did your uncle keep an appointment diary?"

"Not that I know of."

"I will search his desk just the same." Officer Riley made a note, then asked the servants, "One of you must have seen this man entering. Can any of you give me his name or description?"

The housekeeper, maid, and manservant shook their heads.

"Or the name of anyone else with something against Percival Norris?"

Around the room, heads shook once more. Only Mr. Hardy remained still, eyes alight, Benjamin saw, with an idea, or a suspicion.

He said, "I hate to speak ill of someone not present to defend herself. But Percival traveled to Belle Island recently, and he and Miss Wilder argued. He mentioned it to me with some concern."

The officer turned expectantly to Miss Lawrence.

The young woman shrugged. "It's possible. They sometimes sparred over management of the estate. But Aunt Belle hasn't come to London in years and would not hurt a soul."

"It's true, sir," the housekeeper agreed.

Officer Riley considered. "Well, I'll make a note of it. Although I shall start searching for a more likely local offender first."

The officer looked through his notes and seemed satisfied. "I think Constable Buxton has it right. A thief sneaked through the unlocked garden door, lifted a few pieces of silver, then entered the office, where he was surprised to find Mr. Norris. Norris reached for a pistol he kept in his top drawer, but before he could shoot, the intruder struck him with a hard object, perhaps one of the silver pieces in his possession."

Officer Riley snapped shut his notebook. "I will see if the missing silver turns up at any nearby pawn sellers. Could be we'll find our thief and killer that way. For now, you are all free to leave. Though I reserve the right to call on you if further questions arise. Understood?"

Around the room heads solemnly nodded, and the servants filed out.

Miss Lawrence bestowed a charming smile on the officer. "Actually . . . we are planning to travel tomorrow into Berkshire, near Maidenhead."

"Leaving town? Why?"

"My aunt was not able to join us for our engagement party here, so we are going to her. I hope we shan't need to delay our trip." She fluttered her lashes at the officer and asked tentatively, "May we please travel to Belle Island tomorrow?"

The officer hesitated, his gaze lingering on the pretty young face. "I don't see why not. Berkshire is not so far away, should I need to contact you again."

"Excellent." Rose Lawrence beamed. "My aunt would worry were we delayed."

He returned her smile, bowed, and walked from the room.

Benjamin followed the officer into the corridor. "One flaw in your theory, Officer Riley. I noted signs of poisoning, but a thief would not bother with poison."

The officer turned back. "*If* the coroner's inquest concludes the use of poison, of course I will pursue that then."

As they walked down the back passage toward the scene of the crime, Benjamin saw something small and shiny on the carpet and squatted down to study it more closely. A garnet earring, the blood-red gem set amid small leaves of gold. Probably of no significance, but he pointed it out anyway.

"Mislaid by Miss Lawrence, I'll be bound." The officer bent to retrieve it. "But I will show it to the coroner, just in case." He gingerly opened the office door, and Benjamin heard his brother's low voice pontificating within.

As he slipped into the room, Riley turned back and whispered, "Now, good night"—he winked—"benish Ben."

Summarily dismissed, Benjamin hesitated near the garden door, vacillating about what to do. Mr. Hardy joined him there, and they watched as the servants disappeared in various directions, assumedly returning to their duties or going to bed for the night.

Mr. Adair led Miss Lawrence into the corridor and said gently, "You had better stay with us tonight, Rose. It may not be safe here."

Miss Lawrence managed a wobbly smile. "Thank you."

Her companion nodded her agreement and started up the

servants' stairs. "Give me five minutes to collect a few things for Miss Rose."

With her chaperone out of sight, the young man stole a kiss.

Benjamin averted his gaze and shifted foot to foot, feeling restless to be standing there doing nothing. "Shall we search the house? Take another look in the office?" He gestured toward the closed door.

Mr. Hardy held up his hand. "Your brother would resent our interference. Perhaps even lodge a complaint."

"True." Ben sighed. "But there must be something we can do. I am not convinced some unknown assailant is to blame."

His mentor studied him, then ran a hand over his weary face. "You are not satisfied with that theory, and neither am I. You and I both know Bow Street officers rarely have time to be as diligent in tracking down offenders as we would like. Especially if doing so would require them to leave the familiar comforts of London to search farther afield."

"What are you suggesting?"

"That there will be no justice for my friend if we don't do something. Did you notice the look that passed between Miss Lawrence and Adair? There is more going on here than they let on."

"I did notice."

"And now Riley has approved their request to leave town, to visit her aunt, Isabelle Wilder. Perhaps even to . . . warn her."

"Warn her?"

Hardy nodded grimly. "She not only argued with Percy when he was last there, but she also sent him an angry letter afterward."

Benjamin felt his brows rise. "Should we not have told the officer?"

The older man grimaced, the expression emphasizing his

thin lips and long, narrow nose. "Perhaps I should have done. But you saw how little interested Riley was in hearing about Miss Wilder."

"The letter would provide physical evidence of her resentment."

"If we had it."

"Where is it?" Benjamin again gestured to the closed door. "If it's in his office, then—"

Hardy shook his head. "It's been destroyed. He read parts aloud to me, then in his anger wadded it up and tossed it onto the fire."

Benjamin huffed. "Why? What did she write?"

"She disputed his management of their affairs and threatened to have him removed as trustee. Nothing illegal, but that sort of family drama becoming public would be irresistible to journalists, and I don't know that our firm can weather another scandal at present."

Benjamin's stomach knotted. "Because of my recent very public failure."

Hardy's expression gentled. "I would not put it that way, my boy. Nor would I raise the sore subject again if circumstances had not compelled me. But I cannot deny our reputation has suffered. We will recover, but the timing of another scandal coming to light now could not be worse. Percival's death will be bad enough. If my suspicions about Miss Wilder turn out to be baseless, we would have given the newspapers more fodder for nothing."

Hardy paused, then added with resolve, "If we find corroborating evidence to suggest she had a hand in Percival's death, then of course I would not hesitate to mention the letter, but as it is, I don't believe it worth the risk. Unless you think we should?"

Benjamin considered, then shook his head. "Without supporting evidence, it would do us no good. It would be your word against Miss Wilder's."

"True." Hardy's expression brightened, and he raised an *aha* finger. "Except . . . she does not know Percy destroyed it. As far as she knows, the letter is here among his many papers."

"Ah." Benjamin nodded, grasping the significance. "And believing we have the letter, she will not deny writing it and will perhaps admit to more as well."

Hardy nodded, eyes narrowed in thought. "Here's what I want you to do. Go to Belle Island, and quickly. Introduce yourself as a member of her uncle's firm. She won't suspect why you are really there. Leave as soon as possible, so you arrive before the niece can give her any warning."

"Wait, you want *me* to go?"

"Yes, Ben. I know you are not fond of travel, but it would be a great personal favor to me and to the firm. I can't get away at present, not with the Monkford case pending and Cordelia expecting any day. And you must admit, it might be a relief to be out of town until the scandal and jests die down."

"True."

"It isn't far. You can go by stage as far as Maidenhead and hire a hack from there."

"Just show up on her doorstep? You know I have no reason to be poking about, asking questions."

"Of course you do. It's only professional courtesy that someone from our firm should deliver the sad news of his death in person and see if she requires any help with arrangements."

Hardy warmed to the idea. "Besides, are you not the perfect person to go? You saw Officer Riley. Miss Lawrence has only to bat her lashes and he believes her every word and bows to her every wish. But you have learned a timely lesson. You are not apt to be taken in by a guilty female again, are you?"

Benjamin hesitated, clenching his hands behind his back to hide their tremble. Dread and rising duty warred within him.

When he said nothing, Robert Hardy leaned near, pale eyes downturned, expression beseeching. When had so much silver invaded the man's sandy side-whiskers?

"Will you do this for me, Ben? Percival was not a perfect man, I know, but he was my oldest friend."

Benjamin thought of all the ways Mr. Hardy had helped him over the years, taking him on as an articled clerk when he was an inexperienced youth, teaching him and encouraging him. The older man had responded with resilient patience when his young protégé made mistakes and with warm praise when he succeeded. What balm and motivation both had been, when Benjamin had known only distance and cool disapproval from his own father.

Would he suffer the discomforts of travel, leave the familiarity of London where he'd lived all his one and thirty years, to help this man who had done so much for him? And in the bargain, maybe even bring a murderer to justice?

Yes, he would.

CHAPTER
three

Isabelle Wilder vaguely realized she was dreaming, but it seemed so real. In the dream, she was dressed in a flowing gown of red silk—the very gown Carlota wore when she performed at the Theatre Royal. Wearing it, Isabelle felt beautiful as she floated down the stairs of their London townhouse, eager to join the party.

Evan Curtis stood at the bottom of the stairs, waiting for her, so dashing in his infantry uniform. He smiled up at her, blue eyes simmering with passion. Her heart raced. Uncle Percival must have changed his mind and invited him after all.

In her hurry to descend, Isabelle tripped on the long gown and felt herself fly through the air. Slowly, weightlessly, she fell, her skirts a billowing curtain carried aloft by the breeze.

Evan stretched out his hands, and she settled into his arms like a bird coming home to its nest. She wrapped one hand around his neck and rested the other on the lapel of his uniform. She tried to feel his heartbeat but felt . . . nothing. For a moment, he cradled her close, and they gazed into one another's eyes.

Then, abruptly, he dropped her.

She landed hard on the stairs, the bottom step digging into her tailbone, her elbow smacking against the newel-post.

She yelped in pain, but no one came running to see what the matter was. She looked down the empty passage, confused by its silence. The guests should have been there by now.

Where were Rose and the servants? And Uncle Percival?

Percival. Isabelle wrinkled her nose. She doubted he would be mingling cheerfully among the guests. No, more likely he'd be sulking in his office, grumbling over the bills.

Isabelle pulled herself up to her hands and knees and crawled the few feet to his office. Uncle Percy had taken over the morning room near the back door, where he could meet with tradesmen without their having to traipse through the whole house. Finding the door unlatched, she pushed it open, and an empty wine bottle on the floor went rolling away. Rising up on her knees, she looked inside the room . . . and drew in a sharp breath.

Uncle Percy sat slumped forward, head on the desk, arms sprawled across its surface, a pistol in hand, one eye open and unseeing, blood at his temple.

Isabelle blinked and blinked again, trying to clear the gruesome image, but it stubbornly remained, like a stain. A bloodstain.

Overwhelmed, her vision tunneled to blackness, and she crumpled to the floor.

Isabelle awoke with an ice pick in the back of her skull. At least that was how it felt. She suppressed a groan, relieved to awaken and realize it had only been a dream, although the headache was real enough. *Only a dream*, she reassured herself again, yet the foul image clung to her and made her queasy.

She was not in London, of course, but in her own bed on

Belle Island, miles from the London townhouse, which she had not visited in years. What a dream, so vivid and strange. How odd that she'd been wearing Carlota's red gown. And she had not seen Evan Curtis in nearly a decade.

Isabelle opened her eyes, but harsh shafts of daylight assaulted her, and she squeezed them shut again, the suppressed groan now escaping.

"Miss?" Carlota asked, and in her mild Spanish accent, the word sounded like *mees*. "Are you awake?"

"Mm-hmm," Isabelle murmured.

"Doctor came by."

"So early?"

"Actually . . . it has just gone one."

Isabelle's eyes jolted wide. "In the afternoon?"

Carlota chuckled. "Yes."

Isabelle tossed back her bedclothes. "Oh no. I wanted to be in the workshop this morning. The master weaver is due today."

"I did try to wake you earlier, but you shooed me away. Don't worry, I talked to Mr. Linton for you."

Isabelle rose stiffly from bed, thinking of their dour though capable foreman. "What did you tell him?"

"I told him you were indisposed and asked him to greet the master weaver in your stead when he arrives. Apparently, his coach is running late. Mr. Linton grumbled something about *women's troubles*, which I did not confirm or deny. Mrs. Philpotts and I served the midday meal, and the weavers are eating while they wait."

"Thank you, Lotty. You are a treasure." In most houses, lady's maids were called by their surnames, but Carlota Medina was not most maids.

Lotty added, "The doctor went to see Abel and the Howtons and will come back later."

"Good." Rubbing her elbow, Isabelle hurried to her dressing chest. She slipped into a fresh shift, while Carlota brought over a pair of stays and stockings.

"I feel terrible not being there on such an important day. Especially when the weavers have given up part of their day off to meet him."

"Don't punish yourself so," Carlota said as she laced the stays. "You had a late night. And a rough one in the bargain."

Isabelle pressed her throbbing temples. "Don't remind me."

Last night . . . the evening of her dear niece's betrothal dinner, and Isabelle had not been there. She had foolishly attempted to drown her sorrows and today was paying the price.

As Carlota helped her dress, a cherished memory returned to Isabelle. Of crossing the island bridge with her parents to attend her sister's wedding in the village church, surrounded by friends and neighbors. After the service, they had all walked home together for the wedding breakfast, happy and laughing and simply relishing one another's company. Oh, what she would give to relive that memory, to see Rose married in the village church among their friends and neighbors and then welcome them all back to Belle Island for a joy-filled wedding breakfast.

But that dream, Isabelle feared, was forever out of reach.

-◈ CHAPTER ◈-
four

That afternoon, Benjamin found himself bounced, jostled, and thoroughly shaken on the *Emerald*, a day coach traveling westward from London. The journey into Berkshire was only some thirty miles, but it felt interminable. Ben worried he would become ill or, heaven forbid, have one of his . . . episodes.

Across from him in the coach sat a stoic old cleric and a severe-looking woman in black. And beside him, a young gentleman with a countenance almost as green as his natty frockcoat confessed deep regret about an overindulgence of port the night before. Suddenly, the gentleman's cheeks bulged and he retched, not quite making it out the window. The sound and smell nearly overcame Benjamin's restraint.

Embarrassed, the young man apologized to the other passengers. Benjamin opened the window on his side—just in case—then handed the gentleman his handkerchief with an empathetic grin.

Ben closed his eyes, drawing deep breaths of fresh air, trying to stave off his own nausea. Again and again, he inhaled deeply and exhaled with a long "Hooo." The spell began to pass.

He hoped the worst was over, for he wanted to perform this assignment well and make Mr. Hardy proud. To do so, he needed to arrive on Belle Island looking the picture of a competent, composed lawyer.

If he concentrated, he could still feel Mr. Hardy's comforting hand resting upon his shoulder after his failure. It was the closest thing to fatherly affection Benjamin had experienced in years. He supposed he should have been the one offering comfort, since Robert Hardy had lost not only a partner in the law firm but also an old friend.

You can do this, Benjamin admonished himself. *For his sake, you must.*

The road the *Emerald* traveled paralleled the River Thames for a time. Ben stared out at the sun-dappled water, noting the boats and occasional fishermen, and his mind traveled back to a few summers from his childhood when his father had actually closed his practice for several days and taken them to a fishing lodge. Benjamin and his brother had spent many sanguine hours along the picturesque shore, racing rowboats, learning to fish, and gathering firewood while his surgeon-father expertly filleted their catches and Mamma cooked them, all of them talking and laughing together as a family. A happy family. How long ago it seemed.

Finally reaching Maidenhead's Bear Inn, Benjamin hired a driver—a young man with a small gig pulled by a single horse—to take him the rest of the way. The rickety vehicle listed to one side and possessed not a single spring or ounce of comfort.

After fifteen bone-jarring minutes, they reached the outskirts of Riverton. The little hamlet curved around the riverbank, its church, homes, and shops situated on a low rise and, at present, enveloped in fog.

The driver pointed to a wooden bridge spanning the river, just wide enough to allow a carriage to pass.

"That takes you to the island, sir," the young man said. "The Wilders have lived there for ages. You'll see the house better once the fog burns off. All right if I set you down here?"

"Hm? Yes, all right." Benjamin paid the man, climbed down on rubbery legs, and turned to study the scene. He faintly heard the driver's "Walk on," and the gig continue on its way, but his gaze remained fixed on the opposite shore.

Through the filmy grey fog, he made out a tall stone manor house shrouded in climbing vines and mist. Nearer shore, trees overhung the river—prickly junipers and chestnuts, weeping willows and elms, their hoary heads bowed in grief, their arms reaching out, pushing him back. Warning him away.

Benjamin frowned. What a foolish notion. The journey had clearly addled his brains.

As he stood staring across the bridge, it seemed to undulate, the rails to compress to a narrow tunnel and then widen again. He grasped a post for support. *Good heavens.* No wonder he rarely traveled.

Movement caught his eye. Across the bridge, a figure appeared through the mist—a woman in a long red coat, her deep bonnet concealing her face. She stood out against the grey background like a rosefinch in winter.

Benjamin blinked and looked again, and the woman was gone. Disappeared into the fog . . . or had it been an apparition? He shivered.

Stepping onto the bridge, he felt it tremble beneath his feet. For a moment, he stopped where he was, everything in him longing to be back in his shabby, comfortable rooms in London. Something told him if he crossed the bridge his life would never be the same again.

He closed his eyes, breathed deeply, and prayed for wisdom and direction. He again reminded himself of his purpose in coming. He was there on behalf of the firm—to offer legal advice to Miss Wilder after Percival Norris's death, and to discreetly discover if she or a member of her family was to blame for it. His success would go a long way toward redeeming his recent mistakes.

Soon he felt a bit steadier. When he opened his eyes again, the fog was beginning to lift.

He wondered about the female figure he'd glimpsed—or imagined. Had it been Isabelle Wilder? He had not seen the woman's face. He wondered how old Miss Lawrence's maiden aunt would be. Forty? Five and forty? For some reason, he imagined an angry spinster with a hooknose and an evil glint in her eye.

Through the lingering mist, a few more details of the island began to emerge. Beyond the bridge, a lawn led up to a broad veranda that wrapped around the front and side of the stone manor house. Columns flanked its entryway, and a three-story bay projected on the right. His gaze traveled up to a high rooftop parapet, and an unpleasant jolt of nerves shot through him. Not fond of heights, he quickly looked away and walked on.

As he stepped from the bridge onto the island, a woman near his own age appeared from behind the house, a shaggy dog trailing slowly behind. The woman was tall and slender. Light brown hair with streaks of gold shone from beneath her dark red bonnet. Now that he could see her face, he realized she was far too young and attractive to be the spinster he'd imagined. A companion, perhaps?

She noticed him and stopped. "Oh. Good day."

He took a deep breath and began, "I am here to see Miss Wilder."

The woman replied, "I am she."

Incredulity flared. Her face was oval and smooth, her eyes large and blue, though dark circles shadowed them at present, like faint crescent bruises. She seemed a pretty, pleasant young woman, not evil looking at all. Though he knew too well that looks were often deceiving.

"*You* are Isabelle Wilder?"

"Guilty."

Interesting word choice, Benjamin thought. A wave of dizziness washed over him, but he tried to ignore it.

She looked down. "I'm sorry. You've caught me."

"Caught you?" he echoed stupidly. Was she going to confess on the spot?

"Just coming down for the day. I usually rise early, but I was not quite the thing this morning." The dog lay at her feet, tongue lolling, as if as weary as she.

"Oh? I . . ." he stammered lamely. "I have just arrived myself."

"Late start for you as well? I believe Mr. Linton expected you a few hours ago."

"Expected me?"

"Yes. Aren't you the master weaver here to teach lessons?"

"I am not."

"Oh. Sorry. Then, who are you?"

He set down his valise and gave her his card, hoping she did not notice the slight tremor of his hand. "Benjamin Booker. With Norris, Hardy, and Hunt."

She glanced at it. "Uncle Percy's firm, of course." She started up the veranda steps and gestured for him to follow.

"Oddly enough, I was just thinking about Percival. In fact, I dreamt about him last night."

"You did?"

"Um-hm," she replied casually. "Not surprising, I suppose. He was just here a few weeks ago."

"So I heard."

As they crossed the veranda, she asked, "What brings you here? I suppose you brought something I need to sign?"

Benjamin hesitated. He recalled Mr. Hardy's advice to more than one young barrister. "*State what you* suspect *as fact with confidence, and nine times out of ten people will believe you in possession of the evidence and respond accordingly.*"

With this in mind, he said, "The two of you had quite a row, I understand. And afterward, you sent him a rather unpleasant letter."

She grimaced. "Yes. I suppose he told you all about it."

Benjamin sketched a noncommittal shrug.

She sighed. "I was angry. He is insisting we lease part of the island to a . . . stranger. It would spoil everything I have tried to do here."

"Well, with him dead, there's that problem sorted."

Her head whipped toward him, mouth parted, face elongated in shock or a convincing imitation. "What? Percival is dead?"

He nodded, the dizziness mounting. *No, no, not now. Hold yourself together, Booker.*

Taking a deep breath, he asked, "Where were you last night?"

"Here on the island."

"Can anyone vouch for that?"

"Um . . . yes."

Suddenly unsteady, Ben teetered and grasped a nearby column for support.

Her eyes widened in alarm. "Are you all right?"

He shook his head, the act making him woozier yet. Heaven help him, he was going to faint. Not in front of this woman of all people!

"Are you unwell, Mr. Booker? Truly, you look very ill."

He pressed his other hand over his eyes. "Just . . . dizzy. It will pass."

"Do sit down, before you fall down." She took his arm and guided him to a nearby chair, her grip surprisingly strong.

Strong enough to kill a man?

Isabelle studied the man seated on the chair—elbows on his knees, head in his hands—and felt a water-and-oil slurry of pity and fear wash over her. *Why fear?* she asked herself. She had nothing to be afraid of. It was only the remnants of that horrid nightmare clinging to her and making her uneasy.

"I suppose I am the only one to feel the earth spinning?" he murmured. "The ground is not actually quaking?"

"No, it isn't," she gently replied. She sat down on the veranda sofa near him, clasping her hands and looking about her, unsure what to do.

How strange that she had dreamt of Uncle Percy only last night. A violent dream at that.

She murmured, "I can't believe Percival is dead."

"Yes. He was killed."

She reared her head back, stunned anew. "Killed? Are you sure?"

He nodded, and a low groan escaped him. He extracted a handkerchief from his valise and mopped his brow.

"How?"

He sent her a pained glance. "Perhaps you could tell me."

She sucked in a breath. "What is that supposed to mean?"

He grimaced. "Not certain yet. Awaiting coroner's report."

Isabelle slowly shook her head, stomach knotted. A killer in their townhouse? Her chest tightened at the thought. "And my niece, Rose Lawrence. Did you see her? Is she well?"

"Yes, perfectly."

She exhaled a long breath. "Good."

Movement catching her eye, she looked and saw a man's high-crowned hat beyond the veranda railing.

"Teddy!" Isabelle waved her friend over, remembering Carlota mentioning the doctor had gone to call on her tenants—the Howtons and Abel Curtis.

Curtis . . . The name delivered a prick to her heart, but not the lance it once had. Abel was their groundsman and the father of the young man she'd once fancied herself in love with—the one who'd dropped her in the dream.

Dr. Theodore Grant mounted the stairs and crossed the veranda with his long-legged stride, auburn hair and side-whiskers showing beneath his hat, green eyes narrowed on the man seated near her. Teddy was almost two years older than she was, but his face retained a boyish appearance. He and Evan had both grown up with her on the island.

"What is it, Isabelle? What's wrong?"

"Mr. Booker seems to be having a dizzy spell."

At his raised-brow glance, she explained, "He is visiting from London—a lawyer from Uncle Percival's firm."

She looked again at the hunched man. "Mr. Booker, this is Dr. Grant, local physician and family friend."

Again the lawyer groaned. "I don't need a doctor."

"Dr. Grant is an excellent physician. I'm sure he can help you."

She turned to Teddy and saw his shoulders straighten and chest expand at her words of praise.

"Indeed, I will endeavor to ease your discomfort, if I can."

"It will pass," the lawyer insisted. He stood, faltered, and teetered again.

Teddy took his arm. "Come, Mr. Booker. You will feel better once you lie down."

Isabelle hesitated. "Oh . . . yes, of course," she said. "One of the guest rooms upstairs."

Mr. Booker shook his head. "I planned to take a room at the inn."

"No need," she said. "Unless . . . can you manage more stairs, do you think? If not, perhaps our footman can help carry—"

"I can manage," Mr. Booker gritted out between clenched teeth, his face damp and pale.

While Dr. Grant took one arm, she took his other, and together they helped the lawyer inside. For some reason, she quailed at the thought of inviting this man into her home, but charity and duty overrode her desire for self-preservation.

CHAPTER
five

Benjamin lay atop a made bed in trousers and shirt-sleeves, his coat hung over a nearby chair. He looked around the pleasant chamber with its faded but attractive carpet and bedclothes. The room smelled faintly of dried roses, dust, and old money.

"Have you been ill lately?" the physician asked.

"Only a trifling cold."

"That would not explain the dizziness."

"Look, I am laid low with vertigo now and again. Though not this bad in years."

The physician nodded sagely. "Your ears seem congested. That could set it off."

"Yes, and all that lurching about on the journey here worsened it." Benjamin wiped the handkerchief over his sweaty neck, hoping not to mar the pillows.

"You don't travel often?"

"No. I live near the office. I occasionally must take a hackney, but the cobbled streets of London are smooth as glass compared to the rutted roads that brought me here. The coach gave me a thorough shaking, I can tell you. One man was sick on the journey. A second almost followed his example."

"Was the second one a lawyer?" Dr. Grant quipped.

"Yes."

"I'm sure the other passengers appreciated your restraint." The doctor snapped his medical case shut. "I confess I don't know a great deal about vertiginous conditions, though I briefly studied under an expert on melancholies and hysterias."

Benjamin pressed his hands together. "As I said, it is nothing so serious. Simply vertigo."

"Nothing simple about it." Dr. Grant drew himself up. "Well, I will consult my texts and see what I can discover to help you. Rest here today. Remain as still as possible, and I shall be back to see you in the morning."

"Very kind of you, and of Miss Wilder, but I am not an invalid."

"Doctor's orders." At the door, Theodore Grant turned back. "What brings you here, if I may ask?"

"The death of Percival Norris. He was murdered."

The physician's green eyes widened. "Murdered, you say? Good heavens. I would think that a matter for Bow Street."

"An officer is investigating the death in London. I am here at the behest of our senior partner—to inform the family and offer legal advice in Mr. Norris's stead."

The doctor absorbed that, then said, "I thought Mr. Norris had retired from law, save for acting as trustee to the Wilder estate."

"Well, now he has retired in every sense of the word."

Dr. Grant joined Isabelle in her father's study, which she now used as an office for her burgeoning basketmaking business. The family dog, Hamish, lay on a rug near the fire.

"And how is Mr. Booker?" she asked.

Teddy set down his case. "He says it's nothing serious, but I am not sure. I have ordered bed rest for the remainder of the day as a precaution."

He looked her in the eye. "Isabelle, how well do you know this man?"

"Not at all. I have only just met him."

He tucked his chin in surprise. "Oh? I assumed you must be some acquainted with him."

She shook her head. "No."

"Mr. Booker mentioned your uncle's death. I am sorry. He said he came to deliver the news in person and offer legal advice, but I wonder . . ."

"So do I. I almost think he suspects *me* of killing Percival. He mentioned our argument and the angry letter I sent."

Her friend's thin face lengthened all the more, his mouth a long oval of shock. "What?"

Isabelle shrugged, lifting a nonchalant hand.

"But . . ." he sputtered. "That is ridiculous!"

"I know it is. That is why I am not overly concerned."

Dr. Grant shook his head, nostrils flared. "Had I known, I certainly would not have suggested he stay."

"Yes. Inconvenient, that."

"I shall remove him to the inn at once."

"No need. He is here now. And as you saw, he seems rather harmless."

"At present, perhaps, but not for long."

"And he's right. With Percival gone, there will be legal matters to sort out. Especially with Rose about to marry. And we'll have his will and the trust to deal with. It's probably good he came here, as I have no plans to travel to London, as you well know."

He murmured, "I do indeed."

Isabelle glanced at the mantel clock and nibbled her lip. "I do hope Rose and Mr. Adair are all right. I thought they might be here by now."

He stepped nearer. "Don't go borrowing trouble. No doubt they are perfectly well and will arrive in time for dinner."

"I am sure you are right. But you know how I worry."

"I do know." He studied her face. "How are you feeling, by the way?"

"I am well. Bit of a headache."

"You drank a great deal of wine yesterday."

"You needn't remind me."

"I meant no censure. I know how difficult it has been for you. Wanting to be in London for Rose but unable to be."

She made a face. "You needn't remind me of that either."

"Sorry." He dipped his head, then looked up at her from beneath golden eyelashes. "Just a headache? No stomach upset?"

"Well, I am not ready to sit down to a plate of eels, but my sour stomach will pass more quickly than my regret. I hope I did not embarrass myself—or you."

"No, of course not," he replied, but Isabelle was not convinced.

"In all honesty, I didn't think I drank that much. Perhaps the last batch was more potent than usual. You didn't help me finish off the bottle, did you?"

He shook his head. "You know I don't drink."

"And my behavior last night no doubt affirmed your resolve."

He laid a comforting hand on her sleeve. "Don't be too hard on yourself, Isabelle. You are usually quite temperate."

"And will endeavor to remain so in future."

His touch reminded her, and she rubbed the aching joint. "I managed to hurt my elbow somehow. Probably just slept on it wrong."

He looked from her arm to her face. "May I?" When she nodded, he gently pushed up her sleeve and studied her elbow. "Just bruised, I think. Nothing serious."

"Good. Though I don't recall hitting it on anything."

His fingers lingered, gently stroking her skin. "Perhaps out in the weaving shed?"

"It's certainly possible."

Dr. Grant, the most eligible bachelor in the village, was touching her bare arm. She ought to feel . . . something, should she not? But when she looked at him, she still saw Teddy, the boy with ginger hair and freckles and bony ankles showing beneath too-short trousers and slipped-down socks. She smiled at the image, and he smiled back, his gaze glimmering with mischief.

"By the way," he said. "I have a present for you in my cart."

"Oh?" Isabelle replied. "How intriguing."

"Shall we go and see it?"

"Very well." She walked toward the door, calling to the sleeping dog, "Come on, Hamish. Let's go, boy."

But the dog only thumped his tail and continued his nap.

Teddy shook his head, lips wry. "That old dog is on its last legs."

"I know, but he was Father's. Barely more than a pup when he and Mamma . . ." She let the words drift off, unspoken. No need to explain. Teddy knew.

She followed him out to his cart, where he removed a lap rug from a wooden crate.

"What is this?" She heard a whine through the slats and a scratching of claws. "Sounds alive."

"It had better be. Jack Pearson promised me he was perfectly healthy when I bought him."

"He?"

"Look for yourself."

She opened the lid, and a brown-and-white head popped out, with floppy ears, bright eyes, and lolling tongue, its sharp-nailed paws clawing at the top edge of the crate.

Isabelle bent and stroked his head. "Aww . . . he's adorable."

"Glad you think so. He's yours. A gift."

She looked up at him in surprise. "But I already have a dog."

"I know. But Hamish is more of a fixture than a companion. Barely moves off his rug most days."

"Maybe, but I was not planning to even consider another dog while he is still . . . with us."

"I saw him at Pearson's and thought he'd be perfect for you."

"He is sweet. And so energetic!" She rubbed the pup's ears, then asked, "Are you sure there is nothing more you can do for Hamish?"

His expression soured. "I am a physician, Isabelle. Not a magician. I did try, you know. But if you insist on feeding him table scraps and not making him take exercise or the tonic I prescribed . . ."

"I do try! But he doesn't like it."

"Well, then there is nothing more I can do for him."

"Please, Teddy."

He sighed and his expression softened. "Oh, very well. I will take another look at him. But in the meanwhile, what will you name this creature?"

She stroked the pup's muzzle and was rewarded with several damp licks. "That will take some thought."

Benjamin reclined atop the bed per doctor's orders but felt frustrated to be so unproductive. A manservant named Jacob came in and asked if he needed anything.

"No, thank you."

Benjamin decided to gather some information from the young man. "Have you been in service here long?"

"About four years, sir. It's a good situation."

"Just out of curiosity, does Miss Wilder keep a carriage and coachman?"

"No, sir. Not since I've been here."

"Then . . . how does she travel. By stage?"

Jacob shook his head. "She stays here."

"She has not left the island recently?"

"No, sir. Well, I had better get back to work."

The loyal servant could not leave the room fast enough. Clearly Benjamin would not learn anything useful from him.

Ben pulled out a favorite book he'd brought along and read to pass the time.

Sometime later someone knocked on the doorframe, and he looked over, expecting to see the young manservant again.

Instead, Miss Wilder stood there, and beside her was a second woman, carrying a tray. "We have brought you some dinner, Mr. Booker, if you are feeling up to it."

He looked forward to the prospect of asking her questions more than consuming food but straightened to a sitting position against the pillows. "Thank you. Come in."

The second woman entered first, setting the tray on the bedside table, while Miss Wilder hesitated just over the threshold. "I hope you don't mind us coming to your room, but Jacob is busy out-of-doors at present."

"Not at all." Ben's frockcoat still hung over the chair, but otherwise he was fully dressed.

Miss Wilder gestured to her companion, who he'd assumed was a servant. "This is Miss Carlota Medina. She works for me but is also my friend."

He nodded to the woman, giving her a longer look. She

had Mediterranean coloring—cream tea skin, dark eyes, and black hair, pinned back. She was attractive, but her face held a world-weary look, and up close she appeared perhaps a few years older than Miss Wilder.

Under the gazes of two females, Benjamin felt at a distinct disadvantage, suddenly wishing he were wearing his coat as well. "Please forgive my shirt-sleeves, ladies."

"That is all right," Miss Wilder said. "I am not so easily shocked. I did have a brother, after all."

Her friend added in a light Spanish accent, "And I have seen men in far less, I assure you."

"Lotty!" Isabelle exclaimed on a laugh, half-indignant, half-amused.

"I refer only to my years in the theatre, of course."

Miss Wilder grinned at her. "You forget Mr. Booker is not yet acquainted with your particular sense of humor."

Turning back to him, she studied his face. "How are you feeling?"

"Better. Though your doctor-friend insists I lie still until he returns."

She nodded. "Dr. Grant gives excellent advice. You are wise to follow his instructions."

The other woman gave a little snort at that, but when Benjamin glanced over, her expression gave nothing away.

Miss Wilder said, "You mentioned seeing my niece in Town yesterday. Is that right?"

"I did, yes. She and Mr. Adair were questioned by a Bow Street officer at the house, and she and her companion planned to spend the night with his family afterward. Mr. Adair thought she would be safer there than in the house where Mr. Norris was killed."

Miss Wilder winced at the word. "Understandable." She

gripped the back of a chair near the door. "And did you . . . see . . . Mr. Norris?"

"Yes." Unbidden, the scene reappeared in his mind. "He was found lying over his desk, pistol in hand."

Miss Wilder sat down heavily on the chair, eyes wide. "Was he shot?"

"No. He apparently grabbed the pistol from his desk drawer, but it had not been fired."

"Then . . . how?"

"As I said, we are awaiting the coroner's verdict, but apparently Mr. Norris was struck in the head with something. We don't know what."

"With a wine bottle, perhaps?"

He stared at her. "Why on earth would you guess that?"

She blinked. "I . . . don't know. Never mind."

He studied her face a moment longer, saw confusion and concern. "There was no bottle in the room," he said. "Only an empty decanter. There was, however, a drinking glass smashed against the wall, as though it had been thrown in anger. Or at someone in self-defense."

"I see." She swallowed and asked, "And how did Rose seem when you saw her? Shocked and upset, I don't doubt."

"On the contrary, she seemed remarkably composed. I take it there was little love lost between her and Mr. Norris."

"Well, I . . ."

"Who can blame her?" Miss Medina hotly retorted. "The man was odious."

"Why 'odious'?" Benjamin asked.

"Lotty, please," Isabelle interjected. "He was a relation, after all, though we did not see eye to eye."

Isabelle glanced at the clock and fiddled with the chatelaine of keys at her waist. "Speaking of family, I do hope Rose and

Mr. Adair are all right. They planned to travel here for a visit. I thought they would have arrived by now."

Benjamin nodded. "As did I. They told the Bow Street officer they planned to leave today."

Isabelle clasped her hands together. "You are not helping allay my worries."

He shrugged. "Perhaps the officer returned with more questions for them. Perhaps he suspected they knew more about the death than they let on."

"If that is supposed to make me feel better, it does not."

"I was merely attempting to explain."

"I wonder if you have many friends, Mr. Booker. The ability to comfort is a virtue in a close companion."

"Well . . . thankfully you have Dr. Grant for that," he said evenly.

"True. And Lotty."

Taking her cue, the other woman said, "I am sure Rose is well, miss."

"No doubt you are right. You know how I worry."

Benjamin said, "You mentioned a brother, Miss Wilder. Where is he?"

"Gone, I'm afraid. Went to sea to find adventure as a young man and died instead."

"I'm sorry."

"Thank you. We lost him years ago. And the rest of my family rather all at once."

"Oh? I recall your London housekeeper mentioning Miss Lawrence's mother has passed on?"

"Yes. Grace and I were inseparable, though she was six years older. But then she met Harry Lawrence and that was that. Off she went with him to India—she who hated spiders and snakes and dirt. That's true love, I suppose."

"I wouldn't know," Benjamin murmured dryly, then added, "Of course I knew your parents are deceased, hence Mr. Norris acting as trustee. Remind me, how long have they been gone?"

"Over ten years." Miss Wilder stepped to the window and looked out, probably hoping to see her niece arrive. "I still remember it so clearly. . . . We had just received a letter from Grace, with the awful news that her husband had died of some foreign disease, and she was ill as well. She informed us she was sailing back to London with her young daughter and hoped we would come to the East India Docks to meet the ship. Her letter only reached us the evening before the ship was due to arrive, and Mamma was wild with worry. Papa tried to convince her to get some sleep, promising to set out first thing in the morning.

"I wanted to go along, but Mamma insisted I stay home and stay safe. While she packed and paced, Papa ordered a groom to prepare the traveling chariot and shut himself up in the study to 'put their affairs in order.' In the end, although it was after midnight, Mamma could wait no longer and demanded they leave. Papa gave in, wakened the coachman, and off they went. A disastrous decision, as it turned out. They collided with a speeding mail coach and were killed instantly."

Benjamin grimaced. What a tragic loss. He could not imagine losing his parents and sibling all at once. "Again, I am sorry."

"So am I. But I thank God the collision happened before they retrieved little Rose, or I should have lost her too. I learned later that Grace died during the voyage. Thankfully, they were traveling with an English governess Grace had employed for Rose. When no one came to meet the ship, competent Miss O'Toole found an inn and eventually procured passage on a stagecoach. By the time they reached the island, I was frantic with worry. For word had reached me about my parents' fate, but I had no idea what had become of my sister and her child."

Isabelle turned and met his gaze straight on. "So you see, Mr. Booker, my fears for Rose are not completely unfounded. I have lost everyone else in my family when they embarked on one journey or another."

Her maid spoke up. "But remember, Miss Rose was not born here on the island—the so-called curse does not apply to her."

"Curse?" Benjamin echoed in surprise.

Miss Wilder waved a dismissive hand. "Some of the locals have started saying our family must be cursed, because any Wilder born on the island who leaves it dies young. Of course it is not logical, but you can see how such a thing might get started. First my brother dying, then my sister, then my parents. . . . Yes, they left the island on occasion over the years without mishap, as has Rose, so I should *not* worry, I know. But I do."

His hostess stepped to the door. "Well, we shall leave you to enjoy your dinner in peace, Mr. Booker. Anything else you need, just ring the bell there."

"Thank you, I shall."

As the women started through the door, Benjamin called after them, "What about Percival Norris?"

Isabelle Wilder turned back. "What about him?"

"He was part of the family too, was he not, as your uncle?"

"Actually, he was only Father's second cousin. We called him 'uncle' out of respect for his age."

"Was he born on Belle Island?"

"No. Why do you ask?"

"Just wondering if the curse applied to him as well."

CHAPTER

six

In the morning, Benjamin awoke feeling both refreshed and confused. He looked around, not recognizing the room or the foreign sound of waterfowl quacking and honking outside the window. The shutters were open, and sunlight spilled inside—so different from the gloom of the afternoon before.

When the doctor told him to rest, he'd never imagined he would sleep away the entire evening and all night as well. The journey and vertigo episode had clearly sapped his strength.

He rose tentatively, testing out the strength of his limbs after yesterday's tremors, relieved to find them steady. Mortification heated his ears to think of how he had embarrassed himself upon arrival, showing his every weakness to Miss Wilder and her physician-friend.

Today will be different, he promised himself. He would make sure of it.

Dressed in a nightshirt he barely recalled donning, he stepped to the window and looked out. He stilled, marveling at the view before him. Gone were yesterday's fog and grey pall. Everywhere was color: lush green lawn stretching down to a gently flowing river of a darker hue. Vibrant yellow daffodils lining the bank and blooming cherry trees adding splashes of pink and white.

Across the Thames, the village of Riverton appeared a charming hodgepodge—stone church with ivy-mantled tower, the mill and village shops, thatched- and tile-roof cottages agreeably situated on a gentle slope rising beyond the road he'd arrived on.

Crowded, sooty London seemed suddenly a lifetime away. A world of darkness and shadows compared to this vivid watercolor painting.

Careful . . . he cautioned himself, remembering his purpose in coming there. This was no social call, however pleasant the prospect might seem. Especially if the lovely scene harbored a killer.

After he washed, he shook out a shirt from his small valise, wrinkled but clean, and dressed for the day, his hands thankfully steady when he shaved and fastened buttons. As he tied his cravat in a simple barrel knot, the sound of a carriage arriving drew him to the window. A sleek chaise driven by mounted postilion crossed the bridge to the island.

Anticipation coursed through him. Things were about to become more interesting. . . .

When Benjamin left his bedchamber a short while later, he walked along the corridor, noticing formal portraits of Wilder ancestors adorning the walls. A wide, carpeted stairway led him down to a grand entry hall with several doors and passages leading from it. Hearing female voices, he followed them toward an open doorway.

From within, Miss Wilder said, "I am so relieved you are here at last. I began to worry. We expected you yesterday."

"I know. I am sorry." Miss Lawrence's voice sounded tentative. "We were . . . unavoidably delayed."

"The party went well, I trust?"

"Well enough, considering the last-minute change in location. But that's not why we were late. Aunt Belle, I'm afraid I have some rather shocking news."

"If it is about Uncle Percival's death, I already know. It is dreadful."

A moment of respectful silence passed, then Miss Wilder asked abruptly, "What do you mean about a change in location? Was the party not held at our London house as planned?"

Benjamin reached the threshold of an informal morning room. Inside, Isabelle Wilder and Rose Lawrence sat companionably drinking tea, their heads near one another in animated conversation. Mr. Adair sat slouched, half-hidden behind a London newspaper.

Miss Lawrence shook her head, eyes sparking with ire. "No. In the end Uncle Percy refused to host it, bemoaning the expense."

"But . . . ! It is family tradition. Just as we celebrated your parents' engagement there, and my parents' before that."

"I know. I tried to explain, but he would not listen."

"My dear, I am sorry to hear it. You ought to have written to tell me."

"It all happened so quickly. There wasn't time. Thankfully Christopher's parents stepped in and offered to host it in their home. What a mad rush it was, sending round notices and carting over extra dishes and the foodstuffs Mrs. Kittleson had already ordered."

"Was it all terribly awkward?"

"Not too bad. I explained it by saying Uncle Percival's health was declining." Rose clapped a hand to her cheek. "Oh! Never did I guess how prophetic that was!"

Rose looked back to her aunt, hand lowering. "But it can't

have been in the papers so soon. How did you hear about Uncle Percy?"

Clearing his throat to announce his presence, Benjamin stepped into the room.

Seeing him, the young woman's mouth parted in surprise. "Oh . . . Mr. Brooks, was it?"

"Booker."

Mr. Adair lowered the newspaper and scowled. "What is he doing here?"

Benjamin adopted a casual air. "Good day, Miss Lawrence. Mr. Adair. Pleasant journey?"

The two only stared at him in reply.

Isabelle breached the awkward pause and explained, "Mr. Booker is a lawyer with Uncle Percy's firm. He came to give me the news in person. How are you feeling this morning, Mr. Booker? Better I hope?"

"Yes, thank you." Miss Wilder also looked more refreshed today, Ben noticed, her blue eyes bright and well rested.

Mr. Adair snapped his paper closed. "Humph. You wasted no time. I suppose you vultures are eager to name a new trustee?"

Concern dulled Miss Wilder's expression. "Oh. I had not thought of that."

"Knowing Uncle Percy, he had already assigned someone." Rose Lawrence pouted. "Someone more controlling and miserly than he was."

Miss Wilder pressed her niece's arm in mild warning. "My dear. Shh. Let us hope not." She looked up at him. "Are you here to unveil a new trustee, Mr. Booker? You did not mention it."

He shook his head. "No. First, there is the more pressing matter of Mr. Norris's death to deal with, and"—he chose his words with purposeful discretion—"who stands to benefit from it."

But Miss Wilder turned to her niece and said bluntly, "Mr. Booker knows Percival and I argued. He apparently thinks I may have killed him myself."

"What!" Rose blurted.

Benjamin braced himself for a verbal attack. But instead of the shocked outrage he expected, Miss Lawrence giggled. "That's rich! You have taken a wrong turn there, Mr. Booker. Aunt Belle? Can you just imagine her sneaking off to London, doing the deed, then sneaking back, no one any the wiser?" The young woman bent forward at the waist, laughter shaking her slight figure. "I am sorry, but it is too ridiculous!"

Mr. Adair, however, did not look amused. "Rose, contain yourself. This is no laughing matter."

Benjamin lifted his chin. "Why is it out of the question? Your aunt admits she was angry with Mr. Norris and had reason to wish him gone."

Rose looked at him, eyes alight, then looked to her aunt for confirmation. "Does he not know?"

Miss Wilder shrugged uneasily. "I suppose it's possible my reputation precedes me. Percival may have mentioned it."

"Mentioned what?" Benjamin snapped, irritated to be the cause of Miss Lawrence's mirth and not knowing why.

"My aunt has not stepped foot off this island in almost ten years."

He turned to stare at Miss Wilder in disbelief. The London housekeeper mentioned she had not been to London in years, but nothing about this!

Miss Wilder fidgeted and looked away, self-consciously rubbing her neck. "Goodness. Hearing it aloud makes me sound like a freak of nature."

Clearly noticing her aunt's discomfiture, Miss Lawrence changed the subject. "How long will you be staying, Mr. Booker?"

"Not sure yet. A day or two. Though I shall remove to the inn this morning."

Miss Wilder straightened. "Mr. Booker. About the trust. Is there a way to revoke it? Rose and I can look after ourselves."

Taken aback by the unexpected legal question, Benjamin paused to consider. "It would depend on how the original grantor—your father, I assume—created the trust. I would have to review the terms."

"Would you do that for us? I would be happy to cover your usual fees, of course."

Mr. Adair hissed, "Take care, Miss Wilder. I hardly think he is the best choice. Why do I not write to my father? His attorney would be more objective."

"But Mr. Booker is here, and a member of Percival's firm with access to the trust papers, wills, and any other documents he might need. Would you, Mr. Booker? I would like to know what lies in store for Rose and me and the estate."

"Do you not have your father's copy of the trust documents?"

She shook her head. "As far as I know, Uncle Percy has them—had them—in London."

Benjamin hesitated. Her request would give him an excuse to look through correspondence and papers and perhaps unearth some evidence in the bargain. Besides, the firm needed all the paying clients they could muster at present.

"Very well," he replied. "I will see what I can find out."

Isabelle smiled at the man and thanked him, hoping it was not a mistake to invite him to remain there longer.

Rose looked at their guest and said impulsively, "If you are to stay, Mr. Booker, then you must attend our party!"

Isabelle spoke up quickly, apology in her tone. "Rose, I have been thinking. With Uncle Percy's death, I am not sure another party would be quite the thing."

"I am sorry he's dead, truly, but he was only a distant relative. He controlled too much of our lives while he was alive. Shall he continue to control us now by his death? He would have loved to be the cause of another canceled party! No."

Rose took Isabelle's hand. "I know you hated not being there with us in London, not acting as hostess for the traditional Wilder engagement dinner. And I know you have consoled yourself, and me, by planning a second party here. How much you have been looking forward to it!"

Rose leaned close. "By the way, we passed Miss Truelock in the village, and she called out to us, telling us how much she is looking forward to it as well."

Arminda Truelock was the vicar's daughter and Isabelle's closest female friend. A spinster, like her, who enjoyed far too little society or amusement in her life. Isabelle hated to disappoint her.

She hesitated. "Well, I suppose a dinner would do no harm. Though I am not certain about dancing. . . ."

"Oh, we must have dancing! Just like an old-time *rèiteach*."

Mr. Booker asked, "Rare-choch?"

"Gaelic. A betrothal party," Isabelle explained. "A long tradition in our family."

"And we can't postpone it," Rose added, "because I shall be an old married woman soon, and the time for celebrating betrothals shall be passed."

Isabelle's stomach pinched, but she managed a smile for her beloved niece, who had so carefully raised the topic of her upcoming wedding. Isabelle had hoped Rose would marry on the island, in the manor's small chapel. But Rose had gently protested that the chapel was far too small for all the guests they and the Adairs would invite. Isabelle had countered that perhaps they might marry in St. Raymond's across the bridge and afterward come over to the island for the wedding breakfast, which Isabelle would happily host for as many as wanted to attend. Rose had seemed amenable to the idea, but Mr. Adair argued that it was too far for all of his London relatives and friends to travel.

Rose had ended the argument, saying they would discuss it later. But later was rapidly approaching. How could Isabelle bear to miss her niece's wedding? Rose was more like a daughter to her than a niece, as she had all but raised her after her parents died.

Her heart hitched. *Why can I not get over this fear?*

Isabelle decided she could not disappoint Rose again. Nor herself. "Very well. If there are no objections, we shall proceed with the party." Isabelle looked from face to face, but no one protested.

"There, it's settled!" Rose enthused.

Isabelle stood and started across the room. "I shall let Mrs. Philpotts know. If you will excuse me."

Mr. Booker followed her out. "Your niece invited me out of politeness, I know, but you needn't include me."

"It isn't politeness alone, I assure you." Isabelle sent him a sly grin. "We could use another man to even our numbers. Have you evening attire?"

"Not with me."

Isabelle's gaze swept his form in a measuring look. Fine, handsome features. Deep brown eyes. Dark hair with some curl to it. Tall, well built, and lean, with a long torso and confident bearing. "No matter. I think you are nearly my father's height. And men's fashions change so little compared to ours. I shall ask Mr. Adair's valet to pick something from among

Papa's things to brush out and press for the evening. If you don't mind, that is."

"Not at all."

"Good." She hesitated. "And . . . since you will be remaining for the party and helping us with the trust, you might as well stay here on the island. There is no need to remove to the inn."

One dark brow rose. "Are you certain?"

Isabelle nodded.

"Very well. Thank you."

Miss Wilder started toward the kitchen, then turned back. "Actually, since you are looking into the trust for us, I wonder if you might help me with something related to it?"

Wariness tingled through him. "What might that be?"

"Come with me."

She led him to a masculine chamber dominated by a large mahogany desk, with floor-to-ceiling bookshelves lining the walls. "This was my father's study. I use it now as my office." She shut the door behind them, opened the shutters to let in light, and began. "You may recall I mentioned my father wanting to get his affairs in order before that last journey?"

"Yes . . . ?"

"I distinctly remember him telling me that he was revising his will that night, as it related to the trust. As a lawyer, you probably encourage people to write their last will and testament before setting out by coach. You know firsthand how dangerous road travel can be. As I learned to my great sorrow the next day."

"True."

"Papa had revised his will once already when he learned of Rose's birth abroad. That's when he set up the trust to provide for me and Grace, and Rose through her. He named Percival trustee in the event of his death, granting him a modest stipend.

We haven't much family, and Papa had no reason to question Percy's honor or ability at the time.

"But when he learned Grace's husband had died and Grace herself was ill, he told me he thought it prudent to revise the terms so that if the worst happened, I would become Rose's guardian when I reached my majority, and the mistress of my own fate, instead of Percival going on as trustee indefinitely. After all, I was already twenty by that time."

"Did your father ever finish this newer will?"

"That is the question. If he did, we never found it. Perhaps he meant to write it but, in the rush to leave, neglected to do so. And in all honesty, I was not overly concerned about it initially. At first, Uncle Percy performed his role dutifully and remained in the background, uninvolved in our day-to-day lives. I raised Rose here with little interference until she moved to London.

"However, during one of Uncle Percy's recent visits, he spent hours in here, going through every drawer and file, looking for something. In fact, I came down at three in the morning for warm milk and found him still at it. He seemed quite concerned. Frantic, almost."

"You think he was looking for this will?"

"I believe so."

"You mentioned your parents have been gone for over ten years. Why would Mr. Norris suddenly be looking for a possible newer will?"

She ducked her head and said sheepishly, "Perhaps because I hinted that my father had written something that dissolved the trust, which I would produce as evidence, effectively eliminating his position."

"But you don't have any such document."

She shook her head. "No. I was angry and scared and desperate. He was threatening to ruin my way of life. My island.

I wanted to stop him. It was all I could think of at the time. I knew my father would never have stood for it, were he here. And if he'd foreseen the underhanded things Percival would do, he would never have appointed him trustee in the first place."

Benjamin wondered if threatening Percival Norris was all she had done. Or had she carried out a more effective, permanent solution? He looked around the room, at the desk and cabinets. "Would your father have left such a document here, in his study?"

"I thought he would have had it with him in the coach. I understood he planned to deliver it to the lawyers in London after meeting Grace's ship, but they never made it that far. Perhaps I was mistaken. For their valises were returned to us, and we found no such papers inside. Then again, I was consumed with grief, not thinking of mundane things like legal documents."

"Forgive me, but your . . . Were your parents returned here as well?"

She winced. "Yes. They are buried in St. Raymond's churchyard in Riverton. The undertaker returned a few personal effects to me—Papa's purse and watch, Mamma's reticule and ring—but no papers."

"Why are you concerned about this now that Mr. Norris is dead?"

"Because if I do nothing, I will be saddled with another trustee and required to submit to a stranger controlling what I do and what I spend. A stranger who will dictate Rose's dowry and marriage settlement and all the rest. I need to know. Have I grounds to refuse such a successor, to be the mistress of the estate without outside interference?"

"Is the estate not half Rose's?"

"The island and the London house are tied up in the trust, I believe, but in the end, Rose is my heir, so she will inherit everything when I die in any case."

"I am not sure I would bandy that about."

"Why?"

Ben made a mental note of this possible motive but decided to let it pass. "Never mind. Getting back to your question—you're right, your father, as original grantor, probably appointed a successor trustee in the event Mr. Norris was unable or unwilling to serve. Otherwise the court must do so."

"But why do we need a trustee at all? Or a guardian, for that matter? Rose is not yet eighteen, but she is about to marry, and that, of course, means her husband will then own all of her property."

"True. *Unless* a marriage settlement is enacted before the wedding."

"Which is why Percival was insisting on one, though the Adairs were not pleased with the terms."

Benjamin nodded. "Your niece is very young. It's not surprising Mr. Norris would think she needs a settlement to protect her, and an older trustee to advise her."

"And what about me? I am thirty years old."

"I admit you seem altogether capable."

"Thank you. My goal is to preserve this house and the island for future generations. For Rose's children."

"And your own?"

She blinked her large blue eyes. "I . . . have no plans to marry at present."

"Does Dr. Grant know that?"

With a huff, she sputtered, "You are impertinent!"

"Forgive me. I am tactless, I know."

She lifted her chin. "Dr. Grant and I are old friends."

His gaze traced her face, the graceful curve of her neck. "He seems to admire you."

She fiddled with the wax jack on the desk. "Perhaps. Yet we . . . remain friends."

"I wonder why."

She shrugged and avoided his gaze.

Benjamin's heart softened toward her, and he instantly bristled. She was already casting her spell on him, just as Susan Stark had. Was he a fool to help this woman? Would he regret staying here longer, to be taken in by her? Then again, there might be unexpected benefits to being a guest in the Wilder house. He would have more access to the people who lived there, more opportunity to discover any secrets they might be hiding.

He squared his shoulders, sliding into a professional demeanor as he would a stiff tailcoat. "Very well. I will look for a newer will and also research the matter of a successor. I will write to Mr. Hardy, our senior partner, and ask about the terms of the existing trust."

"Thank you." She extracted a key from the chatelaine at her waist and unlocked the desk and file drawers. "Please do let me know what you learn." She departed, leaving Benjamin alone in the study, wondering how in the world he had come to be a guest among people he barely knew and trusted less.

Until recently, he had thought himself good at reading people, of knowing whether someone was telling the truth or lying. But the Susan Stark case had shaken his confidence. Now he was not at all certain what to believe.

Benjamin spent some time sorting through papers and then wrote to Mr. Hardy, asking about the terms of the Wilder trust and letting him know he would be remaining on Belle Island for a few more days.

He was sealing the letter when barking drew his attention to the window. From there he looked down and saw Miss Wilder frolicking on the lawn with two dogs. The old dog he'd seen before held a stick in his mouth, and Miss Wilder playfully tried to pull it from him. She skipped in a circle around the canine in an exuberant dance of sorts, smiling and laughing, while a puppy barked and chased after her.

Isabelle Wilder seemed to be a woman without affectation, not overly concerned about appearing proper or elegant. He found that refreshing. He found *her* refreshing. In the past, he'd harbored a somewhat prejudiced view of country rustics. Perhaps he'd been wrong. He squeezed his eyes shut. *Don't jump to conclusions about her, one way or the other.* He might admire her spirit, but that didn't necessarily mean she was innocent of wrongdoing.

After a few minutes, the old dog lay down and would not play for all her coaxing. Tongue lolling, he seemed to smile at the antics of his mistress and wagged his tail appreciatively. Finally, she gave up, tossed the stick aside, and patted the dog's head before leading the puppy back inside.

A short while later, Benjamin left the house, planning to post the letter himself. As he crossed the wooden bridge to reach Riverton on the opposite shore, he decided the hamlet was an attractive place. Its homes were bedecked with climbing plants and many boasted colorful spring flowers in their front gardens. One humble cottage near the church offered bouquets for sale. A village shop stood on the corner opposite, its window displaying a jumble of items to entice passersby: candles, tobacco pipes, tops and balls, sugar loafs, tin and hardware, buttons and tapes.

Farther down the bank stood the old mill, its wheel churning the water white with foam. Beside the mill sat a wagon with red wheels, piled high with sacks of flour. Its team of horses fed on a truss of hay.

While the river road paralleled the Thames, a cross street led uphill away from it. There Benjamin saw his destination—the White Hart Inn, which also served as the local post office. It made an inviting picture with its warm yellow wash, red tile roof, and a courtyard where elderly people sat beneath an ancient walnut tree, gossiping over village news.

Benjamin entered the inn and posted his letter. While he was there, he asked the innkeeper if he or a livery in the village offered chaises for hire if someone—like Miss Wilder—wished to go to London.

The innkeeper looked at him as though he were daft. "You're not from around here, are you? Nearest coaching inn is in Maidenhead. That's where our post is delivered, and we pick it up with our donkey cart. But you wouldn't get far in that."

"No. Well, thank you."

Errand completed, Benjamin entered the taproom on a whim and sat next to a solitary silver-haired man.

Hoping to glean a little information about the Wilders, he casually addressed the oldster. "Good day to you, sir. What's the news here?"

The grizzled head turned, and rheumy eyes swept over him. "Not much. Never seen ye afore."

"I am visiting from London."

"Then I hope ye don't mean to stay long."

Benjamin reared his head back in surprise. "Oh? Why?"

"Foul weather coming. Almanac ain't always right, ye know. Feel it in my bones. Gonna be worse than '11 or the flood of '08."

The barman approached with a tolerant grin. "Don't let Mr.

Colebrook worry you, friend. He's always predicting doom and gloom."

"Ach." The man waved a dismissive hand, lip curled in disgust. "You'll see I'm right."

Benjamin ordered a coffee for himself, and a second pint for Mr. Colebrook.

His silvery eyebrows rose in appreciation, and he nodded his thanks. "Don't mind if I do."

Benjamin sipped, then asked, "You have lived here a long time, I take it?"

"That I have, young man. Since afore ye was born, I wager."

"This is my first visit. I am staying on Belle Island for a few days. I heard a rumor that the mistress hasn't left the island in ten years. Surely that's an exaggeration?"

"No, sir. She likes to stay home. No crime in that."

"I have never heard of such a thing. Is she . . . ill?"

"Not as such."

"Then . . . why? If you had to guess?"

"On account of the curse. Any Wilder born on the island who leaves it dies young."

"I heard about that. Surely no one really believes it?"

For a moment the old man's bleary eyes sharpened with suspicion. "What's it to you?"

Benjamin shrugged. "Merely curious. You must admit it's strange."

The old man's eyes narrowed, then cleared in resolve. He withdrew a coin from his pocket and pressed it onto the counter with a resounding snap. "I admit nothing. And I can buy my own pints and keep my own counsel, thank ye very much. I suggest you do the same. You won't hear me say another word against the mistress. I regret I said anything at all."

"You said nothing unflattering, sir, I assure you. Please sit down. Pray do not be offended."

But the man rose on wobbly legs and walked out the side door to join the others in the courtyard. Benjamin sighed. What an oaf he felt. Apparently, he would have made a terrible barrister, pleading cases in court. His ability to question witnesses certainly left a great deal to be desired.

CHAPTER

seven

On his way back over the bridge a short while later, Benjamin saw Miss Wilder walk out of the house with a large basket in her arms.

He met her at the bottom of the veranda steps. "Miss Wilder, I have a few questions for you, if I may."

"Of course, but might you do so while we walk? I am supposed to be in the weaving shed in two minutes."

"Oh. All right."

She had already turned and was striding across the lawn, rather quickly for one in skirts. Just how long were the legs beneath? He banished the unwise thought, or tried to.

"What is the hurry?" he asked, jogging to catch up with her on the shore path.

"I am bringing the midday meal for the weavers." She lifted the covered basket in her hands.

"Here, allow me." He took it from her and carried it, finding it surprisingly heavy.

"Thank you. I confess I also want to see how it is going. We have brought in a master weaver to help our workers improve their technique."

"How did you manage that?"

"Our vicar, Mr. Truelock, knew of him and arranged the introduction."

As they followed the path upriver, Ben asked, "Why baskets?"

"Because it makes sense. The osier beds were already here, though I hired traveling cutters to harvest the rods for us. Hard work, that. And now we are making them into something useful, marketable, and profitable."

"You need money?"

"Apparently, according to Uncle Percy. He insisted the estate must become more self-sustaining. That's why I started our little business here. I thought it an ideal plan, but he did not agree. He said our problems were bigger than a few baskets could solve. He brought a man here. Wanted me to sell or lease part of the island to him. Can you imagine? Dozens of strangers here on my family's island, cutting down trees and putting up outbuildings where our osiers grow?"

She shook her head. "I would rather employ my neighbors— many of whom struggle to support their families. I know weaving is usually done by men, but since the war, we have fewer men and more widows and adolescents in need of work. I help them, and they, in turn, help the estate."

"Good of you."

She glanced over at him, perhaps sensing his skepticism. She smirked. "I am no saint, Mr. Booker. My father was one of the area's leading landowners, as were his parents before him. They always saw it as their duty to help their neighbors, to contribute to the church and the poor fund, to help rebuild after floods and visit the sick and the like. I am simply following in their footsteps."

"Does the area flood often?"

She nodded. "Every four or five years, it seems. Fortunately, the water doesn't usually rise high enough to endanger the house. Even so, I dread them. Beyond the damage to property, people suffer as well. Especially the elderly. When the river floods, crippling rheumatism and fevers are sure to follow." She added, "Thankfully, Dr. Grant is here to help."

"You admire him."

"Of course. He does a great deal for our community. It is a real boon to have a doctor in our small hamlet."

"Yes, unusual, when physicians are in short supply compared to surgeons and apothecaries."

"I agree. I never thought he would practice here so long. But I am grateful."

Benjamin studied her profile, wondering if gratitude was all she felt for Dr. Grant, or if the hope of romance was what kept the man here in relative obscurity. For an attractive, genteel woman like Isabelle Wilder, a man would be willing to sacrifice a great deal careerwise. Again he inwardly chastised himself. *Stop it, Booker! Have you learned nothing?*

He forced his gaze away from her to his surroundings instead. He saw many trees, immense weeping willows among them, their long manes of fine green branches swaying to the ground. Squirrels scampered beneath them, and the air was filled with birdsong.

The path curved, and she pointed out a copse of cut-back stumps. From each one, dozens of thin osier rods had sprouted like a head of wild, silvery green hair. Meanwhile, the withies cut that winter stood in great bundles, left there to dry.

She explained, "The new growth should reach seven or eight feet before summer is over. Some growers coppice their willows almost to the ground, but our sheep like to eat the shoots, so this method keeps them out of reach, although our groundsman harvests some for winter feed."

They reached a large shed built near the river's edge. A smaller building—a privy, he guessed—stood to one side.

"We originally had only a few acres of basket willows or osiers. But I have devoted more land at the far end of the island." She gestured beyond the shed. "In fact, I had ten loads of manure delivered recently. When the wind blows from the north you can still smell it."

He looked at her, shaking his head in amusement. "Of all the topics I anticipated discussing with the lady of the island, manure was not one of them."

She chuckled, and her cheeks turned pink, or perhaps it was a play of the sunlight on her smooth, lovely skin.

He cleared his throat. "What kind of baskets do you make here?"

"Common bushel baskets for farmers and fruiterers, and large hampers like this one. But we want to expand our offerings, include some baskets made of osiers peeled white, which bakers use to carry bread, and flat broad clothes baskets. Perhaps later, eel traps, lobster baskets, and salmon traps."

"Ambitious," Benjamin allowed, impressed in spite of himself.

They approached the shed, which was two steps up from the ground on low pilings. Through the open double doors, he saw perhaps ten people—women, adolescents, and a few older men sitting on stools or rugs on the ground, the spidery starts of baskets in their hands, long willow spokes projecting from a center base. Before them stood a man in his mid- to late thirties, broad shouldered and simply dressed in a dark coat and trousers. He had a head of shaggy brown curls in need of cutting and a pair of colored spectacles screening his eyes.

He demonstrated the proper technique for a sturdy base, instructing in a low baritone voice.

"That is Mr. Christie," Miss Wilder said quietly. "The master weaver."

"He is younger than I'd imagine a master would be. Is he . . . blind?"

"Um-hm. Mr. Truelock tells me he contracted ophthalmia while working as a sailor in the West Indies."

"He can teach though he cannot see?"

She nodded. "Apparently he taught for several years at the Liverpool School for the Indigent Blind before coming here."

She gestured for Benjamin to set her hamper on a side table, then picked up one of the baskets from a nearby stack. "Here is one of his baskets. Intricate, is it not?"

He studied the pleasing pattern, created with different colors of willow. "Yes, and surprisingly . . . symmetrical."

They watched the lesson for a few minutes, and then Miss Wilder quietly began laying out the contents of her hamper: a heaping pile of buns, butter, sliced meat and cheese, and several urns of milk and tea. "We serve breakfast and midday nuncheon and then send home larger dinners the workers can share with their families."

"Good night! Your Mrs. Philpotts must be the saint."

"I won't argue with that. Lotty and I help. We all do."

She glanced up at him as she worked. "Perhaps you think I ought to weave as well. But the truth is, I am all thumbs. My talents are put to better use in ordering supplies, corresponding with potential customers, paying wages and bills, and helping to keep our workers well fed."

"And ordering manure."

She grinned. "Exactly."

The foreman, Mr. Linton, announced a short respite, and

the weavers sighed with relief, rising and stretching aching limbs.

"It will get easier, I promise," Mr. Christie called after them.

A youth bounded over to the table, an eager smile on his face and a book under his arm.

Miss Wilder smiled back. "Goodness, Joe, you seem to grow every time I see you. You are nearly as tall as I am."

"It's on account of the good food you feed us, Mum says."

"I am glad to hear it." She handed him a sandwich and cup of milk.

He thanked her and moved off. Curious, Ben followed him. Joe sat on a bench that overlooked a picturesque stream, but he clearly had eyes only for his book. Ben sat beside him and asked what he was reading.

Swallowing a bite, the lad replied, "It's an adventure story called *The Notorious Highwayman*."

"The hero is a highwayman?" Benjamin asked in surprise.

Joe nodded. "I know it's wrong to steal, but he's such an amusing fellow, it's hard not to like him."

"Well. It's good to see a young man reading. I always had a book in hand at your age."

The boy nodded, took a hearty bite, and turned the page.

Benjamin returned to the shed. There Miss Wilder greeted two of the women as they stretched their necks and flexed stiff fingers.

"Good afternoon, Mrs. Winkfield. Jenny."

The older woman waved and continued to the privy, but the younger woman—large with child—came over to the table for a cup of tea and lingered to talk. He thought of Mr. Hardy's daughter, Cordelia. Tried to imagine her in a similar state, carrying her husband's child. He had once thought he might have that role in her life, but it was not to be.

Miss Wilder asked the young woman, "How are you feeling, Jenny?"

The expectant mother shrugged, her expression stoic. "This babe is restless and keeping me up nights, truth be told. But I'm glad for every little sign that he or she is alive and well."

Miss Wilder nodded. "Have you decided on names yet?"

"Louis or Louisa, named for my poor husband, God rest his soul."

Surprise flared through Benjamin. She was so young to be a widow.

Another woman in middle age went through the line. Isabelle asked her, "How is Mr. Jones today?"

"Low indeed, miss. But where there's life, there's hope. Aye?"

Miss Wilder opened her mouth, and Benjamin expected her to say something comforting, to offer to pray for the ailing Mr. Jones, whoever he was, but she hesitated. Instead, she squeezed the woman's hand and said, "I shall remind Mr. Truelock to pray for him."

The woman nodded. "Oh yes, he has been good about re-membering us and visiting. And Miss Truelock often brings a loaf or pie."

"I am glad to hear it. Arminda and her father are both so kindhearted."

"Yes." The woman grinned and gave Miss Wilder a saucy wink. "And you ain't too bad yourself."

Benjamin secretly agreed.

When the brief meal was over, Miss Wilder packed up her hamper and turned to him. "Would you like to see the rest of the island while we are out here?"

"Yes, if you have the time to show me."

"It won't take long. And it's such a beautiful day."

Benjamin again carried the covered basket—far lighter now. He looked around and heavenward. It was indeed a beautiful, sunny day. The blue skies were webbed with wispy white clouds stirred by a gentle breeze.

They walked a little farther on the shore path, leaving the weaving shed behind them. Here, several paths diverged from the main one, cutting across the island's wooded interior.

Miss Wilder directed their steps onto one of these, its cobbles grouted in moss. "The island isn't terribly wide, but it's long. This end is given over to the osier beds, weaving shed, and tenant cottages. At the other end are the house, stables, and boathouse. Here in the middle is mostly woodland. Many birds and small animals take refuge here."

"As do you."

She looked over at him and for a moment held his gaze. "Yes, I suppose I do."

They continued across the island, Benjamin recognizing cedar, chestnut, and Scots pine among the willows, the trees filtering the sunlight and dappling the bright green grass with patches of shade. The air smelled of tangy pine and daffodils.

They soon reached the opposite bank. To the left, she pointed out the new osier bed, the rows of planted cuttings already sprouting with spring growth. To the right, a row of attached limestone cottages with slate roofs. "Those are the tenant cottages," she explained. "Our groundsman, Abel Curtis, lives in one. Roy and Frances Howton in another. Oh, and Mr. Christie, while he's here."

They turned and headed downriver. The path here was simply a narrow track worn in the grass, bordered by lush green ivy. After several yards, they crossed a low stone bridge. Beneath it, the stream ran peacefully, tumbling over rocks in a mini waterfall before widening into a lagoon.

This bridge, Benjamin noticed, she walked over without hesitation.

A statue stood in the midst of the lagoon, the figure of a young woman feeding swans.

"Is that meant to be you?" he asked.

"No. My great-grandmother Isabelle was the model for that sculpture when she was young. The island and I were both named after her."

They walked on, passing a small flock of grazing sheep. Beyond the lagoon, where the stream met the Thames, a boathouse huddled on the riverbank. They veered from the path toward it.

As they neared, he asked, "Do you have a boat?"

"Just an old rowboat."

Benjamin thought again of racing rowboats with his brother and found himself grinning.

Miss Wilder studied his face with interest. "Like boats, do you?"

He shrugged. "My brother and I used to race." And while Reuben seemed to best him at most things in life, Benjamin had won every time. He had even competed with an amateur rowing club for a few years, before his responsibilities at the law firm increased, limiting his free time.

"You are welcome to take the boat out while you are here, if you would like."

"Thank you. I just might do that. For old times' sake."

Reaching a wooden pier beside the boathouse, Ben looked out at the water. The river rippled in shades of yellow green and moss green, aquatic plants visible below the surface.

"Take care," she said. "The river is shallow near shore, but it drops off sharply."

Boats passed by on the winking water. Narrowboats, punts, and skiffs.

89

She pointed out a few species of birds to him. There a great crested grebe, with dark head plumes and orange neck ruff. And there a shy kingfisher flashing past at high speed, then plunging into the water to catch a small fish.

She drew a quick intake of breath and pointed. "There's another kingfisher. On that willow branch hanging over the water . . . ? I don't often see them, and two in one day? A rare treat."

When the bird flew off, she turned toward two large white swans. "Those are mute swans. Very common on the Thames, especially near Windsor. Most mate for life."

The pair of regal birds faced one another forehead to forehead, orange beaks pointing down, their long necks curved in the very shape of a valentine heart.

"Beautiful, are they not?" she murmured.

"Yes," he agreed, admiring their elegance and fidelity.

Finally, she pointed out a European coot—a water bird with a "bald" forehead and brilliant white bill. She said, "Coots are famous for punishing boisterous chicks. Their young often go off and hide, sometimes never returning."

"Sounds familiar."

"Hm?"

"Oh. Nothing."

Continuing along the shore, they came to the stable building and fenced paddock.

"Do you have many horses?" he asked.

"Not now. We keep a horse to pull the wagon to market, but that is all. Our chaise and carriage horses are kept in London these days, except when Rose visits. We had more in the past. My brother was an avid rider."

"No separate carriage house?"

"No."

He gestured toward the stable door. "Do you mind if I take a look?"

She hesitated. "If you would like."

He opened the door, the smells of hay, dust, and dung assaulting him. He hoped he would find a second carriage inside, bearing evidence of a recent trip to London, like toll receipts. He stepped over piles of droppings and looked around. Dust motes danced in shafts of sunshine streaming in through a loft window. By this light, he saw a farm wagon, and the sleek chaise he'd seen arrive that morning.

A few horses nickered at them from the nearest stalls, while the remaining stalls were unoccupied. Benjamin walked slowly down the aisle to the building's end, but Miss Wilder lagged behind.

He looked back at her, noticing her discomfort as she twisted the ring on her finger, her gaze sliding to and away from the last stall.

He looked closer. Something was in there. Tarpaulins covered a large heap, but it was too dim in the shadows to make out any details.

"Shall we be getting back?" she asked, turning toward the door.

He nodded and followed her out. It was probably not related to Norris's death, but he decided to return and investigate later with a lamp.

They strolled a little farther to the downstream point of the island, where another bench sat overlooking the water. "Of course you know Riverton is there on the right," Miss Wilder said, then pointed across the wider expanse of river on the left. "And on the opposite shore is Taplow, though you can't see it for the trees."

They walked back toward the front of the house, completing

the circular tour, their shoes crunching over pebbles and pine needles, many trees in full leaf and more spring flowers blossoming as the April days warmed and lengthened.

"It's beautiful here," he murmured.

Miss Wilder smiled softly. "Thank you. I think so too."

She turned back to him, adding, "Oh. You said you had a few questions for me, but I quite forgot."

He grinned a bit sheepishly. "I did too."

Isabelle expected Mr. Booker to start asking his questions, but he remained silent. As they neared the veranda, she spied a familiar figure crossing the bridge and her heart lightened. "Ah. Miss Truelock is here."

Isabelle walked over to greet her friend. Arminda Truelock was short and plump, with a sweet face and cheerful disposition. Isabelle loved her.

"Good afternoon, Arminda."

"Isabelle. I've only come to see how you are."

"Well enough. Better than a few days ago, at least."

Mr. Booker, she noticed, hesitated a few steps behind. She turned to include him.

"Miss Truelock, allow me to introduce Mr. Booker, a lawyer with Uncle Percival's firm. Miss Truelock is our vicar's daughter and my dear friend."

He bowed and she curtsied.

Interest and curiosity dancing in her eyes, Arminda looked from the handsome, gentlemanlike lawyer to Isabelle and back again. "And what brings you here to Belle Island, Mr. Booker?"

Isabelle answered for him. "Unfortunately he came to deliver the sad news of Percival's death. He is remaining a few days longer to help me with a few legal matters."

"Oh no!" Arminda's face fell. "How unexpected. Your uncle was here not long ago. Was he in poor health?"

"No. Mr. Booker says he was killed, of all things. Struck down a couple of nights ago. I believe he counts me as one of the suspects."

Her friend's thin eyebrows rose, and her mouth parted. "You? Unbelievable."

"I know. Especially as Percival died in London."

"In London? Well, still . . ." Arminda shifted, glanced at Isabelle, then returned her focus to Mr. Booker.

He gave her a tight-lipped smile and said, "The authorities are pursuing other possibilities as well."

Arminda clasped her hands. "I can tell you that it is not in Isabelle's character to harm anyone."

"I am glad to hear you think so. But in my experience, people will do all sorts of uncharacteristic things if the threat is dire enough."

Arminda's gaze darted to Isabelle, then away again. "I see. I am stunned, truly."

Isabelle looked at her friend in consternation. Though Arminda was generally reticent and reserved, as befitted a clergyman's daughter, Isabelle had still expected her to protest more vehemently, insisting Mr. Booker's suspicions were outlandish and impossible. But she did not. Instead, Arminda's face puckered, and she looked far away in thought.

Then, as if becoming aware of two pairs of expectant eyes watching her, she blinked and said, "Again, I don't believe Isabelle would harm anyone. I will pray the authorities find whoever is responsible. In the meantime, is there anything I can do to help? I suppose the party is off?"

"No, it goes on as planned. Rose insists, and I haven't the heart to disappoint her. Please don't refuse for propriety's sake."

"I shan't. I shall be there for Rose's sake. And for yours."

They talked for a few minutes longer, and Isabelle invited Arminda to drink tea with them. But insisting errands prevented her, the vicar's daughter quickly retreated across the bridge. After Isabelle and Mr. Booker returned to the house, her thoughts remained on her friend. Did Arminda know something she did not?

That evening, Isabelle, Rose, and Mr. Adair gathered in the drawing room, dressed for dinner. Mr. Adair drank brandy he'd brought from London, while she and Rose sipped tea. It would be a long time before Isabelle wanted to drink anything stronger again. Mr. Booker had remained ensconced in the study all afternoon. She was just about to go and ask how he fared when he wandered into the drawing room.

"Ah, Mr. Booker. I was just about to send out a search party. You will join us for dinner, I hope?"

"Yes, I confess myself starved. Thank you."

"Excellent. May I offer you something first? I'm afraid we don't keep many spirits here, but I could send Jacob to fetch a bottle of orange wine, if you'd like."

Mr. Booker stilled. "Orange wine . . . ?"

"Yes. It is quite good, though I say it myself. From an old family recipe. My third year attempting it. I think the last batch is my best yet, though perhaps a bit more potent."

"Potent is right," the lawyer murmured.

Confusion swept over her. *What does he mean by that?*

Mr. Booker asked, "Did you give any wine to Mr. Norris?"

She looked at him in surprise. "I did, actually. I sent two bottles as a peace offering. Did he mention the wine? I do hope he enjoyed it."

"I think that highly unlikely."

She frowned. "Why do you say that?"

He opened his mouth, then apparently thought better of what he'd been about to say.

Isabelle looked at Rose, wondering if her niece would mention her part as courier when she was last home. Rose met her gaze, then glanced at Mr. Adair, who gave a subtle shake of his head. Both remained silent.

Isabelle turned back to Mr. Booker and saw that he had not missed any of it.

"What sort of container did you send the wine in?" he asked.

"Green glass bottles. In the past I used simple silver rings to identify the type. But this year I made my own paste labels with little watercolor oranges and the name *Belle Island Wine*. It is as artistic as I get these days."

"So Mr. Norris would have known the wine came from here."

"Yes. Anyone would have."

"Where are the rest of the bottles now?"

"In the cellar," she answered without hesitation. "Beyond the few we've already consumed. Why do you ask?"

Ignoring the question, his gaze shifted from person to person. "Miss Wilder, no one else has chosen to drink your *potent* homemade wine. I wonder why?"

"I prefer tea," Miss Lawrence said.

Mr. Adair held up his glass. "Brandy for me. Orange wine is too sweet for my taste. Pray do not be offended, Miss Wilder."

"Not at all." Isabelle confessed, "And truth be told, I overindulged recently and am loathe to repeat the experience. But I guarantee the wine is perfectly good to drink."

Mr. Booker studied her face and said dryly, "Well then, tea it is."

The conversation at dinner was rather stilted, the trio clearly uneasy in the company of their unexpected guest. But then Miss Lawrence raised the topic of her aunt's new pet.

"Have you decided what to name the new puppy, Aunt Belle?"

"Not yet. But I am thinking perhaps Oliver or Ollie."

"Oh yes, I like that. He looks like an Ollie. But is poor Hamish jealous?"

"Actually I think he is relieved to be left alone to sleep to his heart's content. Until the puppy decides to nip his tail, that is."

"Speaking of sleep, where does the pup bed down at night?" Rose asked. "With you?"

"Goodness no. My father would never have allowed a dog in one of the bedchambers. He will sleep in the laundry room until he is old enough and well-trained enough to have free rein of the house."

"Poor thing. He is probably scared down there all alone with the mangle. I know I would be."

Miss Wilder gave her a fond smile. "That is because you have always been tenderhearted where animals are concerned, but a firm hand is the only way to raise a well-behaved dog."

"I am sure you are right." Rose turned to Benjamin. "Had you a dog growing up, Mr. Booker?"

"Me? No. Too difficult to keep a dog in London."

"Yes, I can see that."

The conversation became stilted once more.

Benjamin excused himself from coffee and dessert and returned to the study to let the others enjoy the remainder of their meal in peace.

Later that night, Benjamin lay in bed reading his book, *Gulliver's Travels*. He paused midpage and looked up. What had he heard? Footsteps outside his bedchamber? Probably just a servant.

He continued reading.

Eventually he set aside the novel and blew out his candle. He pulled up the bedclothes and closed his eyes. A door creaked somewhere nearby, and he abruptly opened them. He felt wide awake and restless, every sound in the house an alarm bell. Probably because he'd slept so much the day before, obeying the doctor's order to rest.

Giving up, he climbed from bed, tied a dressing gown around himself, and slid his feet into shoes. He thought he would try to find a glass of milk or something more to eat from the kitchen. That would help him sleep.

He relit his candle by dipping a long matchstick into the fire, then opened his bedchamber door and listened. Silence. He walked quietly along the corridor and down the stairs, his candle casting ghoulish shadows on the portraits of Wilder ancestors on the walls. Reaching the ground floor, he turned in the direction he had seen the servants coming and going and made his way belowstairs.

He paused at the bottom of the basement stairs. Was that a voice? Surely none of the servants would be up at this hour. He began to feel uneasy, hoping he wouldn't interrupt a clandestine meeting or tryst.

Then he heard a strange high-pitched whine, and a shiver ran over him. Someone was in distress. His heart began to beat a little faster.

Concerned, he followed the sound to a door left slightly ajar. Weak light leaked from it into the passage.

"Shh . . ." someone inside said. "Hush. You're all right. You're safe."

Miss Wilder's voice. Curiosity mounting, he tiptoed to the door and peeked inside. From the light of a candle lamp, he saw her lying on the floor next to a bed set up for the new puppy, stroking his fur. The puppy whined again, then burrowed close to her side with a sigh.

Apparently Benjamin had not been the only one struggling to sleep in his new environment. He recalled what Miss Wilder had said at dinner about needing a firm hand to raise a well-behaved dog and found himself grinning in the dark.

A firm hand, indeed.

CHAPTER
eight

The next morning everyone was up and about early, busily preparing for the party that night—everyone except for Benjamin and perhaps Mr. Adair. Jacob and the housemaids finished cleaning, Mrs. Philpotts and the kitchen maids prepared vast quantities of food, and Miss Wilder and Rose polished silver, wrote place cards, and debated seating arrangements.

After helping himself to tea and toast, Benjamin tried to work in the study but felt guilty sitting there while everyone rushed madly about. From the windows, he saw the groundsman scything the lawn where the sheep had missed a weedy patch, and an older man in the kitchen garden behind the house. He decided to go out and offer his assistance. He had no experience with grounds keeping, but he knew his way around a garden. Though admittedly, he was more familiar with the medicinal herbs that grew in his father's physic garden than vegetables.

Benjamin let himself out the rear door and approached the low-walled kitchen garden. Among its rows of plants and staked vines, the old man moved slowly, bending and straightening arduously, hands gnarled with arthritis.

"Morning, sir. May I help?"

The man looked up. "Did Miss Wilder send you out here? I told her I could manage it. But she will fuss so about my rheumatism."

"She did not, sir. I am asking for myself. A man does not like to feel useless."

"Don't I know it." He sent a doubtful glance at Ben's suit of clothes. "Ever picked asparagus before?"

"No, but I can learn."

"Very well. You snap off each stalk at the ground, like so."

He bent to demonstrate, and then together the two men set to work, talking companionably as they did so. Benjamin learned that Roy Howton had been the head gardener during the estate's former days of glory.

"How long have you lived here?" Benjamin asked.

"More than five and twenty years. My missus too."

"So you know Miss Wilder well, then."

"Suppose I do. Though my wife knows her better. She worked in the nursery when the girls were young."

Ben added another few stalks to the basket. Not wanting to raise the man's ire, he said without derision, "So you knew Miss Wilder when she would still leave the island?"

Roy nodded. "That I did. She and her family would cross that bridge every Sunday on their way to church. We all followed them, proud to be part of the estate. Those were happy days for us. My wife and I still had our health. The Wilders were alive and well. Mr. Wilder was an excellent master—Miss Isabelle is very like him. Though times are leaner now than they were in his day."

Benjamin snapped another stalk, his fingernails already tinged green. "Did she change immediately or gradually?"

Roy considered. "It began fairly soon after their deaths, if I remember right. She went to church a few times to put flowers on their graves or attend a service, but less and less as the months passed and soon not at all. She grew more afraid to leave the island, and the bridge became the line she would not cross. As though it were quicksand, waiting to swallow her whole."

The old man paused to wipe a handkerchief over his perspiring face. "It's sad to see her so frightened. She's a keen, kind mistress, but an anxious woman, like her mother was."

"She doesn't appear anxious to me."

Roy shrugged. "For the most part, she's not. Belle Island is her home. Here, she feels safe and is everything gracious and benevolent. But don't ask her to cross that bridge, or you will see another woman entirely."

"Extraordinary . . ."

The gardener looked at him in mock severity and shook a stalk in his face. "Now, enough gossip, young man." He sat down on the low garden wall, wiped his face again, and fanned himself with his hat. "You take this basket and that one with the peas to Mrs. Philpotts for me, will you?"

"Happily." Ben rose on knees already stiff and carried the baskets down to the kitchen. He was glad to be of use, although he wished he'd learned something more useful about Miss Wilder.

Late that morning, Mr. Booker left the house to visit Riverton, saying only that he had an errand to complete. Isabelle offered to send Jacob on his behalf, but he declined. He seemed happy for an excuse to walk into the village again. She should be relieved to see the inquisitive lawyer leave . . . but she was not.

She followed him as far as the veranda steps, watching wistfully as he crossed the bridge so effortlessly.

At its center, Mr. Booker turned back. As if reading her thoughts, he rapped the wooden railing and called to her, "Seems perfectly sound to me!"

Making a funny face, she pressed the back of her hand to her brow in a melodramatic pose. He chuckled.

"How you do enjoy tormenting me, Mr. Booker," she called after him, waving to shoo him away.

He tipped his hat and continued into the village. His teasing had surprised her, but she found she rather liked it.

Feeling suddenly restless, Isabelle brought Ollie outside to play, thinking a great deal of exercise might calm his exuberant behavior so he would hopefully sleep through the party later that evening.

The young dog ran happily over the lawn, chasing a squirrel. She called his name, urging him to return to her, to no avail. She clapped her hands and called him again in a louder, higher voice. "Come here, boy. Come!"

Finally, the squirrel disappeared up a tree and her voice seemed to penetrate. The pup turned and ran toward her.

Isabelle lowered herself to her haunches and spread her hands. The overgrown puppy bounded into her embrace, all legs and ears and eagerness. She rubbed its head and tilted up her chin in a vain attempt to avoid his licking tongue.

Teddy, in black frockcoat and hat, walked over to join her, medical case in hand.

She looked up at him from her squatting position. "Visiting Mr. Curtis again?"

"Yes."

"How is Abel?"

"Hearty and hale, unlike poor Mrs. Howton, who is suffering a cold at present." He extended his hand and helped her up.

"I don't know why you visit Abel so often when he is the

healthiest of my tenants." Reluctantly, she added, "Is it because you miss your own father?" It was the first time in recent
memory she had mentioned the man.

Her companion winced. "More because Abel misses his own
son."

"He would never say it to me, but I suppose he blames me
for Evan staying away?"

Instead of answering, Teddy bent to the ground and picked
up a stick. He stood and tossed it, and the pup bounded after it.

Isabelle watched Ollie fondly. "He is a dear. Thank you again,
Teddy."

"I am glad you are enjoying him."

Tail wagging, the dog retrieved the tossed stick and returned
it—not to the man who had thrown it but to his mistress. The
pup was clearly besotted with her, and Isabelle didn't mind
that at all.

She smiled at her old friend. "What I like best about dogs
is that they are so loyal. They love us unconditionally, just as
we are."

The doctor frowned. "That is because they are simple crea-
tures, Isabelle. It is not wrong to wish to help someone to
change, to overcome whatever weaknesses are holding them
back from living life to the full."

She sifted his words and felt a pinch of hurt. "Am I not living life to the full?"

"You know you are not."

"Being a homebody is not the same as being ill or weak."

He looked at her, one brow raised, but wisely kept silent.

As they talked, Teddy continued the idle game of fetch
with the dog, which led them slowly across the lawn, nearer
the bridge. Teddy offered her the stick to throw. She reached
for it but hesitated. On the opposite bank, she noticed a man

half-hidden by a tree. Was he watching them? Feeling suddenly self-conscious, she dropped her hand. "You go ahead."

Teddy reeled back and threw the stick, hard. A gust of wind seemed to catch it and carry it high and far. Or perhaps in his frustration with her, he had whipped the stick farther than intended. The stick flew in an arc over the water, clattering off the railing of the bridge before bouncing and landing on the road beyond it. The man watching them retreated farther behind the tree.

As the pup took off running across the bridge in lusty pursuit of the stick, Isabelle became aware of a sound, the thunder of horse hooves approaching on the river road.

Isabelle sucked in a breath, then shouted, "No . . . !"

She started toward the bridge, stopping dead at the first plank as though at a cliff's edge. Only her voice followed the puppy over. "Ollie, no! Come back!"

But the eager pup bounded with single-minded determination toward the stick, heedless of the approaching carriage. She turned her head toward the speeding stagecoach. The driver, whip in hand, was clearly unaware of all but a schedule to keep. She gauged his rate of speed against the dog's, and panic squeezed her chest. She felt Teddy's watchful gaze on her profile, but he said nothing, did nothing.

"Do something!" she cried.

"I'm sorry. I did not mean to throw it to the road."

Finally, he leapt into motion, starting across the bridge. But it was too late. The horses were nearly upon the defenseless puppy. Isabelle stood there, feeling helpless.

At the last second, the man behind the tree lunged, hat flying, grabbing the small canine as though a damsel in distress and rolling out of harm's way. The pup yelped. The driver shouted curses as he passed, the wheels dangerously close to the man's head.

When the carriage had gone, the man released the startled dog. Ollie snapped up the stick and ran back across the bridge, joyously unaware of his near demise. The man retrieved his hat and replaced it on his head. Pulling the brim low, he walked in a surprisingly nonchalant fashion back toward the tree.

Her heart lurched. Sunlight had shone on his exposed profile before he put his hat back on, and a flash of recognition bolted through her. Pulse pounding, Isabelle stood there frozen, ignoring the returning dog and her companion. The man remained where he was but did not wave or otherwise acknowledge them.

"Who is it?" Teddy asked, returning to her side.

Isabelle did not answer. She knew who she'd thought it was, but she was probably mistaken.

She stared silently a moment longer, but the man turned away and disappeared from view.

Teddy stepped in front of her, grasping her shoulders. "Will you now admit you have a problem? An innocent creature was in danger, and you would not step one foot onto the bridge to rescue him."

Isabelle looked up at him, irritation mounting. "You didn't exactly hurry to his rescue until I prompted you. And you are the one who bought the dog and threw the stick in the first place!"

She turned away in a swirl of skirts and rushed across the grass, onto the veranda, and back to the house. The pup followed eagerly behind. Her human companion, less so.

Since he would be staying on a few days longer, Benjamin needed to pick up more tooth powder and shaving tonic, and perhaps an extra pair of stockings. He wished he'd visited his barber before leaving London.

While he awaited his turn at the counter, he thought about the man he'd seen loitering near the bridge when he'd passed, leaning one shoulder against a tree. The man had clearly been watching the island. Benjamin had looked back to see what might have arrested his attention, and there she was . . . Miss Wilder. She was easily recognizable even from across the river, though his memory no doubt filled in the smaller details. Her golden brown hair, blue eyes, fair skin, small nose, and curvy mouth.

A sudden smile had split her lovely mouth that distance could not disguise. What had prompted it? The physician beside her or the stranger on the opposite bank? Then the puppy bounded into view, and Miss Wilder bent to pet it. This, then, was the recipient of her beaming expression and not either man.

Satisfied, Benjamin had continued to the village shop.

When he stepped outside after making his purchases, the man was still there, half-hidden by the broad tree trunk, dusting off his trousers and coat sleeves. What was he doing? Benjamin wondered, suspicion flooding him.

Feigning interest in the wares on display in the shop window, Benjamin surreptitiously watched the tall, dark-haired man, near his own age.

With a final look across the bridge, the man turned his back on the island, picked up his walking stick, and strolled toward the inn, a slight limp to his gait. Benjamin waited a few moments for discretion's sake, then followed him inside.

He found the man in the taproom, seated in an inglenook with Mr. Colebrook—the same old man Benjamin had tried to talk to the day before.

The newcomer asked Mr. Colebrook a question, and Benjamin waited for the cranky old man to deliver the same sharp setdown he had received . . . but no.

"She has never married?" the younger man asked.

"No, sir. Hard to find a husband when she don't step foot off that island."

The dark brows rose in reply. "What?"

The old man nodded. "That's right. She hasn't crossed that bridge in ten years. Not even once."

"Why?" the man asked, clearly thunderstruck.

"Can ye blame her? When every Wilder dies young when he leaves it? Her brother, her father, her sister . . ." The old man shook his head. "I suppose ye think it's down to you. Ye want to hear that her heart were broken after you left, and she vowed to remain alone on the island all her days. Is that it?"

The younger man smirked. "A flattering scenario, I admit. Though I always imagined Theo Grant would be there to comfort her and offer his shoulder . . . and the rest of his sorry carcass."

The old man snorted and took a long draw from his ale. "Oh, he's worn a path over that bridge sure enough, but no wedding bells in the offing, leastways that I've heard about."

The barman took notice of Benjamin standing there and raised his eyebrows in question. Sheepishly, Benjamin waved a greeting and turned to go. But he found himself irrationally peeved. Who was that man that the old curmudgeon would answer his questions when he had rebuffed Benjamin? And more importantly, who was he to Miss Wilder?

As he left the inn, the postmaster called out to him. "Mr. Booker, is it?"

Benjamin turned. "Yes?"

"I've a letter for you. Was planning to send it with the rest of the Belle Island post, but since you're here . . ."

Benjamin walked over to the counter and accepted it, fishing out his coin purse to pay the postage. "Thank you."

He recognized Mr. Hardy's handwriting and opened the letter immediately.

Benjamin,

New development. Officer Riley has turned his attention to a different suspect. Housekeeper Mrs. Kittleson reports that the maid, Mary Williams, has absconded. Kittleson also suspects her of pinching the missing silver. Riley theorizes that perhaps Percival caught her in the act of stealing, and she silenced him. Riley is also searching for Williams's beau. She'd given his name and direction, but when Riley went there, no one answered the door, so the two may have left town together.

Stay your course for a day or two until we know more. I am not yet convinced Miss W or Miss L not involved.

Robert Hardy

Benjamin lowered the letter with a sigh of relief. Then he caught himself. Was he so glad the lovely Miss Wilder was no longer the primary suspect, so hopeful she was innocent and already admiring her against his better judgment? *Careful, Booker, you've made this same mistake before.* He reminded himself that they had yet to receive the coroner's report. At least, Mr. Hardy had not mentioned it. Perhaps it had been inconclusive or delayed for some other reason.

Benjamin drew a long inhale. He would stay the course as Mr. Hardy asked, and continue to search for the missing will and for evidence. But in the meanwhile, this news made him feel slightly less guilty about attending Miss Wilder's dinner party. Who knew? He might even enjoy it.

CHAPTER

nine

Isabelle slipped down to the dining room with a sigh of pleasure. How lovely to see the long table laid with all the fine family china and silver they so rarely used these days. Their cook-housekeeper, Mrs. Philpotts, fairly glowed with exertion and enjoyment. How she had bustled about, setting the table, inspecting the glasses for spots, and selecting only the straightest wax candles for the candelabra and chandelier. She'd arranged flowers from their garden and fruit from the greengrocer in lovely displays, now and again dashing back to the kitchen to look at this roast or that fowl or observe the progress of the side dishes or sauces.

Isabelle and Lotty had offered to help, but Mrs. Philpotts wanted to see to everything herself. It was such a treat for her to prepare a formal meal after so many simple breakfasts, plain midday repasts, and boxed dinners for the workers.

At Isabelle's prodding, she *had* engaged two additional girls from the village to help with all the chopping and cleaning, and a waiter from the inn to act as second footman and help Jacob serve.

Together Isabelle and Mrs. Philpotts had planned a lovely

menu: a first course of asparagus soup and turbot with lobster sauce, followed by roast sirloin of beef, leg of lamb, larded guinea fowls, peas and stewed mushrooms, and finally a dessert course of meringues, orange jelly, and raspberry-rhubarb ices.

Isabelle surveyed the room one last time, touching up the flower arrangement and straightening the silverware.

Finally, she switched two place cards, then on second thought, switched them back. Did she want Mr. Booker seated next to her or directly across from her, watching her every expression? A difficult decision.

She might have stood there vacillating longer, but Carlota appeared and gently turned her toward the door. "The table looks lovely. Time to worry about your own appearance. Your bath is ready." Isabelle allowed her friend to lead her upstairs.

Lotty helped her undress and took her hand to steady her as she stepped into the tub. As Isabelle sank into the warm water, her muscles relaxed and her worries faded away. She had been foolish to allow a dream to bother her so much. Her anxiety over Rose's engagement and Percival's death had clearly left her overly emotional. Of course she had not somehow sneaked away to London and seen Percival dead. *Foolish, irrational creature.*

After Isabelle had soaked for a time, Lotty helped her wash her hair. *Heavenly.* She leaned forward, bowing her head as Carlota poured warm rinse water over her hair.

Carlota paused. "Miss? How did you get that bruise on your back?"

"Hm?"

"A nasty bruise. Near your tailbone?"

Isabelle stiffened, her pleasure evaporating. The dream came back to her—falling on the stairs, hitting her tailbone on the bottom step, her elbow on the newel-post.

She rose abruptly in the tub, and Carlota hurried to retrieve a towel and help her out. Isabelle stepped to the long mirror and twisted to the side. Sure enough, a purple bruise marred her lower back.

"I don't remember doing anything to cause this. And that scares me."

"Perhaps you knocked against something the other night, coming in from the boathouse in the dark."

"I suppose so . . ."

But a chill shivered over her, dispelling the warm comfort of the bath. What else might she not remember doing?

Lotty helped her into an evening gown of duck egg–blue taffeta with gold satin trim. Isabelle hoped the style and color were not too young for her. The more typical ivory worn by many women gave her complexion an unflattering sallow tinge.

Next Isabelle sat at the dressing table while Lotty curled her hair. Normally, Isabelle scoffed at too much fuss, but now she pushed aside her worries and said, "Why not? It is a festive occasion after all."

Lotty pressed her advantage. "And a touch of rouge?"

"Very well."

At the appointed hour, Isabelle made her way downstairs. For a moment, she remained on the bottom step, watching the scene in the entry hall as guests began arriving. At the door, Jacob took hats, greatcoats, and capes. He looked like a stranger, dressed as he was in foreign-looking livery.

The guests of honor stood waiting to meet the new arrivals— Mr. Adair in elegant evening attire, and Rose resplendent in shimmering ivory satin with an embroidered bodice. Her hair had been curled in tiny ringlets by Miss O'Toole, a woman of many talents, who had kept her place with Rose all these years by learning new skills as the need arose.

Dr. Grant arrived, wearing customary black and white. She realized anew that the stark colors were not flattering to Teddy, with his pale complexion and auburn hair. Nor was the cut of his coat as impressive as Mr. Adair's. She supposed the country physician had few occasions to dress formally.

The squeak of shoe leather caught her ear, and she turned with a little gasp. "Oh, Mr. Booker, you startled me."

The lawyer, striking in evening attire, came down the stairs looking a bit self-conscious. "Will I do?"

Her gaze traveled over him, heartbeat quickening. The coat emphasized broad shoulders and narrow waist. The high white shirt collar accentuated his strong jawline and cheekbones. "My goodness," she breathed. "My father never looked half so good in those as you do." She stopped herself. "That is, you look quite . . . tolerable."

"Thank you. If true, the credit goes to Adair's valet, who insisted on helping me dress and doing *something* with my hair. Did you ask him to do so?"

"No. I am afraid I did not think of it."

"He pressed the trousers, pinned up the waistcoat to better fit me, and polished the shoes. He also gave me the best shave of my life and tried to tame my hair. I hope I don't look the poodle or the fop."

Dark hair curled over his brow, and his side-whiskers had been trimmed to a fashionable point. She shook her head. "Neither one, I assure you."

His gaze moved from her hair to her face to her dress and back again. "And you, Miss Wilder. You look quite . . . tolerable too." But the light in his eyes told her he found her pretty.

Her cheeks grew warm. "Thank you, but you needn't flatter me. I know I am a woman of a certain age."

He continued down the stairs until he stood on the same

step. "A certain age? You mentioned you are only thirty, and as I am a similar age, I call that young indeed."

She smiled. "I admire your logic. Well, we had better go in. I'm meant to be the hostess, after all, and I am late to my own party."

As Isabelle descended the last step onto the marble floor, her shoes slipped on the highly polished surface. Instinctively, she flailed for a handhold and ended up gripping Mr. Booker's arm.

"Sorry. These new slippers are just that—slippery."

He laid a firm hand over hers. "All right?"

She nodded, but somehow she felt more at risk of falling than before.

He teased, "I would offer you my arm, but you have it in a death grip already."

"Oh! Forgive me!" She released him, but he grinned and jutted his elbow toward her. At this parry of humor from the serious solicitor, amusement overcame her embarrassment. She took his arm, a girlish giggle escaping as they gingerly crossed the hall together.

A stern-looking Theodore Grant appeared in their path.

"You needn't scowl so, Teddy," Isabelle said. "I slipped on the marble, and Mr. Booker was kind enough to . . . em, offer his arm."

The physician's brow furrowed with concern. "Are you all right?"

"Yes, yes. Perfectly. I did not fall, thanks to Mr. Booker. Now, is everyone here?"

Isabelle moved on to greet her guests: Mr. and Mrs. Truelock and their daughter, Arminda. Her mother's old friend, Lady Elliott. Rose's childhood friends, the Miss Faringdons, and their brother, George. And of course, Dr. Grant, Mr. Booker, Rose, and Christopher Adair.

113

The twelve of them took their seats around the beautifully set table lit by many candles, their flames spangling the silver tureen and serving dishes.

After the soup course, the meal was served in traditional French family style, with dishes arranged on the table and everyone helping themselves and their neighbors to whatever they wished to eat.

Noticing Isabelle eyeing the roast, Mr. Booker reached for the serving fork, but Teddy circumvented him, saying a bit too loudly, "What can I serve for you, Isabelle? Some roast and the horseradish sauce? I know you are partial to it."

He put a slice of meat on her plate and spooned the sauce on for her.

"Thank you, Teddy. I could have managed the sauce on my own."

"I don't mind. I like helping you."

Aware of Mr. Booker watching with studious interest, Isabelle was embarrassed by Teddy's doting behavior. She turned her attention to Rose and instantly felt better. How pretty and happy she looked, talking with the Truelocks and Faringdons and smiling often at Mr. Adair.

After the final course, Isabelle took a deep breath and rose. Tapping her glass with a spoon, she soon claimed everyone's attention.

Self-conscious with so many pairs of eyes upon her, Isabelle felt her smile waver. But the faces were all friendly, familiar ones. Even Mr. Booker appeared less suspicious than when he'd first arrived. Emboldened, she began, "I realize it is more traditional for the man of the family to toast the health of the young couple we are here to celebrate tonight, but I hope you don't mind listening to me instead."

Arminda smiled encouragement and Isabelle continued, "The

last time we celebrated an engagement in this family was when my sister, Grace, became engaged to her dear Harry Lawrence. It was my father standing up, raising his glass. How long ago it seems. How I miss them all still."

Her throat tightened, and she swallowed the rising lump. "Grace and Harry were very much in love and eager to serve God and country, even though it meant going far from home. Seeing Rose tonight, none of us can doubt how much in love she is with her dear Christopher as well."

She met Rose's gaze and continued, hoping to get through her speech without crying. "I know from my sister's letters how much she and Mr. Lawrence loved you, Rose. How they prayed for you and hoped you would have a good, long, meaningful life. They would be so happy for you, were they here. So proud of the wonderful young woman you've become." Isabelle's voice hitched, and she pressed her lips together to halt their tremble. Across the table, Rose's brown eyes glistened with tears.

Isabelle forced a smile. "I hope, Mr. Adair, that you will endeavor to deserve her. For she has the most beautiful, loving heart I have ever known."

"I could not agree more," Adair said, then added with a roguish wink, "And the most beautiful everything else!" He put his arm around Rose's shoulder, and she playfully pushed him away.

Isabelle continued, "I congratulate you, Mr. Adair. And, my dear Rose, I wish you every happiness in the world."

She raised her glass higher. "To Christopher and Rose."

"To Christopher and Rose," the others echoed. Around the table, guests lifted their glasses and nodded their heads to the couple in acknowledgment.

Shortly thereafter, Isabelle stood again, this time signaling it was time for the women to withdraw. "Well, ladies, shall we leave the men to their port and vile cigars?"

Mr. Truelock teased, "What? Are we to have none of your famous orange wine tonight?"

"Not this time." She darted an awkward glance at Mr. Booker. "There is some concern that the latest batch might be a little strong."

"Don't tarry too long," Rose urged the men. "For we are to have music soon. Aunt Belle thought we ought to limit the party to dinner only, for propriety's sake after recent . . . news. But I insisted. So if you must blame anyone, blame me. But for now, rest up, for dancing begins soon!"

Rose had asked Carlota to play the pianoforte in the drawing room while the women sipped tea and their food settled. When the men joined them half an hour later, Isabelle rose and said, "Many of you have met Miss Medina, my companion and friend. But you may not know that she is also an accomplished actress and singer. And though she is reluctant, she has agreed to sing for us. Please offer her your encouragement."

Around the room, polite applause rose. Carlota began to play and sing "Deh vieni, non tardar" from *The Marriage of Figaro* by Mozart and Lorenzo da Ponte.

As Carlota sang the love song in her pure, lush soprano voice, Mr. Booker leaned near. "What in the world is she doing here as your maid? She belongs on the stage."

"That is where I first saw her," Isabelle whispered back.

"Why did she give it up?"

"You shall have to ask her. Though I will say her choice of song is rather ironic. In the opera, it is sung by the countess's maid while pretending to be a lady."

His lips pursed in appreciation. "I don't understand Italian. What do the words mean?"

"I am a poor translator, but something like, 'At last the moment arrives. I will experience joy without worry in the arms of my beloved. Fearful anxieties, get out of my heart!'"

For a moment Isabelle stilled, silently echoing the words. *"Fearful anxieties, get out of my heart!"* Would she ever experience joy without worry?

She felt Mr. Booker's thoughtful gaze on her profile. She sent him a small smile and then returned her focus to the music.

Carlota sang a second piece, and after a hearty round of applause, she rose and curtsied. "Now, enough of singing. The bride-to-be wishes to dance!"

"Hear, hear!" Rose enthused, rising to her feet and taking Christopher's hand.

The furniture at the end of the long room had already been placed around the perimeter in preparation, and the large Turkish carpet had been rolled up and taken away.

Rose called the first dance, the Leamington, and she and Mr. Adair stood at the top of the set as lead couple. Other couples filled in, forming two facing lines for a longways dance. Teddy claimed Isabelle, and Mr. and Mrs. Truelock joined them. George Faringdon politely asked Lady Elliott, but she waved away his offer, protesting she was too old to dance, so he turned and asked one of his sisters instead. His other sister, a budding musician herself, stood beside Carlota at the pianoforte to watch her flying fingers and turn the pages of music.

That left Mr. Booker and Arminda Truelock standing alone.

Mr. Booker, looking ill at ease, turned to her. "I am afraid I am out of practice."

Arminda smiled bravely. "That is all right. I don't mind sitting out if you'd rather not dance."

"I am willing if you are," he said. "I am simply warning you to beware your feet."

Arminda's face pinkened with pleasure. "Oh. Then, yes. I would love to. Thank you."

Seeing her friend's happiness, Isabelle's regard for Mr. Booker instantly grew. She watched him covertly as they danced. He moved with natural, athletic ease, and while he made a wrong turn now and again, he recovered quickly and soon mastered the patterns.

They completed a set of country dances, then paused to change partners.

Mr. and Mrs. Truelock begged off to rest, joining Lady Elliott in comfortable chairs around the perimeter. Isabelle secretly hoped to dance with Mr. Booker, but Mr. Adair politely asked for the next, and Teddy dutifully danced the second with Rose. George and Miss Truelock paired up, leaving Mr. Booker to dance with one of the young Miss Faringdons.

Carlota launched into a lively cotillion, and the four remaining couples danced another set.

When the dance ended, they were all overheated by their exertions. Rose threw open the garden door to let in some cool air. Mrs. Philpotts brought in punch and lemonade, and everyone paused to take refreshment, talking and laughing and catching their breath.

Lady Elliott took Isabelle aside and said, "I gather that handsome Mr. Booker is your lawyer. I had hoped he was a new admirer."

"I am afraid not."

"Pity. Of course I would prefer a gentleman for you, but at your age, my dear, it does not do to be too exacting."

"I quite agree."

Lady Elliott sent her a mischievous grin and pressed her arm.

As she walked away, Dr. Grant approached and placed a shawl around Isabelle's shoulders. "Don't want you to take a chill."

"Oh. I am not . . . well, thank you." She smiled at the thoughtful gesture and stepped to the sideboard to refill her lemonade.

Mr. Booker stood nearby, glass in hand. He nodded toward the physician. "He is something of a mother hen, is he not?"

Isabelle glanced over at Teddy. "I suppose he is. He has been looking after me for a long time."

She turned back to Mr. Booker, found his warm eyes fastened upon her, and wondered what it would be like to be cared for by such a man. She *was* fond of Teddy and would probably even have agreed to marry him, if he'd asked, assuming his father remained elsewhere. But she could not honestly say she was *in love* with him. She had fancied herself in love only once, and that had been years ago. She thought again of the man who had rescued Ollie. For a moment, she'd imagined it was him. Would Evan Curtis one day return to Belle Island? Did she want him to? Isabelle was not certain.

Stepping closer, Mr. Booker asked, "May I have the next, Miss Wilder? Your friends survived dancing with me, although I cannot guarantee your toes will."

Isabelle's stomach tingled with anticipation. "With pleasure. I consider myself and my toes duly warned."

Carlota played the introduction of another country dance, and Isabelle recognized it as Prince William of Gloucester's Waltz.

The couples took their places. First, they faced their corners, balancing right and left, then turned and changed places. Mr. Booker took both of her hands in his, and together they moved around their neighbors. Although she was wearing gloves, the lawyer had discarded his, and Isabelle noticed how easily his larger hands enveloped hers. Finally, they joined four hands across and circled right, then left.

The simple pattern repeated, and each time Mr. Booker faced

her or took her hand, his gaze held hers. He really had the most arresting eyes. . . .

Moving forward the second time, he stepped on her hem, causing her to stumble.

Grasping her hands to steady her, his face reddened. "Sorry."

She smiled reassurance. "That's all right."

When the set ended, Mr. Booker offered his arm and escorted her to her seat. "You are a beautiful dancer, Miss Wilder. Very graceful—even when some clod steps on your dress."

Her cheeks warmed with pleasure. "Thank you."

He grinned. "And how are your toes?"

She looked up into his deep brown eyes, thinking, *In less danger than my heart.*

When next they rested between sets, the guests begged Carlota to sing again. She modestly resisted their entreaties, though Isabelle, who knew her so well, could see the attention pleased her. She added her own encouragement. "Do sing for us. Perhaps something from *Don Giovanni?*"

It was after this opera that Isabelle had first met Carlota Medina, though she was using her stage name at the time. She had performed the role of Donna Elvira, a woman abandoned by her lover and seeking revenge.

Now their eyes met for a meaningful moment, and then with a somber nod, Carlota began to sing, but then she broke off midsong, staring at something.

Isabelle turned to see what had arrested her attention. In the open garden door stood a man in a greatcoat, walking stick in hand. Isabelle gasped, palm instinctively pressed to her heart. Evan Curtis. The man she had once thought she'd marry.

She had not spoken to him in nearly ten years. Not since Uncle Percy persuaded her to refuse him. It *had* been him on the other side of the bridge.

He looked somewhat different. Shoulders broader. Jaw stronger. More a man than the rash youth she recalled. His hair was still black, his face devilishly handsome, his eyes piercing blue and more sardonic than ever.

"Ev . . . um, Mr. Curtis," Isabelle faltered.

He stepped inside. "It's Captain Curtis now. I meant to stay away, but I heard the most singular voice." He turned to Carlota at the pianoforte. "My compliments, madam."

Lotty darted an uncertain glance at Isabelle, then back to him. "Thank you."

Isabelle struggled to think of what to say. Especially with an audience witnessing their awkward reunion, including Mr. Booker. "You . . . have been to see your father?"

"I have. He is the reason I've come, after all. I hope you didn't think I'd come to see . . . anyone else."

"I . . . no, I . . ."

"That is all in the past of course. Ah . . . Miss Truelock." He bowed to Arminda, and she curtsied but did not smile. Evan turned and added, "And here is the great physician himself."

Teddy walked forward to stand beside Isabelle, his mouth pressed into a prim line. "Curtis. About time you showed up. Your father has been worried sick."

"Good to see you too, Theo. Haven't changed a bit, I see. Except your hair is thinner—as is your wit, I imagine."

Teddy stiffened, but Curtis raised a consoling palm. "Forgive me. My father says you have been kindness itself to him all these years, and I sincerely appreciate it."

Dr. Grant held his gaze a moment, perhaps gauging his sincerity, then relaxed. "It has been my pleasure. He is a good man. And he has missed you terribly."

"Yes, well. I had good reason to stay away." He sent a telling glance toward Isabelle.

Evan walked farther into the room, and she noticed a slight limp.

He added, "I speak of duty, of course. Duty kept me away. But I am back now."

Dr. Grant frowned. "The war has been over for some time."

"Has it? I beg to disagree. Some wars are just beginning."

The two men stared at one another, until Isabelle cleared her throat and said brightly, "For those of you who haven't met Captain Curtis, he is Abel Curtis's son. He and Dr. Grant and I have known each other since childhood."

Rose stepped forward with a ready grin. "I knew you only briefly when I was young, but I remember you. You always had a liquorice drop for me in your pocket."

She curtsied and he bowed, his eyes remaining on her face. He slowly shook his head in awe. "She is the picture of her mother."

"Yes," Isabelle acknowledged.

Curtis patted his pocket. "I'm afraid I've no candy today."

"That's all right." Rose winked. "You may remedy that to-morrow."

He chuckled.

Isabelle added, "We are celebrating Rose's engagement to Mr. Adair."

His surprised glance swept over Isabelle, Teddy, and Arminda. "How can it be that Grace's wee girl is old enough to marry, when we four, so stricken in years, are yet unwed?"

Isabelle laughed softly. "That is an . . . interesting question."

For a moment Evan's gaze remained on her, then he turned again toward Lotty. "And may I ask the name of your song-bird?"

"Of course. This is Carlota Medina. Miss Medina, Captain Curtis. An old . . . friend."

"Yes, I have heard him spoken of."

One side of Evan's mouth lifted in a lazy grin. "All bad, I trust?"

"Not all."

The two regarded one another a moment. Evan looked away first, bowing again to Rose. "Please excuse me, Miss Rose. I am sure the last thing you want is an uninvited, unwelcome guest at your party."

"Uninvited, maybe," she said. "But that does not mean you are unwelcome. I was just about to beg for another dance. Will you join us?"

He made a face—part grimace, part smile. "Thank you. But my dancing days are over, thanks to Bonaparte." He tapped his walking stick against his ankle. "My last injury did not heal well."

Isabelle swallowed. She wanted to speak with him alone, even though the prospect made her nervous. Gathering her courage, she said, "You lead another dance without me, Rose. I will just see Captain Curtis out."

Around the room, looks were exchanged, and Teddy began to protest, but Arminda grasped his arm, forestalling him. *Dear Arminda.* Mr. Booker watched it all with a curious expression on his face.

Evan followed her out of the room without comment.

In the shadowy hall, Isabelle began, "You . . . joined an infantry regiment, I understand."

"Yes. Because Percival Norris purchased my commission. Started as an ensign, thanks to him, but advanced thanks to no one but me. Or maybe Boney, who killed one superior officer after another."

Behind them, the notes of a Scottish reel could be heard. Isabelle said, "That's right. I do recall hearing that."

"You knew he sent me away? Did you also know he made sure I would be assigned to a distant regiment about to be shipped off to war-torn Spain and Portugal? He didn't care where I went, as long as it was far from you. You *knew*, and you said nothing? Did nothing?"

Again she swallowed. "I . . . was glad Uncle Percy did something for you, though I did not know the particulars of the posting. Even so, I felt terrible about how things ended. I knew you were disappointed, so I—"

"And you were not—is that it? You were glad to be rid of me?"

"No, but . . . we were so young. And Percy so adamant."

Evan waved a hand, feigning unconcern. "That's all right. I should be thankful. It was a great opportunity for a *poor lad* like me. Father only a groundsman to the lofty Wilders. A chance to travel. See the world and move up in it. And I have done."

He sent her a sidelong glance. "I *was* surprised to hear you had not wed."

Isabelle shook her head.

He studied her face, then added dryly, "You need not worry. I have no wish to rekindle old feelings. I realize I was just a green, stupid boy and you the only female my age on the island. It was only natural I should fancy myself in love with you. It was an illusion, of course. I got over it as quickly as you did, no doubt."

Stung by his words, Isabelle licked dry lips. What to say? "I . . . I am relieved you are alive and well. When you did not return after the war, we worried about you."

"Did you indeed?"

"Yes."

He held her gaze a moment, then looked away. "Well, I cannot say the same. I only came here tonight because I saw the lights and heard the music. Merely curious. Your Miss Medina is a gem." His voice held a brittle quality. Was he purposely aiming to hurt her, or was he disguising his own pain?

"That was you on the road today, was it not? Thank you for saving my pup."

He shrugged. "It was nothing." Taking a deep breath, he said, "Well, I had better get back to my father. Thought I would stay with him for a few days. That is, if the mistress of the island does not mind."

"Of course not. You are welcome."

"Am I? How kind. Are you sure Mr. Norris will not jump out of the shadows and send me packing once more?"

She shook her head. "He cannot. He is dead."

Evan stilled. Sobered. "When?"

She told him what she knew.

"Dash it." He rubbed a hand over his face and muttered, "I was afraid of that."

She looked at him in surprise. "What do you mean?"

"Never mind. Good night, Isabelle Wilder, and good-bye. Again."

ten

The next morning, Benjamin lingered over coffee in the breakfast parlour. The simple buffet of fruits, cheese, and breads had been laid out the night before, to allow the cook-housekeeper and most of the servants to sleep in after their hard work for the previous evening's party.

Jacob—footman and all-around manservant—brought in a fresh pot of coffee, barely stifling a yawn.

Benjamin asked, "Are you the only one up and at it this morning?"

"I am, sir. But that's all right. I have the afternoon off instead and am already planning a nice long nap." He grinned and left the room.

Benjamin understood the weavers had been given the morning off as well.

He had seen none of the family yet and guessed they were sleeping in after the late night. His thoughts circled back to Miss Wilder's reaction when Captain Curtis had appeared like a ghost from the past. She'd been stunned, yes. Happy? He thought not. Or was that wishful thinking on his part?

He recalled the conversation he'd overheard at the inn, when the old curmudgeon said, *"Ye want to hear that her heart were broken after you left, and she vowed to remain alone on the island all her days."* Curtis had flippantly replied that he'd always imagined Miss Wilder would turn to Dr. Grant in his absence. A commonly held theory that had not come to pass. At least not yet.

Again Benjamin wondered why. He was no judge of what appealed to women, but Grant appeared to be an esteemed, reasonably good-looking physician near her own age. Grant clearly admired her and was protective of her, even possessive. Which of them hesitated to commit? Or were they really "just friends," as Miss Wilder had said? He doubted it was that simple. Might Curtis's return spur the doctor to act? And why did the thought of Isabelle Wilder married to either man leave Benjamin feeling so . . . empty? What a romantic fool he was. He'd only known her for a few days, whereas those three had been close for years.

Jacob returned and extended a silver tray toward him. "A letter for you, sir."

"Thank you."

Benjamin recognized the scrawled writing with surprise. The letter was not another from Mr. Hardy, as he'd expected, but from his brother. From the markings, he saw that it had at first been missent elsewhere. And little wonder, as Reuben had written the direction remarkably ill.

Ben opened it and read:

B.B.,
  Your Mr. Hardy told me where to write to you.
  As I suspected, P. Norris fatally poisoned before being struck. Organs inflamed. Wine in his stomach. Arsenic

detected using Orfila's methods: the sulphuretted hydro-
gen test and by subjecting the insoluble stomach contents
to burning charcoal. Results took time.

Upon receiving my report, Officer Riley has questioned
the household staff again. Manservant now claims Miss L
delivered wine to P.N.'s office the day of his death.

Take care what you eat and drink.

R.B.

As he *suspected?* Benjamin thought acidly. That's not how he
remembered it. How like Reuben to claim the credit. Ah well,
that was hardly the point at present. And it *was* good of his
brother to write and let him know. To warn him.

His sibling might be conceited, but Benjamin knew he himself was not perfect either. He recalled the last time he had seen
his brother socially. They had happened into one another near
the Old Bailey, and Reuben suggested they have a pint together.
Once in the public house, his brother began, "Father's taken
on a new apprentice, by the way."

And Benjamin had quipped, "Training another youth to separate a man from a week's wages for a futile nostrum of bear
grease and ground mummy?"

He'd meant it to be humorous, but his brother had frowned
at him, irritation in his eyes. "That is unfair and unkind, even
from you. Our father is no charlatan, like some I could mention, and you know it."

Benjamin had feigned unconcern, but his brother's correction had stung.

The memory faded as the words Reuben had written sank
in. *Poisoned . . . wine in stomach and arsenic detected.*

Ben felt more idiotic than ever to realize he had been thinking warm thoughts about Miss Wilder only moments before. He clearly remained the world's worst judge of character where attractive women were concerned. Would he never learn?

Anger propelling him, Ben went looking for Miss Wilder. He thought she might be in the morning room but found only Christopher Adair within, bent over *The Times* again, hair rumpled.

"Good morning, Mr. Adair. You must have breakfasted early."

The young man shook his head. "Could not stomach any food this morning. Something I ate last night did not agree with me."

Benjamin doubted the food was to blame. He'd noticed Adair refill his glass many times during the party.

"Have you seen Miss Wilder yet today?"

"Briefly. She went out with that talented companion of hers."

"Where?"

"I don't know." The irritating young man didn't even look up from the paper.

Frustrated at this delay, the news burning within him, Benjamin turned his attention to Mr. Adair instead. Deciding an indirect approach might be more fruitful, he began, "Then, may I ask you a few questions?"

The hands holding the broadsheet tensed. "You may ask anything you like. Does not mean I will necessarily answer."

"Very well. Miss Wilder mentioned you were not happy with the terms of the marriage settlement Mr. Norris proposed. Is that right?"

Adair shrugged. "That's no secret. Neither were my parents or their solicitor."

"Are not marriage settlements rather typical among people of rank?"

"Yes, but not like this one. I understand wanting to provide for Rose, but his terms reserved the lion's share for her pin money, jointure, and future children, leaving next to nothing to benefit my family."

"They are in need of financial benefit?"

Adair shifted. "Not proud of it, but yes. We own property but have very little income. A generous dowry would have helped a great deal. But Percival reduced the amount and tied up the majority in the settlement."

"On what grounds?"

"On the grounds that he dashed well felt like it!" Adair ran a hand over his face. "He thought I was marrying Rose for personal gain. Money would have come in handy, I don't deny, but I love Rose. He probably thought I would break off the engagement without the financial incentive, but he was dead wrong. I plan to marry her, dowry or not."

"Dead wrong? Interesting choice of words."

Adair's jaw clenched. "Just a saying."

Benjamin considered. "Hmm. I can ask Mr. Hardy to verify the details of the settlement—I assume he has seen a copy—but perhaps you could give me a summary."

"Well, I am no jackleg lawyer, thankfully, but as our solicitor explained it, Percy was insisting on equity rather than common law."

Ben nodded. "Separate property for the wife's sole use, held and managed by a trustee."

"Correct. With Percy acting as trustee, of course. Rose thought she'd be getting out from under his grip once she married me, but he'd found a way to maintain control."

"Did you sign the settlement?"

The young man hesitated. "I did . . . not."

"Did he give you a copy to review?"

"Yes."

"Where is it now?"

Adair fisted his hand. "Destroyed. I threw it on the fire in a fit of pique."

Benjamin thought of Percival Norris destroying Miss Wilder's angry letter in the same impulsive manner. The two men were more alike than he would have guessed.

Avoiding mention of the letter, he said instead, "Rather like Percival throwing his drinking glass in a fit of pique?"

"Madness more like."

Benjamin cocked his head to one side. "What do you mean by that?"

"I don't know. He must have been mad."

"Perhaps he threw it in self-defense."

Adair scowled. "With a gun in his desk?"

"Perhaps it was instinctive. Perhaps it took him a moment to recall the weapon, while the glass was already in hand?"

The younger man's eyes narrowed. "Are we theorizing what may have happened when a thief entered?"

Benjamin hesitated, suspicion flaring. "I don't know. Are we?"

For a moment their gazes locked, and then Benjamin changed tack.

"You knew Miss Wilder made orange wine here on the island?"

"Yes, I even drank some when Rose and I were here for Easter." Adair rose and paced across the room. "In fact, the longer you talk to me, the more I want a drink right now."

Benjamin continued, "Did you also know that Miss Wilder sent two bottles to Mr. Norris?"

"So? What is your point?"

Benjamin watched his face. "I have just received a note from the coroner confirming my suspicions. Percival Norris was poisoned. Wine and arsenic were found in his body."

The young man's lips parted. "But they said he was hit on the head."

"He was. After he was poisoned. But the poison, not the blow, was the cause of death."

Mr. Adair sank slowly onto a chair, as though a balloon deflating before Ben's eyes.

Interesting . . . Benjamin thought, then added, "He probably ingested the poison via the wine—wine made by Miss Wilder and handed to him by Miss Lawrence herself."

Adair stiffened once more. "That's preposterous. You can't know that."

"Old Marvin reported seeing her do it."

Adair shook his head. "Rose never said anything about it. Sounds like a hum to me."

"Does it? Why?"

"Because Rose Lawrence would never hurt anyone, knowingly."

"And her aunt?"

"I can't speak for her aunt. I don't know her as well as I know Rose. Though of course, Rose thinks the world of her."

"You don't?"

"I didn't say that. Dash it, don't put words in my mouth. I would never say anything against *dear* Aunt Belle. I would not dare."

"But you might *think* something against her?"

"Well, come on, man. You must admit it's all rather odd, not to mention deuced inconvenient, having one's sole living relative anchored to such an out-of-the-way place, unwilling or unable to come to Town for important events. It's caused more than one row between Rose and me, I don't mind telling you. And don't get me started on the arguments over wedding plans."

"You don't wish to marry on Belle Island?"

"No, I don't. Too inconvenient for my friends and family. Riverton is not exactly rife with fashionable lodgings, is it?"

"No, I suppose not. Though if it will make your bride happy . . . ?"

"My bride, yes. My mother, no." Adair groaned and ran a hand over his face.

Benjamin gentled his voice. "I have no wife. But I do have a mother I like to please."

"Then you understand. And heaven help me please them both."

For the first time, Benjamin felt a sliver of pity for the privileged young man. Even so he asked, "Remind me of your actions the day of Mr. Norris's death."

Adair huffed. "As I told the runner, I was home all day, until I escorted Rose and O'Toole home after the party."

"Were you with Miss Lawrence all that time?"

"Yes, as I said, except for a few minutes while we both dressed for dinner. Between Rose, my parents, and my valet, the officer should have no trouble accounting for my whereabouts."

Benjamin guessed Officer Riley had verified the young man's account already. Even so, he had the distinct impression Adair was lying.

Isabelle and Carlota sat side by side on chaise longues in the boathouse, the double doors thrown wide to reveal the morning sunshine shimmering on the gently rippling water of the Thames.

A tray of tea things sat on the small table between them, along with a plate of muffins. Isabelle had toasted them herself and filled the kettle. They had given Mrs. Philpotts and most of the servants the morning off. The weavers too. A leisurely morning was a rare luxury on Belle Island since they'd begun the basket business, and Isabelle and Lotty were determined to enjoy it.

The only sounds were the lapping water, birdsong, and the occasional call of a duck.

"So peaceful here," Lotty murmured.

"I have always thought so." Isabelle sighed. "At least the party went off well."

"Yes. Most . . . interesting."

She felt Lotty's gaze move to her face.

"Are you all right? Seeing Evan Curtis again must have been a shock."

"Yes. But I am all right."

"Good. I remember you telling me about him years ago— how that devil Percival sent him away."

Isabelle nodded. "I was angry with Uncle Percy at the time, but a small part of me thought it might be for the best. Even so, I admit I have often wondered what might have happened had he stayed."

Carlotta sipped from her cup. For several moments the two women sat in companionable silence.

Then Isabelle turned to study Carlota's pretty but pensive profile. "Speaking of staying, I cannot believe you are still here with me. I am glad of it, don't mistake me. But when you first came to the island, I never thought you would stay so long. Do you never miss London? The stage? The applause?"

The woman languidly lifted one shoulder. "Sometimes. Life here is rather quiet and uneventful." She sent Isabelle a smirk. "At least until recent visitors enlivened the place."

Isabelle returned her wry smile. "Agreed." She wondered if her friend was speaking in general terms, or if one visitor in particular had caught her interest. "You must miss having admirers, hidden away here as you are."

Another sanguine shrug. "I miss little of that life. The grasping, demanding men. The pressure. The expectations. Yes, I miss the admiration, the innocent flirtation, that first spark of attraction. . . ." She gazed off into the distance, a dreamy look on her face.

Then Lotty redirected the same question to her. "And do *you* wish for an admirer? You seem to have two at the moment."

Isabelle raised one brow. "Who do you mean?"

"Mr. Booker and Captain Curtis."

"Mr. Booker? You include him but not Dr. Grant? Most people would, you know."

Lotty waved a dismissive hand. "I don't count him. If he wants to marry you, he has a most peculiar way of showing it."

"By caring for me without demands? By giving me years of friendship and support?"

"By dragging his feet and treating you more like a patient than a desirable woman."

Lotty had never expressed her opinion of Teddy quite so bluntly. The words stung, but Isabelle could not refute them.

"At all events, I don't think you can call Evan a suitor. Last night, he made it clear he has no interest in me. He was hurt, and I can't blame him for that. Now I sense more bitterness than admiration from him."

Carlota nodded thoughtfully. "And Mr. Booker?"

Isabelle chuckled. "Mr. Booker lives in London. Besides, he suspects me of murder. I hardly think you can count him as an admirer."

"Oh, I don't think he really suspects you. I think he likes you. But you must admit you had good reason to want Percival dead."

Isabelle looked at Carlota Medina and whispered somberly, "So did you."

CHAPTER
eleven

Benjamin worked in the study, going through papers as Miss Wilder had requested but struggling to concentrate. Could she have done it? Did she?

He'd left the door open, hoping to hear her return. When he saw Rose Lawrence walk by, he hailed her instead.

"Miss Lawrence? Might you spare a few minutes?"

"Good morning, Mr. Booker," she cheerfully replied. "I would be happy to talk with you, but might I just nip into the breakfast parlour first for tea and toast? It will only take a moment."

"Of course. I did not realize you had not yet eaten."

"Just up, I'm afraid. And I am starving. What a night!"

"Yes, indeed. Again, congratulations."

She held up her index finger, eyes impishly bright. "Right back."

Miss Lawrence certainly was a likable young woman. He truly hoped she'd had nothing to do with Percival's death.

Rose returned shortly, as promised, teacup in one hand, plate of toast and jam in the other. She balanced the plate on the arm of the chair and sat back with her cup.

"Ready."

He began, attempting an open, easy demeanor. "Your aunt mentioned sending two bottles of orange wine back to London for Mr. Norris. A peace offering."

Her smile faltered. "That's right."

"In fact, I understand you carried one of those bottles into his office the day of his death."

She stared, lips parted. "How did you know that?"

"Apparently, Marvin mentioned it upon further questioning."

Miss Lawrence blinked wide eyes. "Oh . . ."

Christopher Adair appeared in the doorway. "Thought I heard your voice, Rose. Remember, you don't have to answer his questions. He's only a lawyer, not a Bow Street officer or magistrate."

Benjamin retorted, "If she is innocent, why hesitate?"

Miss Lawrence lifted her head high. "I did nothing wrong, Mr. Booker. Yes, I took a bottle to his office before I left for the Adairs'. I heard him shouting at poor old Marvin, berating him that we were out of gin again and it was all his fault, when I knew full well that Marvin had tried to buy more, but the merchant refused to extend us any more credit.

"Where all our money went, I don't know. But I grew frustrated listening to his caterwauling, so I retrieved one of the wine bottles from the butler's pantry, carried it to his office, and thumped it down on his desk. I'm afraid I said something rather saucy like, 'Drink this and leave poor Marvin alone. It is not his fault our accounts are in arrears.' And I stalked out before he could fashion a reply."

"Why the butler's pantry?" Benjamin asked. "Has the London house no wine cellar?"

She shrugged. "Yes, but the cellar there hasn't been used in years. Uncle Percy had long ago consumed any bottles worth drinking. And as he preferred gin, he had little interest in keeping the cellar stocked. On the rare occasion we entertained, Marvin found it easier to store the wine and decant it right there in the butler's pantry. It's where we kept the decanters and glasses anyway."

Benjamin was aware of Adair, leaning his shoulder against the doorframe, but he kept his focus on Rose. "Was the second bottle of orange wine still there at that time?"

Rose frowned in concentration. "I think so. . . ."

Benjamin picked up the letter from his brother. "As I told Mr. Adair earlier this morning, I received confirmation from the coroner that Percival Norris was indeed poisoned."

Miss Lawrence's mouth dropped open. "How?"

Adair gave a bark of dry laughter. "He thinks one of us poisoned the wine, Rose. Do keep up."

Ignoring him, Benjamin asked her, "Did you suspect the wine might be poisoned?"

"Of course not. Come, you can't really think Aunt Belle poisoned the wine."

"If not, someone else might easily have poisoned it in the butler's pantry. Someone like you."

She gasped. "I wouldn't know how."

"What's to know? Just pour white arsenic into the bottle and replace the stopper. Easiest thing in the world."

Rose's eyebrows rose. "Says the voice of experience?"

"No, but I've attended many trials at the Old Bailey, where one hears all sorts of confessions. And my brother is coroner for the borough of Westminster. Unfortunately he shares details of his inquests."

Rose shuddered. "Sounds ghastly."

Benjamin thought, then said, "I wish we had that second bottle. Either bottle, actually."

Adair asked acerbically, "And would you volunteer to sample the second bottle if we had it?"

"No, but a rat might do." He sent the young man a pointed look, then added, "Some dispute their validity, but there are a few tests for arsenic. If we compared the remaining bottles here to that one, it might help us determine if the wine was poisoned on the island or after it reached London." He turned back to Miss Lawrence to gauge her reaction.

Under his scrutiny, the young woman again lifted her chin. "Why would I poison a bottle of wine clearly marked as being made by my beloved Aunt Belle?"

"Perhaps because you will inherit everything after she is gone."

Rose huffed and shook her head. "No. I love my aunt. She was a second mother to me after my own died. You are mistaken, Mr. Booker. I had nothing to do with Uncle Percy's death. When I left the house at half past three that day, he was alive and well and grumbling as usual. I took my gown and Miss O'Toole and together we went to the Adairs' to dress for the party."

"Why so early? Why dress there?"

"It looked like rain, so I decided to change and curl my hair there. Miss O'Toole brought a case with hot irons and brushes and powder and things. When we arrived, Mrs. Adair insisted I take tea with her before we started, and then gave us a guest room to use."

"And you remained there the rest of the evening?"

"Yes, as I told the officer. We stayed until Mr. Adair escorted us home. That's when we came upon all of you there in the townhouse."

"And what was Mr. Adair doing while you curled your hair and whatnot?"

"He was already dressed when we arrived, so probably having a drink with his father. I'm afraid I took rather a long time at my toilette. O'Toole will fuss so—we were at it nearly two hours." She lifted her hand. "He's right here. Ask him yourself."

From the corner of his eye, Benjamin noticed Mr. Adair stiffen.

"I did ask him. He said he was with you the entire evening except for a *few minutes* while you both dressed for dinner."

Again Rose blinked in surprise. "Oh . . ."

Adair shifted in the threshold, arms crossed. "Then I simply lost track of time and misspoke. I had no idea females could take so long dressing."

Rose looked at her young man, hesitated, then turned a forced smile on Mr. Booker. "There, you see? An innocent mistake."

Benjamin looked from one to the other, unconvinced. Had it been an innocent mistake, or a purposeful deception?

After relaxing with Carlota, Isabelle went to the garden to clip a bouquet of spring flowers for her ailing tenant, Mrs. Howton. Rose came out and joined her. Isabelle glanced at her niece and then quickly turned to study her anxious face.

"What is it?"

Rose yanked a weed. "Did you hear? Mr. Booker received a letter from the coroner. Uncle Percy was poisoned. They think by orange wine."

"Good heavens." Isabelle's heart thudded hard, and she pressed a hand to her chest. Had Percival been poisoned by *her* orange wine? Impossible! She squeezed her eyes shut, recalling the dream. There *had* been a wine bottle on the floor. . . .

It was only a dream, she reminded herself once more. Merciful heaven, how had it happened? What had she done?

Rose went on to tell of her conversation with Mr. Booker, including the fact that one of the servants had seen her carry a bottle into Percy's office. She described Mr. Adair's responses as well.

Isabelle looked around for anyone nearby, then said, "Did you happen to mention to Mr. Booker that you delivered the bottles from here to London? I believe he assumes Percival took them back with him, but I did not think to offer them until after he left."

Her niece pulled another weed and stripped leaves from its stem. "No. I didn't think it was important. Should I have?" She shrugged it off, or at least pretended to.

Isabelle's concern for Rose grew. She set down her basket and scissors, took Rose's hand, and led her to a nearby bench. "You know I don't suspect you for an instant. But did you take those two bottles directly from here to the London house? Or might someone else have interfered with them on the way?"

Rose shook her head. "Directly from here to London. When we stopped to change horses, I dashed out to the privy, but Christopher stayed with the chaise the entire time, so it was never left untended. He was reading the newspaper when I stepped down and had not moved when I returned. I don't know how men wait so long."

Isabelle considered. "Were the bottles out with the baggage, or inside with you?"

"Inside. I was afraid they might break being tossed about in the boot."

"Good thinking," Isabelle murmured, but her thoughts took a darker turn.

Mr. Adair had been left alone with the bottles for several minutes at least. Probably not long enough to adulterate the wine. Or was it . . . ? If he had acquired the poison ahead of time and taken it with him, it might be possible. She hated even imagining him the culprit, but better Adair than Rose. . . .

Rose said, "I am so sorry you have become embroiled in this. I wish both of those bottles had been smashed during the journey! I never dreamed that by delivering them to London and later taking one to Percival's office that I might implicate us both in his death."

Isabelle laid a hand on hers. "Of course not. How could anyone have foreseen this? And we are not implicated . . . officially." *At least not yet . . .*

"As I've said before," Rose continued, "when I left the house that day, Uncle Percy was alive and well and predicting an unhappy future if I went through with my marriage to Mr. Adair."

Isabelle studied the dear girl's face. "And what do you think about that? Is there any kernel of truth in his warnings?"

For a moment their gazes held. Then Rose looked away first. "Of course not. You know I love Christopher and he loves me."

Isabelle asked gently, "And you have no . . . fears . . . for your future together?"

Rose swallowed. "Goodness, I suppose we all have fears about the future. Who knows what tomorrow will bring? I admit Christopher is not as . . . sound . . . financially as I originally believed, but I am sure we shall deal very well together."

"Of course you know I will help you any way I can. Though in all honesty, I don't know what our financial situation is now that Percival is gone."

Rose leaned her shoulder against her aunt's. "Hopefully, Mr. Booker will help us sort things out. In the meantime, don't worry about me. Christopher and I shall manage."

"I would still feel better if you had a marriage settlement. If the one Mr. Norris drafted was unfair to Mr. Adair, perhaps we might ask Mr. Booker to draft a new one with more liberal terms. Would Mr. Adair be amenable to that?"

"I don't know. I could ask Christopher about it."

Isabelle nodded, then thought aloud, "I wonder where the settlement Percival wrote ended up? Might give Mr. Booker a starting place and help him avoid whatever terms proved objectionable to your intended and his parents."

Rose sighed. "I am ignorant in such matters, I'm afraid."

"As am I, unfortunately. But perhaps it is time we both learned something about the legalities controlling our finances and our futures."

Rose did not appear eager at the prospect. "If you think we should."

"I do."

Isabelle pressed her lips together, choosing her words carefully. "Something you said in your recounting is troubling me. I know from personal experience how long it takes you to get ready. . . ." She gently nudged Rose beside her. "But Mr. Adair told Mr. Booker that he was with you the entire evening except for a few minutes while you both dressed?"

Rose looked down at her hands. "I was a little surprised by that myself. I think it was merely a . . . simplification on his part. He says he lost track of time. I had thought he was already dressed when we arrived, but I must have been mistaken. Men's dark coats look so alike. And we *were* together the rest of the evening, after the party began."

Isabelle slowly nodded. "I see." But she couldn't help wondering if there was more to it than that. Was Rose protecting Mr. Adair as she herself longed to protect Rose? *Oh, please don't let my precious Rose be engaged to someone capable of murder!*

She squeezed her niece's hand. "I just want you to be happy and safe and loved. You know that, don't you?"

"Of course I do. And I want the same for you."

CHAPTER
twelve

After Miss Lawrence and Mr. Adair departed, Benjamin remained in the study. He sat at the desk, files open and pages spread before him. Eyes soon growing weary, he donned the spectacles he often wore for reading.

He came across an architect's plan for the house and on it identified the location of the wine cellar. He considered searching it himself, although he doubted there was any point. Miss Wilder had made no secret of where the remaining bottles were, and both she and Mr. Adair had mentioned drinking some of the orange wine, to no lasting harm. Even if she were guilty, it seemed highly unlikely that she would have poisoned more than the two bottles she'd sent to Mr. Norris. Might he find some evidence of that act down there? He supposed it was possible. Perhaps he should just ask Miss Wilder to show him the cellar. He doubted she would refuse to do so, knowing it would only make her appear suspicious.

Some time later, Miss Wilder knocked on the doorframe. She did not look pleased. "May I interrupt?"

"Of course." Benjamin removed his spectacles and sat back in the chair.

She stepped inside. "Rose told me the news. I wish you would have told me first, instead of interrogating my young niece without me present."

Chagrin washed over him. "I did try to find you, but Adair told me you and Miss Medina had gone out."

"Only to the boathouse."

"Then perhaps I should have waited. Forgive me. Mr. Adair joined us, if that eases your mind."

"Unfortunately, it does not." She took a deep breath and began, "Mr. Booker, my niece would never hurt Uncle Percy or anyone else. This is the girl who captured spiders and released them out-of-doors instead of smashing them to bits as most people do. She has a quick tongue, I allow, and often speaks without thinking, but that just shows you it is not in her nature to dissemble.

"No, she did not always get on with Uncle Percy. But she liked him more than I ever did. He was her legal guardian, after all, and they spent a great deal of time together in London. Yes, he irritated her when he refused her requests for this falderal or that, but what young girl enjoys being refused anything? She would not have liked her parents denying her whims either, had they lived."

Miss Wilder paused to catch her breath, then continued. "If anyone had something against Percival Norris, it was me. For it was my island he was threatening with his talk of shipyards and boatbuilders and leases and profits. Remember I sent him that angry letter?"

Benjamin was surprised she would raise that topic on her own. She must be desperate indeed to protect her niece. "I did not read the letter myself, but Mr. Hardy told me about it."

"Then he probably told you what I wrote."

Benjamin hedged, "Not in detail. Though he mentioned its threatening nature."

"I was upset. I told Percy to desist or I would engage my own lawyer and have him removed as trustee. It was probably a foolish threat, for Percival once hinted that if I tried anything like that, he would testify that I was not of sound mind and unable to manage my own affairs."

"On what grounds?"

A mirthless chuckle escaped her. "On the grounds that I have refused to leave this island for any reason."

"Being reclusive does not make one insane."

"He called it some sort of female hysteria." Miss Wilder began pacing across the room. "I had to do something. I hated feeling so powerless about my own home. My own fate."

Was she mad? Suffering from hysteria? Benjamin didn't think so, but he was no expert. Nor, considering his own episodes, was he in any position to judge. "A court case would have been drawn out, publicly embarrassing, and expensive. You can see why someone might suspect you of deciding it would be easier to kill him."

She gaped at him and slowly shook her head. "You astound me. What sort of world do you live in where killing someone is the easier option? Every life is precious, even that of someone we don't like. I could never do it."

Testing her reaction, he asked, "Would you show me the wine cellar?"

"Of course," she replied, with no sign of distress. "Any time you like."

He drummed his fingers on the desk and changed tack. "Let's talk about the day of the betrothal party in London."

"What about it? I already told you I was not there for it."

"Tell me what you did instead. Was it just an ordinary day for you?"

She sketched a small shrug. "No, it started out ordinarily enough, but then I recalled what day it was and the party. That made me think ahead to Rose's wedding and fear that I shall miss that as well. I know I should not borrow trouble, but in practice, it is difficult not to worry."

"I understand. I tend to be a worrier myself. How often my poor mamma tried to encourage me as a boy, reminding me not to worry but to pray instead. At the time, it vexed me. Now, whenever I grow anxious, those words from Philippians four go through my mind and put things in perspective."

"Perhaps I should learn those myself." She sighed. "At all events, on that day I felt as low as I have since the deaths of my parents and sister. I was unable to attend to anything—not the baskets or my responsibilities. Not my favorite books or my other friends."

They shared small smiles at that, then she walked to the window and stared out as she continued.

"Dr. Grant came to check on me midafternoon and did his best to comfort me and keep me company. We sat out in the boathouse for hours, the doors flung wide, looking at the water. The river usually soothes me. As a rule, I do not overindulge, but I confess, low as I was, I did drink rather a lot of orange wine that day, hoping it would ease the pain. Ironically, yet unsurprisingly, the 'cure' left me with a stabbing headache the next morning, or should I say afternoon, as I slept embarrassingly late."

"Did you stay in the boathouse all night?"

"I went to bed at some point, though it's all a bit foggy. I apparently fell asleep out there, and Dr. Grant had to help me inside."

"Did he share the wine?"

"No. He never has a drop."

"Religious conviction?"

She shook her head. "He simply saw its effects on too many patients and determined to have nothing to do with the stuff. Probably wise."

Tentatively Benjamin asked, "You don't worry people will talk about you and the doctor being out together all night? Fear your reputation will be ruined?"

"As I said, that day did not represent my usual behavior. But no, I don't worry overmuch about what people think about Teddy and me. Nor of my reputation—not at my age. Besides, there were not many people on the island to see us. The weavers return to their homes by late afternoon. Abel Curtis and the other tenants were no doubt already tucked into their own cottages for the evening, and the servants were probably either too busy to notice or in their beds, for they rise early."

"And Miss Medina? Did she not remain awake to help you . . . undress for bed?" His foolish neck heated to say the innocent words. Why must he find her so attractive?

"She does usually, but when she came to the boathouse to look in on me that afternoon, I told her I wanted no dinner and not to wait up for me. I said I would see her in the morning. I didn't want her to stay up late on my account."

Miss Wilder looked off in thought. "I vaguely remember Dr. Grant helping me to my bedchamber. Goodness! How scandalous that sounds. But I promise you, in my state, there was absolutely nothing romantic about the situation."

Isabelle glanced over and noticed Theodore Grant hovering beyond the threshold, his face grim as he looked from her to Mr. Booker. She wished she'd thought to close the study door.

"Isabelle, may I speak to you a moment? It's important."

"Oh . . . of course. If you will excuse me, Mr. Booker?" Isabelle rose and joined Teddy in the corridor.

Taking her arm, he led her down the passage and hissed, "Why are you answering his questions? You needn't, you know. He cannot compel you. He has no authority."

"He is trying to help discover the identity of Percival's killer. And although Uncle Percy and I did not see eye to eye and I was not fond of him, he was still a human being and a relation. He deserves justice. That is why I am answering Mr. Booker's questions."

"Even if you end up implicating yourself or someone you love?"

Isabelle's heart twisted. "What are you saying? How could I?"

He shut his eyes and ran a hand through his hair. "Just be careful, Isabelle. That man is poking into a hornets' nest, and I don't want you to get stung."

Long after Teddy had left the house, his words remained, running over and over again through Isabelle's mind. What had he meant? By answering Mr. Booker's questions, had she somehow put Rose in jeopardy . . . or Teddy himself?

Yes, she might implicate Rose if she told Mr. Booker her niece had delivered the wine to London and therefore had ample opportunity to poison it had she wanted to. His suspicion would certainly increase, especially as Rose had avoided mentioning that detail. But really it proved nothing. The wine could have been tampered with after it reached London.

And what about Teddy? Was he worried his professional reputation would suffer if people found out they'd been alone together most of the night, or was he worried about something else entirely? Had he something against Percival Norris too?

Unbeknownst to her, had Percy refused his consent to Teddy as he had to Evan? She wanted to know the truth . . . but wasn't keen on being stung by it.

Who else might Teddy have meant by "someone you love," now that most of her family were gone? Of course she loved Arminda and Lotty, but surely neither of them had been involved. Isabelle doubted he would include Evan Curtis in that number, even if he wondered how she felt about her former beau.

Isabelle went to her bedchamber and closed the door behind her. She didn't know how soon Lotty would return but was glad for a few minutes of privacy.

She crossed the room and pulled a small box from the bottom of her dressing chest. In it were several pieces of memorabilia from her younger days. A brittle fan of her mother's, a few letters from her brother when he'd been away at sea, her father's small copy of the New Testament and Psalms, a hand-sewn needle case given to her by Arminda, and a silk scarf of her sister's. Beneath this she found the items she was looking for.

First, a tin star. Second, a river rock worn smooth by the current of years and unmistakably heart shaped. Isabelle stroked the glossy surface and remembered Evan pressing it into her hand, his fingers lingering, caressing the sensitive skin of her palm. *"I will put a ring on this hand one day, but for now this will have to do. You hold my heart in your hands, Isabelle Wilder. Take care what you do with it."*

The recollection brought a stab of guilt.

Finally, she picked up the shriveled bud of a dog rose complete with stem and prickle—a wild climbing variety with hooked thorns. When given to a lover, it meant pleasure mixed with pain. The thorn pricked her finger even now, all these years later, and a tiny mound of blood dotted her skin. *Pleasure and pain . . .* That certainly described her memories of Evan Curtis.

Benjamin thought about going back to the stables to look under the tarpaulins but through the window saw Miss Wilder's lady's maid out on the veranda and decided to talk to her instead. She sat on the sofa with a heap of blue material on her lap and a basket beside her.

He walked outside and said, "Good afternoon, Miss Medina. I like your sewing room."

She lowered her needle and thread. "Glad you approve. Miss Isabelle tore her hem dancing. And since it is such an unseasonably warm day, I decided to work out here."

"Ah. My fault, I'm afraid." He took a step closer. "May I ask you a few questions while you work?"

"If you'd like." She moved the dress out of the way to make room for him.

He sat down and turned to her. "After hearing you sing, it is clear you are a woman of remarkable talent."

"Thank you."

"How long have you lived here?"

"Nearly seven years."

"And before that?"

"I performed as an actress and singer for several London theatres."

"Had you worked in that profession for long?"

"My whole life. My grandparents managed a theatre. My mother made costumes, and I grew up backstage."

"Medina . . . Is that a Spanish name?"

"*Sí*," she replied with a sly grin. "My father was Ferdinand Vega Medina. An actor. He married my mother but soon strayed, leaving her for some young dancer. After my grandparents died, it was just *Mamá* and me."

"How did you come to work on Belle Island?"

"Miss Wilder invited me. I met her about three years before I came here, during one of her last trips to London, I believe. She attended one of my performances at the Theatre Royal. Afterward, she came out to the back door to congratulate me, as people sometimes do. Unfortunately, she came upon me arguing with someone. He was my . . . benefactor . . . at the time. I wanted to end our relationship, but he threatened to ruin my career if I did. I thought he would strike me, but he realized we had an audience, so he stormed off instead. That's when I saw her. So elegant. Such posture! I knew in an instant she was a real lady, unlike me.

"We stood there awkwardly for a time. I braced myself, waiting for her to turn up her nose at me, to say something like, 'I regret interrupting such an unsavory scene.' Instead she came near to me, eyes wide with concern, and said, 'I came to congratulate you, but if there is anything I can do to help you, you need only ask. If you need somewhere to go . . . please let me know. Anytime.' She handed me one of her calling cards.

"I kept the card but brushed off the offer. After all, I was much in demand as a performer. I could not imagine leaving London for some remote island in Berkshire. Could not imagine needing to."

For a moment the woman gazed off into her memories, but then she turned back to him.

"Unfortunately, my former benefactor made good on his threats to ruin me and saw to it that I never worked in any of the better theatres again. A few years later, I was down to my last few pounds and unable to pay my rent. By that time, my mother had died as well. Then another man—a dangerous man—began making my life difficult, and I realized I needed to get out of town and quickly. I dug through my many reticules until I found her calling card, went to the nearest coaching inn, and bought my fare, which left me with only a few shillings to my name.

"I confess I came here hoping the generous woman would remember and help me. But when I arrived, I discovered Miss Wilder was the one who needed help. Her parents and sister had died. The man she thought she'd marry had been sent far away to *España*. This was during *la Guerra de la Independencia Española*, or what you call the Peninsular War."

He nodded his understanding. He had lost a childhood friend in that war.

Miss Medina continued. "Miss Isabelle seemed so . . . diminished . . . since I had last seen her. Lost. If not for little Rose, I believe she would have curled up into a ball of grief and remained there. But for her niece's sake she forced herself to go on with life, or at least, her version of life, limited to the island."

She slowly shook her head. "When I learned of her losses, I felt terrible to intrude, but true to her word, she took me in. I insisted on earning my keep, so I became her companion and lady's maid." She lifted the sewing in her lap as though proof. "I had never been in service, but I knew how to sew, help people dress, and arrange hair from my years at the theatre. I learned the rest as we went. I helped her, listened to her, read to her, brushed and powdered her through the lingering grief, and we became friends. Of course, she had Miss Truelock. But as a vicar's daughter, Arminda has many duties in the parish, so she cannot come here as often as she'd like."

When she stopped, Benjamin asked, "Did you not think it strange that Miss Wilder keeps herself to the island?"

"Yes. I was worried for her. Miss Truelock too. We discreetly discussed the change in her, her unwillingness to leave the island, even to go into the village or to church. But despite that, we have both done our best to support her over the years."

"Dr. Grant has been a longtime friend as well, I understand."

The pretty woman's face puckered. "I suppose so."

Benjamin noted her reaction with interest. "You don't like the good doctor, do you?" He felt odd satisfaction at the question.

She shook her head. "He doesn't like me either. But we both want to help Miss Wilder, so we tolerate one another and get on as best we can."

"I see." He tucked that away for later. "And have you no plans to return to London?"

"I have thought about it a time or two, but no plans at present."

"Very well. Tell me what happened the night Miss Wilder fell asleep in the boathouse."

"Did she not already tell you?"

"Yes, but I would like to hear your version of events."

"It will be the same as hers."

"That's all right. Tell me everything that happened."

Miss Medina looked off in thought. "Let's see. I remember Miss Wilder wanted to wear a new favorite dress that day, in honor of Rose's engagement, even though she would not be attending the dinner party in London. Despite the pretty dress, she seemed sad and subdued. Then I saw her walking down to the boathouse, a bottle in one hand and a glass in the other. Please don't think she makes a habit of drinking a lot or alone. She rarely imbibes."

"I understand. Go on."

"I was concerned about her, truth be told, so I went out to look in on her an hour or so later. I brought her a pillow and a lap rug to keep her warm. She thanked me kindly and said she wanted no dinner that night and that I should return to the house and not wait up for her. She told me she planned to sit out there all evening and wouldn't be able to relax if she knew I was staying up to help her undress for bed. She insisted she would make do on her own for one night and I could help her in the morning. As I was leaving, Dr. Grant came out and joined her. There was a second chair there, but I didn't offer to fetch him a pillow."

Miss Medina paused to think, dark eyes flickering with memory. "Later, after supper, I turned down her bed for her and then went to my room. And I . . . went to sleep."

Benjamin heard a slight hesitation. "You did not come down again? See that she made it to bed all right?"

"I . . . did not."

There it was again. Benjamin had the distinct impression the woman was lying.

Carlota finished, "But she was in her bed in the morning when I went in, suffering a headache but otherwise unharmed."

"Unharmed? Why should she be harmed?"

"I only meant . . . well, she had a fair amount to drink the day before."

Is that what Miss Medina had meant? Benjamin guessed there was more to the story than she was willing to tell him.

He returned to the former topic. "May I ask why you dislike the doctor?"

"I don't like the way he patronizes her. So condescending, when she is far above him in many ways. I don't trust him."

Benjamin felt his brows rise. "Did he do something that makes you distrust him?"

Carlota shook her head. "He's never done anything to me, but even so I can't like him."

"Why?"

She sent him a pointed look. "Have you visited his surgery?"

"No."

"Perhaps you should. Miss Wilder has not, of course. If she had, she might think differently of her old friend. I know I do."

"When were you there?"

"Several months ago. I cut myself sharpening a pair of shears." She regretfully shook her head. "Miss Wilder sent me to Dr. Grant's surgery."

"What was wrong with it? Not tidy enough for you?"

"It was not that. I happened to look into his private office." She shuddered. "Something's not right there."

"What do you mean?"

"That's all I will say. Go and see it yourself."

"I shall. Anything else?"

"Just this. I'd swear on my life Miss Wilder is innocent."

But Benjamin had all too recently risked all, believing a pretty woman was innocent. He was not about to take this former actress's word for it now.

⊶⊰ CHAPTER ⊱⊷
thirteen

The next day, Benjamin wrote again to Mr. Hardy, summarizing what he had learned while questioning various members of the family and staff. He had uncovered a possible chink in Mr. Adair's alibi, but otherwise, he'd discovered precious little. He assumed Mr. Hardy had already heard the information Reuben had sent him—confirming poisoning and the news that Miss Lawrence had been seen taking a bottle of wine into Mr. Norris's office—but he included these points just in case he had not.

Benjamin decided to walk to Riverton to post his report to Mr. Hardy without delay. He donned his coat and hat and started outside. Recalling Miss Medina's suggestion that he visit Dr. Grant's office, he made up his mind to stop there on his way back.

He passed Miss Wilder on the veranda, trying to coax her old dog to play catch with a leather ball, while the pup circled the lounging oldster, yapping encouragement.

"Where are you off to?" she asked. "Posting another letter?"

"Yes, and visiting your friend Dr. Grant as well."

"Oh? I hope you are not feeling poorly again."

"No, I feel perfectly well. Care to join me? A lovely day for a walk." He grinned as he said it, unable to resist teasing her.

"Ha-ha. Thank you, but I have taken enough exercise already, retrieving the ball for this lazy dog!"

Benjamin waved and continued over the bridge. Innocent or not, he liked that she could laugh at herself.

After posting his letter at the inn, he continued up the cross street. Here were the bakery, greengrocer, and he'd been told, the doctor's surgery. A few narrow winding lanes led from this street to small cottages and outbuildings. What the structures lacked in architectural grace or recent paint, they made up for in charm, with an abundance of hanging pots and window boxes bursting with spring blooms.

Several yards farther on, he saw a small plaque that modestly announced *Theodore Grant, M.D.*

Did one knock at a physician's door or let himself in as one would at a shop? Benjamin was not certain. He'd had rare occasion in his life to call on a lofty gentleman-physician.

Because his own father was a surgeon-apothecary, people had come and gone through his door as though to a confectioner's shop or hardware seller. Thomas Booker had taken care of all of Benjamin's and Reuben's childhood ailments and injuries himself, not having much affection for learned physicians who often loathed touching their patients or doing anything resembling "work."

Benjamin knocked once, then tried the latch. Finding it unlocked, he let himself inside. There he found a pleasant sitting area, its chairs presently unoccupied, and two doors leading from it.

Hearing the murmur of voices behind one of these doors, Benjamin sat down to wait. As he did, he became aware of the office smells—herbs, salves, mustard plasters—and the old memory returned. . . .

The butcher's boy, Davey Paulson, was only eleven or twelve—near Benjamin's own age at the time. He had cut off part of his finger with a deadly sharp cleaver. When his parents brought him in, the lad's sleeves and midsection were covered in blood, where he'd clutched the injured appendage to himself, trying to protect it. Benjamin's father bandaged the finger but could not stop the bleeding. He called for Reuben, but Ben reminded him that he'd gone off on a delivery. So his father had ordered Benjamin to put pressure on it while he prepared his instruments.

Ben pressed the wound, the viscous red slurry quickly seeping through the bandage and running down his fingers.

Davey's face became more ghostly white by the minute. The lad's frightened mother cried, "Oh! He looks very bad. Please, Mr. Booker, don't let my boy bleed to death!"

Between clenched teeth, his father had said to the butcher, "Mr. Paulson, please take your missus into the shop. I can't think with her shrieking so."

The butcher put his arm around her shoulders and firmly led her out.

Everything in Benjamin wanted to follow them. How hot and stifling the room suddenly seemed. The warmer he became, the harder it was to breathe and the more light-headed he felt.

His father then tied a linen tape around the lad's arm and commanded Benjamin to "Hold the ligature—tight." He hurried to comply but was so nervous his hands shook.

Frustration mounting, his father's voice rose. "Hold it tighter, Benjamin. I want to stitch the fingertip back in place, but we've got to stop the bleeding so I can see properly."

Davey's eyes fluttered and then closed.

Panic jolted Ben. "Is he dead?"

"Of course not. Only fainted. Slap his cheek—not too hard."

Benjamin did so, leaving blood-stained handprints on the boy's white cheeks. Davey didn't respond. Ben was sure he must be dying, and it would be his fault.

"Oh, where is your brother?" his father lamented. "I need him here."

"I'll get him," Ben said, and bolted from the room. In his dizziness, he tripped and hit the side of his head on the doorframe but kept moving, ignoring his father's calls to come back and assist him.

In the end, Davey Paulson recovered, but Benjamin had done everything in his power to avoid being asked to assist again.

The memory faded, leaving Benjamin feeling uneasy. Not long after that, bouts of what he now knew as vertigo had begun to plague him.

Ben forced his attention to one of the medical journals in the waiting room. Flipping through its pages, he saw an advertisement for instruments and receptacles for bloodletting. Wrong choice. He picked up a newspaper instead.

A few minutes later, the door opened and an elderly man stepped out, followed by Dr. Grant. "You take care, Mr. Jones, and remember to abstain from fermented drink and cheeses." He looked up. "Ah, Mr. Booker. Thought I heard someone knock."

"I hope you don't mind I let myself in."

"Not at all." The doctor waited until the outer door closed behind his patient, then asked, "How can I help? Are you feeling dizzy again?"

"No, I am quite well, thank you, but . . ." Benjamin hesitated. Aware the man was already set against him, he decided to try friendly conversation first. "I realized I never"—he bit back the word *paid*, knowing physicians found talk of payment for services beneath them—"properly thanked or reimbursed you for your kind attentions."

Dr. Grant waved a casual hand. "No need. I am on retainer with the Wilders."

"Retainer?" Benjamin echoed, thinking, *For one Wilder?* Isabelle must suffer from more illnesses than her healthy, not to mention attractive, appearance suggested.

"Yes. Isabelle suggested it. This way, I can attend to her or the servants or tenants as needed without fuss."

"I see . . . A lot of illness on the island?"

"A fair amount. The damp winters bring their dangers, especially for the three elderly tenants who live there. Have you met them?"

"I've seen Abel Curtis and met Roy Howton."

Dr. Grant nodded. "Old Roy used to be head gardener until rheumatism stole his strength. And his wife was once nursemaid to Isabelle and her sister. They have lived in the tenant cottages on the island for years. And Abel acts as groundsman, groom, whatever is needed out-of-doors these days."

He shook his head, a wistful expression on his fair face. "My goodness, in the past, the Wilders employed an under gardener, coachman, stable hands, two footmen, several more maids . . . but those days are long gone, sad to say."

"I am surprised former servants are allowed to live on the estate when they are no longer able to work."

He shrugged. "Isabelle is kind that way. She looks out for her own. Once a friend to Isabelle, always a friend to Isabelle."

"And you . . . see . . . Miss Wilder too?"

The man held his gaze. "Yes. I see her and care for her."

A silent tension buzzed between them.

Dr. Grant was perhaps a year or two older than Benjamin, of similar height and build, although he had lighter hair, green eyes, and the fair skin of a redhead. His hands were long and almost elegant compared to Benjamin's perennially ink-stained, knobby knuckles from years bent over quill and paper. This man was more successful than he was, but Benjamin thought he could best him in a fight if he had to. He had Reuben to thank for his early training in fisticuffs.

Benjamin reminded himself of his mission and continued casually, "And you attended her companion, Miss Medina, for an injury, I understand."

"Yes. She cut herself. Nasty gash. I'm the only medical man for several miles so must at times act the part of surgeon as well as physician." A frown flickered over his face, clearly not pleased about it.

"My own father is a surgeon-apothecary."

"Ah. But you didn't follow him into the family profession."

"To his disappointment, I'm afraid." Benjamin diverted the conversation back to safer shores. "Miss Medina happened to mention she'd had occasion to see your private office. She seemed . . . impressed."

"Yes. Would you like to see it? I confess I am rather proud of it."

"If you don't mind."

"Not at all. Right this way." He opened the second door for Benjamin and gestured him through it.

Inside, Benjamin stood to one side, surveying the scene. The shutters were closed for privacy but plenty of light shone in from high transom windows above them. A large desk and leather chair dominated one side of the room, backed by a bookcase filled with weighty medical tomes. Nothing unusual there.

Then he saw.

On the other side of the room stood a tall counter lit by lamplight. On it sat a few animal skulls, odd specimens in jars, mice in a cage, and two potted plants—one green and thriving, the other brown and shriveled.

Noticing the direction of his gaze, the doctor walked over to the raised work surface. "I see you have noticed my experiments. Considering your background, you may find them as fascinating as I do."

He gestured toward the specimens preserved in spirits—a fetal pig, a kidney, and a few others Ben could not identify. Several sketches of human organs lay on the counter nearby.

"Some of my dissections from medical school and sketches from anatomy lectures," Dr. Grant explained. "I went to Edinburgh. Not my first choice. But in the end it proved an excellent turn of events, for the medical school there is far advanced compared to those in England. Much more hands-on than theoretical."

Benjamin glanced again at the contents of the murky jars. "And you keep them here to . . . ?"

Grant lifted an expressive hand. "As a symbol of my education. And occasionally to explain a point of anatomy to a patient. Although I have been told illustrations alone would work just as well."

"And the plants?"

"Various experiments. Light and darkness. Various substances and their effects on the plant's health. Though I find animal experiments far more indicative of the human condition."

"I see." Benjamin gestured to the mice. "Like these?"

The doctor nodded. "Currently I am trying to find a cure for gin addiction."

Benjamin turned to stare at him. "These mice are addicted to gin?"

"Yes. I've made sure of it. There's a reason they call it 'blue ruin.' Gin has ruined many a life, and I hope to discover a treatment for those in its grip."

"Laudable," Benjamin murmured, though he could see why a woman might find the displays rather gruesome. He found them somewhat gruesome himself.

"Thank you. I admire the work of James Lind, another Edinburgh-trained physician. You may have heard of his scurvy trials. And I am not the first to study mice. Hooke, Priestley, and Lavoisier have all done so before me."

"Has Miss Wilder seen all this?"

"No. But Miss Medina must have described it to her as she did you, for Isabelle asked me about my experiments."

"You and Miss Wilder are old friends. She depends on you a great deal, I think."

He nodded. "We are. And I value her opinion and counsel as well."

"I understand you were with her the afternoon and evening of Mr. Norris's unfortunate demise. Trying to comfort her, I believe she said."

"Yes. She was upset. She knew her niece was celebrating her engagement in London and was distraught to not be there with her."

"What have you advised her to do, to overcome the fear that traps her on the island?"

He shook his head. "There is little I can say. Logic and rationale don't have much effect in such situations, I find. I was there with her as her friend, not her physician, that night."

"All night?"

The man shot him a hard look. "I hope you are not insinuating anything. I won't hear a word against Miss Wilder or any slights to her character."

164

Benjamin raised his hands. "None intended."

"Good. No, not all night, though a good deal of it. She was suffering a noticeable depression of spirits and wanted only company and a listening ear."

"And wine."

"Yes, though I was too gentlemanly to mention it to you. Don't worry, Miss Wilder is not one I consider addicted to drink in the least. Usually she is perfectly sober. But it was not a usual day."

Dr. Grant thought and added, "We sat out in the boathouse until quite late, and then afterward, I saw her safely to her room. That is all."

"And you went straight home?"

"Yes."

"Can anyone verify that?"

He hesitated. "My father could. He is here visiting."

"Oh? I have not heard him mentioned before."

"He retired to the coast years ago, to live with his sister. I rarely see him."

Benjamin echoed the man's earlier words. "But you didn't follow him into the family profession?"

The physician's mouth thinned. "No, I did not. My father was . . . he is not an educated man, nor had he the means or connections to see me educated. Thankfully, Mr. Wilder saw my potential. He sponsored me through grammar school and later university. In Edinburgh, I got on famously with one professor in particular. A physician and lecturer who has since offered me a partnership in a lucrative practice."

"But you did not take it."

"Not yet, no."

"May I ask why?" Benjamin thought of Miss Wilder. "Or is the answer the one that obviously presents itself?"

The doctor gave him another hard look. "Things are rarely as simple as we think, Mr. Booker. Surely you have learned that in your practice of the law, with its nuances and changes."

"Perhaps."

"Suffice it to say, I had my reasons. One being that I have felt duty-bound to offer my services here in Riverton in honor of Mr. Wilder, who made my education possible in the first place."

"Would he have expected you to remain here forever?"

"No, not forever."

"How long?"

A muscle in the man's jaw pulsed. "As long as it takes."

CHAPTER

fourteen

On his way back to the house, Benjamin saw young Joe playing on the lawn with Miss Wilder's puppy. It must be the weavers' mealtime.

Benjamin asked him, "What, no book today?"

"I finished it."

"And not yet started another?"

"I've read them all."

"Oh? And where did you find such a treasure trove of books?"

"Miss Wilder, sir. They were her brother's. She let me borrow them, but I've read them all now, sad to say."

"That was good of her."

The youth shrugged. "Yes. She is good. And kind." The lad looked at him closely. Too closely. "You don't believe me, do you?"

"I . . . don't know her very well."

"Well, I have known her all my life, and I like her and trust her."

"I am glad to hear you say so. But you see, I liked and trusted a woman once, and it turned out badly for me."

"That's not Miss Wilder's fault."

Ben looked at the youth, impressed. "You're right. It's not."

He changed the subject. "So, how did the book end? Did the highwayman go free?"

Joe shook his head. "No. He got justice in the end." The boy sat cross-legged on the grass, and the puppy climbed onto his lap to be petted. "In the last chapter, he holds up the same gentleman's chaise a second time. He disarms the guard and takes the ladies' jewels while the dandy sits there, helpless once more, or so you believe. But that dandy has learnt his lesson. He had hidden a gun and shoots the highwayman straight through the heart. It was justice, I know, though still a sad ending." Joe sighed. "Never cared much for the dandy."

Benjamin thought, then asked, "Have you read *Gulliver's Travels*?"

"No, sir."

"I have a copy with me. I will loan it to you, if you promise to take good care of it."

"I will, sir. I promise!"

Benjamin ruffled the boy's hair and continued toward the house. As he entered, he heard voices coming from the drawing room. He paused at the threshold and looked inside, his head rearing back in surprise.

Robert Hardy sat on a chair near Miss Wilder, the two talking and laughing like old friends.

She glanced up and noticed him. "Oh, there you are, Mr. Booker. Mr. Hardy was just sharing a few memories of my father. I did not realize they were acquainted, though perhaps I should have."

Hardy nodded, eyes warm with nostalgia. "Oh yes, Jonathan Wilder would drop by our offices when he was in London. He came to see Percy, of course, but he and I became acquainted during those visits as well. He once brought me a box of the best cigars I ever had. From India, I believe he said."

Miss Wilder nodded. "Yes, my father was partial to those. My mother, less so."

She smiled and gestured Benjamin closer. "Join us."

Benjamin sat, feeling oddly disoriented to see two previously separate parts of his world collide.

Mr. Hardy leaned forward, eyes alight. "One evening, Percy was keen to play cards, but your father was not a gambling man. We needed a fourth, so he begrudgingly consented to play, but only on the condition that all the winnings be donated to Coram's foundling hospital."

Isabelle chuckled. "Sounds like Father."

Hardy nodded. "Percy, Hunt, and I moaned and groaned but eventually agreed. And at the end of the evening, your father might have had cause to repent that decision. He'd won four hundred pounds! True to his word, he donated every farthing. The governors were very grateful."

With a closed-lip smile and tears in her eyes, Miss Wilder's face shone with poignant pleasure.

After a moment of respectful silence passed, Benjamin spoke up. "I am happy to see you here, sir, though also surprised."

"Are you? But you wrote and asked about the terms of the Wilder trust. I thought it best to bring you the documents myself. Some things one does not trust to the post."

"Very true. Thank you, sir."

His mentor gestured to Isabelle. "Miss Wilder has been graciousness itself and invited me to stay for a few days while you and I work through the details. I'm afraid Hunt Senior composed the original documents, and as he was known for verbosity and painstaking thoroughness, it may take some untangling." He smiled at her. "But if anyone can make sense of it, Mr. Booker can. Never knew a young man with a keener mind."

Miss Wilder sent Benjamin an appraising look at that, then rose. "Well, I shall leave you to it. Mr. Booker can show you the way to the study. Anything you gentlemen need, just let me know. I will ask Jacob to build up the fire."

Benjamin and Mr. Hardy rose as well.

"Very kind, madam. Very thoughtful," the older man said warmly. "You remind me of my own dear daughter."

She turned back, her countenance alight with interest. "Have you a daughter? How lovely. What is her name, if I may ask?"

"Indeed you may. It is a proud father's pleasure to describe his children, after all. My Cordelia is a fine, accomplished young lady. She married Mr. Ralph Farnsworth some eighteen months ago, and I'm delighted to say the happy couple have just given me my first grandchild."

"How wonderful!" Isabelle enthused. "And mother and babe are well?"

"Indeed. Perfectly well."

"What a blessing. I am so happy for you."

Benjamin cleared a sudden lump in his throat. "And I, sir. Congratulations."

Mr. Hardy clapped his shoulder, holding his gaze in a long, understanding look. "I had hoped for a different son-in-law, but in the end I must be grateful."

"Yes, of course you must," Benjamin said with more conviction than he felt. He became aware of Miss Wilder's sympathetic gaze, and his ears heated in embarrassment. *Now she will know Miss Hardy chose another man over me and is no doubt not surprised.*

When Miss Wilder left them, Benjamin led Mr. Hardy to the study. There he faced his mentor feeling ill at ease, wondering if the man was displeased with him, despite his praise to their hostess.

"I know I have been away longer than anticipated, but—"

"Never mind that." Mr. Hardy waved away his excuses. "I've come with news." He shut the door securely and took a seat, directing Benjamin to sit as well. "There's been a development. I thought of writing to you but felt you should know directly."

"What is it?"

"There has been another death. Mary Williams, the maid employed in Percival's household."

"The Wilders' household, I believe you mean."

Another dismissive wave. "He lived there too. This is no time for splitting hairs."

"Sorry. How did she die?"

"Poisoned. She was found in a lodging house, in a room rented by a young carter named Lester Crabb. Her beau, apparently. He reported the death himself. He'd left her sleeping, or so he thought, and went off to make an out-of-town delivery. He was shocked to return two days later to a dead woman in his bed, as you can imagine. And her only twenty. A bottle was found on the side table bearing a Belle Island label."

Benjamin took the news like a punch to his gut. *A second poisoning* . . . He drew a shaky breath and tried to keep his expression and tone even. "How is it the young man was spared?"

"Never cared for wine, apparently, and didn't take any. Wise choice in this case."

"Is he a suspect in her death?"

"Ordinarily he would be. But a man would be a fool to poison a victim in his own room and then alert the constable himself. He made no effort to remove the bottle or any evidence of their . . . previous activities. And considering the extenuating circumstances—the fact that this is the second suspected poi-soning by Wilder wine—I don't think he'll be charged."

Benjamin's mind whirled. "Why would anyone want to harm the maid? Do you think she might have seen something that night? Knew more than she let on about Mr. Norris's death? Perhaps she got greedy and tried to extort money from some-one."

Mr. Hardy stared, taking it all in. "Goodness, how your mind works."

"Have you another theory?"

Hardy rubbed his jaw. "Actually, you may be right. Do you recall when the maid told the officer she'd heard Percival arguing with 'some fellow' before she left the house? When the officer asked who it was, she hesitated before saying she'd never heard him mention a name."

Benjamin nodded. "I do recall that. Though we both know it is hardly solid evidence."

"True."

Benjamin's mind continued to spin with possibilities. He said, "Perhaps there is a far simpler explanation. Perhaps both bottles were poisoned to assure whichever Percival drank would be his last. And if Miss Williams helped herself to the second bottle not realizing the risk, her death was accidental, or at least not planned by the poisoner."

Mr. Hardy slowly nodded. "I agree, that sounds more likely."

Benjamin shook his head, guilt pinching him. "We ought to have considered that. Warned the staff and searched for ad-ditional bottles."

Mr. Hardy laid a hand on his arm. "The coroner should have done so. He is the one responsible for preventing further harm. Or perhaps the Bow Street officer, but not you. This is not your fault, Benjamin. Your brother dismissed your poisoning theory initially, remember? And assuming the maid stole the bottle, she is not a completely innocent party."

"I hardly think the fatal punishment fits the rather minor crime."

"No." Hardy sighed deeply. "It is an unfortunate business."

"I agree. The question remaining is, Who poisoned the wine and where?"

"Is not the most likely scenario that the wine was poisoned here by Miss Wilder especially for Percy?"

"I don't know, sir. I don't think Miss Wilder would have done so, but . . ."

Worry lined his mentor's face. "Careful, Ben. Remember what happened the last time you trusted a pretty woman."

"You needn't remind me. I am hourly aware. But any of the servants or Miss Lawrence or even Mr. Adair might have tampered with it in London."

"Good point." Mr. Hardy nodded, then added, "Before I left town, I asked their housekeeper to make sure no other bottles were in the house. She reported finding none. Have you inspected the wine cellar here?"

Benjamin swallowed another guilty lump. "No. I judged it unlikely she would poison bottles made for her own use. Besides, I would not know what to look for. I am not an apothecary."

"But your father is, as was mine. Like yours, my father wanted me to follow him into physic, but I chose a different career as you have."

"Yes . . ." Benjamin murmured. He had never told Mr. Hardy the real reason he had shunned the medical profession—his inability to measure up to his naturally gifted brother or their father's expectations.

Thinking of the congenial scene he'd interrupted between

Mr. Hardy and Miss Wilder, he quickly changed the subject. "Why did you say nothing of the maid's death to Miss Wilder?"

"Because I wanted to speak to you privately first. I didn't want to warn her—give her cause to scurry about getting rid of evidence before we have a chance to search for it."

"I see . . ." Benjamin hesitated. He hated the thought of sneaking around another person's house, especially hers.

Mr. Hardy said kindly, "I understand your reticence, but we are justified. Our goal is to protect anyone else from poisoning— accidental or otherwise."

"Very well. I found an architect's plan for the house when going through the papers in the study. I think I could find the door. Or we could simply ask her, you know. She would not prevent us from going down there."

"After she had removed all traces of poison, perhaps."

"Then should we go down there now?"

Hardy thought. "Not yet. I've just arrived, and she may be watching. I'll take a look at that plan, but let's get you started on the trust first, so if she asks, you can report on our progress. We don't want to raise suspicion unnecessarily."

Ben agreed, relieved to put off the prying task for as long as possible.

Hardy pulled a folder from his brief bag and laid it on the desk. Then he looked at Ben with sympathy. "I know it seems intrusive, but don't feel guilty. It's only a matter of time until someone searches the place. With Mary Williams dead, I imagine Officer Riley will be coming here any day."

His mentor had intended to comfort him, Benjamin knew, but his words had the opposite effect.

Mr. Hardy sat on the velvet sofa near the window. Benjamin handed him the rolled plan, then returned to the desk and centered the leather folder before him. The folder was an inch thick, so Benjamin put on his spectacles in readiness for a lot of tedious reading.

"Have you already gone through this?"

Hardy wafted his hand. "Skimmed only enough to confirm my memory. I vaguely recalled Mr. Wilder asking if he could list my name as a possible successor, in the event Percival was unable or unwilling to serve. Apparently I agreed without giving it another thought. I knew Percy was willing, so I never imagined this day would come."

"No, of course not," Ben murmured, absorbing the news. Mr. Hardy was the successor. Ben understood why the man's memory might be foggy. The senior partner had probably composed and reviewed a thousand legal documents in the years since.

Mr. Hardy sighed, looking tired. "In all honesty, I wish I had not agreed. I have my hands full with the firm and looked forward to spending all my leisure hours spoiling my new grandson. I won't be able to devote nearly as much time to the Wilder estate as Percy did."

Ben knew Miss Wilder, Miss Lawrence, and even the London servants disapproved of how Mr. Norris had carried out his duties but did not say so to his old friend.

Hardy added, "In your letter, you mentioned Miss Wilder hopes to go on without a successor. I don't know if the trust includes contingencies for bringing that about. I planned to study the details on the journey here, but reading while in motion makes me ill. All right if I leave it to you?"

"Yes, of course."

Mr. Hardy glanced at the house plan, then set it aside. "Will you think me terribly doddering if I close my eyes for a few minutes? I didn't sleep well last night and shared a coach with two screaming toddlers."

"Not at all. I know how tiring travel can be." Ben licked dry lips, then added lightly, "Though I suppose you shall have to grow accustomed to such sounds in the near future."

Robert Hardy stretched out on the sofa, keeping his shoes considerately clear of the upholstery. "Very true. Though somehow I think it will be more endearing from one's own grandchild." He grinned at the thought, laid his head on the plush arm of the sofa, and closed his eyes.

Banishing the image of Cordelia's face from his mind, Benjamin opened the folder and began sorting through the documents within. The folder included a copy of Mrs. Wilder's simple last will and testament, bequeathing her personal possessions to her daughters, followed by Mr. Wilder's longer will, which directed that his estate, assets, real and personal property be disposed of as directed by the established trust. Benjamin turned to it next. He first skimmed through the articles describing the establishment of the trust—*Grantor: Jonathan Wilder, Trustee: Percival Norris*—then flipped past the articles about the rights and methods to amend, revoke, or terminate the trust agreement. It took some time as the language was complicated and the organization convoluted, as Mr. Hardy had predicted, but eventually he came to what he was looking for.

Successor Trustee.

He ran his finger along the text and read quietly to himself, "'In the event Percival Norris is deceased, unwilling or unable to serve, etc., etc., then . . . Robert Hardy shall serve as successor trustee.'"

Just as Mr. Hardy had said. He read a bit further. "'In the event Robert Hardy is unable or unwilling to serve, etc., etc., then I authorize the firm of Norris, Hardy, and Hunt to appoint a qualified Successor Trustee.'"

Benjamin sat back. He removed his spectacles and considered the situation.

His initial reaction of surprise was followed by relief. They were not dealing with some stranger or impersonal bank or corporation. Rose's fear that the successor trustee would be more controlling and miserly than Mr. Norris was unfounded. Robert Hardy was firm yet fair, even generous.

Miss Wilder's hopes that there would be no successor at all were not realized, but her concerns should be at least partially alleviated by learning Robert Hardy was the successor. She seemed to like him already.

Whether she had grounds to refuse a new trustee was more complicated. He would have to review the lengthy articles that prescribed the rights and methods to amend, revoke, or terminate the trust agreement. Mr. Wilder, as grantor, could have done so at any time were he alive, but it would be much more difficult to do now that he was gone.

A growl of his stomach alerted Ben to his mounting hunger. He glanced up at the clock. The family would soon be dressing for dinner. He would try to catch Miss Wilder alone and give her the news in person. Even though Mr. Hardy was not eager for the role, Ben knew his mentor well enough to know he was not one to shirk his responsibilities. He glanced across the room again, tempted to confirm his willingness. But Mr. Hardy's mouth had fallen slack, and a soft snore rumbled from his throat. *Oh, let him sleep*, he told himself. There would be time enough for legalities later.

Looking fondly at the man, Ben thought of a long-ago memory—of Mr. Hardy asking him, perhaps a year after he'd started at the firm, why he had chosen law over medicine.

Ben had replied, "I never cared for any of it. Not the work itself, nor the accompanying smells and sights. I swept and dusted and completed tasks in the physic garden when required but could not wait to leave it all behind me. All I wanted to do was read and study the law."

Hardy had nodded approvingly. "Just as I did at that age. We are men more at home with legal language, leather volumes, and lengthy rhetoric. I applaud you for charting your own course in life." He'd squeezed Benjamin's shoulder with affection. "Like the son I wished I had."

Benjamin's chest had expanded with pleasure and pride at the words. He had long seen himself as the second-best son, the son who would always be a disappointment. It felt good to be the wished-for son in his respected mentor's eyes. He'd walked with his head held higher for days afterward.

Even now, Ben was proud to have earned Mr. Hardy's trust and esteem. He hoped he had not jeopardized both by his recent failure. With renewed determination, Benjamin resolved not to let his attraction to Miss Wilder impede his search for the truth.

CHAPTER
fifteen

Almost dressed for dinner, Isabelle put on one earring, then ran her finger through the jumble of earbobs in her jewelry box. "Lotty? Have you seen my other garnet earring? I can only find one."

"No, miss." Lotty came forward to help her search. "Perhaps it fell behind the dressing chest?" She dropped to her knees to look. "When was the last time you saw it?"

Isabelle squinted her eyes shut, trying to remember.

"Oh, I know." Lotty rose, answering her own question. "You wore them with your new dress with the red embroidery."

"That's right. The day of Rose's party—the one in London, I mean."

Lotty nodded. "I remember thinking how pretty you looked. *Que linda.* I was sure the doctor would propose, but . . . thankfully not."

Isabelle let the comment pass, searching her memories of that particular day and night. "Perhaps it fell off in the boathouse. I shall go and look."

"I'll go, miss."

"No, you have more than enough work to do as it is, helping with a houseful of guests. But thank you for offering." Isabelle started toward the door.

Carlota called after her, "About that night, I . . ."

Isabelle turned back. "What about it?"

Her companion hesitated, then nibbled her lip. "Oh, never mind. A night better forgotten, probably."

Isabelle nodded. "I agree."

She walked down to the boathouse and opened the creaky side door, leaving it open to let in the light. She walked past the two chaise longues and opened one of the wide, riverside doors as well, then began searching the ground.

A footfall startled her, and she looked up. The tall lawyer stepped inside, expression quizzical.

"Oh, Mr. Booker. You gave me a start."

"Looking for something?"

"Yes, I lost an earring. I thought I might have dropped it out here."

"An earring?" A strange look passed over his face. "What does it look like?"

"Like this." She removed the single earbob and handed it to him.

He frowned down at it.

Before she could ask him what was wrong, another voice interrupted them.

"Halloo?" Rose slipped in through the open door behind him, eyes darting from the man to her aunt. "When I saw Mr. Booker follow you down here, I couldn't imagine why." Her high laugh sounded a little false to Isabelle's ear.

Was her niece trying to protect her reputation, or something else?

"I lost one of my garnet earrings," Isabelle explained. "I thought it might be out here, since I can't find it in the house."

Mr. Booker walked toward the open door, entering the shaft of light and examining her earring more closely. "I recently saw one exactly like this."

"Really?" she said, hope rising. "Where?"

"In London."

Confusion flared. "What?"

"In the back passage of the townhouse. The night of your uncle's death."

She stared, uncomprehending. "You must be mistaken."

He shook his head. "A garnet set amid leaves of gold. I pointed it out to the officer as possible evidence. I imagine he still has it, unless he gave it to the housekeeper."

"But . . . how did it get there?"

"You tell me."

"Aunt Belle!" Rose blurted. "You forget! You loaned those earrings to me, remember? I said how well they would look with my red spencer, and you agreed to send them to London with me. When I came back here this time, I returned only the one to you. I am so sorry."

Isabelle stood there, dumbfounded into silence.

Rose went on, "I must have lost it on my way down to speak to Uncle Percy on some matter or another. Silly me. I am forever losing things." She beamed up at Mr. Booker. "Thank you, sir. I am so relieved to know the lost sheep has been found." She held out her palm to him. "I shall ask Mrs. Kittleson for its mate when I get back to Town."

He glanced at Rose's outstretched hand and instead turned to Isabelle. "I think I had better hold on to it for the time being. Officer Riley might find it most interesting. Unless, that is, you object?"

Isabelle hesitated, pulse pounding. "I . . . No. Of course not."

He held her gaze a moment and then placed the earbob into his waistcoat pocket. "Good. I would hate for this one to somehow go missing as well."

Benjamin walked back to the house, the earring like a bur in his pocket, pricking him through the fine fabric. Anger pricked him too. All her claims of not leaving the island, of not being in London for years, and then . . . this? He'd immediately recognized the garnet-and-gold earring, and he didn't for a moment believe Miss Lawrence's explanation, and clearly Miss Wilder had not either. Her bewildered expression showed she had no idea what her niece was talking about. Perhaps she was even now chastising herself for not falling in with Rose's attempt to explain away the earring's unexpected appearance in London.

Benjamin had seen Miss Wilder walking toward the boathouse and decided he would take advantage of the private moment to tell her about the successor trustee. But the earring had chased all other thoughts from his mind. Now, going back upstairs, he knocked at the guest room Mr. Hardy occupied.

"Come."

Benjamin entered. Mr. Hardy had changed for dinner and was adjusting his cravat. Years of dining with upper-class clients had honed his ability to dress the part. His brief nap had clearly refreshed him, and he looked better than he had upon arrival.

"I saw you go outside," the older man began. "I suppose you told Miss Wilder the news?"

"No, I . . . didn't have a chance."

"That's all right. You can mention it at dinner. And let's hold off on announcing the maid's death until we've had a chance to search the wine cellar. Probably best not to spring too much startling news on the family at once."

Benjamin nodded. The revelation about the earring was there, coiled on his tongue, but he held it back. Why did he feel so illogically protective of Isabelle Wilder? It would probably be his ruination.

A short while later, Benjamin and Mr. Hardy joined the others for dinner. If their irritable expressions were any indication, Miss Lawrence and Mr. Adair did not seem pleased to find another lawyer sharing the table with them.

Aware of their chilly reception, Mr. Hardy tried his best, warmest charm. "A pleasure to see you again, Miss Lawrence. Mr. Norris spoke of you often and fondly."

"I doubt that, Mr. Hardy, but thank you. My aunt tells me you are here to help us get out from under the yoke of that horrid trust."

"Well, I wouldn't put it quite that way, but yes, I hope to help."

"Then if so, you are most welcome."

Mr. Hardy glanced at Benjamin, brows high. They had decided the news would be better received from him.

Benjamin cleared his throat. "Mr. Hardy brought the trust documents from London, and I have begun going through them. More to untangle, but the document did reveal the successor trustee as expected."

Rose groaned and laid a hand over her aunt's.

He continued, "The good news is, it is not some stranger or impersonal corporation, but Mr. Norris's old friend and my trusted mentor, Robert Hardy, senior partner of Norris, Hardy, and Hunt."

Adair swore under his breath.

Miss Wilder looked at Mr. Hardy, wearing a hurt expression. "You did not mention this when you arrived."

"Forgive me, my dear. As I told Benjamin, I only vaguely recalled being listed in the event Percival was unable to serve, and as I never thought that would happen, I have not thought about it in years."

Aware of the lingering tension in the room, Benjamin said, "May I gently remind you that your own father, Miss Lawrence's grandfather, appointed Mr. Hardy?"

Adair frowned. "Yes, but he also appointed Percival, who turned out to be a scoundrel!"

"Christopher . . ." Rose hissed, with a significant look at her uncle's friend.

Mr. Hardy did not appear offended, however. "I understand your concern, Mr. Adair, ladies. Although I was fond of Percy, I realize he had his faults and weaknesses, which I do not share. If you want my help, Miss Wilder, I will endeavor to carry out your father's wishes in a responsible, considerate manner. But if you object, we will happily investigate options for having me replaced."

He gazed earnestly at Miss Wilder, and she looked away first.

"It is nothing personal, Mr. Hardy. I barely know you. I only hoped to be mistress of the estate myself. No one loves the island more than I do."

"I cannot argue with that." He smiled warmly at her, then looked around the table. "Well, shall we leave the topic for the time being? As Mr. Booker said, many more pages and clauses to review before we know all we are dealing with, and meanwhile, our soup is growing cold. Shall we turn our attention to the first course? Everything looks delicious."

Isabelle managed a small smile in return. "Yes. Of course."

Benjamin distractedly spooned his soup, his gaze now and again drawn to Christopher Adair across from him. Looking pale, weary, and less polished than usual, Adair seemed to consume more brandy than food as the meal progressed.

Benjamin thought again of what Mary Williams had said about hearing Mr. Norris arguing with a man the day of his death. When the officer asked her who it was, he thought the maid's gaze had darted to Mr. Adair. At the time Benjamin told himself he might have imagined it, but Mr. Hardy had noticed it too. Mary also said she'd heard a glass shatter, so she had been in the house when Mr. Norris was still alive, and perhaps even at the moment he had been killed. Oh, if only they had asked her more questions . . . when they'd had the chance.

Adair's sullen lip curled. "What are you staring at, Booker?"

"Hm? Oh, sorry. Only remembering something."

"Something about me?"

"Something Miss Williams said."

"Who?"

"The housemaid in London. She said she heard Mr. Norris arguing with 'some fellow' that day. I was wondering who it was. Whoever it was might have been the last person to see Percival Norris alive."

Christopher Adair lifted a pugnacious chin. "And if I remember right, she said she didn't know who the man was. Which is . . . a pity."

"Actually, her reply was rather ambiguous. She said, 'I never heard him mention a name.' But she might have recognized the voice and felt duty-bound to keep quiet."

The young man held his gaze, and if anything looked even paler than before. Rose looked uneasy as well, and Miss Wilder not much better.

Mr. Hardy nudged Ben's shoe under the table. He was edging awfully close to the news of Miss Williams's death.

"Do pass me the peas, Benjamin," Mr. Hardy said. "Fresh from the garden, I think. Delicious."

Later that night, Isabelle stood on the veranda gazing at the golden moonlight reflected on the Thames. Rose came outside, dragged the cushion off the veranda sofa, and laid it on the paving stones, as they had done so often when her niece was a girl.

Rose lay down first and patted the space beside her. "Come, Aunt Belle. Just as when I was little."

"Very well. But don't tell Lotty I am lying on my best satin or she'll box my ears."

She settled down beside Rose, and together they looked up at the night sky. Innumerable stars shone in the dark canopy, some twinkling, some steady and unwavering. In the distance, crickets chir-chirred along with an invisible orchestra of frogs.

Rose asked wistfully, "Do you remember when I would try to count the stars?"

"Yes. One night you made it to nine hundred ninety-nine."

Rose chuckled. "Or we would just talk. About the future. About our dreams. You were always such a good listener."

"Thank you. Your mother trained me well. She and I used to look up at the stars too and whisper about whom we might marry one day or all the wonderful places we might travel."

Rose turned her head to look at her, but Isabelle kept her own eyes on the stars above. She knew what was coming.

"Do you ever regret not going to those places?"

"Sometimes."

"Are you truly happy here on the island?"

"I am. For the most part. Or I was, until you left." Isabelle raised a hand. "No guilt, I promise. I am happy for you and Mr.

Adair, truly." She lowered her hand, found Rose's beside her, and clasped it. "I miss you, though. And I miss your mother. But when you are here, it is almost as if she's here too."

Rose mused, "I wonder if she and Papa can see me? As a girl, I thought they were up in heaven like two of the stars, winking down on us, watching us."

"I don't know about that, but Arminda believes God watches over us."

"Mamma and Papa taught me God was loving, but sometimes I wonder. If He is so loving, why did He take my parents from me, and yours from you?"

Ah, the age-old question. "I don't know," Isabelle answered honestly. Did she believe God was loving? Perhaps. Trustworthy? No, she did not trust Him with the lives of those she loved. Was that blasphemous to admit? She wanted to trust, but fear and worry all too often won out.

Isabelle gently changed the subject. "I didn't really lend you those earrings, Rose."

The girl sighed. "I know. But I also know you didn't do anything wrong. I couldn't stand the way Mr. Booker was looking at you. Eyes narrowed. So suspicious. So sure he'd caught you. I had to say something to wipe that reproachful look from his face."

"I don't think he believed you."

Rose shrugged, unconcerned. "He can't prove I was not telling the truth either."

Isabelle didn't like that her niece could lie so easily. "Perhaps not, but that still doesn't explain how that earring ended up in the London house."

Rose turned on her side, head propped up on her hand. "I have a theory about that. Did you not tell me those were Grandmother's earrings?"

"Yes. One of her favorite pairs. She gave them to me when I was thirteen."

Rose nodded. "So here's what I think happened. She lost one years ago while in London for the season. They were her favorites, so she asked a jeweler to make a duplicate to match the one she'd lost. And all this time that lost earring has been hiding somewhere in the London house . . . under a carpet or cushion or in some dusty corner that has long escaped Mrs. Kittleson's notice. Then it was finally unearthed with all the cleaning she and Mary did when they thought we were hosting the engagement party. All sorts of drawers were turned out and carpets taken up and beaten that have not been touched in years. Things have become rather lax there since Grandmother's passing." Rose looked at Isabelle, pleased with herself. "It *could* explain it."

"It is certainly creative, my love, though not very likely."

"More likely than you sneaking off to London to kill Uncle Percy."

"True."

"Can you think of a better explanation?"

Isabelle shook her head, her gaze once more drawn to the stars. "No. I wish I could."

Rose took herself inside eventually, but Isabelle remained out on the veranda for a long time, her mind uneasy. She thought of Rose delivering the wine to Percival, Mr. Adair's strange behavior, and Teddy's warning about implicating someone she loved. She also thought of the coldness in Mr. Booker's eyes when he'd recognized her earring. She missed the warm teasing light that had been there before.

Oh, how in the world had her earring ended up in London? *Was* it her earring, or merely identical to the one she'd lost? After all, there was nothing so unusual about the setting. Perhaps she would find the missing one yet and prove Mr. Booker wrong and herself . . . sane.

She squeezed her eyes shut. Must there always be something new to worry about? What was that verse Mr. Booker had mentioned? Be anxious for nothing, but pray instead? Something like it, at any rate. Oh, what she would give for a little peace. . . .

The sound of boot steps on the paving stones caught her ear. She turned her head and saw Evan Curtis approach, wearing a coat but no cravat, his waistcoat casually unbuttoned.

"Oh . . . Evan." She struggled up into a seated position.

"Good evening, Belle. How strange to hear you call me by my given name after so many years."

"Forgive me. I should probably not do so."

"Why? We are old friends. Or at least, we were."

An awkward silence followed, and she grasped for a neutral topic. "And how is your father?"

"He is well, except for a trifling cold. Nothing to poor Mrs. Howton's condition, yet it causes him to snore worse than a whole regiment of foot soldiers. I gave up trying to sleep and decided to go for a walk. And you? Why are you out here so late?"

She shrugged. "Just thinking."

He looked up at the stars. "We used to look at the stars together, remember? We planned to chart our course by them and sail away somewhere beautiful and exciting."

Isabelle nodded, thinking of the tin star in her keepsake box. "How young we were then. How naïve. Though I should speak only for myself, as you did make good on those plans to see the world. Was it as beautiful and exciting as you hoped?"

He shook his head. "Not most of it. Spain and Portugal were beautiful, I suppose, but I was too busy trying to stay alive to appreciate it."

189

"I am glad you survived. Though I am still surprised you came back here."

"Are you? Of course I came back. My father lives here."

"Is that . . . the only reason?" She wished the words back as soon as they slipped past her lips. How forward they must have sounded.

He looked down at her, studying her face. She tried to hold his gaze, appear innocently, casually interested, even as her cheeks heated in embarrassment. She hoped the shadows hid her blush.

"Of course that's the only reason. What else could it be, after all this time?"

She looked away. The word *revenge* whispered in her mind, but this time she held her tongue. Was it possible he bore her or Uncle Percy a grudge?

Eventually, she said, "I *am* sorry, you know."

"Are you?"

"I hope you are not still angry with me."

She felt his gaze sear her profile, and then finally he looked away across the lawn to the water beyond. "I transferred my anger to your *dear* Uncle Percy long ago."

He sat on the arm of the veranda sofa and sent her a sidelong glance. "I can guess what you are thinking. No, I did not kill him, except biblically speaking, I suppose. What's the verse? 'Whosoever hateth his brother is a murderer'? Thankfully I do not consider him a brother."

He sent another sidelong glance. "I have often wondered, though, if you allowed Percy to be your scapegoat. Perhaps you didn't want me here, pestering you for an answer, so you asked him to send me away."

"Never! I did have reservations about a match between us. But I never said anything to Uncle Percy about sending you away. In fact, when I learned of it, I was furious with him. It was the beginning of the breach between us."

"Yet he still came here regularly as a guest over the years, according to Papa."

"Because my father named him trustee. I had to honor that. I could not tell him he was unwelcome, although he no doubt felt the chill between us whenever he came on some estate business or other. And the last time he was here, we argued terribly. No doubt one of the reasons I am a suspect in his murder."

"I can't believe you did it. Though I wouldn't blame you if you had."

"No, I did not, though like you I certainly thought some unkind things about the man."

They were quiet for several moments, then he looked at her, one brow high. "You mentioned reservations. I thought you were drawn to my devilish good looks and confident, adventurous spirit."

A setdown leapt to her tongue, but she glimpsed a sheen of vulnerability in his eyes and the urge to humble him evaporated. Instead she said, "You are good-looking, as you very well know, and I always admired your confidence. But you . . . frightened me too. I knew you would go off to the wild unknown somewhere, and I had little desire to do the same. I have always been a homebody, even before the deaths in my family."

His lips quirked. "You're saying I was too wild for a Wilder?"

She grinned. "Exactly."

"Nothing to do with the fact that I was only the groundsman's son?"

"No—at least not in my case. I cannot speak to Percival's objections."

He nodded thoughtfully. "I sincerely thought I would return

to find you married to Theo Grant. Have you two an understanding?"

Have we? Isabelle asked herself. "No. Nothing formal."

His eyes glinted by moonlight. "What's the fool waiting for?"

She shifted, feeling suddenly chilled. "Teddy and I are just friends."

The captain did not look convinced.

CHAPTER
sixteen

In the morning, Benjamin and Mr. Hardy lingered over break-fast. When they saw Mrs. Philpotts and Miss Wilder leave the house with baskets of food and urns of tea for the weavers, they judged it safe to go down to the cellar unnoticed.

Armed with candle lamps, they walked quietly belowstairs. Following the dim passage, they heard the gentle splash of water and rhythmic *clack, clack* of crockery being stacked. A scullery maid washing breakfast dishes, no doubt. A pot clanged and Benjamin jumped, scuffing the floor.

"Shh . . ." Mr. Hardy admonished.

"Sorry."

Mr. Hardy led the way to the cellar door and tried to open it. It would not yield.

"You try."

Benjamin tried the latch without success. It was locked.

Footsteps tap-tapped down the stairs behind them, and Benjamin jerked alert. Feeling like a disloyal friend and misbehaving boy all at once, he held his breath as someone descended into the passage.

He expected Miss Wilder, perhaps having forgotten something. Instead, Miss Lawrence appeared, drawing up short to find the two of them at the cellar door.

Her eyes shifted from man to man. "What are you two doing skulking around down here?"

Mr. Hardy said earnestly, "Forgive us, my dear, but Percival Norris was my friend, and I feel duty-bound to do all I can to bring his killer to justice."

She arched one brow. "So you are sneaking down to the cellar to look for evidence that my aunt poisoned his wine?"

"Or that someone did, yes."

"Meaning me?"

"You did carry a bottle into his office."

"True." Rose hesitated, then gestured toward the door. "So what are you waiting for?"

"The door is locked. Is it usually?"

Her brow furrowed. "I would not have guessed so. I have gone down there only once or twice, helping Aunt Belle move bottles from the stillroom. You might as well search there for now, for that is where she actually makes the wine."

Rose led them to a small ancillary kitchen adjacent to the scullery, complete with stove, sink, and worktable. "She and I dry flowers here and make our jams, cordials, and salves. Keeps us out of Mrs. Philpotts's way."

Benjamin halfheartedly joined the search as Mr. Hardy looked in various cabinets and drawers, but they found nothing unusual.

"Who keeps the key to the cellar?" he asked.

"My aunt, I suppose. Or perhaps Mrs. Philpotts. I don't have one, if that's what you mean." Rose lifted her chin. "If *I* had poisoned the wine, I certainly wouldn't have done so in that nasty cobwebbed cellar. After all, I might have done it anywhere—even waited until Uncle Percy's office was empty and poisoned it there."

What game is she playing? Benjamin wondered and shook his head. "I don't think so. If someone poisoned it in London, I'd wager the poison was introduced in the butler's pantry, where . . . others would have ready access to that second bottle."

She frowned. "Did that second bottle ever turn up?"

He glanced at Mr. Hardy, who gave an almost imperceptible nod. Benjamin said, "Yes, it has."

Rose Lawrence clasped her hands and waited.

Mr. Hardy said, "There has been a second poisoning by a bottle of Belle Island wine, which spurred our search down here today."

"Good heavens, no." Rose's fingers went to her throat. "Who?"

"Mary Williams."

Her eyebrows rose. "The housemaid?"

"Yes."

"But why would anyone want to . . . ?" She broke off mid-sentence, her wide eyes flashing to Benjamin's face. Was she recalling his conversation with Adair at dinner last night? He certainly was.

Mr. Hardy added, "The bottle may have been meant for someone else. Your aunt sent only the two bottles to London—is that right?"

"Yes, two," she murmured. After a moment, she added, "And you may as well know that Mr. Adair and I delivered the bottles to London for Aunt Belle."

Benjamin tipped his head back. Why had she and her aunt neglected to mention that detail earlier? It was less condemning, he supposed, than the fact she had taken the bottle directly to Mr. Norris's office, but still questionable that Rose should conceal it, only to reveal it now, when her aunt was under suspicion.

An hour later, Isabelle Wilder sat slumped in the study, slowly shaking her head. Her niece sat beside her, holding her hand. Benjamin and Mr. Hardy stood like somber guards, both with their hands behind their backs.

"I can't think how such a thing happened," Miss Wilder said. "That poor girl."

"Were you acquainted with Mary Williams?"

Again she shook her head. "I never met her."

"Mary had only lately come into service with us," Miss Lawrence explained.

Miss Wilder's voice rose in incredulity. "But why would anyone want to kill her?"

"That's what we need to find out," said Mr. Hardy. "Though her death may have been accidental. Mr. Booker tells me the remaining bottles are in the wine cellar?"

"Yes. I filled them in the stillroom, then carried them down there to store. Rose helped me, as did Mr. Adair."

She looked up at Benjamin, and he saw betrayal in her expression. "Rose told me she found you trying to sneak into the cellar. I told you I would show it to you anytime you wanted."

He looked down, shame heating his face.

Mr. Hardy said, "We were surprised to find the door locked. Do you always keep it so?"

"No. I locked it after Mr. Booker told us Percival had been poisoned. I thought it a wise precaution, just in case. To protect everyone."

"Perhaps to protect yourself, most of all?" Mr. Hardy asked, his tone matter-of-fact. "Have you something to hide down there?"

Miss Wilder's mouth tightened, and her nostrils flared. She unclipped the chatelaine from her bodice and tossed her keys—hard—not at the man who asked the question but at Benjamin. He deftly caught them, the metal keys stinging his palm, perhaps as she'd intended.

"There. Happy hunting." She stalked from the room.

Needing to calm down, Isabelle walked out to the boathouse to be alone. For several minutes, she continued her search for the missing earring, cut short by Mr. Booker's appearance the night before. Perhaps it was futile and foolish, but she just couldn't believe her own earring had ended up in London.

Opening all the doors and windows wide, she searched every corner but found nothing. Nor had Lotty found anything in her thorough search of the bedchamber and dressing room.

Giving up, Isabelle sat on the pier. Seeing no one about, she slipped off her shoes and stockings and let her feet dangle in the cool water. Completely perplexed, her mind whirled, searching for possible explanations for the earring, for the poisoned wine, for . . . everything.

Mr. Booker came walking along the shore a short while later. As he neared, she called, "Come to search for poison in the boathouse too?"

He winced. "No. Sorry about all that."

"You made quick work of your search."

Nearing, he explained, "Actually, we haven't gone down yet. We decided to wait until you were free to go with us, if you will."

"I will, though I don't know what good it will do. I don't understand what's happened, let alone how."

His gaze swept the boathouse behind her. "And what are you

doing out here—hiding from me, I suppose? Or searching for another earring?"

"I've given up on that. Presently, I am searching for peace by watching the ducks swim."

Without waiting to be asked, he sat down beside her, near but not too close, crossing his legs like a boy. He asked, "Do you swim?"

"Me? Goodness no. Do you?"

He shook his head. "Not since boyhood. I enjoy rowing, but no one wants to swim in the Thames near London. Filthy water."

She nodded her understanding, suddenly aware of her own feet in the same river, which was fairly clean this far upstream. Isabelle felt self-conscious about her bare feet and ankles in his presence, but thankfully between the long skirt and the water, her skin was mostly covered. "Teddy swims, but I never learnt."

"Most people don't."

A memory struck her. "I shall tell you a secret, however. When we were girls, my sister and I went wading into the lagoon in only our shifts and stays. It was after a dry summer, so the water was only waist deep, but still we enjoyed splashing around. It's the closest I've come to swimming."

She'd begun the story without thinking it through, and now her face heated to realize she'd mentioned undergarments to a man like Mr. Booker.

Isabelle stole a sideways glance at him. Were his cheeks red from embarrassment as well, or had he stayed too long in the sun? She swallowed and returned the conversation to safer ground. "Teddy's father insisted he learn to swim. Said anyone who lived near the river ought to know how, for his own safety."

"Probably good advice." Mr. Booker narrowed his eyes in

thought. "I believe Mr. Hardy can swim. As a youth, he spent summers near a lake, if memory serves."

Isabelle studied his profile. In spite of her anger, she thought Mr. Booker remarkably handsome. She liked his full lower lip, strong cheekbones, and brown eyes—especially when they looked at her with admiration. "You speak of him a great deal," she observed.

He looked at her, lips pursed. "Do I? I suppose I do. He has been my mentor for years now. Taught me most of what I know about the law. Almost a second father to me."

"And he obviously thinks very highly of you." She added gently, "I gather he hoped for a match between you and his daughter?"

Mr. Booker dipped his head, clearly embarrassed. "Yes, the objections were all on the lady's part, not his. And she was right to refuse me, no doubt. She has married a man far more gentlemanlike and accomplished than I am."

"I am sorry."

"Never mind." He shifted uneasily on the pier, then asked a question in return. "And Captain Curtis . . . I gather he hoped for a match with you at one point?"

"Um-hm. Percy objected, and truly, I had reservations of my own. Though I am fond of him."

Curious, she returned to a former subject. "You mentioned Mr. Hardy is like a second father to you. Is your actual father still . . . with us?"

"Yes. In London. We don't get on."

"I am sorry to hear it. Did something happen?"

He shrugged. "We are quite different and have never seen eye to eye, a gap that only widened as I grew into adulthood. He and my brother are very much alike. Both medical men, confident and outspoken. Father wanted me to follow the family line, but I . . ." He hesitated, then said, "I was too bookish for them."

"You . . . bookish?" she said in faux surprise. "I had not noticed." She smiled as she said it, hoping he could take teasing as well as he dished it out.

"Ha-ha," he said with a crooked grin. "At all events, I had no interest in medicine."

"Your father did not approve of the law for your vocation?"

"No. He did not forbid me to be articled to Mr. Hardy, but he didn't like it. Doesn't like Hardy either, for some reason."

"Perhaps he feels Mr. Hardy has replaced him in your affections or taken his role in your life."

"You think my father is jealous? Not likely. Probably relieved to shift responsibility to someone else so he could focus on my over-achieving brother. Reuben has recently been appointed coroner."

"Elected, you mean?"

"No, Westminster appoints theirs. I doubt my curmudgeonly brother could win enough votes to become coroner otherwise. Even so, my father is very proud."

"I'm sure he is proud of you too."

"Are you? I think not."

"Forgive me. I don't mean to pry or criticize. It's just . . . if my father were still alive, I would not let petty disagreements or misunderstandings stand between us."

Mr. Booker stiffened beside her, his profile tight as he stared straight ahead, probably offended by her words. But at the moment, Isabelle was too swamped with emotion to pay much attention. Oh, how she missed her father! Tears filled her eyes and ran down her cheeks.

Mr. Booker turned to her, face stern, and opened his mouth to deliver a sharp setdown, she guessed. But he took one look at her face and closed his mouth without a word.

She swiped at wet cheeks with the back of her hand and managed a breezy tone. "And your mother?"

Before her eyes, his tense features softened. "A dear woman. I know it bothers her that my father and I are not close. You remind me that I should visit her when I return to London."

Isabelle nodded her approval, thinking, *Dear Mamma, I miss you too.*

Benjamin's mother's face shimmered in his mind's eye. Plump cheeks, warm intelligent eyes, a ready if slightly crooked smile. Benjamin missed her. His father? Not so much.

He'd been offended when Miss Wilder had challenged the rift with his papa. He'd turned to her, a rebuttal on his lips, *Easy for you to say, to "saint" a father long dead*. But then he saw her tears and stifled his retort, wishing he could comfort her instead.

He could have told her his father was not proud of him, nor all that understanding about his episodes, but instead he changed the subject. "By the way, I paid a call on Dr. Grant yesterday. I went to thank him for his services and to see his office. Miss Medina mentioned finding it quite . . . interesting."

"Disturbing, I think you mean," Isabelle said wryly. "I have never seen it, of course, but I did ask him about it. I tried, tactfully, to suggest he might store his specimens and experiments away from public viewing, but he did not take my hint, apparently."

"At least they are in his private office and not his waiting room."

"True." Miss Wilder chuckled and splashed her feet in the water. He'd been trying not to stare at that tantalizing glimpse of ankle and leg, but it was dashed difficult.

"He mentioned he'd spent time with his father recently,

after keeping you company here in the boathouse. Are you acquainted with his father?"

Miss Wilder turned to stare at him, clearly stunned. Anger sparked in her wide eyes.

"He did not mention that to me. His father is not welcome here." She slapped her hand against the planks.

Benjamin blinked. "Why?"

"He did not tell you?"

"No. He said very little about him, except that he retired to the coast."

Her small nostrils flared. "His father was our coachman. He was driving the night my parents' carriage collided with a mail coach and they both died."

Now it was his turn to be stunned. "Oh . . ." Benjamin breathed, stomach sinking. "No wonder you don't speak of him."

She nodded. "It is a sore subject. I have no doubt Mr. Grant is remorseful. And I know it was an accident. Carriage wrecks are far too common for me to doubt that. He was thrown clear and somehow escaped with only minor injuries. He felt terribly guilty and has never come back here before now, to my knowledge. Couldn't face me, I suppose. And I didn't want to see him either, or hear his apologies. Teddy told me he decided to retire, which was a relief, as I would have had to let him go, for we'd had little need for a coachman while my parents were alive, and far less after they were gone. Still, I am surprised Teddy didn't mention his father was here. I know he has visited him and his aunt a few times, at Christmas or whatnot, but I didn't realize his father ever came to Riverton."

"Perhaps he didn't want to upset you further, so he didn't mention it."

"Very likely." Miss Wilder gathered her shoes in one hand and swung her feet to the pier.

He quickly stood and offered her a hand. She hesitated only a moment, then put her hand in his. He helped her up, foolishly wishing he could keep holding on. Wishing she was innocent. Wishing they were not at cross-purposes.

She avoided his eyes. "Well. Almost time to deliver the midday meal, I think." She pulled her hand from his and stalked away, leaving a trail of wet footprints, and leaving Benjamin sorry he'd mentioned Mr. Grant when she'd seemed ready to forgive their trespassing.

It was interesting though. . . . Benjamin sat back down, steepling his fingers as he considered. The proud and proper physician was a coachman's son. How unexpected. No wonder he tried so hard to seem respectable and uphold gentlemanly propriety. For he was no gentleman at all, at least by birth. Neither was Benjamin, of course, but he made no pretensions to being one. Or did he? Much to ponder.

In his heart of hearts, he didn't think Isabelle Wilder had poisoned anyone, at least not intentionally. And if somehow arsenic used as, say, rat poison, had accidentally ended up in the bottles of wine? Two people were still dead, but it would reduce the charge to manslaughter instead of premeditated murder. Deep down, he believed she was innocent of that as well. She did not seem like a woman who would make such a careless mistake. He sighed deeply, uncertainty and worry twisting his insides.

His mother's face flashed into his mind again, gentle with that long-suffering smile she wore whenever she had to exhort him. He could almost hear her voice in his ear. *"Benjamin, Benjamin, worry does no good. It saps your strength and joy. Instead pray."*

Speaking to Miss Wilder about his parents reminded him of the unpleasant scene the morning of his departure for Belle

Island. His father had stopped by his rooms as he was packing to leave. . . .

"Where are you bound?"

"Berkshire. An assignment for Mr. Hardy."

"Ah. Your mother suggested I call. We heard what happened in court yesterday, and—"

"I suppose you rejoice in my failure. After all, you always said it was a mistake to pursue the law."

His father frowned and shook his head. "Do you know me so little? Or has that man prejudiced you against me so thoroughly?"

"*That man* took me in and taught me everything he knows."

His father opened his mouth, hesitated, and seemed to think the better of whatever he'd been about to say. Instead he said, "I do not rejoice in your *failure*, as you call it. We have all made mistakes. It's how we respond to them that shows our character. At our best we learn from them, make recompense if possible, and behave better in the future. Not blame anyone else, or make excuses, or hide away in shame."

"Is that what you think I am doing? Hiding?"

His father cast a significant glance at his shabby valise. "You tell me."

"Mr. Hardy thinks it wise that I absent myself from London for a time, but more importantly, I am looking into the death of his former partner."

His father's brows rose. "I am sorry to hear of it. But that's a task for Bow Street. Or your brother."

My brother, yes, always my brother . . . . "Reuben is handling the inquest. And an officer has been assigned, but he is focusing on local suspects. Mr. Hardy is not satisfied that justice will be done."

"And he believes you are the man for the job?"

"Mr. Hardy has confidence in me, even if you don't."

"Ben, I know I have made mistakes too, especially where you are concerned. Mistakes I regret. I regret this . . . distance between us. This enmity."

"So do I. But is it not to be expected, when you have made your disapproval of me evident for so many years? Thankfully you have one ideal son in Reuben."

His father slowly shook his head. "I care for you and your brother equally. Yet you must allow that Reuben was easier to raise—wasn't forever running off instead of helping, or wearing on your mother's nerves, as you seemed bent on doing. But we care for you both and always will."

He took a deep breath, then added, "And yes, I was disappointed when you chose law over physic. I was angry and raised my voice more than I should have. I saw it as a rejection of me and my life's work."

His father's eyes glittered with intensity. "Was it so wrong to want my sons to learn the profession beside me? To take over my practice and care for my patients one day? But now the shop is not smart enough for your brother either."

"It's too late for me as well," Ben said. "I'm too old to change courses—to take the part of adolescent apprentice compounding medicines and pressing pills."

"I know that. I have accepted your chosen profession. But would it kill you to spend a little less time with Hardy and a little more time with your mother and me? Even your brother wishes he could see you more often."

That gave Benjamin pause. "Does he? He's never said."

"It isn't his way. Booker men have never been good at expressing themselves or in showing emotion. But he cares for you and worries for you. We all do."

"You need not worry about me. I am perfectly well."

His father glanced at Benjamin's trembling hand. "Are you sure you are equal to the journey? Had I known you planned to travel today I would have brought ginger lozenges for your stomach."

"As I said, I am perfectly well. I'm an adult, remember, not the weak child you seem to think me."

His father raised both hands. "I don't. But does being a good parent mean *never* expressing concern, never attempting to check our offspring when they are on a dangerous heading? If so, then I cannot be a *good* parent."

Ben grimly replied, "No, apparently not." He wished the words back as soon as they slipped from his mouth, regret washing over him.

"I didn't mean that." He ran a hand over his face. "Look, I have no wish to fight with you. I am resigned to things as they are between us. But I will come and see Mamma when I return."

Sitting there on the Belle Island pier, Benjamin held his head in his hands and prayed. He asked forgiveness for his harsh words to his father and his neglect of his mother. He prayed for wisdom, and answers, and for the truth to set them all free.

Then, wanting to expend some pent-up energy and remembering Miss Wilder's offer, Benjamin hung his coat in the boathouse, rolled up his shirt-sleeves, and untied the rowboat.

Young Joe came walking up the pier as he prepared to climb in. "Going fishing, sir?"

Benjamin hesitated. He had not planned to fish, but the eager look on the adolescent's face could not be denied. "I might, if I had a fishing partner."

Joe's eyes brightened. "Could I come along, sir? It has been a long time since I fished from a boat, but I still remember all the best spots, if you don't mind some rowing."

Ben grinned. "I don't mind at all."

After dinner that evening, Mr. Hardy went out to the veranda to smoke a cigar. Benjamin did not smoke, but he went out to keep him company.

Across the Thames, the setting sun hovered over Riverton, gilding the clouds and rooftops. Crickets began to chirp, and twilight descended like a filmy grey curtain. As the two sat companionably, Abel Curtis walked past with a fowling piece and a black-and-white sheepdog, probably on his way back to the tenants' cottages.

Hardy asked quietly, "Who is that man?"

"Mr. Curtis."

"Curtis? That name is familiar. . . . Was that not the name of the young man who wanted to marry Miss Wilder years ago?"

"Yes. That is his father. Evan Curtis became a captain in the infantry."

Hardy nodded. "That's right. He came to see Percival as her closest male relative shortly after her parents died. He refused his permission."

"On what grounds?"

"On the grounds it would be a disastrous match. Curtis was only a shepherd's son. No prospects. Nothing to commend him. Percy sought my advice, and I agreed with him. But we did not send him away empty-handed. I have friends in the military. I suggested a commission in the infantry might keep him at a safe distance for a few years."

"How did Miss Wilder take it?"

"Not well. She was angry with Percival for sending him away. I said he could tell her it was my idea, but he chose not to."

Suddenly a dark figure stepped from the gloaming—Evan Curtis himself. Had he been purposefully eavesdropping? How much had he heard? Benjamin felt sheepish to be caught talking about the man, but Mr. Hardy seemed unaffected. Ben wished he had half his confidence.

Mounting the veranda stairs, Curtis said, "Well, that's one mystery solved. I wondered how Percy managed it. I should have guessed you were his right-hand man. Why did you do it?"

Hardy rose to face the young man. His tone was unruffled, even fatherly. "Surely there was no mystery about our motive. Sad as it may seem, a shepherd's son does not marry an heiress."

"Groundsman," Evan corrected between clenched teeth. "My father is groundsman on this estate. A longtime, trusted retainer. Ask Miss Wilder. Ask anyone."

Hardy waved a dismissive hand. "No need. I recall the particulars."

The man slowly approached. "Now I learn it was your idea to offer me a commission."

"Only trying to be helpful."

Anger flashed over Curtis's face. "You sent me as far away and to as dangerous a posting as you could manage."

"I don't know about dangerous, but distant, yes. Can you blame us? Miss Wilder was young and impressionable. We didn't want you to sway her to accept you against her family's wishes. Or heaven forbid, convince her to elope with you."

Every muscle tensed, and Evan's hand fisted. Benjamin leapt to his feet, just as the man lunged, and grabbed hold of him.

"Arrogant toff!" Curtis seethed. "Let me go. I want to punch that smug look from his face."

Benjamin barely managed to hold him back.

Curtis strained against his grip, glaring at Hardy. "How dare you? You knew nothing of me. Nothing of Isabelle or our plans. What gave you the right to decide I was unworthy of her—and worse, to send me away before I had a chance to prove myself?"

"Come now. It was a good offer, you must admit. You could have declined, yet you did not."

"Because I did not know the regiment was about to be sent to the war-ravaged peninsula. But you knew." Evan cursed and shook his head. "And all along I blamed Percy, when it was you who hatched the scheme. And there you stand, so dashed proud of yourself."

Hardy shrugged. "My friend asked for my advice and I gave it. There is no shame in that."

Curtis's nostrils flared. "When I returned to London, I paid old Percy a visit to express my grievances. He tried to pass the blame to you then, but I didn't believe him."

"Did you kill the wrong man?" Hardy challenged.

"I've killed no one, except in battle. So far."

Benjamin looked from one to the other. Was Hardy on to something? Might Curtis be responsible for Percival's death?

Ben asked, "Were you in London the night he died?"

He jerked from Benjamin's hold. "Yes, I was. But I did not kill him." The captain's eyes glinted. "Although I have an idea who did."

"Who do you mean?" Benjamin asked.

"I couldn't say. Not to you two sons of prattlement." He straightened his lapels. "Good night, gentlemen, and I use that term loosely."

He turned on his heels with military precision and stalked off into the night.

Mr. Hardy stepped nearer and lowered his voice. "What do you think, Ben? Is he a possible suspect?"

Benjamin hesitated. "I could certainly see him striking Percival in a passionate rage, but poisoning him with Belle Island wine? That seems less likely."

"Unless . . . does he resent Miss Wilder as well? If so, setting her up to take the blame would allow him to kill two birds with one stone, as it were."

An interesting theory, Benjamin allowed. Was it true?

In the morning, Benjamin ate a solitary breakfast, then took his coffee and a newspaper out to the veranda. He guessed Miss Wilder had already left for the weaving shed.

It was a cool, breezy morning and he hoped the fresh air would help him think and keep a clear head. But instead of any revelations, he simply sat on the outdoor sofa and soaked in the peace of the new day, listening to birdsong and watching the boats passing by on the river. Occasionally one of the crew raised a hand in greeting as they passed, and Benjamin returned it as though he lived there, his hand remarkably steady. *Thank you*, he murmured to his Creator. *And help me.*

Miss Lawrence came out of the house, wool shawl wrapped around herself and teacup in hand. "May I join you?"

"Of course." He was surprised she would want to talk to him after their confrontation outside the cellar door.

As if reading his thoughts, Rose said, "I am sorry I was cross with you. I know you are trying to help, but it sometimes does not feel that way."

"I understand. I am sorry too."

She sat on the opposite end of the cushion, pulling her feet under her to keep them warm under skirt and shawl. "Bit chilly this morning. But so beautiful." She inhaled deeply, surveying the scene much as he had done. "I love it here. I miss it when I'm away."

"Yet you live in London most of the time." He quickly raised a palm. "I am not criticizing, I assure you. After all, I live there too."

"Then you know London has its own kind of beauty. With its squares and parks, museums and magnificent buildings . . ."

"And its shops and theatres and society."

She sent him a dimpled grin. "Those too, now that you mention it."

"What was it like, growing up here?"

"Hmm. Good question. In most ways idyllic. Of course at first I was scared and sad and missing my parents. Thankfully, I didn't lose O'Toole as well, or I really would have been terrified. I was six, almost seven, when I arrived here. Being relatively young, the pain faded quickly, and Aunt Belle was everything loving and affectionate. Well, you see how kind she is. So I had a happy childhood despite my losses. The Miss Faringdons came often to see me—you met them at the party—and there was another girl in the village, the schoolmaster's daughter, who would come over to play. Aunt Belle preferred my friends to come to the island, of course, but she didn't forbid me to cross the bridge. Though naturally both she and O'Toole warned me to avoid the river.

"My aunt knew her fears were not completely rational, and she didn't want me to be so encumbered, but for the most part I willingly stayed on the island. It was a heavenly playground for a girl. At one point I even had my own pet duck! It followed me everywhere."

He chuckled, imagining the scene.

"But when I was fifteen or so, I began longing to experience more of the world, wanting a bit of freedom and diversion and social life. . . ."

"And admirers?" Ben added helpfully.

"Exactly." Another dimpled grin appeared.

"Later, an old friend of my grandmother's, Lady Elliott—you met her too—agreed to host me in London for a season. She had a house in Town near ours. Aunt Belle had spent several seasons in London herself as a young woman, so how could she forbid me? Of course we both thought I would come back after the season, but then I met Mr. Adair, and that was that." She sighed dreamily.

"How did your aunt feel about your staying in Town?"

"She didn't like it. And in truth, I missed her too. Lady Elliott was polite and generous, but she had her own life to live, so eventually Uncle Percy moved into the townhouse as my guardian and set up an office there."

"And how did *you* feel about that?"

She wrinkled her nose. "I wished Aunt Belle could live with me instead. If she could have at least visited me from time to time, it would have been perfect. But she could not."

"Could not or would not?"

Rose looked at him, expression earnest. "I understand your question, Mr. Booker. But my aunt is not pretending to be unable to leave. She honestly feels she can't. And as far as I know she hasn't. Not in many years."

She leaned a bit closer. "I can see in your eyes that you want to believe me. That you want to believe *her*. You admire her, I think."

It was her turn to hold up a hand. "Ah-ah, don't answer. But if you do admire her, you are a very wise man." The young woman unfolded herself and stood. "Now, please excuse me. I promised to sort through my mother's jewelry this morning and pick some things to take back with me. I shall leave you to think it over."

Benjamin rose as well. He thought of following her, of refuting her claim, but the echoing thud of footfalls crossing the bridge caught his ear. He turned and saw a man wearing a dark coat step from the bridge and cross the lawn. A familiar man. Anxiety needled his stomach.

"Officer Riley, is it not?"

"That's right." The Bow Street runner ascended the veranda steps.

Benjamin kept his tone light. "What are you doing here? You're a bit far from home."

"I could say the same of you, sir."

"Yes, well, the Wilder family are longtime clients of our firm."

"Including the pretty Miss Lawrence you were chatting with all familiar-like?"

Ben stiffened. "It was merely friendly conversation."

"Um-hm." He did not appear convinced. The officer looked around him. "Never been out this far. Beautiful country."

"So you've come to admire the views?" Benjamin said dryly. "I thought you were pursuing the missing silver in London?"

He nodded. "I was. I did. Traced them to a pawn seller not far from the Wilder townhouse. I was hoping he would tell me the silver had been brought in by some notorious thief, but alas, no. Brought in by someone who actually works for the family. My first thought was Mary Williams, since she'd disappeared. But as I'm standing there in the pawnshop, who should come in but the manservant, Marvin. He ambled in, as proud as you please, with a silver candlestick. When he saw me, he looked startled indeed, but held his ground. Insisted the master himself had told him to see what he could get for the silver pitcher and candelabras."

"You didn't believe him."

"Not at first. But I took him with me to talk to the house-keeper again, and she admitted she'd overheard Mr. Norris say, 'I don't care what you have to sell. Just get the money to pay the man.' Apparently, the stipend he received as trustee did not stretch far enough.

"Still, I said to Marvin, 'And today? Do you expect me to believe Mr. Norris told you to sell that candlestick from the grave?'

"At that, ol' Marvin finally looked guilty. But he lifted his whiskered chin and said, 'No, sir. But no one is payin' my wages now he's gone. I only took what I had coming to me.'"

"Mrs. Kittleson confirmed that no money is coming in for wages or household expenses. Would have thought you lawyers would have seen to that, representing the Wilder family all these years and all."

Benjamin was surprised as well.

The officer continued, "Mrs. Kittleson had already told me about the housemaid leaving her employ without so much as a by-your-leave. I searched for her, but—"

Benjamin interrupted him. "Yes, Mr. Hardy told me about her disappearance. And her death."

Officer Riley nodded. "I stopped by the hallowed offices of Norris, Hardy, and Hunt, but only Mr. Hunt was in, and he pleaded ignorance of the whole affair, though he did tell me where I could find you and Mr. Hardy."

"Yes, well, thank you for coming all this way to let the family know. I am sure Miss Wilder will make amends to the London servants as soon as possible."

"Oh, but that's not the reason I'm here. Now that I've run the absconding-housemaid and theft-gone-wrong theories to the ground, I am here to pursue other suspects among the family."

"That is what I have been doing."

"Oh?" Officer Riley's expression conveyed disbelief, his tone sarcasm. "And have you any evidence for me?"

Benjamin considered mentioning the garnet earring, but when he hesitated, the officer continued.

"You looked awful cozy when I arrived. Made yourself quite at home here. Probably present the family with a lengthy bill for the privilege of hosting you, too, as snipes do."

Lawyers were said to resemble those birds due to their "long bills." Benjamin gritted his teeth at the officer's mocking. Yet could he blame the man? What a picture he must have made, lounging on the veranda, talking and laughing with Miss Lawrence as if they were old friends.

The man's eyes twinkled. "Well, excuse me if I don't rush back to Bow Street and tell my superiors that the infamous benish Booker has the matter in hand. Lulling the Wilder ladies into a false sense of security, are ya? Just waiting for the right time to spring your trap?"

Benjamin inwardly seethed, yet shame held his tongue. He was the one who'd been lulled into a false sense of security.

"No, sir." Officer Riley hitched up his trousers and squared his shoulders, adding an inch to his small frame. "I've come to take in Miss Wilder for questioning."

Shock jolted Benjamin. Take in Isabelle? Off the island . . . ? A slew of dread and protectiveness washed over him at the thought.

Riley slowly shook his head, eyes alight with humor. "Fell for another conniving female, did ya?"

Benjamin fisted his hands. "Why Miss Wilder and not Miss

Lawrence or Mr. Adair? Based on what evidence? Did the house-keeper identify that earring we found as belonging to her?"

Riley shook his head. "Didn't recognize it. Assumes it must belong to Miss Lawrence."

Benjamin hesitated, gallantry wrestling with conscience. He asked God for wisdom but heard no clear answer. If Riley had brought that earring with him, he would feel duty-bound to hand over the matching one. Benjamin pressed dry lips together. "Do you still have the earring?"

Riley shrugged. "Gave it to the housekeeper. Nothing useful there. I haven't ruled out the pretty young miss yet as far as the poisoning is concerned, but as for the bludgeoning, she and Adair have alibis. Has Miss Wilder?"

"I . . . believe so," Benjamin faltered. Had she? Was falling asleep in the boathouse sufficient alibi? Not likely, especially as she would be reluctant to admit a man had been with her most of the night.

The officer smirked. "Well, let's go and ask her, shall we?"

Benjamin led Officer Riley into the house. He saw Mr. Hardy coming up from the kitchen, a biscuit in hand. "Just talking to Mrs. Philpotts. Excellent woman." Then he noticed the Bow Street runner behind Ben. "Ah, Officer Riley, we were expecting you." He joined them as they walked to the study.

Benjamin hoped he might have time to come up with a plan before the officer confronted Miss Wilder, but upon entering, he saw that she had already returned from the weaving shed, apparently through the garden door. She sat at the desk, a few bills of lading before her.

Mr. Hardy made the introductions, while Benjamin stood stiffly mute, feeling like a failure and a betrayer. He was aware of her wary glances in his direction, looking for reassurance. Reassurance he could not give.

Hardy explained, "Officer Riley is with the Bow Street office in London. He has been assigned to investigate Percival's death."

"Oh." Another glance at Benjamin. Then she entwined her long fingers on the desk and faced the officer. "I thought you were pursuing suspects in London."

"I was indeed," Officer Riley replied. "I have now turned my attention elsewhere."

Benjamin quickly summarized the situation with Marvin and the pawn seller and the servants' lack of wages.

"Oh no!" Miss Wilder exclaimed. "With everything going on here, it did not cross my mind that poor Mrs. Kittleson was having to struggle on with no income. Thank you for coming to alert me to the situation, Mr. Riley."

The officer looked to Benjamin, as if waiting for him to explain his real purpose. Was Riley suddenly hesitant in Isabelle's presence, surprised by her genteel nature and attractiveness as he had been, or did he simply enjoy watching Benjamin squirm?

He swallowed. "Em, that is not the only reason Officer Riley has come."

"No?" She turned to the weasellike man, brows high in expectation.

Riley cleared his throat. "I am here to ascertain, that is, to inquire as to your whereabouts on the night of Percival Norris's death."

"I was here, Mr. Riley. On the island. As anyone can tell you, I never leave it."

"Is that so?"

"It is."

"And why is that?"

"Because I . . . cannot. You will think me very strange, but

I have lost nearly my entire family when they ventured from home."

"At your hand?"

"Wha . . . ? No! That is not what I meant at all. My brother and sister died hundreds of miles from here, he somewhere at sea and she en route from India. My parents died in a carriage accident, driving to the London docks to meet her ship. I can hardly be blamed for any of those deaths, but the fear of meeting with a similar fate has taken hold, and the very thought of leaving brings on a disabling fit of panic."

"Very convenient."

"Not at all, actually. Quite the opposite. I should have dearly loved to attend my niece's engagement dinner in London, and long to be there for her upcoming wedding, but I fear it will prove impossible."

"And I am to take your word for it?" The man's reticence faded as he continued to question her.

"You may ask anyone you like. The servants, my friends, villagers . . ."

"I will do. But even if I find no one willing to speak out against the local *squire-ess*, I believe you were in London that night. In fact, I have evidence to prove it."

Miss Wilder shot Benjamin a look. He felt the earring pricking a hole in his pocket. She must think he'd handed it over. He subtly shook his head, hoping she'd understand his meaning.

She looked back at the officer. "What evidence?"

Riley pulled something from his pocket. Not an earring, but paper. He unfolded it and held the letter before her face.

She reached for it, but he shook his head. "Uh-uh-uhn."

She leaned nearer and squinted at the page, growing pale as she read. Then the officer shifted the letter toward Benjamin and Mr. Hardy.

Ben bent and read the scrawled message.

I seen Miz Wilder in London the night P. Norris died.

Beside him, Hardy gave a low whistle. "From where was it posted?"

"Lombard Street post office, London."

"No signature?" Ben scowled. "You're going to believe an anonymous, barely legible note like that?"

"Benjamin . . ." Hardy's low voice reminded him to stay calm.

Riley stiffened. "I am not on trial here, Mr. Booker. Miss Wilder is."

"She is not on trial either!"

"Not yet." Officer Riley turned back to Isabelle. "How do you explain this, Miss Wilder?"

"I don't know. How strange. Do you think someone wants me to take the blame for his death for some reason?"

"Or perhaps you deserve the blame for some reason?"

"I don't! Even if I were in London, that is not a crime. It would not mean I killed anyone."

"If you would lie about the one, why not the other?"

"I didn't lie. I am just saying . . . I did not kill Uncle Percy!"

"We know you were angry with him. Argued with him."

"I did, yes. I don't deny it. I may have threatened him with words, but that is all I did."

"I have a wine bottle marked with a Belle Island label that says otherwise. Wine very likely responsible for poisoning not one but two persons. Perhaps your niece took the bottle into his office, but then you went to Town to make sure he died."

"I would never do such a thing. I swear it."

"You may very well have your chance to swear, in court. I

220

would like you to come with me to London, Miss Wilder. See if any of the neighbors remember seeing you near the house the day Norris was bludgeoned. Find us a real live witness to go along with this letter."

"What? No!" She grabbed hold of her father's desk as though it were an anchor.

The officer took her elbow and pulled her away, escorting her out of the study. As they crossed the hall, she looked back over her shoulder at Benjamin following behind, his mind whirling to think of some way out of this.

Drawn by the hubbub, Rose and Adair came out of the morning room, and Rose's eyes widened. "Aunt Belle?" She looked at Benjamin in alarm. "Mr. Booker, what is going on?"

Riley opened the front door and dragged his captive through it. Isabelle cried out. She grabbed hold of one of the columns flanking the door and sank to the ground. She looked and sounded like a terrified, wounded child.

It propelled Benjamin to step forward between officer and woman, and only after doing so, did he think of what to say.

"Have you an official warrant or summons? Is Miss Wilder under indictment by a magistrate?"

"Well, not exactly. I haven't found witnesses yet, but I shall."

"Then as her lawyer, I must insist that you wait until you have a warrant or duly authorized summons."

Mr. Hardy spoke up. "Officer Riley will at least want to search the wine cellar while he's here to look for evidence of poison."

Benjamin reiterated, "*If* he has the appropriate warrant."

Riley fluttered the letter. "I have just cause, and—"

"And if the magistrate sees it as you do, then he will no doubt send you back with the proper paperwork. If so, we shan't hinder you further." He glanced at Hardy, but it seemed Benjamin was the only one fighting this.

"Come now, be reasonable," Riley said. "He shall not look kindly on my returning empty-handed, only to be asked to be sent back again with a piece of paper."

Benjamin set his jaw. "Miss Wilder is a woman of influence in this county. If you besmirch her reputation on such flimsy evidence, I will make sure your superiors hear of it, and what a row her well-connected friends shall raise."

Rose chimed in, "And her family!"

"I doubt you shall keep your position when I'm through with you," Ben insisted.

The officer's eyes narrowed. "You're not serious. That's all bluster."

"Are you certain? Do you want to take that risk? Especially when the court will pay for the miles you travel in pursuit of your duties? An additional shilling a mile, is it? You can't mind that, I'm sure."

The man hesitated. He was in a vulnerable position, and he knew it.

The officer held Benjamin's gaze a moment longer, then said, "Very well. I won't mind the extra pay—you're right. But I shall return. Can I trust Miss Wilder not to run off before I get back?"

He surveyed the crumpled figure huddled around the column. His lips quirked as he dryly answered his own question, "Yes, I think it a safe assumption."

After the officer left, Benjamin helped Miss Wilder to her feet. She avoided his gaze. He longed to soothe her embarrassment and distress, but resisted, conscious of the senior partner beside him. Thankfully, Rose embraced her aunt and led her back inside.

For a few minutes the two lawyers remained where they were. Noticing Mr. Hardy's watchful gaze on his profile, Ben said,

"You think I'm doing it again, don't you? Defending another woman who is not as innocent as she appears."

"It sure looks that way, though I hope I'm wrong for your sake." Mr. Hardy sighed, then said, "Even so, I admire what you did there—standing up to that runner."

Benjamin looked at the older man in surprise. "Thank you, sir."

"I just hope you haven't antagonized him to the point that he's more determined than ever to gather evidence against your Miss Wilder. Perhaps partly to spite you."

What a dreadful prediction. Benjamin hoped he was wrong.

Isabelle and Mr. Booker sat on the veranda together later that morning. The sunshine and birdsong were peaceful and relaxing after her panic-filled ordeal. Isabelle felt wrung out, every muscle weary. Yet she also felt an exhilarating ripple of something she had not felt in a long time. Hope.

She glanced over at Mr. Booker—casual posture, one ankle crossed over his knee, gazing out at the water. She thought of how he had looked rowing on the river. Broad shoulders taut, pulling with skill and strength, the boat gliding effortlessly through the water, his wavy dark hair tousled by the wind. It had warmed her heart to see Joe in the boat with him, the two talking and laughing as they went off fishing together.

Now she said softly, "Thank you again for intervening."

Benjamin turned his head. "I am sorry I didn't react more quickly."

"You rescued me, and that is what counts."

His gentle gaze lingered on her face. "Have you tried to leave—to cross the bridge yourself?"

"Yes. Unsuccessfully."

"When did you first realize you were unable to do so?"

"It was, oh, a few months after the funeral. Rose and I were going to the churchyard to lay flowers on my parents' grave, but I had to turn back."

He sat forward, elbows resting on his knees. "What does it feel like? Can you describe it?"

Isabelle reflected. She laid a hand to her abdomen, then drew two fingers forth as though pulling a thread. "It is a nervous, panicky feeling in my stomach trying to hold me back as I walk toward the bridge. It's as if the house has me on a leash, and I can only go so far before it catches me up. I feel the tugging first. Then the cord tightens and binds around my chest until I can hardly breathe."

She drew in a shaky inhale before continuing, "The closer I get to the bridge, the longer its span appears to be, until the space between Belle Island and Riverton seems a wide, treacherous chasm. My heart beats like a crazed bird trying to break free from my chest. I have to fight with every ounce of my being the alarm clanging in my brain, screaming at me to run back into the house.

"If I don't retreat, I become nauseous and dizzy. I perspire and shake. I can't move, can't see properly. I feel as though I must be dying because that is the only explanation I can think of for feeling so ghastly."

She steeled herself and glanced over, expecting to see shock or revulsion. But she saw only warm sympathy and perhaps . . . empathy.

He whispered, "I'm sorry."

She straightened and said lightly, "Well, now that I've told you all that, you no doubt think me a lunatic, and I can't blame you."

"No, I don't. I experience something similar with my vertigo, though to a lesser extent."

"Poor Mr. Booker," Isabelle murmured sincerely. "I wouldn't wish that on anyone."

He humbly dipped his head. "I live in fear of having an episode in public. In fact, the very thought of it can bring on the symptoms."

"Then don't think about it!" Isabelle said with a teasing wink. "And stay off the roof."

He gave her a self-deprecating grin. "Oh, I think it safe to say you will never see me up there."

A short while later, Mr. Booker returned to the study, but Isabelle lingered on the veranda, remembering that day she first realized she could not cross the bridge.

She had missed church the previous few weeks, due to inclement weather and then because she had come down with a bothersome cold. By the following week, however, she felt better and decided to venture forth despite the typically damp, grey English weather. She gathered flowers from the border of the kitchen garden and handed Rose a pair of daisies. She wanted the little girl to grow up knowing her grandparents, even in this small way. To know how much they had cared for and prayed for her, even though they had never met.

Isabelle also wanted the child to remember her own parents, of course. But Rose's father had died in India and Grace at sea. Isabelle still cringed at the thought of her dear sister's body being wrapped in canvas and tipped overboard, committed to the deep, and left to sink with the fishes. She wished she'd had a chance to claim Grace's body and give her a proper burial.

Rose had skipped ahead but tripped and fell on the grass. Isabelle followed, concern hastening her steps. "Are you all right?"

The little girl sat up, tears running down her dirt-smeared face. "Owwwie . . ."

"Let me see." Isabelle crouched beside her. Observing the fallen stocking and scraped little knee, a bud of maternal tenderness blossomed in her breast. "I imagine that stings, my love, but you are all right. When we get back, I shall wash it up and put some lavender salve on it. Remember, we made some in the stillroom?"

Rose nodded, tears ceasing.

"Shall we go and lay our flowers first?"

The little girl vigorously nodded, blond curls bouncing. "And may we buy liquorice from the shop?"

"I believe you have already eaten all the liquorice in Riverton, but we can ask."

"When will Mr. Evan come back? He always gives me candy."

"Not for a long time, I'm afraid." *If ever.* The thought came unbidden. It was a dangerous world out there at any time. And with a war on . . . ? Isabelle shivered.

Rose picked up the fallen flowers, which looked a little worse for their accident, and clambered to her feet.

Accident . . . The word echoed in her mind. Taking her niece firmly by the hand, her own bouquet in the other, they walked on toward the bridge.

But something was wrong. Each step seemed more arduous than the last. Unease hung heavy on her, like a weighted cloak. A distasteful, itchy sense of having neglected some important task or of an impending and dreaded obligation. What was happening? Her niece's injury was minor indeed, so that was no cause for concern.

Even so, sweat dampened Isabelle's forehead and prickled her underarms. As a dutiful daughter, she ought to be eager to go and put flowers on her parents' grave. Yet fear and guilt, like a ball of toffee boiled rock hard, filled her stomach.

Reaching the bridge, Isabelle stopped as though at a glass

wall. Her nerves tingled messages of: *Danger. Alarm.* And her mother's final, anxious words ricocheted through her brain: *"Stay home, stay safe!"*

Rose looked up at her, confusion puckering her little brow. "Are we not going to the churchyard?"

Isabelle swallowed and forced a cheerful tone. "The morning is damp, my dear. I fear it shall rain any moment. Let us return to the house and take care of your knee. We shall go another day instead."

But that day never came.

After a few minutes, Isabelle rose and walked gingerly to the rear of the house. She still didn't feel quite the thing since her encounter with Officer Riley, but she wanted to retrieve Ollie from where she'd tethered him beneath a shade tree, contentedly gnawing a bone from the kitchen.

Rounding the house, she saw Evan Curtis and Carlota speaking to one another in the garden, their voices weaving together in pleasant harmony. The words, however, were indecipherable. As Isabelle neared, she realized they were not speaking English. Spanish, she assumed. Although she did not understand that language, she knew Carlota's father was a Spaniard, and her mother had spoken Spanish as well.

A branch snapped beneath her feet as she approached, and the two took a guilty step apart.

Isabelle said in a friendly manner, "Evan? I did not realize you spoke Spanish."

He shrugged. "A little. A little Portuguese too. I fought in the Peninsular War, after all. Came in handy."

"Sadly, your accent is not so good," Lotty said in teasing tones.

He grinned at her. "Are you offering to tutor me?"

Perhaps realizing they were flirting in front of Isabelle, Lotty looked self-conscious and the captain cleared his throat.

Isabelle said, "It must have been difficult to learn amid all that fighting. Were you not primarily with your own country-men?"

He nodded. "Yes, until I was left for dead near Talavera. A Spanish couple found me and nursed my wounds. I was with them for some time and learned more of the language then. They saved my life."

"Thank God," Isabelle breathed.

Carlota nodded her agreement, then said, "My father came from Madrid, not far from there, I don't think."

"Oh? Where is he now?"

"No idea. He left *Mamá* when I was quite young. I have not seen him in years."

"How despicable. I would never do that. Never betray some-one I loved." He sent a veiled glance at Isabelle.

"Easy words to say, Captain," Carlota said mildly.

"How did he end up in England?" Evan asked.

"He was an actor. My mother's parents were also from Spain and happy to hire a fellow from their homeland. They managed a theatre off Covent Garden."

"You performed there as well—is that right?"

"Yes. And for several other theatres."

"She was quite famous," Isabelle said, "though she used a stage name then."

"Oh? What was it?"

"Maria Carlita Vega."

"Ah! I have heard of you."

Lotty made a face. "I won't ask what you heard. For I doubt it was good."

"I heard that you were talented and . . ." His eyes narrowed

228

as if recalling something else he had heard, but he did not repeat it. "And as I've listened to you sing, I know that much is true."

"Thank you, Captain. I hope you don't believe everything you hear. A certain type of man tends to boast about conquests to impress other men, whether true or not."

"Yes, I imagine you encountered quite a few of that sort in your former profession. But I am not one of them." He drew himself up. "Well, I'm off to London on some unfinished business, if you will excuse me."

He turned away, then looked back at Carlota. "May I bring you anything from Town? Anything you are missing?"

Her eyes sparkled. "Oh, I would love some *pimientos de Padrón*. A costermonger in Covent Garden sells them. Delicious."

He touched his heart and bowed, gaze locked on Carlota's. "Your wish is my command."

Did he or Teddy ever look at me *like that?* Isabelle wondered.

Evan hesitated, then glanced at Isabelle. "And sugar plums from Fortnum and Mason for you, Belle?"

He remembered. "How thoughtful. Thank you."

Captain Curtis took his leave with a tip of his hat. "*Adiós,* ladies."

They watched him go.

"A handsome man," Lotty mused. "And charming. I imagine he looks dashing in uniform."

Isabelle turned and studied her friend's profile with interest.

"Probably. Too bad officers only wear them while on duty and perhaps on formal occasions."

"Yes, a pity."

Isabelle gazed around the garden. She remembered hiding behind that big topiary bush with Evan while Teddy counted and then searched for them. It was the first time Evan had held her hand.

She became aware of Carlota studying *her* profile.

"How do you feel about him, now that he is back?" she asked.

Isabelle thought. Then she looked behind her in case he might be near enough to overhear. She didn't want to hurt him any more than she already had.

Isabelle said solemnly, "Guilty, if I am honest."

"You are not pining for him, not hoping to rekindle the old flame?"

Isabelle searched her heart. She had no hopes of Evan for herself, she didn't think. So why was she struggling? Was she afraid of losing Lotty? Or was it because her friends may have found something she wanted for herself?

"I told you I have often thought about him over the years. I suppose I have romanticized him, built him up into more of a romantic hero than flesh-and-blood human. But now that he's here . . . I care for him of course, as a friend, but no, I don't . . . pine for him. I don't know if it is because of Teddy or Mr. Booker's arrival and all that may bode, or what."

"My money is on Mr. Booker." Carlota grinned, then sent her another measuring look. "Whatever the reason, I am relieved to hear you say so. When you told me Percy sent him away, I too conjured an image of a tragic hero. But now that I have met him, I don't see it as a tragedy or a grave injustice."

"Oh? Why?"

"Because you are not suited, in my view. I admire you both, but not together."

Again Isabelle raised her brows. "Do you admire him?"

"I . . . Well, of course I admire any man who serves his king and country."

It was Isabelle's turn to grin. "Right. Very patriotic of you."

Watching Carlota's reaction, she asked, "He seems to return your admiration, does he not?"

Carlota raised an uncertain hand. "Not really. I think he sees only you. I am lost in your shadow."

Isabelle considered, then added, "Or the shadows of the past."

eighteen

After nuncheon that day, Mr. Hardy set down his table napkin and asked, "Shall we search the wine cellar since Riley did not?"

Benjamin frowned. He glanced at their hostess and then replied, "Sir, Miss Wilder has been through a great deal already today. Perhaps we ought to wait till tomorrow or for Officer Riley's return."

"And give the ladies time to destroy the evidence?"

"They've had sufficient time already if they'd intended to do so."

Miss Wilder rose. "Thank you, Mr. Booker, but I have nothing to hide."

Rose made to follow her, but Adair kept hold of her hand. "You need not go, my love."

Rose turned questioning eyes to her aunt.

"You may stay here, as far as I am concerned," Miss Wilder said. "Unless the lawyers insist on your presence . . . ?"

Hardy replied, "I don't mind. It is the cellar we are interested in at present." He turned to Benjamin. "Do you still have the key?"

Ben hesitated. After Miss Wilder had thrown the key at him, he'd left it in the side table in his room. As far as he knew it was still there. "Just give me a moment to fetch it."

When Benjamin returned with the key, Miss Wilder led the way belowstairs.

They stopped in the kitchen long enough to light a few lanterns, and then walked across the passage to the cellar. Benjamin unlocked the door and pushed it open with a whining creak. Lanterns held high, they carefully made their way down the narrow stairs, the musty smell of dust and sour oak barrels rising up to greet them.

Benjamin swung his light in an arc, surveying the dank space with its shadowy corners. He saw large barrels lying on their sides, rows of cobwebbed shelves with ceramic labels, and bins marked by plaques painted with terms like *Lafite 1805*. At center stood a table made from a wide board nailed to a standing barrel.

Benjamin lowered his lantern near this worktable, inspecting the surface. Was that a dusting of grey powder there? Arsenic could be grey or white in powdered form.

Miss Wilder gestured to one of the bins. "Here are the others I bottled the same day."

Benjamin held one to the light. "No obvious sediment."

Mr. Hardy directed his lantern toward a set of shelves and a tall cabinet.

"I'll search these shelves," he said to Benjamin. "You have a look in that cabinet."

Mr. Hardy turned and began sending shafts of light along each shelf.

With an inward sigh, Benjamin opened the cabinet doors and looked within, lowering himself to his haunches to search its lowest shelves. Tools, containers, bottles. At the back of the bottom shelf something caught his eye. A label printed with a skull and crossbones. Stomach sinking, he reached for it and pulled out a container of rat poison. He was tempted to shove it back in and pretend he'd never seen it. . . .

Too late. Hardy joined him at the cabinet. "What did you find?"

Benjamin held it up to the light.

Miss Wilder stared at it in disbelief. "I did not know that was in there. Though I suppose we may have had problems with rodents down here in the past. Certainly a likely place for them."

Hardy peered closer. "This container looks rather new."

"Well, I didn't put it there," Isabelle insisted. "I have never used the stuff. Abel would do that, or Jacob, perhaps, but not I."

Alarm bells rang in his head. "It doesn't prove anything," Benjamin said. "Many people keep rat poison in their cellars. We would have to find it in the casks or the bottles themselves."

Mr. Hardy nodded. "There are new tests for arsenic, but I am not familiar with the process. Perhaps we had better leave everything as it is and keep the cellar door locked until Officer Riley returns."

"Very well," Miss Wilder replied.

"Good idea," Benjamin agreed, although nothing about this situation was good.

Unsettled by the results of their search, Ben decided to undertake a second search on his own. Taking the lantern with him, he walked toward the stables. He noticed the horses outside in the paddock, and there was Joe reading on the bench near the point.

He made a detour in his direction. "Good day, Joe."

"Mr. Booker. Glad I am to see you, sir. I must thank you for loaning me this book." He lifted it high. "I am at the part where Gulliver finds himself a giant on an island of little people. He puts out a fire in the tiny village by, well, making water. I laughed so hard I snorted."

Benjamin grinned. "Thought you might like that."

"What boy wouldn't? It's almost better than fishing!" Joe's smile softened, and he tipped his head thoughtfully to one side. "But some of the story seems to be . . . making sport of people, I think. Like people fighting and taking sides over which end of an egg to crack. That sort of thing."

"Yes, there is a great deal of satire in it—political and otherwise."

Joe shrugged. "I don't understand all of it, but I am enjoying it immensely."

"Glad to hear it. And I am enjoying the book you recommended as well."

"Have you reached the end yet?"

"Not quite."

"Just wait. That dandy has a surprise up his sleeve, you'll see."

"Is that where he hid his pistol?"

Joe chuckled. "You'll have to read and find out. I don't want to spoil it for you any more than I already have." He pointed to the lantern. "What's that for?"

"Oh. I am, uh, looking for something in the stables."

Joe rose. "I'd help you, but I have to get back to work."

"That's all right." Ben said good-bye and continued into the stables. Reaching the rear stall, he hung the lantern on a hook to illuminate the tarpaulin-covered heap.

Benjamin pulled up one corner, and an eruption of dust mushroomed into the air. He waved a hand before his face and coughed to clear his throat. Rethinking his strategy, he opened the stable door to allow the dust to settle, then slowly and gingerly pulled the cover away.

When he saw what lay beneath, his heart constricted. It was the twisted body of a traveling chariot—wood, leather, springs, its wheels long gone—crouching in this dark corner as though in shame. How it must have grieved Isabelle to see it, to imagine her parents trapped inside. Killed on impact. No wonder she'd had it covered up and stored out of sight. Seeing it felt like visiting a solemn site, a graveyard or family tomb, although he knew Mr. and Mrs. Wilder were actually buried in the churchyard across the river.

He remembered what Isabelle said when they'd discussed the missing will. *"I thought he would have had it with him, in the coach. . . . Their valises were returned to us, and we found no such papers inside."* Had she searched the ruined chariot herself? More likely a servant had done so, and who knew how thoroughly?

Ben tried to open the carriage door, found it stuck, but pulled hard until it gave way. Inside, the once-fine upholstery was moldering over seat backs broken and sagging. The velvet curtains were moth eaten and shredded over cracked windows. But he saw nothing of interest.

A low voice broke the silence. "Who's there?"

With a start, Ben turned and saw a dark figure haloed in blinding sunshine from the open door, like an avenging angel.

"What are you doing?" The disapproving figure came closer, stepping into the lantern light. Ben saw it was the groundsman, Abel Curtis, armed with a shotgun aimed at his chest.

Ben slowly raised his hands. "It is only me, um, Benjamin Booker. Miss Wilder's lawyer."

"I know who you are. What is your business here? Why are you disturbing things better left alone?"

Ben's hands began to tremble. "Sorry. Miss Wilder has asked me to find a missing document of her father's. She thought he might have had it with him in the coach the day they . . . met their unfortunate end."

For a moment, the older man stared at him, steely-eyed and unyielding.

A little help here, Lord?

Then Abel slowly lowered the barrel. "She asked me to go through everything after the accident, and I did. Not one to shirk, am I? Brought in all the belongings worth saving."

"And did you see any papers?"

"Not that I recall. But anything I found I gave to the mistress."

"Of course you did. Well. Thank you."

Abel turned to go, jerking a thumb toward the chariot. "You will cover that back up on your way out?"

"I will indeed," Ben assured him.

With a sigh of relief, he spread the tarpaulins back over the wreckage and returned to the house.

The next day being Sunday, Benjamin walked into River-ton to attend church. He left early and stopped first at Mrs. Winkfield's humble cottage near St. Raymond's. He recalled seeing flowers for sale atop her low garden wall. Fresh offerings awaited that morning as well, tied with twine and set in jars of water. Propped beside them was a hand-lettered sign, *Poseys 6p*, and a simple honor box with a slit on top. Benjamin dropped in a sixpence and selected a bouquet. Then he continued on through the gate into the walled churchyard—a peaceful place of uneven paths, well-kept newer headstones, and listing lichen-spotted ancient monuments. Here and there he saw wildflowers bobbing their heads in the breeze and a few bouquets like his own. Yew trees stood straight and solemn along the back wall, while a graceful oak spread sheltering arms over precious memorials below. A mourning dove cooed from its branches, and two white butterflies flitted past.

Benjamin walked slowly from grave to grave, seeing many names unfamiliar to him, and some he already recognized: *Howton, Winkfield, Colebrook, Jones.*

Arminda Truelock came around the side of the church, wearing a bonnet and gloves, prayer book in hand.

"Good morning, Mr. Booker. I'm afraid the service does not begin for another half hour."

"I came early, hoping to find Mr. and Mrs. Wilder's grave."

"Ah." Glancing from his face to the flowers in his hand, she nodded. "I'll show you. It is over here."

She led him to a group of stately headstones of various ages, then pointed out the Wilders' grave. It had a rounded top carved with the emblem of a weeping willow.

In Loving Memory
Elizabeth Wilder
Died 1808
Aged 46 years
and
Jonathan Wilder
Died 1808
Aged 48 years
Beloved Parents and Grandparents

An urn-like stone vase formed part of the monument. Wilted lilies of the valley stood shriveled within.

"I thought Miss Wilder no longer came to put flowers on their grave?"

"She does not, although I know she wishes she could." Miss

Truelock bent and removed the spent blooms. "I pick something from our own garden now and again, in her place."

"That is kind of you."

She modestly shrugged. "I do what I can to tend the graves. Our sexton is rather infirm."

Benjamin lowered himself to his haunches and set the flowers in the waiting receptacle.

"And that is kind of you," she added.

His shrug echoed hers. "I feel as though I have come to know them somewhat—staying in their house and becoming acquainted with their daughter."

Arminda studied his face with interest, and Benjamin looked away, feeling self-conscious under that gentle, knowing gaze.

An idea struck, and he asked, "Might I trouble you for a large piece of paper?"

On Sunday morning, Isabelle spent time in the family chapel reading from a book of Edward Cooper's sermons. Then, after donning bonnet and pelisse, she climbed the stairs to the roof.

She slowly walked along the low railing. From that height she could see much of the island: to the north, the roofs of the weaving shed and tenant cottages peeking out from the trees; to the east, behind the manor, the garden and boathouse; and to the south, the stables, paddock, and tail of the island. Picking up the field glasses she kept up there—her father's—Isabelle looked west toward Riverton, noticing a sailing barge moored at the village pier, and then focused on the farms in the distance. She often came up here to gaze at the world beyond her reach, to expand her horizons at least visually. Especially when she was feeling lonely.

Her sense of isolation was sharpest on holy days and Sundays.

Isabelle stood watching families on their way to church—men in Sunday best, ladies in their finest frocks and bonnets, holding their young ones by the hand or slicking down unruly hair. Two friends waved to one another, and Isabelle thought of Arminda, imagining her fingers poised above the keys, ready to play the opening psalm. In her mind's eye, she saw them all sitting down in their pews, singing together, repeating the prayers, and sharing communion.

It reminded her, as always, of the old days when her parents and siblings were still alive, of her family walking over the bridge to attend church, their loyal retainers and tenants following behind. All of them talking and worshiping together and relishing one another's company.

She thought of Mr. Booker. Would someone direct him to the Wilders' pew? Or had it long ago been relegated to another family? Her niece had stopped attending St. Raymond's when she had. But at least Rose was home now, she reminded herself. Although not for long. And not for her wedding.

Isabelle groaned. How she wished she might rip this fear from her body and throw it over the rail. She had missed too much as its prisoner.

With a sigh, she set down the glasses and went downstairs to take Ollie for a walk.

Retrieving the puppy, the two started up the shore path together. Isabelle's gaze was drawn to the large weeping willows along the way, their branches bowing low, as though burdened under the weight of grief. No wonder the trees were used as a symbol of mourning. In fact, she had chosen that emblem to be carved on her parents' headstone. Isabelle closed her eyes, trying to remember what it looked like. She would like to see it again but doubted she ever would.

Turning inland, they crossed the island, Ollie eagerly sniffing as they went. At the stream, he ran off happily on the scent of something. Hopefully he would not harass the sheep, or Abel would not be pleased. Isabelle stood atop the small stone bridge, gazing over the lagoon and at the statue of her great-grandmother feeding swans. Around her, the island was quiet, save for bird chatter. The weavers were off enjoying their Sabbath rest. For a few moments, Isabelle tipped her face up to the sun, enjoying its warmth and the peace of being alone in a lonely place.

Or was she?

A footstep scuffed a stone nearby. Opening her eyes, she saw a man in a frockcoat and beaver hat walking along the stream from the direction of the boathouse. As he neared, she recognized the broad-chested man as Enos Redknap. A jolt of dread seized her. The last time she'd seen him, he'd visited the island with Uncle Percy, who had introduced him as *"one of the King's Watermen, a professional sculler, man of business, and boatbuilder."* She had thought—hoped—she would never see him again.

Reaching the footbridge, the man doffed his hat and bowed, sunlight flashing on his red hair.

"Miss Wilder. Pleasure to see you again, ma'am."

Enos Redknap was in his midthirties. He dressed like a gentleman, but his massive shoulders and thighs were at odds with his professional appearance. She'd thought he had a certain masculine appeal when she'd first met him, but after Carlota's warnings, he seemed far less attractive. In fact, he put her in mind of a devious red-haired pirate.

"Mr. Redknap. I am surprised to see you." Isabelle sent a nervous glance behind her.

"No reason you should be." He followed the direction of her gaze. "Are you all alone out 'ere?"

"No, I . . ." She swallowed. "My watchdog is with me."

He chuckled. "You mean 'at little scamp of a pup? Saw 'im down at the boathouse. Licked me hand." His accent identified him as an East Londoner.

Isabelle lifted her chin, feigning confidence she did not feel. "What brings you here?"

"I have yet to receive me answer. At least, not the answer I wanted." He grinned as he said it, but his eyes remained cold.

"Then perhaps you have not yet heard," she said. "My uncle has died."

"Yes, I know." He picked a stray hair from his sleeve. "Killed. Poisoned."

Isabelle looked at him sharply. Had this man done it?

She clasped her hands. "Even so, I have not changed my mind about leasing any land. I am sorry you've come all this way for nothing."

"Not at all. Good timing, I'd say. Now we can negotiate just the two of us. We shall no doubt deal very well together." Innuendo sweetened his voice, sending a repulsive shiver down her neck.

He looked around and added, "I still say Belle Island is an ideal place for me enterprise. Though that statue may have to go."

Isabelle felt annoyance rise. "But as I said, the island is not for sale or let."

"Now, Miss Wilder. Do be reasonable. Everything is for sale, I find, if the price is 'igh enough."

"Not in this case, Mr. Redknap. I need all the acres we can spare to grow basket willows."

"A resourceful female. I applaud you. Truly I do." He flashed a broad smile at her, forming dimples in chiseled cheeks. His teeth, however, were dingy and chipped, spoiling his well-groomed appearance.

His appreciative gaze made her uneasy. Oh, where was Mr. Booker when she needed him?

Redknap gestured toward the manor. "Will you not invite me in, so we can discuss 'is proper-like?"

It was the last thing Isabelle wanted to do, but she also didn't want the man to think that she was a defenseless female alone on the island. Remembering Carlota's fear of Mr. Redknap, she hoped her companion would remain out of sight. This was the man, after all, whose threats had spurred Lotty to leave London nearly seven years ago.

"This way." She strode up the path, and he followed, the back of her neck prickling all the while. Nearing the house a few moments later, she glimpsed a face in the window. With a flick of a curtain, Carlota disappeared.

Relieved, Isabelle said, "I can offer you some refreshment before you return to London, if you'd like."

"Thank you, but I have no plans to return just yet."

"Oh. Well . . ." Not knowing what else to say, she led the man inside.

Crossing the hall, she heard low male voices in the morning room. Relief flooded her. Inside she found Hardy and Adair, reading newspapers. Hardy rose when she entered.

"Mr. Hardy and Mr. Adair. May I introduce Mr. Redknap from London."

Redknap's gaze flicked over Christopher, then quickly returned to the older lawyer. "Oh, I know who Mr. Hardy is. 'Course I do."

"And how is that?" Hardy eyed the man coolly. "I have never met you, I don't believe."

"Percy mentioned you several times."

Isabelle explained, "Mr. Redknap came here with my uncle a few weeks ago, with the aim of letting part of the island. I turned down the scheme, but apparently Uncle Percy did not convey that to him before he died."

Mr. Hardy nodded. "How unfortunate."

Isabelle turned back to their unwanted guest. "Mr. Hardy is the successor trustee now that Percival is gone. But I am sure he will support my decision."

Mr. Hardy's gaze rested on her face, and Isabelle saw understanding kindle in his eyes. "Yes. A pity you have come all this way for nothing, Mr. Redknap. I wish you a safe and speedy journey back to Town."

Enos gave them another lazy smile. "Oh, I'm in no 'urry to go back."

"The last stage leaves Maidenhead in two hours," Hardy added helpfully.

Redknap shook his head. "I came by water with me men. 'At way, we can come and go as we please."

His reptilian eyes darted back to Isabelle. "I urge you, miss, to reconsider. You 'elp me protect my interests . . . I'll 'elp you protect yours."

Isabelle frowned. "How so?"

"We were keeping track of Percy Norris, see. Making sure 'e didn't try to walk out on 'is obligations. Watching 'is 'ouse as we were, we saw many interesting comings and goings."

At this, Christopher Adair's head snapped up, and he stared at the man, newspaper forgotten.

Isabelle said, "If you saw something related to my uncle's death, you should take the information to Bow Street."

"Are you sure you'd want me to do that?"

Isabelle stilled. What did he mean? Had he seen something that implicated someone she wanted to protect? Like Rose or Mr. Adair, or maybe even herself?

Seeing his words had produced the desired effect, the man

smirked. "I'll leave Bow Street out of it for the present. Not on the best of terms with that lot, nor the marine police, for that matter. This will remain between us. For now."

Redknap lifted his chin in Mr. Hardy's direction. "In the meantime, I trust you'll 'elp your client see the merits of our proposal. Being protective of all the females in your life, as you are."

Hardy's nostrils flared. "I hardly think threats are going to help your cause with Miss Wilder, or with me."

"I disagree. I find 'em exceedingly effective." His eyes glinted. "Especially as I never deliver idle ones."

Fear washed over Isabelle, prickling her skin with gooseflesh.

Abel Curtis appeared in the doorway, his fowling piece in hand. "Everything all right, miss? Jacob mentioned some, um, stranger had come to call."

Expelling a relieved breath, Isabelle said, "Thank you, Abel. It was kind of you to look in, but Mr. Redknap was just leaving."

Redknap looked from the armed, steely-eyed man back to Miss Wilder. "Indeed I was. But never fear, I shall pay another call when it's more . . . convenient." He replaced his hat with a jaunty tip to its brim. "For now, I bid you all good day."

He swept from the room and out of the house. Isabelle walked to the window to watch him go, then she went searching for Carlota. She found her locked inside Isabelle's bedchamber, armed with a pair of shears.

"Is he gone?"

Isabelle nodded.

"What did he want this time?"

"The same thing he wanted last time."

"Still pretending to be a respectable boatbuilder?"

"Yes."

"Ha! If he's a boatbuilder, I'm a crown princess." She looked at Isabelle, expression pained. "Does he know I am here?"

"Not that I know of."

"I sent Jacob to fetch Abel, since Captain Curtis is gone to Town."

"Good thinking. Abel certainly spurred him on his way. I should warn you, however—he promised to return."

"If he does, I shall have to leave."

"No, Lotty. You are safe here."

"None of us are safe with that man around. I know how he is. Don't be taken in. I remember thinking him handsome once. And he can be charming when he wants to be. Women always fall for him. Foolish women like me. But he *is* dangerous. Why did you invite him inside the house?"

"Because I wanted him to see that I am not alone here. He met Mr. Hardy and Mr. Adair as well as Abel."

"A priggish lawyer is not likely to scare Enos Redknap. Adair less so. Abel is better, but too bad Captain Curtis was not here."

"True. Or Mr. Booker," Isabelle added.

"Mr. Booker? Pray, do not be offended, but what could he do? Read him to death? Throw a book at his head?"

Isabelle gazed out the window. "I don't know. I just feel . . . safer . . . when he is near."

Exiting the churchyard, Benjamin saw a stranger step from the bridge, tip his hat to Miss Truelock, and continue on his way. He didn't recognize the man, but he didn't like the look of him either. What was his business on the island? Benjamin turned to watch his retreating back, then hastened over the bridge, the roll of paper in hand. Mr. Hardy met him on the veranda and described the encounter.

"Enos Redknap?" Benjamin echoed with a frown. "That was the name of Susan Stark's first husband. She told me after the trial that he was dangerous, claiming that's why she changed her name—to protect herself. I don't know if it's true, or if this is the same man. . . ."

"Seems probable," Hardy said. "It is not a common name."

Ben's mind raced. "*This* was the man who came here with Mr. Norris, hoping to secure the use of Belle Island for his business, whatever it is?"

Hardy nodded. "And now he is back."

Benjamin grimaced. "That does not bode well for any of us, I don't think."

Hardy considered, then drew himself up. "Well, I wouldn't lose sleep over it. He came back here expecting to find Miss Wilder alone and unprotected. Instead he found me here, not to mention an armed Abel Curtis, and beat a hasty retreat. We probably won't see him again."

But Benjamin was far less certain.

CHAPTER
nineteen

That evening, Arminda Truelock joined them for dinner as she sometimes did. And with her sweet, sunny presence, the mood around the table was lighter than usual and the topics pleasant. They avoided mentioning Mr. Redknap's visit, Percival's death, or Mr. Grant's return. Instead they talked of fond memories, village news, an upcoming fete at the church, and Isabelle's rambunctious puppy. Only Mr. Adair seemed immune to the general cheer, sitting quietly and not taking part in the conversation.

After the meal, the ladies withdrew, leaving the men in the dining room for a time as was customary. In the drawing room, Arminda acquiesced to Isabelle's request and played a piece for them on the pianoforte. Though not as skilled as Carlota, she was accomplished in her own right and a pleasure to hear.

When she reached the final notes, Rose applauded. "I still remember when you tried to teach me to play as a girl, but I never could sit still long enough to practice."

Arminda nodded and continued to play softly. "I remember. Too busy with that duck of yours and, later, poring over fashion plates."

Rose's dimples appeared. "Then apparently I have not changed at all. For I still adore fashion plates, and I still adore ducks. They are delicious."

Isabelle chuckled. Arminda had been something of a second aunt as well as godmother to Rose, and Isabelle enjoyed seeing the affection between them even now. "Can you believe our little Rose is engaged to be married?"

Miss Truelock shook her head and asked in teasing tones, "Tell us old tabbies, among all the young men you undoubtedly met in London, how did you know Mr. Adair was the one?"

Rose looked up in memory, and her eyes shone. "He was so handsome and gallant. And his address! Such the gentleman. I am embarrassed to admit, I was so flustered to dance with him that I turned the wrong way more than once. He assured me I had nothing to be embarrassed about and insisted the mistakes had all been his. Many young ladies flirted with him that night, and the mammas were eager to introduce their daughters to him, but the way he looked at me . . . It was as if I were the only woman in the room. When he came to call on me the next day, he said, 'Miss Lawrence, I feel as though I have been waiting to meet you my entire life.' How my heart leapt! For I felt the same way!"

Isabelle and Arminda shared a look over her niece's head, part amusement, part wistfulness. Oh, to be young and in love and so sure of your admirer's devotion. It was something the two old friends could only imagine.

Soon after that, the vicar's daughter stood to take her leave, turning down their request to play again because she had promised her father a game of chess that evening. She bid Rose a fond farewell, and Isabelle walked her out.

As they crossed the hall, Arminda said, "By the way, Mr. Booker came to the churchyard today."

"Yes, he mentioned he planned to attend the service."

Miss Truelock nodded. "He also laid flowers on your parents' grave."

Isabelle stopped near the door, looking at her with wide eyes. "Did he? He said nothing about it to me. I did tell him I regretted neglecting that task. Even so, it surprises me."

"Does it?"

"Yes. I can't imagine why he would."

A teasing smile played about Arminda's mouth. "Can you not?"

The men spilled out of the dining room at that moment, on their way to join the women in the drawing room. As if sensing they were talking about him, Mr. Booker paused and turned toward the two ladies standing near the front door. Isabelle looked at him, gratitude warming her heart, followed swiftly by attraction. Her gaze swept over his dark hair, broad shoulders, and tall athletic form before lingering on his face.

"Are you taking your leave, Miss Truelock?" he asked.

"I am."

"Then I bid you good evening." He bowed. For a moment he held Isabelle's gaze, then he continued into the drawing room.

Isabelle turned back to Arminda and found her friend studying her with humor and speculation in her eyes.

She repeated, "Can you not indeed?"

After Arminda left, the rest of the company gathered in the drawing room as usual.

Isabelle sat with Mr. Hardy on the sofa, listening to him describe his first glimpse of his first grandchild with affection and pride. Perhaps, Isabelle thought, he *would* be a good trustee, though she would still prefer to have no one at all. Across the room, Mr. Adair and Rose played a game of draughts, Rose all eagerness, while Mr. Adair looked far less enthusiastic, head resting on his hand, a glass of something nearby. Mr. Booker sat alone near the fire, reading one of her brother's old books—an adventure story Joe had recommended to him.

Noticing a figure in the doorway, Isabelle looked over and was surprised to see Miss O'Toole, Rose's longtime companion and lady's maid, hovering outside the drawing room.

"Miss O'Toole, did you . . . need something?"

"I have something to say. To everyone. May I come in?"

"Of course."

Isabelle and Rose exchanged raised-brow looks. The men turned in their seats to face the newcomer.

The thin woman stepped just over the threshold. She stood there, hands clasped, clearly ill at ease.

Isabelle prompted, "What is it, Miss O'Toole?"

"That officer who came here yesterday. I overheard some of what he said. I gather you and perhaps even Miss Rose are suspected of killing Mr. Norris, and perhaps Mary Williams too. Is that true?"

Mr. Hardy answered for them all. "I'm afraid so. After all, Miss Lawrence *was* seen delivering a bottle to Percival's office, though Officer Riley seems to be focusing his investigation on Miss Wilder at this point."

Miss O'Toole lifted her chin, and Isabelle saw stoic resolve in her eyes. It reminded her of all those years ago when the woman had shown up on the island, valise in hand and child in tow, pale and weary but determined to see her charge safe.

"I was not going to say anything," she began. "For I know Miss Rose has her heart set on him. But I can remain silent no longer—not when Miss Wilder and Miss Rose are being accused of something so vile. And not when my dear girl is soon to marry a man who has lied to everyone . . . and perhaps done far worse."

Scowling, Adair stood, hands on slim hips. "O'Toole, what are you talking about?"

She ignored him and looked at Rose. "Can you deny that he has been acting strangely? Guilty?"

Rose blinked. "Well no, he has not been himself since Percival's death, but that is understandable. You can't blame him for that."

"Can't I?" The woman turned to the two lawyers. "Miss Rose told the officer that she and I were at the Adairs' home all evening, which is true. Mr. Adair said he was as well—dressing and then in the library with his father the entire time Rose and I were upstairs. But that is not true."

"It is," Adair insisted. He began pacing the room like a caged tiger in a menagerie. "I may have underestimated the duration, but we *were* in the library together. He wanted a good long father-son chat. A chance to give me marriage advice."

Miss O'Toole shook her head. "No. I saw you from the window. Crossing the mews at half past six."

Mr. Adair squinted, his lips pressed tight, and then said calmly, "My dear Miss O'Toole, you must be mistaken. The guest room faces the front of the house."

"Yes, but I went across the corridor to borrow more hairpins from your mother's maid. I happened to look out the window. Imagine my surprise to see you stealing furtively back toward the house, wearing a greatcoat, collar turned up, hat pulled low. I was confused but told myself there had to be a simple explanation. You must have dashed out for something. A last-minute gift, perhaps, though I saw nothing in your hands. For a moment I stood there watching you, but then Miss Rose called out, urging me to hurry back and finish her hair."

Rose looked from one to the other. "Miss O'Toole, I don't

know what to say. When I went downstairs a short while later, Mr. Adair was there, coming out of his father's library."

"Perhaps, but he had not been there long."

Isabelle's pulse pounded as she watched Christopher Adair. His Adam's apple convulsed up and down his white neck, but he said nothing.

Miss O'Toole continued, "I wasn't overly concerned until he escorted us home that night and we were met by the constable and the news that Mr. Norris was dead. Then a darker suspicion came to me. I knew Mr. Adair was still angry about the settlement and the party. I wondered if he had sneaked off to the Wilder house to confront Mr. Norris in secret."

She faced the young man. "I saw you, trying so hard to look shocked at the news, but you were not. You already knew."

Rose turned wide, pleading eyes to her intended. Her voice hitched. "Christopher . . . ?"

"It is not what you think!" he blurted.

"No?"

"No. I swear it."

Rose said somberly, "Then you had better tell us the absolute truth. Or our engagement, our . . . *us* . . . is over."

He ran an agitated hand over his face. "That is why I didn't tell you. Though I fear we shall be over anyway."

Benjamin listened with keen interest as Christopher Adair heaved a sigh and began his account. "I did go to see Percy. I was upset. I saw my mother trying to stretch the meat and count the bottles of champagne, wringing her hands and worrying we wouldn't have enough. Found my father up late the night before, fretting over bills, wondering what to sell to cover the added expenses. So yes, I was angry, and I wanted to give the miser a piece of my mind. I was already dressed for the evening and had time to kill since Rose was still busy having her hair arranged and whatever else females do for so long."

"You thought you had an alibi," Hardy said, "so you sneaked out."

"No, man. Must you lawyers twist every word? We are not in court, dash it."

"Sorry. Continue."

Adair ran a hand over his face. "I was frustrated, and I wanted Percival to know it, to understand how everyone in our house had to bustle about, sweating and fussing and trying to organize a formal party because at the last minute he spitefully refused to do so, like a toddler throwing a fit when he doesn't get his way. I wanted him to know how not only my mother and our housekeeper but also the Wilder servants had worked together frantically so the guests would never suspect all the drama and discord going on behind the scenes. Frankly, it was embarrassing that Rose had no family to host her. Pray don't be offended, Miss Wilder."

"I am not," Isabelle said. "I was disappointed and embarrassed myself not to be there."

"At all events, I slipped out and stalked over to your house. I went there to rail at him, yes, but please believe me, I never meant to lay a hand on him. I planned to tell the man in no uncertain terms what I thought of him and his settlement—which I had destroyed after unwisely signing."

Adair looked to Rose. "If your grandparents were alive, they never would have stood for his broken promises and shoddy hospitality. Percival ought to have been ashamed to pretend to represent Mr. Wilder's wishes for you. And I intended to tell him so."

Looking pale, Rose listened but didn't interrupt. Benjamin noticed her white knuckles as she gripped the arms of her chair.

Adair continued. "I knew Mrs. Kittleson and Marvin were at our house but figured the housemaid would still be there to let me in. Instead, I found the garden door ajar and walked inside. I heard Percival in his study, grumbling and talking to himself and almost . . . gasping.

"I pushed open his office door and saw in an instant he'd been drinking again. An empty wine bottle sat there along with his usual decanter. He held his head in his hands, a half-full glass at his elbow. I foolishly thought he might be remorseful for his treatment of Rose. But then he looked up, and I was stunned to see him red-faced, cords in his neck standing out, frothing at the mouth like a mad dog! I don't exaggerate. He looked like a madman. I tried to deliver my setdown, but the words stuck in my throat.

"He saw me and his rage exploded. 'You!' he shouted, his voice full of venom. 'I knew it was one of you! Come to finish me off?'

"In my confusion, I shouted back, 'What? No!'

"He looked like a devil, eyes flaming and spittle flying. He threw his glass at my head. I ducked, and it flew past me, smashing against the wall instead. Then he lunged into his desk drawer and pulled out a gun. I couldn't believe what was happening.

"He pointed it at me, and I thought I was a dead man. His grip on the gun wavered—he was that drunk, or so I thought. I had only an instant. I reacted quickly, barely thinking. I had to defend myself, did I not? I grabbed the nearest thing—the wine bottle—and swung in a blind panic. I meant to hit the gun from his hand, but at the last second, he fell forward, and I struck the side of his head with a sickening *whack*." Adair shuddered, his countenance taking on a greenish cast.

"Percival fell to the desk and didn't move. I thought I'd killed him. For a minute I stood there, frozen in shock. I never intended to hurt him, only to protect myself! I dropped the bottle and hastened out of there, shaking so hard I could barely open the door."

Benjamin said, "There was no wine bottle in the room when we arrived."

"Then someone else removed it, for I did not. I'm not sure I even shut the door. Didn't want anyone to see or hear me leaving. I crept through the back garden and all but ran home. I hurried inside, hung the coat on a peg, and sped to the library. My hands would not stop shaking. My father put it down to a case of engagement nerves."

Rose murmured, "That's why you smelled like oranges that night. I asked, but you dismissed it as a new shaving tonic."

He nodded. "Some must have spilled onto my evening clothes when he threw the glass at me."

Mr. Hardy spoke up. "The housemaid said she heard Percival arguing with a man that night. Perhaps she recognized your voice and that's why she's dead. Poisoned as well."

"That has nothing to do with me!" Again Adair shook his head. "I was never so relieved in my life when Mr. Booker announced the coroner's verdict that Percival had been poisoned, for I knew I had not done that."

Mr. Hardy said, "How can you expect us to believe that you sneaked over there only intending to *talk* to the man? I think you knew he had been poisoned, and you went back to see if it had worked, and to finish him off if it had not."

"No! That is not true." Adair blanched, his freckles standing out against white skin.

Benjamin winced at Robert Hardy's harsh accusation. But was he right?

Hardy continued, "How can we trust you? We thought you

had an alibi for the entire evening, but clearly we were led a merry dance. Why should we believe anything you say?"

"Because it is the truth!" Adair cried. "God help me, I have been in torment. When I learned my blow had not killed him, I felt like I could breathe again after days of suffocation." He looked down at his hands. "Though I've still been living in fear of what I did do becoming known."

Rose slowly shook her head. "I knew you were not yourself. I thought you were having second thoughts about marrying me."

"Never. Except that I wondered how in the world I could keep such a dreadful secret from you all our lives. I was trying to rouse my courage to confess, but I . . . failed."

He knelt before Rose and grasped her hand. "Please say you believe me, Rose. I don't care if they do, but *you must* believe me."

"Oh, Christopher. I want to believe you. But why didn't you tell me any of this before now?"

"Why do you think? I was terrified. Afraid of arrest and scandal and prison. Afraid of ruining my parents' lives and losing you. My dearest, please forgive me."

Rose swallowed. "I will . . . try."

Benjamin felt sorry for the frantic young man. Even if Miss Lawrence forgave him, would she ever be able to trust him again? Trust—in another or yourself—was difficult to rebuild. As Benjamin knew all too well.

Mr. Hardy said, "No doubt Officer Riley will be eager to hear your account when he returns."

Mr. Adair met his gaze but said no more.

Later that night, Benjamin tossed and turned, unable to sleep, his mind full of Adair's confession and the discovery of poison in the wine cellar the day before. And something else was bothering him. Was it Enos Redknap's visit? He wasn't sure.

Ben put on his dressing gown and decided to go down to the kitchen as he had once before, hoping a glass of milk or a slice of bread and cheese might help him sleep. The dog, Hamish, saw him descending the stairs and lumbered to all fours to meet him at the bottom, offering the top of his head to be petted.

"Evening, ol' boy," Ben whispered. After an obligatory pat, Ben made his way belowstairs, the dog following companionably behind him.

Reaching the servants' area, Ben heard something and peeked into the laundry room, wondering if Miss Wilder might be there again with her puppy, but the young dog slept peacefully in his bed alone.

He continued down the passage, hearing a *glug-glug* sound of . . . running water? Or perhaps a washtub being filled. He knew from his previous visit that the scullery and stillroom had sinks with hand pumps to draw water from a spring, but who would be up doing dishes at this time of night?

The kitchen was dark, but faint light leaked out from the door to the stillroom Miss Lawrence had shown them—the small workroom where Miss Wilder made wine and preserves.

He quietly approached the threshold. The door was open a crack, and through it he looked inside.

Miss Wilder stood at the sink in a dressing gown. On the counter beside her stood nine wine bottles with watercolor labels. She had pulled out the stoppers and was dumping them down the drain two at a time.

His heart sank. Why was she disposing of them, and in such a clandestine fashion? The sour-sweet smell of oranges filled the air. Four bottles, six, eight . . .

With his head, the dog nudged the door wide, hinges creaking.

Miss Wilder turned, sucking in a breath. "Oh! Mr. Booker, you scared me to death."

He said, "I suppose I needn't ask what you are doing. The only question is why?"

The dog lay near the stove with a contented sigh, but Miss Wilder kept her eyes on Benjamin. "I . . . thought it a wise precaution, so I borrowed Mrs. Philpott's key."

"In the middle of the night?"

"I had another nightmare. Uncle Percy was in it, serving orange wine to everyone at a party I was not invited to. One by one they all died, and I did nothing to stop it. When I woke, I came down here to make sure no one else gets hurt by these."

"Are you telling me the bottles you made *are* poisoned?"

"No! I did not knowingly poison any of them. But if somehow the bottles or cask I used had been in contact with poison, or if the wine had gone bad . . . fatally so . . . then I couldn't risk keeping these in the house."

Benjamin slowly walked toward her.

Bottle in hand, she asked, "What are you going to do?"

Without a word, he extended his hand.

She met his gaze, her eyes downturned and almost sad as she relinquished the final bottle to him.

"What are you doing!"

Mr. Hardy's sharp voice jolted Benjamin. Whirling to face him, he dropped the bottle. It landed on his toe and rolled to the floor, spilling wine in its wake. Ben stifled the expletive that leapt to his lips but not the low growl of pain. *Hang me, that hurt.*

Mr. Hardy stood there, the biscuit in his hand forgotten. His stare blazed a condemning trail from their guilty faces to the empty bottles and sink.

Miss Wilder spoke up. "Don't blame him. I was determined to get rid of the wine on the small chance it has somehow been tainted."

"Did you poison the whole batch?" Hardy asked, much as Ben had done.

"Of course not. As if I would poison wine I meant to serve to my own family!"

Hardy reminded her, "Mr. Norris was family, was he not?"

"Only distantly—and I did not poison him. At least not knowingly."

Hardy turned to Benjamin. Incredulity dug deep lines into the older man's face. "Why were you helping her destroy evidence?"

He licked dry lips and faltered, "I . . . Because two people have died and keeping the wine here is not worth the risk."

He felt Miss Wilder's surprised gaze on his profile but kept his focus on his superior.

Hardy sighed. "Benjamin, Benjamin. Forever the noble knight trying to protect the damsel in distress . . . innocent or not."

"Sir, please. This is an entirely different situation."

Hardy met his gaze. "Is it?"

"Yes."

Miss Wilder said, "Mr. Booker did nothing wrong. This was all my doing."

Mouth tight, Hardy turned back to Miss Wilder. "Do you know how guilty this makes you look?"

"I am not guilty." She lifted her chin. "But I care more about making sure no one else gets hurt than how I *look*."

As the two argued, another sound penetrated Benjamin's awareness. A lapping sound. He looked over and saw Hamish licking up the spilled wine.

Isabelle followed the direction of his gaze and frowned. "Hamish, no, that isn't good for you."

She walked over to grab his collar and pull him away.

"Afraid he'll be poisoned?" Mr. Hardy asked.

"No, just ill. Old fool will eat anything. Come on, boy. Out you go." She led the dog into the passage and up the basement steps.

"You see?" Hardy hissed. "She didn't want the dog to drink it."

"Sir, you grasp at straws. As Miss Wilder said, she would not have poisoned these bottles and risked endangering herself and others here."

"Are you questioning my intelligence, Benjamin?"

"Of course not." His trusted mentor did not seem his usual calm, logical self. Was he still so distraught over Percival's death? Benjamin gentled his voice. "I understand you are determined to seek justice for your friend. But being so close to him, you are not objective in this case."

"And you are?" Hardy scoffed. "Please tell me you are not in league with her."

"Absolutely not." Benjamin said, hoping that was true. He took a deep breath to steel himself, then said, "Perhaps you ought to go home, sir. I have things in hand here."

"Do you?" Irritation sparked in the older man's eyes. "Having 'things in hand' apparently includes standing by while a suspect destroys evidence in the middle of the night."

It was a valid point. Benjamin had not helped Miss Wilder, but he had not acted quickly to stop her either. Even so, Ben resolutely held Mr. Hardy's gaze, trying to ignore a nagging feeling in his gut. Who was acting more suspicious now—Miss Wilder, Mr. Hardy, or Benjamin himself?

Then Mr. Hardy sighed again, and his shoulders slumped. "You are right. I am tired and overreacted. I think I will go home. Leave this to you, and to Bow Street."

Benjamin nodded in relief. "I think that's wise, sir." He added in mollifying tones, "If someone on the island is dangerous, or if Enos Redknap returns, I wouldn't want you in harm's way. There is your daughter to consider, after all, and that new grandchild of yours."

Hardy pursed his lips and nodded. "True. Very well, Ben. If you think it best, I shall return to London tomorrow. You're right that Cordelia would worry if I stayed away too long."

"Thank you, sir. That would ease my mind."

But in truth, nothing eased Benjamin's mind that night. He returned to his room, where he continued to toss and turn, questioning himself for defending Miss Wilder's decision to pour out the wine—even standing by while she did so. What would he have done had Hardy not startled them, causing him to drop that final bottle? Would he have handed it over to Officer Riley when he had not handed over the earring? He was not absolutely certain.

It had been Mr. Hardy's idea to send Benjamin to Belle Island in the first place. Ben wondered if he regretted that decision. Had Hardy been right to believe Percival Norris's killer would be found on the island? Mr. Adair had certainly played a part, but who else was guilty in the trustee's death? Might Robert Hardy find himself in similar danger as successor trustee?

What-ifs and worries continued to plague him. Growing weary, Ben heard his mother's voice in his mind, reminding him not to worry but to pray instead. He began repeating the old familiar words, like a sacred refrain. *"In every thing by prayer and supplication with thanksgiving let your requests be made known unto God. And the peace of God, which passeth all understanding, shall keep your hearts and minds through Christ Jesus."*

Finally, he fell asleep.

CHAPTER

twenty

In the morning, Carlota helped Isabelle dress and pinned up her hair as usual. She smiled as she did so, mentioning Captain Curtis had returned from London.

When she finished her tasks and left the room, Isabelle lingered in her bedchamber alone, thinking back to the previous night. With the clarity of a new day, she realized how strange her actions must have seemed—pouring out wine late at night in her dressing gown. And first Mr. Booker and then Mr. Hardy catching her in the act. Her neck heated at the thought of what they must think of her.

Isabelle recalled the look on Mr. Booker's face when he'd discovered her in the stillroom—surprise, disillusionment, and something else. Resolve? She didn't know.

He'd been so shocked when Mr. Hardy interrupted them that he dropped the bottle on his foot. Poor man! And he'd been chagrined as well. She had seen it in his red, rigid face. Even so, when Mr. Hardy asked him why he was standing by while she destroyed evidence, he'd echoed back her earlier rationale. She hoped he truly believed her explanation, and even agreed with it. Or did he think she was guilty but defended her actions anyway? Why would he do that, unless perhaps he . . . admired her? Even if he did, she did not think she could respect a man who would defend someone he believed guilty of a heinous crime, simply because he was attracted to her.

Isabelle wondered what Mr. Hardy had meant when he'd referred to Benjamin as *"Forever the noble knight trying to protect the damsel in distress—innocent or not."*

Mr. Booker had insisted this was an entirely different situation. Different from what? Had he been involved with a guilty woman in the past? She didn't hear the rest of their conversation because greedy old Hamish had started licking up the spilled wine, and by the time she'd returned from taking him outside, the men had retired. She hoped Mr. Booker would not suffer repercussions for defending her, nor regret doing so.

Earlier that morning, the housemaid who brought up the hot water had told her Mr. Hardy planned to leave that day. Isabelle was not sure if that was good news for her or bad. Had he decided to return to London to report her actions to the Bow Street officer, along with Mr. Adair's confession?

Hoping to talk to Mr. Booker, Isabelle walked down to the study, but the door was closed. Leaning near, she heard his and Mr. Hardy's voices in low conversation.

With a sigh, Isabelle climbed the stairs to the rooftop parapet again. Pushing open the door, the breeze loosened her carefully pinned hair and whipped it into her face, but she relished the cool, refreshing air anyway. Picking up the field glasses, she surveyed Riverton on the opposite shore and noticed no boats currently moored at the village pier. She looked up and then down river. A few boats were out—a fishing boat, an eel skiff, and there a Thames river barge with red-brown sails. She recalled Enos Redknap saying he'd come by water. Was he already back in London, or was he still lurking about somewhere nearby? Thames river barges were narrow, flat-bottomed boats built for the shallow estuary near London. Their masts could even be lowered to clear bridges. She didn't often see them this far upriver. Might it belong to Enos Redknap, or was she jumping to worrisome conclusions again?

After breakfast, Benjamin and Mr. Hardy met for a last time in the study. The older man seemed much recovered and more his usual self. He had apparently accepted Miss Wilder's word that Benjamin had not aided her in disposing of the wine, for he did not raise the topic again. Instead, Benjamin asked a few clarifying questions about the terms of the trust, and they discussed their plan of action. Ben would stay and continue his search for a newer will, and if unsuccessful, help Miss Wilder navigate the steps if she decided to challenge the trust in court. It would be easier to have Mr. Hardy replaced as trustee than removed altogether, as most judges were skeptical of a woman's ability to manage her own affairs or finances. Benjamin had little doubt of Isabelle Wilder's abilities. But just what was she capable of?

Mr. Hardy said, "If she doesn't want me to serve, I am quite willing to step down."

"Even if you did, it would not give her the freedom she desires," Benjamin replied. "The trust directs that in that case, you appoint someone else from the firm."

"Who would you suggest?"

"There is no one more qualified than you, sir. I'm sure I can convince her of that."

Hardy sent him a wry grin. "Better the devil you know than the devil you don't, ay?"

Benjamin chuckled. "Something like that."

He promised to keep his mentor apprised by writing with any further developments. Meanwhile, Mr. Hardy would return to London and report to Bow Street what they had learned about Adair, and also that Captain Curtis had an idea who might have killed Mr. Norris. With Officer Riley so focused on Miss Wilder, they'd neglected to mention Curtis's surprising statement. Ben had seen the captain return over the bridge last evening and planned to question him as soon as possible.

Hardy also planned to see what he could find out about Enos Redknap, in case the man persisted in threatening Miss Wilder.

After he and Ben had finished talking, Mr. Hardy picked up his brief bag and valise, and together they crossed the hall.

"Safe journey, sir."

"It's not me I worry about," Hardy said. "I can't rid myself of the feeling that you might be in danger here."

"I shall be careful."

The two men shook hands, and Mr. Hardy left the house.

Ben was halfway back to the study when a loud *pop* cracked the air.

A gunshot? A hunter too near the house?

Benjamin stepped to the window and looked out. A flock of startled birds flapped to sudden flight, screeching in alarm. And there on the lawn, Mr. Hardy grasped his arm and teetered, then fell to his knees.

His heart lurched. "No!" Benjamin ran, jumping over the sleeping dog, and bolted outside to his mentor and friend.

"Mr. Hardy! I'm here. Are you badly hurt?"

Only then did he realize he'd put himself in harm's way by leaving the house and joining the man. *So be it.*

Mr. Hardy clutched his sleeve. Blood seeped between his fingers. He'd been shot in the back of the arm.

"What's happened?" A voice called. He looked up. There was Miss Wilder on the roof, field glasses in hand.

"He's been shot! Send for Dr. Grant!"

"I'll send Jacob directly." She set down the glasses and ran off to do so.

"Where did the shot come from?" Benjamin asked, looking all around. From an upper window? he wondered. Or the woods? Could a shot have reached them from across the bridge? Or from a passing boat?

Mr. Hardy panted, "I . . . don't . . . know."

Young Joe came jogging up the shore path from the direction of the point, book under his arm, eyes large and fearful. "Is he . . . Was he shot?"

"Yes."

"I heard the crack," the boy said. "Something whizzed through the bush beside me, and leaves went flying."

"Did you see where the shot came from?"

Joe shook his head. "I'm afraid I ducked."

"Wise move."

Joe looked over his shoulder. "It must have come from behind the stables."

Ben prompted, "Or from a boat on the river?"

"Oh . . . yes, could have been."

Benjamin was tempted to dash around the house to see if any boats were moving away on the other side of the island, but he didn't want to leave the injured man. Instead he held a clean handkerchief to the wound and applied pressure.

Jacob ran out the door and went running over the bridge, casting a concerned glance back at the fallen man.

Where is everyone else? Benjamin wondered. Why were Joe, Isabelle, and Jacob the only ones to respond? But to Hardy he said only, "Come, let's get you into the house."

Miss Wilder and Carlota came out to help. Ben assisted Mr. Hardy to his feet, and together they led the injured man inside and settled him onto the sofa in the morning room. Miss Wilder brought him a lap rug, and Carlota went to ask Mrs. Philpotts for hot water and cloths, just in case.

Dr. Grant hurried into the house a few minutes later, carrying his medical bag. He joined them and quickly assessed the wound.

"A stray bullet, do you think? Someone shooting birds or poaching?"

"We don't know," Benjamin replied, thinking of Enos Red-knap. Or was Captain Curtis, with his bitter grudge against Mr. Hardy—and so recently returned from London—the more likely suspect?

"I don't see many gunshots in my practice," Grant said, "but thankfully the bullet passed through muscle without striking bone."

Mr. Hardy grimaced. "Burns like hades. If you have any laudanum in that bag of yours, I would not say no."

"Right." Dr. Grant dug a vial from his bag and measured out a dose of the stuff. "I won't win any awards for my needlework, I'm afraid, but you'll need stitches."

"Just do what you need to and quickly," Hardy said between clenched teeth.

Half an hour later, Hardy sat atop the bed in the guest room he'd occupied, while Dr. Grant finished the bandaging.

Benjamin said, "Thank God it wasn't worse, sir. You might have been killed."

"Yes, I should be thankful, I know. Would be more grateful if it didn't hurt like the blazes."

"Sorry." Benjamin asked, "Did you see anyone with a gun? Any sign of Captain Curtis? Any boats passing?"

Hardy squinted in concentration. "Might have been . . ."

"Did you notice anyone on the bridge or behind the stables?"

He shook his head. "I saw only Miss Wilder. On the roof."

Benjamin wondered again why no one else had come at the sound of a gunshot. Where were Adair and Rose and Captain Curtis?

Dr. Grant stowed his supplies and prepared to take his leave. "I would stay, but Mr. Jones is doing poorly."

"Of course you must go," Isabelle replied. "Thank you for coming so quickly."

A short while later, the local constable arrived, alerted by Dr. Grant. Miss Wilder introduced Leonard Ray to them, explaining that he was the miller, serving a one-year term as constable.

When she described the shooting, Mr. Ray ruefully shook his head. "Might mean poachers in the area. The magistrate does not tolerate poaching and metes out stiff penalties. I dread reporting this to him."

The miller seemed to find the shooting of a man less objectionable than the illegal shooting of game. The longer Ray talked, the more Benjamin realized that he had little experience or authority. In fact, the man made Constable Buxton and Officer Riley seem like models of efficiency.

Ray asked Mr. Hardy a few questions, and then they left him to rest.

Walking back downstairs with the constable, Benjamin said, "There is another possibility. Someone may have shot Mr. Hardy intentionally. In fact, I witnessed an altercation between Mr. Hardy and Evan Curtis only a few days ago. He was angry with Mr. Hardy and would have struck him had I not held him back. I have no other proof he did this, but you should at least talk to him."

Miss Wilder paled. "Surely not."

The constable sighed. "Very well. Where is Curtis now?"

Jacob was dispatched to summon the captain. As the young man hurried out the garden door toward the tenant cottages, the others gathered in the morning room.

When Captain Curtis joined them a short while later, he winked at Carlota, then smiled at the miller-turned-constable.

"Leo, you old devil. What are you doing here?"

"Parish business, I'm afraid. Where were you about an hour ago?"

Evan shrugged. "In my father's cottage."

"Can he vouch for that?"

"No. He leaves early to do his work. Why? What's going on?"

Isabelle said, "Someone shot Mr. Hardy."

He looked at her blankly. "No."

"Yes. Thankfully, he wasn't badly hurt."

"You think I shot him?"

The constable said, "I've been told you had quite a row with him."

"I was angry, yes, but I didn't shoot him."

"Do you have a gun with you here on the island?"

"Of course I do. And I am an excellent shot. If I had wanted to kill him, he would be dead now, instead of merely whining over a flesh wound."

The constable turned to Miss Wilder. "And you, miss, do you keep a gun?"

"Not for my own use. But my father owned a few for hunting and shooting. Abel keeps them in his cottage to ward off the occasional weasel in the henhouse."

"Would he have any reason to shoot Mr. Hardy?"

"I don't think so."

The constable sighed again. "Better talk to him too, just in case." Jacob was again sent out to summon him.

While they waited, Benjamin thought about Abel coming into the stables with gun aimed, ready to shoot at the slightest provocation.

He asked Miss Wilder, "You were up on the roof when the shot was fired. Did you see anything or anyone?"

She shook her head. "I saw Mr. Hardy emerge from the house. But beyond that, no."

"No one on the bridge? No boats passing?"

"Several boats were on the river this morning. Boats pass by regularly." She tilted her head to one side in thought. "Though I was surprised to see a sailing barge rather near the island."

The captain's eyebrows rose high. "A sailing barge with red-brown sails?"

Isabelle turned to look at him. "Yes, why?"

Before he could explain, his father entered. Abel Curtis held his hat in hand, concern etched into the deep lines of his face. He answered the constable's questions, looking rather bewildered but not, Benjamin thought, guilty. Yes, he had a fowling piece and a rifle Mr. Wilder himself had given him, but he'd not had occasion to shoot either recently. Yes, he would surrender both for examination. He'd been trimming hedges all morning. He'd worked alone, but Mr. Howton had seen him and could attest to this.

The constable nodded. He said he would ask the weavers if they'd seen anything and do a quick search of the island as well.

Before the man left to do so, Benjamin decided to take advantage of his presence. "Captain Curtis, you told Mr. Hardy and me that you had an idea who killed Mr. Norris, but you would not tell us who you meant. Perhaps you would tell the constable?"

"No, thank you."

"Wait. Mr. Norris . . . ?" Constable Ray asked, face puckered in confusion at the apparent change in topic. Benjamin quickly filled the man in on Percival Norris's recent death.

"Evan?" Miss Wilder turned pleading eyes toward the captain. "If you know something, please tell us."

Curtis huffed a long exhale. "Look. I didn't strike Percy or poison him or anything else. But I . . . may have had a hand in his death."

Carlota gasped. Shock creased his father's face, and he gripped a nearby table for support.

"What do you mean?" Isabelle asked.

"After I was put on half pay, I stayed in London for a time."

"Why did you not come straight home?" Abel asked. "You must have known how worried I'd be."

"I know. I'm sorry, Pa. But I left here planning to cut a figure in the world. Show Percy he'd been wrong about me. That did not happen, and I was not eager to return a failure. In London, I met several other fellows in similar situations. Some of them found alternative sources of income. Selling goods they had acquired by, shall we say, dubious means."

The constable asked, "Do you mean sham stevedores, tea-skippers, whiskey-runners, and the like?"

Slang terms for *smugglers*, Benjamin knew.

"Evan, no . . ." his father feebly muttered.

The captain kept his gaze on the constable. "You put it more colorfully than I would, Leo, but yes. Though they prefer the term *free traders*.

"I also began asking around about Percival Norris. It's no secret I held a grudge against him—the man who had me shipped off, or so I thought. I learned he was in debt and looking to borrow money. At the same time, the leader of my new band of friends was seeking someone with higher connections to find buyers for some luxury goods that *may* have avoided customs tax on their way over from France and the Netherlands. The only toff I knew in London was Norris, so I suggested him. Enos met with Percy and found him willing to help. For a price, of course."

"Enos Redknap?" Miss Medina asked, anger flashing in her dark eyes.

He looked at her. "Yes. Have you met him?"

"Unfortunately, I have."

He held her gaze a moment, and when Carlota said no more, Miss Wilder added, "I have met him too. In fact, he was here again yesterday."

The captain muttered an epithet and ran a hand over his mouth. "I did not think it through. It never occurred to me that Percy would boast that he controlled an island on the Thames. We're upriver from Enos's usual foraging grounds around the East India docks and out of reach of the marine police. When he heard about it, Enos thought Belle Island's lagoon might make a good hiding place for his barge and goods."

"No . . ." Isabelle breathed.

Carlota looked at her. "Did I not tell you?"

Curtis went on. "I tried to convince Enos not to pursue the idea, saying Riverton was too far to go and Miss Wilder would never agree to it. But Percival told Enos he was sure he could convince her of the merits of letting out part of the island."

"When the man first came here," Isabelle said, "Uncle Percy told me he was looking for a site to build a boatyard. I believed him. But then . . ." She sent a questioning look at Carlota, who nodded and took up the tale.

"I saw him from the window and recognized him. He'd threatened me when I refused to . . . spend time with him, and that is why I came to Belle Island. I was furious with Percy for bringing him here and also afraid, so I stayed out of sight. I knew he was no boatbuilder, but a dangerous man not to be trusted. And now he's back."

Captain Curtis listened to Carlota with concern on his face, then returned his attention to Isabelle. "He thought you'd be more amenable to the idea of a boatyard than a smuggling operation. And it's a plausible ploy—lots of boatbuilding on the Thames. At all events, Enos liked what he saw and gave Percy some money in good faith. Never a good idea to take money you have not yet earned from Enos Redknap. Worse, apparently Percival used it to pay down what he owed to some other moneylenders. So when Isabelle refused and Enos wanted his money back, Percy had already spent it."

Benjamin said, "I wonder if that gunshot was meant as a warning to her."

Curtis frowned. "I hope not."

Abel looked stricken and pale. "What were you thinking, lad? To lead such men to Miss Wilder's door. To mine? I know she disappointed you, but she did nothing to deserve to have her home—her very life—threatened."

"It was foolish. I see that now. I was blinded by my anger against Percy. My desire for revenge overwhelmed my better sense. I wanted him to lose his home, his hopes, his future, as I lost mine. I never meant to put Isabelle in danger, or you, Papa. I hope you believe me."

Benjamin said, "I am almost surprised you did not take your revenge more directly. Are you sure you did not? Killing him would have been more effective, would have taken all of that from him in one stroke."

Curtis shook his head. "I didn't want to kill him. Well . . . I confess I thought about it many times over those years dodging bullets and having to kill or be killed in Spain, but mostly I wanted to see him knocked down a few pegs."

The captain chuckled, but it was a mirthless sound. "It's funny. I thought I would enjoy his fall, feel some satisfaction, some relief at his death, but I don't. I feel just . . . what a waste of time it has all been. Hating and plotting and longing for revenge. I wish I could have those years back."

"Be careful," the constable warned. "You don't want to spend the years you have left in prison or transported."

"Well, if arranging an introduction between men of business is a crime, then I am guilty. But that's all I did."

Benjamin asked, "Might Enos Redknap have poisoned Mr. Norris in revenge and perhaps shot Mr. Hardy for the same reason?"

Curtis shrugged. "It's possible. But I know he wanted his money back, wanted to squeeze Percy for all he could get, which is hard to do if the man is dead. Unless he's moved on to squeezing Percival's associates or family."

The constable, clearly struggling to keep up with all the volleys of information, asked, "Does this Enos person own a sailing barge with red-brown sails?"

"He does, as a matter of fact."

"Is he known to use guns? Might he have shot Mr. Hardy? Whether he was the intended victim, or someone else, like Miss Wilder?"

The captain considered. "Enos is no stranger to guns. So it is certainly a possibility. A dangerous possibility."

They talked for a few minutes more. Then the constable asked Evan Curtis to stay put on the island until he'd had time to consult with the magistrate.

He agreed, and the two Curtis men left by the rear garden door, just as Rose and Mr. Adair returned through it.

The couple had apparently taken a leisurely stroll around the island and missed all the excitement. At least, Benjamin hoped that was true. Surely Mr. Adair would not do something so rash to keep Mr. Hardy from reporting his confession to the authorities and from becoming successor trustee.

The constable asked them if they had seen anything, and then took his leave as well. He had to step over Hamish on his way out.

Isabelle apologized and called to the dog. "Hamish, move away from the door."

But Hamish would not be moving again. The dog was dead.

twenty-one

Isabelle and Teddy sat side by side in the small family chapel. He laid a comforting hand on her arm.

"He was old. He simply died in his sleep. We've known this was coming."

Isabelle wiped her eyes. "I know. Still, it is hard to lose him. Especially if I somehow poisoned him."

"You did not! It was just his time. That old dog lived longer than anyone expected."

She sniffed and nodded. "Even so, I am doubly glad I dumped out the rest of the orange wine."

Dr. Grant hesitated. "I am not sure that was wise. It makes you appear very guilty."

"I am not guilty."

"I know. I know! I never doubted it for an instant, but destroying evidence like that . . . That was . . . em . . . risky."

"And what would you have advised me to do instead?"

He nodded thoughtfully. "Perhaps nail the bottles shut in a crate and mark it with a skull and crossbones?"

"Oh, that would not make me look suspicious *at all*."

He acknowledged her point with an apologetic grin. "Sorry. Then perhaps I could have tested it on my mice?"

"No, Teddy. You know I don't approve of your experiments."

"Only thinking aloud."

She huffed, shaking her head.

He took her hand in his. "You have Ollie now, don't forget."

"I don't forget. I will come to care for him just as much in time, no doubt, but my heart is still full of Hamish. He is not so easily replaced." She pulled her hand from his and stood.

Remembering something, she looked back at him. "Why did you not tell me your father has returned?"

He pulled a face. "Because I knew it would upset you. He is only visiting. It won't be for long."

Before she could say more, Rose came in and embraced her. "I am sorry, Aunt Belle. I know how much you loved Hamish."

Tears sprang to her eyes anew at the sympathy of one so dear to her. "Thank you, my love."

"Shall we have a burial service for him?" Rose suggested. "Say a few words, share some memories?"

"How thoughtful. Yes, I would like that very much." Bidding Teddy farewell, they went off to make preparations.

Benjamin slipped down the passage to the Wilders' family chapel, taking the rolled paper with him. He felt drawn there to pray. Light from lancet-shaped, stained-glass windows shone on the modest altar and communion table, lending them a golden cast. Plaques carved with the Ten Commandments, the Lord's Prayer, and the Apostle's Creed hung on the walls. Instead of pews, padded oak chairs faced the altar and a simple stand for reading the lessons.

Setting aside the paper, Benjamin reverently approached the

altar rail and sank onto the kneeling pad to pray, elbows on the railing, hands clasped, eyes closed. He thanked God that Mr. Hardy had not been injured more seriously or killed, and prayed for his complete recovery. He prayed for the safety of everyone on the island. He also asked God to comfort Miss Wilder in her grief over the loss of a beloved family pet. Had the old dog really died of natural causes? Ben believed so. Hoped so.

While he was there, he also prayed for wisdom. He'd found no trace of a newer will and had no idea where next to look. Was it time to admit defeat?

The door creaked open, and Benjamin looked over his shoulder.

Miss Wilder entered the quiet room, book in hand, and hesitated upon seeing him there.

"Sorry to disturb you. I did not know anyone was in here. I can leave and let you—"

He rose and turned to her. "No, please join me."

She walked forward. "So you have discovered our little chapel."

"Yes. I hope you don't mind."

"Of course not. It is used too rarely, though Mr. Truelock comes here once a month to read prayers and administers communion on holy days."

She lifted the volume in her hand. "I only came to return a prayer book. Rose read from it for a little graveside service we had for Hamish. I suppose you think that terribly silly."

"Not at all. I am sorry for your loss."

"Thank you. I certainly hope I didn't somehow poison him."

Me too. Ben gestured toward the chairs. She sat, and he took the chair beside her.

"How is Mr. Hardy?" she asked.

"Better. His pain has lessened."

"Good. Were you praying for him?"

"Yes, and for help and wisdom."

"Help in finding the truth?" she asked.

"Yes."

She looked at him earnestly. "Do you really believe the truth sets us free?"

"I do."

"Oh, what must it be like to be free." She closed her eyes. "To trust God and not be trapped by fear and worry."

He hesitated, then reached for her hand. "I understand . . . and I'll pray for you."

"Thank you."

Miss Wilder shifted uneasily, and he let his hand drop. She asked, "How are things going with the search for the will?"

Benjamin shook his head. "I wish I had better news for you, especially after the loss of Hamish. But I have been through all the papers in the study and have not found a will or trust amendment that supersedes the one naming Percival Norris trustee and Robert Hardy his successor."

Isabelle slowly nodded. "I knew it was unlikely. Still, I did hope . . ."

"Anywhere else I can look?" he asked. "Your parents' bed-chamber? A writing desk?"

"I have searched there already. Papa did have an old writing slant he used when traveling, but when I looked, it was empty."

"You told me all their belongings were returned after the accident. Their baggage and personal effects?"

"Yes. Everything, I believe. Even the ruined traveling chariot, though I could not bring myself to look closely."

He stole a sheepish glance at her and admitted, "I looked at it. I hope you don't mind."

"Abel mentioned that. Did you find anything?"

"I'm afraid not."

She sighed. "Too bad, though not surprising after all this time."

Benjamin picked up the roll of paper from the chair beside him, hesitated, and then cleared his throat. "I thought you might want to see this. I hope it is not too morbid or upsetting."

She accepted it from him, eyebrows high. "What is it?"

He made no answer.

As she slowly unrolled the paper, he held one edge to help her spread out the charcoal rubbing.

She drew in a sharp breath, staring down at the headstone rendering in . . . shock? Wonder? Grief? Ben was not sure.

He began to think he had erred and that his idea had been an unfeeling one. "I'm sorry. I hoped it would be a comfort, but if I was wrong, pray excuse me."

Miss Wilder looked up at him, tears in her wide blue eyes. "On the contrary, Mr. Booker. I can't tell you what it means to see it again. I barely remember the inscription I chose so long ago in a muddle of grief, let alone what it looks like." She nodded to the emblem of the weeping willow. "The stone carver suggested it. A common symbol of grief, I know, but how much more meaningful it seems to me now."

She reached out and pressed his hand, the released corner curling. "Thank you, Mr. Booker. It was a truly thoughtful gesture."

Mingled pleasure and self-consciousness rippled through him. "Miss Truelock kindly provided the materials."

"She did not mention it, but I shall thank her next I see her. She did tell me you laid flowers on my parents' grave. I appreciate that as well."

He felt his neck warm, his chest expand. "It was an honor. I know you would do so, if you could."

"Indeed I would," she murmured, her eyes soft and glowing as she gazed into his. The warm way she looked at him did strange and wonderful things to his heart.

The following afternoon, Constable Ray returned to let them know that old Mr. Colebrook, a netmaker, had seen a man standing on a barge with what looked like a gun aimed at the island. He saw a flash and heard the report. Ray told them he would alert the proper authorities and keep an eye out for the vessel but said there was little he could do otherwise.

Isabelle had never truly believed anyone on the island might be responsible, but Mr. Booker had seemed relieved at this confirmation that the shot had not been fired by an island resident. They were still in danger, but somehow danger from within would seem worse.

To everyone's further relief, Dr. Grant came back to see how Mr. Hardy was getting on and reported that the patient was doing well and the wound showed no sign of infection.

After that, the rest of the afternoon passed peacefully, with Abel and Captain Curtis making occasional rounds of the island like sentries. Mr. Booker suggested they begin bolting the doors and urged everyone to remain indoors as much as possible. Isabelle, however, insisted on delivering meals to the weavers as usual.

"Mr. Hardy is asking for me, or I would come with you," Mr. Booker said. "At least take Jacob with you."

"Very well." Isabelle agreed and waved him on his way, telling him she would be fine. She had always been safe on Belle Island and hoped that would never change.

Jacob and Ollie did accompany her out to the weaving shed, but then Mr. Linton, the foreman, asked for the young man's help with something, so Isabelle walked back with only Ollie's protection, such as it was. As usual the pup ran off in futile chase of a squirrel. *Watchdog, indeed.*

Isabelle walked inland, looking for Ollie and calling his name. How far did her voice carry? she wondered, hoping no one watched and noticed she was alone. Looking nervously out at the river, she saw only a passing fishing boat. *All is well*, she told herself.

Reaching the stream, Isabelle again stood on the small stone bridge, surveying the familiar scene: lagoon, statue, and boathouse beyond. No sign of her runaway pup. Belatedly aware of something out of place, her eyes swung back to the statue of her great-grandmother feeding swans. She sucked in a breath, stomach clenching. Hoping it was only a trick of the light, she quickly followed the stream, eyes riveted, breathing fast. Drawing near, she blinked and looked again. No trick.

The statue was missing its head.

A shiver ran over her, and she pressed a hand to her mouth. The sight that had compelled her forward now repelled her. She backed away, her panicked mind faltering for explanation. An accident? A recent lightning storm? No. It would not do. Someone had done this intentionally.

She stumbled over a tree root, righted herself, and ran back to the manor house. Ollie appeared from the direction of the stables, bounding after her as though in a game of chase. Reaching the garden door, she let them both inside and slammed it behind her.

"Ma'am?"

Isabelle whirled, a gasp escaping her. "Oh, sorry. You startled me."

One of the housemaids stood there, eyes wide. "Are you all right?"

"Yes, um. I will be. Excuse me."

Still breathing hard, Isabelle climbed the stairs to her room, wishing she had heeded Mr. Booker's suggestion to bolt all the doors. Someone might have let themselves in as easily as she had just done. Enos Redknap might even now be waiting for her in some shadowy corner with whatever tool of destruction he'd used to knock the head from the statue still gripped in his beefy hand, ready to use it on her. Another shiver passed over her. *Foolish creature. No one has sneaked into your house.* It would be too risky. Jacob or any one of the servants might have caught him. No, she was letting her imagination do its frightening worst.

Reaching her private sanctuary, Isabelle closed the bedchamber door and leaned back against the heavy oak as if it were a gladiator's shield.

She was safe.

Then she saw it and gasped, instantly beginning to tremble.

There on her dressing table was the stone head. The vacant eyes silently mocked her.

Isabelle let out a little cry and yanked open the door.

"Mr. Booker!" she called instinctively, then repeated his name more urgently.

He emerged from Mr. Hardy's room at the end of the passage, concern furrowing his brow. "What is it? What's wrong?"

She waved him into her room and pointed at the offending object. "It was here when I came in. Someone put it there for me to find."

Leaving the door ajar, he crossed the room, regarding the stone more closely. "Is that . . . Is that from the statue in the lagoon?" Incredulity and anger darkened his tone.

"Yes. It's a threat. I am sure of it."

He came back to her, eyes sparking with intensity. Bracketing her trembling shoulders with his strong hands, he looked into her eyes, and she could not look away. Did not want to.

"You are going to be all right. I will do whatever it takes to protect you. And so will Abel and the captain, I know."

"But if Redknap was in my room . . . ?"

Suddenly unsteady at the thought, she felt Mr. Booker's arms wrap around her, holding her close. She laid her cheek on his chest. Hearing the thump of his steady heart, Isabelle felt warm and protected and valued.

Carlota stepped into the room. "Miss, I . . ."

Seeing the two of them embracing, her dark brows rose. "Oh. *Perdóname.*"

Mr. Booker stepped back, and whatever Lotty saw in their faces chased the coy gleam from her eyes.

"You saw it?" Lotty gestured across the room.

Isabelle nodded, the blood pounding in her head.

"Captain Curtis found it on the pier. I brought it up here to show you. I didn't want Abel to add it to the garden wall or toss it into the river, not realizing what it was."

"*You* brought it in here?"

"Yes. Who did you think . . . ? Oh!" Carlota's eyes widened. "*Lo siento.* I never meant to frighten you!"

Isabelle released a pent-up breath. "I thought your old friend Enos broke it off and left it here as a warning."

"Bah." Lotty spit out the syllable. "*Ese diablo* is no friend of mine." She looked again at the head. "But yes, you are right. I can easily believe it of him."

"What do we do now?" Isabelle asked.

"Ask a stone mason if it can be repaired."

"No, I mean about Redknap."

Eyes troubled, Lotty shrugged. They both looked to the tall lawyer.

Mr. Booker slowly nodded. "We pray he does not attempt to make good on his threat, but remain alert, in case he does."

That night, Benjamin sat on the veranda well past midnight. He realized it might not be wise to be outside alone, but he felt compelled to do something. Sitting there in the dark like a guard dog, he watched for passing boats and listened for any footfalls on the bridge but noticed nothing out of the ordinary.

Abel Curtis walked past, lantern in one hand, fowling piece in the other. The sight would have filled Ben with trepidation before the constable's report, but now it seemed reassuring.

The old man nodded in his direction. "Evening, Mr. Booker."

"Abel. You're up late."

He nodded. "Sat up with Roy and . . . a friendly game of cards. Just thought I'd make a final round before I turn in. See anything?"

"No. You?"

"All's quiet. Guess I'll head home."

"Good night."

When his footsteps faded, the quiet continued. With only the chirring of frogs for company, Ben's mind drifted. He thought about his parents, about Mr. and Mrs. Wilder, and the wrecked carriage. He thought about Enos Redknap and Mr. Hardy, and wondered if his mentor might be in danger of another attack. Or if they might all be in danger . . .

A twig snapped, and Ben started.

Across the lawn, a flash of movement caught his eye. A figure walked through a patch of moonlight before disappearing behind the house. Abel had gone home, in the opposite direction, some time ago. Benjamin rose to investigate but hesitated at the edge of the veranda, wishing he had a lamp.

As idyllic as the island seemed during the day, the atmosphere at night was altogether different. In the murky shadows, the swaying willow trees became misshapen monsters, arms bent low and dragging the ground. The water was inky black except where moonlight rippled it silver. Beneath the many trees, darkness reigned and promised danger. The strange cries of nocturnal birds sounded hauntingly over the island.

A door closed nearby. He looked back and saw Miss Wilder stepping out on the veranda.

"What are you doing?" she whispered.

"I saw someone go behind the house."

"Abel, maybe? Or Evan?"

"I don't think so."

"Well, it isn't as though we lock the bridge at night. Anyone could come over."

"Including Redknap."

"True. Why, what do you suspect?"

"Trouble. Go back inside."

"No, I will go with you. I know this island far better than you do."

"And you don't like being told what to do."

"Also true."

"Very well. But stay close." Nothing selfish in *that* request, Benjamin chided himself.

Miss Wilder stepped nearer.

A bird screeched and she jumped. Instinctively, she reached for his arm but found his hand. Or he found hers. He enveloped her fingers in his, pleased when she did not pull away.

"Sorry," she murmured. "Only a barn owl."

They walked like that, hand in hand, around the house and down the path, or at least where he believed the path to be, stumbling off course onto roots or rocks now and again.

She said, "We should have brought a lantern."

"Shh . . . What's that?" Benjamin stopped to listen.

"Don't hush me," she whispered.

"There . . . A door sliding open . . . or shut?"

"The boathouse doors," Isabelle confirmed.

"Stay here."

"No, I—"

"Please," he added earnestly.

"Very well," she whispered back. "But be careful."

Isabelle stood shivering as Mr. Booker disappeared into the darkness.

Then she heard a thud and a grunt. Something or someone fell to the ground, while other footsteps retreated.

Pulse pounding, Isabelle ran toward the boathouse, almost tripping over Mr. Booker's fallen form. "Mr. Booker! Are you all right?" She crouched next to him. In the distance she heard muffled voices and the slap of oars paddling water.

Footsteps came running. "What is it? What's happened?" Mr. Hardy appeared, lamp in hand, arm in a sling.

"Someone attacked Mr. Booker."

"Oh no. Benjamin? Can you hear me?" The older man knelt on the ground on his other side. She was surprised to see him up and about after his recent injury.

Mr. Booker groaned, reached up, and rubbed his head. "Who was it? Who hit me?"

"You didn't see who it was?"

"Too dark."

Mr. Hardy looked at her. "Miss Wilder?"

"I couldn't see either. But I heard someone in the boathouse and the sound of paddling."

Benjamin sat up with a grimace, still rubbing his head. "Goose egg rising already."

Mr. Hardy rose and turned to the boathouse. "I'll go in and have a look."

"I think whoever it was has already left by boat," Isabelle told him.

"Just in case."

Mr. Booker spoke up. "Not alone, sir. You shouldn't even be out of bed. Here, wait for me."

Isabelle protested, "Mr. Booker, perhaps you should lie still."

"I'll be all right. Always have been hardheaded."

Together she and Mr. Hardy helped Benjamin to his feet. Then Mr. Hardy handed Isabelle the lantern and pulled a small pistol from his coat pocket.

"You came armed, sir?" Benjamin asked, taken aback.

"Thought it a wise precaution. I was right to do so, apparently. One partner is dead already, I've been shot, and now another man from my firm is injured."

Together they walked toward the bank and stepped onto the pier. On the river, a boat slipped away into the dark distance, the rhythmic paddling growing faint. The boathouse doors stood open. They were too late. Or were they? Hearing a muffled cough from inside, they all stilled to listen.

"Someone is still in there," Isabelle hissed. Had the boat landed here and left a man behind? Or was the retreating boat a coincidence, unrelated to the attack?

They slipped in through the side door. Mr. Booker tucked Isabelle behind his back and helped himself to the lantern. He lifted it high, sending an arc of yellow light into the black confines of the boathouse—there the fishing boat in its watery bay, there the chaise longues at the river doors, and finally a stack of large willow hampers being stored there.

From behind the stack, a figure slowly arose, hands raised

high. Peeking out from behind Benjamin's shoulder, Isabelle gasped in alarm. Then the light illuminated the man's face.

Silas Grant, Teddy's father. Confusion and disapproval coursing through her, she stepped out from behind Benjamin.

"Miss Isabelle?" he called. "Oh, thank the Lord. I feared it were those men come back again."

"Mr. Grant . . . what are you doing in here?"

"Sleepin' up in the loft. That is, till I heard men on the pier. Then I crept down and hid behin' the hampers to see who it was."

"Why are you sleeping here?"

He looked down, shifting from foot to foot. "I'm sorry, miss. I been spendin' the evenings with my old friends, Abel and Roy, just playin' cards and talkin' of old times. But sometimes we stay up till the wee hours, and I hate to disturb Teddy after he's abed, so I've taken to sleepin' here when the nights grow late. I hope ye don't mind."

Isabelle did not like it, but politeness restrained her tongue. "I . . . I am just surprised. Did you recognize the men in the boat?"

"No. Couldn't make out their faces. I heard one call another Enos, but they were whisperin' and my heart beatin' so loud I couldn't hear everything. Afraid they would hear it too. When they left, I heard someone say, 'Next time, we'll deliver more than a warning.'"

Isabelle shuddered. Had striking Mr. Booker been another warning, as the beheaded statue had been? Beside her, Mr. Booker swayed to one side, and a low moan escaped him.

Mr. Hardy took his arm. "Come, Benjamin, let's get you into the house."

"Are ye all right, young man?" Mr. Grant asked. "Shall I summon my son?"

"No, thank you. Nothing he can do."

"He could give you something for the pain," Isabelle said.

"I think I had better keep my wits about me."

Isabelle nodded her understanding.

As they started toward the house, Mr. Grant followed. Walking beside her, he said, "Miss Isabelle, I . . . wanted to say how . . . sorry I am."

Bitterness soured her throat. "I know, Mr. Grant, but now is not the time. We need to get Mr. Booker inside."

In the lantern's light, she glimpsed the old man's crestfallen expression as he stopped in his tracks. She felt a glimmer of remorse but returned her attention to Benjamin, saying, "I shall see if there is any ice left in the icehouse. That will help with the swelling. And I'll brew some willow bark tea."

"Thank you."

Benjamin felt his mentor's inquisitive gaze slide from Miss Wilder to him and back again, and if he was not mistaken, he did not approve.

With his good arm, Mr. Hardy helped him back into the house. When Isabelle headed for the kitchen, Hardy whispered, "Do you think it wise to drink anything she prepares when two people have been poisoned and possibly a dog as well?"

"She is not the one who tried to harm me tonight. If I am in danger, it is not from her."

"Are you certain?"

"As certain as I can be." Was he? Yes. Benjamin realized he believed her. He hoped he would not live to regret trusting her—nor die doing so either. "What were you doing out there, sir? You should be resting."

"As I told you, I am worried about your safety. And mine, truth be told. I saw a lantern and a couple of shadowy figures moving about and came out to investigate."

"Did you see who it was?"

"No. Though I immediately suspected Redknap."

Ben nodded. "Did you know he and Mr. Norris were working together?"

Mr. Hardy shook his head. "Percy did tell me he was looking into ways to make the estate more profitable but did not give me the particulars. Obviously if I had known about *this*, I would have advised him against it in the strongest terms."

"Remember what Mr. Grant heard the men say? 'Next time we'll deliver more than a warning.' I wish we knew when they plan to return."

"Hopefully they won't. But I shall keep my pistol handy, just in case."

Mr. Hardy saw Benjamin to his room and then bade him good-night, adding, "I advise you to keep a fire iron at your bedside for the same reason."

A short while later, Miss Wilder came to his door, carrying a tray. "May I come in?"

"Of course."

"Has Mr. Hardy gone to bed?"

"Yes."

"How are you feeling?"

"I've been better."

"Any vertigo?"

"Thankfully not. But my head is pounding like a drum."

"Here." She set down her tray. "Willow bark tea and ice for your head."

He sipped the tea and tried not to make a face.

"Sorry, rather bitter, I know."

After he'd drunk most of it, she said, "Now, lie down. Wait, kick off your shoes first. Here, let me help you with your coat."

She tugged the snug sleeves from his arms and hung the coat over the chair. "Lie back."

He felt self-conscious and warm, curious and wary all at once. He'd never had such an attractive woman minister to him before. She sat on the edge of the bed, hair falling loose around her face. At such close proximity, he noticed how long her eyelashes were, how perfect her lips. *Steady, Booker . . .*

"Where does it hurt?"

He touched the goose egg to show her the place.

She had wrapped the ice in a cloth and gently laid it on the throbbing spot. *Ah . . . heavenly.*

"Thank you." He took her hand—it seemed quite natural to do so after all they had been through. "I just want to say that I . . . believe you. Believe you are innocent. And kind. And . . . lovely."

She looked down, but he saw her suppressed smile and blushing cheeks. "I am glad to hear it." She glanced up at him and added wryly, "But then again, you have just suffered a blow to the head. Whoever it was must have knocked you senseless."

He chuckled. "Then I may think quite differently when I recover." He held her gaze. "But I hope not."

CHAPTER

twenty-two

In the morning, Isabelle let the puppy outside, and he dashed off in merry exploration. The day was grey and overcast. Remaining on the veranda, she surveyed the river and woods, eyes keen for anything out of the ordinary. She didn't like feeling uneasy on her own island, but since Mr. Hardy had been shot, a new wariness had crept over everyone. And now that Benjamin had been attacked too . . . ? They had never locked the doors and windows before, but last night she and Jacob had bolted every last one.

The thought of Benjamin Booker sent a warm tingle through her. Mr. Booker believed her innocent. And kind. And lovely. That was a bright spot on this cloudy day.

The telltale *thud-thud* of someone crossing the bridge drew her gaze in that direction. Officer Riley strode across its span, and Isabelle's heart pounded with each step he took. *Already?* She was surprised to see him return so soon, and even more surprised to see who accompanied him—Arminda Truelock and her maid, Martha.

He lifted a document as he neared. "Miss Wilder, I have a warrant for your arrest."

Her stomach sank. She looked around her. Where was Mr. Booker? Still in bed with a headache?

As if summoned by her internal plea, he strode out of the house, Robert Hardy at his heels.

Benjamin called to the officer, "On what grounds?"

"Besides the wine bottle and the anonymous letter, I now have two witnesses who say they saw Miss Wilder off the island, traveling east on the London Road."

Isabelle felt the wind knocked from her. "What? Who saw me? Where?"

Arminda stepped forward, her face puckered in sorrow. "I am sorry, Isabelle. I thought I must have been imagining things, but Martha saw you too. I wouldn't have said anything, but Officer Riley went door-to-door in the village and asked us all outright. I could not tell Martha to lie."

Isabelle stared. "But it couldn't have been me. Where did you supposedly see me? In Riverton?"

Arminda shook her head. "In Taplow. We had been invited to attend the installation of the new vicar there. I glanced through the window of a passing carriage and thought I was seeing things. But Martha remarked upon it too."

"You saw *me* in a carriage?" Isabelle repeated. She heard the sharp skepticism in her tone and saw her friend flinch.

"Yes. A hired chariot or perhaps a post chaise. Painted yellow, at least. Hearing Martha and me exclaim, Papa turned to look as well, but the shade had been pulled closed. He chided us, certain we had both taken leave of our senses. But I wasn't so sure."

Isabelle fell heavily into a chair on the veranda. *Me, in Taplow?* How could this be when she had no memory of traveling anywhere? Again flickering images of the dream returned to her. She may have no memory of a chaise, but she did have a memory of the London townhouse. Of seeing Uncle Percival . . . dead. Was she losing her mind?

Carlota hurried out of the house, her brow lined with concern. "Miss? Are you unwell? May I bring you anything?" She scorched those gathered round her with a fierce, protective look.

"No. Nothing," Isabelle murmured, feeling dizzy and sick, and idly wondering if this was what vertigo felt like.

Isabelle's rest in the chair was short-lived.

Officer Riley said, "I am taking you with me to London, Miss Wilder. For questioning." The officer reached out and grabbed her hand, yanking her to her feet.

Mr. Booker frowned. "Easy, Riley. There's no call for rough treatment."

"Unhand her," Carlota snapped.

The officer cajoled, "Come, Miss Wilder. Don't make this harder on either of us than it has to be."

Isabelle allowed herself to be pulled along behind him, a fish on a line, her senses dazed as her mind reeled, grasping at some explanation. What was real here?

Captain Curtis appeared from around the house, gun in hand. "Belle . . . ?"

Isabelle lifted her free arm. "Don't shoot, Evan. This man is a Bow Street officer. He is only doing his duty."

They continued, the others following, the bridge looming closer. Her chest tightened, and she grew light-headed. She began to shake, light tremors quickly accelerating into vigorous trembling. On legs of jelly, she wobbled to the side and reached out, grasping for something solid to hold on to but finding only air. She craned her neck back toward the house, longing to flee there. The nausea was mounting. Clutching her chest, she panted, "Can't . . . breathe."

"Now, now, Miss Wilder. No need to be dramatic," Riley said. "No one is hurting you."

His voice became a sickening drone in her ears. She pressed her lips together tightly, trying not to be sick.

Benjamin stared at Miss Wilder, torn, stunned, defeated. She had been seen traveling to London in a chaise? And by none other than her dearest friend, the vicar's daughter? He could not conceive of a more reliable witness.

His heart deflated. He'd done it again. Again, he'd believed the protestations of innocence from a woman he found attractive.

As they neared the bridge, the color drained from Isabelle's face. Her eyes were oddly vacant, and she trembled. She looked back at the house, gazing at it with palpable longing. He saw her falter and reach out. His own hand longed to clasp hers, to assure her all would be well. But how could he? Instead he stood there in silent anguish as she fell to the ground and wrapped her arms around herself.

Officer Riley huffed a sigh. "Come, Miss Wilder. Don't make a scene. Must I carry you?"

Captain Curtis stepped forward, saying, "Shall I shoot him now?"

The officer raised his own gun. "I wouldn't try it if I were you. I can take in two as easily as one."

Miss Medina laid a quelling hand on the captain's arm. Then she knelt down and asked Miss Wilder, "Shall I fetch Rose?"

Isabelle grimly shook her head. "Don't want her to . . . see me . . . like this."

How could I have been so blind? Ben wondered. So stupid? So willing to credit her story of never leaving the island. Based on what evidence? Hearsay? The word of a suspected poisoner?

But he *had* believed her. Heaven help him, he still wanted to believe there was some other explanation—that she was the woman he'd come to admire, that she had not lied to them all, sneaked to London in a hired chaise and poisoned the man threatening her way of life, all under the guise of falling asleep in the boathouse after too much wine.

Her closest friend had seen through her claims of innocence, but he had not. Anger rose up in him. At Isabelle, yes, but mostly at himself. How had he let things get so out of hand? Ignored the evidence of the earring for so long? Stood by while she disposed of the wine?

Dr. Grant came walking over the bridge, bag in hand, frowning.

"I didn't do it," Isabelle moaned, her countenance grey now, almost green. "I don't know how to explain what they saw, but I have no memory of leaving the island. And I didn't hurt anyone!"

The doctor said nothing, just stood there, watching with an oddly detached, studious air. Benjamin almost expected him to take out a notepad and pencil and write down his observations.

"Do something!" Miss Medina shouted, looking from man to man.

How Benjamin longed to come up with some legal impediment to stop Riley from dragging her away. But if she had lied about the earring and about not leaving the island, how did he know she was not lying about poisoning Mr. Norris?

He did not.

Isabelle huddled on the ground, every muscle tight, her vision narrowing. *Do. Not. Faint*, she commanded herself. For if she fainted, then he could easily carry her over. . . .

She knew she was making a complete and utter fool of herself but felt powerless to do otherwise. *Breathe*, she told herself. *Breathe through it.* As she did so, she calmed a bit and managed to raise her head in time to see loyal Carlota send Teddy a strange, searing look.

"Dr. Grant," she said.

When he did not react, Carlota repeated more forcefully, "Dr. Grant!"

Teddy stepped forward, Adam's apple moving up and down his pale neck. He sent Carlota a withering look, then addressed the officer. "What is going on here?"

The officer explained the sighting, adding, "We know she lied about leaving the island, and I'd wager, she did so to kill Mr. Norris."

Once again, Miss Wilder beseeched those around her. "I swear to you, upon my honor, I did not leave the island."

"You did." Jaw tense, nostrils flaring, Teddy contradicted her. "You did leave."

Isabelle gasped as though her old friend had kicked her stomach.

He turned back to the officer. "But she did not know it. She thinks she is telling the truth. Can you not stop tormenting her? I took her to London. In a hired carriage."

"*El idiota . . .*" Carlota muttered.

Still on the ground, Isabelle could only stare up at him, speechless.

Mr. Booker, however, looked livid. "What? Why?"

The officer muttered, "Now, that changes things. . . ."

Teddy ignored him. "Because she was distraught not to be able to attend Rose's betrothal dinner. She'd recently said to me, 'If only I could blink my eyes and be there . . . ' I simply meant to help her do that. I knew that if I could just get her there—if she slept through the journey and awoke in a place of fond memories—everything would be well. After all, she had spent many happy seasons in London years ago. I thought I would take her into the house, give her time to wake, and then she could attend the party. A surprise for her and for Rose too. She was already dressed in a favorite gown. The journey is not so long. Of course I did not know that Percival had refused to host the dinner, that the party was, in fact, held elsewhere."

Isabelle struggled upright. Disbelief tying her tongue, she sputtered, "Did you . . . did you . . . drug me?" She could barely spit out the foul word, betrayal stunning her.

The officer gave a long, low whistle.

She raised her hand toward Mr. Booker, and he helped her to her feet to face Teddy.

Dr. Grant's expression remained shamelessly unyielding. "I am a physician, Isabelle. I know how to administer laudanum and other compounds to achieve the desired effect. I would do the same for any patient in pain. 'Drug' sounds so . . ." He grappled for the word.

"Wrong?" she supplied.

"You were perfectly safe. And you didn't even have to cross your dreaded bridge. We were in the boathouse. It was the work of a moment to carry you into the boat, cover you with a blanket, and row you to the opposite shore. I had the carriage waiting in Taplow."

"Who helped you? Who drove?"

"Why do you suggest I needed help? I am quite capable of carrying you myself and have driven my own doctor's cart for years."

She lowered her chin, eyebrows raised in doubt.

He averted his gaze and admitted, "My father drove. I thought it best not to involve postilions."

"Your father? The man who was driving when my parents met their deaths?"

His eyes flashed. "My father is perfectly able to drive. He has not had a drop since."

Shock speared her chest. "*Since?* Are you saying he was inebriated the night of the crash?"

He winced. "I don't believe he was incapacitated, but he'd a few, yes. It wasn't his fault. Your father was planning to leave in the morning, or he never would have had anything to drink. But then your mother panicked, said she couldn't wait any longer. They had to leave right then."

"It was her fault, is that it?"

Another wince. "I didn't say that. It's just . . . Look, what was he supposed to do? She was desperate to get on the road, and he was their coachman. If he confessed he'd been drinking, he feared he'd lose his place."

A chill prickled over her. "He lost it anyway. And so much more."

"I know. He should have spoken up, insisted they wait or hire a postilion in the next village. Something. But he did not. And he has regretted it every day of his life since."

"But not enough to refuse to play a part in this outlandish trick of yours."

"I convinced him it was for your own good, that it would help you, free you from the fear that traps you here."

She threw up her hands. "I don't know what to say. I am astounded." She felt wetness on her face. Cold rain drops, she realized, not teardrops. She was still too stunned to cry. Her teeth began to chatter.

Carlota stepped forward, taking her hands. "Let us move indoors. It is starting to rain, and Miss Isabelle is shivering. She's had a shock."

The officer protested, "But we are not through here. I—"

Carlota cut him off. "We can continue in the house just as well."

He objected no further, and they all went inside, gathering in the morning room. Carlota sent Jacob to the kitchen to request tea while she wrapped a wool shawl around Isabelle's shoulders and built up the fire.

Mr. Hardy and Rose joined them, and Mr. Booker quickly summarized the day's revelations for the newcomers.

Rose walked straight up to Teddy and slapped his face. "You jackanapes!" She glared at the man, then sat beside Isabelle on the sofa, protectively holding her hand.

Isabelle stole a glance and saw the bright red mark on Teddy's face. She supposed she ought to admonish the spirited, impulsive girl, but she did not.

Looking around the room, Isabelle wondered where Christopher Adair was. She guessed that at first sight of the Bow Street officer he had made himself scarce.

Teddy drew a chair close to Isabelle, but she refused to look at him. "It would have worked," he insisted. "It *should* have worked. I planned to arrive early and give you time to recover, but we were delayed and reached London later than I wanted. Once there, things went all wrong. You began to awaken too soon, so I had to give you more than I wished, and I could not understand why the house was so quiet. Where were the guests' carriages, the waiting coachmen? Had I mistaken the date or time?

"We parked in the garden behind the house and found the back door open. We carried you inside and set you on the padded bench in the passage. Father returned to the horses, while I went to find Rose or your uncle."

That's when I must have lost my earring, Isabelle thought.

He pressed his lips together before continuing. "When I found Percival in his office, I could hardly believe what I was seeing. Instead of a party, a death. I made sure there was nothing I could do for him. He was already dead, though recently. And I knew then what a mistake I'd made."

He looked at the others. "I never had any intention of getting Isabelle involved in something like that—or suspected of murder. Good heavens, how could I have foreseen it? All I knew then was that I had to get her out of there and quickly. Before someone saw us and suspected the worst."

Mr. Booker asked, "Was it you who took the wine bottle from the room?"

"Yes, I went back for it. I didn't know then that he'd been poisoned, but I didn't want anything to implicate Isabelle." He sighed. "We drove straight back, only stopping to change horses once, and how the ostlers scalded our ears to receive such frothing beasts."

His eyes slid to her again. "I'm afraid I had to give you one more dose, to get you back into the boat and to the house without you waking."

He turned again to the officer, shoulders squared. "So, yes, Miss Wilder was in London. We were both there, very briefly. But she did not kill anyone. Neither did I. Percival was already dead when we arrived."

Carlota scowled at him. "I knew something was wrong. Late that evening, I went back out to look in on her again and found the boathouse empty. I wondered if you had convinced her to go off on some romantic assignation, but no."

She turned to Mr. Booker. "I know I told you I went to see her only once, but I didn't want you to think the worst about her and the doctor. *Lo siento* . . . I'm sorry."

She continued, "I hurried back to the house, thinking I had

missed her. But her bedchamber was empty as well. I tried to sleep, but worries plagued me. I went downstairs again a few hours later and saw Dr. Grant carrying her to her room. I waited in the shadows, preparing to interrupt if need be. But he came out just a minute later and quietly closed the door. He nodded to me as though nothing was unusual, then tiptoed downstairs. I slipped into the room to make sure she was all right. I found her lying atop the bed, fully dressed and sound asleep, breathing hard and deep but otherwise well. I removed her dress, then left her to sleep."

"And what time was this?"

"According to the hall clock it was just after one."

Isabelle shook her head over and over again, staring at her old friend Teddy as though he were a stranger. "I cannot believe you would do such a thing. No wonder I felt so ill and confused the next day. And so embarrassed to think I had become *that* inebriated. I must have regained my senses at some point while I was lying on that bench and looked into Percy's office, because I saw him, dead, I know I did. Just as Mr. Booker described the scene."

She shuddered. "I thought I was going mad or having prophetic dreams. But no, I really was there. Against my will, but I really was there."

She looked tentatively at Benjamin, feeling sheepish and vindicated at once. "I am sorry, Mr. Booker. I thought I was telling you the truth."

He nodded. "I know you did."

"Thank you, God," Arminda praised. "I knew there must be some explanation. You won't try to take her to London now, will you, Officer? She hasn't done anything wrong."

"If you take anyone, it should be Grant here," Evan interjected.

He turned to Mr. Booker. "What's the penalty for abduction these days?"

"I don't know," Benjamin said. "But I will be happy to find out."

"I did not *abduct* her like some strange assailant with evil intentions," Teddy insisted. "We are friends. I took excellent care of her and returned her safely, no harm done."

Indignation burned through Isabelle. "No harm, Teddy? Really? No harm?"

The officer turned another hard gaze on the physician. "I could also charge you with withholding evidence."

Teddy stoically met his stare and said nothing.

Mr. Booker said, more kindly, "I understand why you didn't say anything for Miss Wilder's sake, but you *were* probably one of the first to stumble upon the scene of the crime."

He didn't, Isabelle noticed, mention Mr. Adair.

"Think back," Mr. Booker continued. "You must have seen something, noticed something, with that medical mind of yours, that might give us a clue to the poisoner."

"I have been trying to remember," Teddy allowed. "At the time, all I thought about was getting Isabelle out of there. Covering our tracks, for both of our sakes. I wasn't surveying the scene with a calm professional eye as I might otherwise have done."

"And now?"

He looked off into the distance, blinking as the memories shuttled past.

Benjamin prompted, "Did you hear anything? Voices? Footsteps? See another carriage waiting outside?"

"No."

Mr. Booker glanced at Officer Riley. When he remained quiet, Benjamin persisted. "Did you notice anything, something out of place or a smell . . . ?"

Teddy slowly nodded, eyes narrowed in memory. "I smelled oranges and maybe . . . pipe tobacco."

Benjamin nodded. "I did as well." He turned to Rose. "Did Mr. Norris smoke a pipe?"

Rose shook her head. "I never saw him do so."

Mr. Hardy asked him, "As a physician, to what did you attribute the cause of death?"

Theo shrugged. "I saw the gun in his hand. The wine bottle on the floor. The head wound. I supposed a robbery gone wrong or something like that. I am no coroner."

"What time were you there?"

He looked up, considering. "A little after eight. I would guess the man had been dead an hour or two."

The officer said, "And the servants found the body and raised the alarm around nine. You barely escaped in time."

Teddy lowered his head, looking sheepish for the first time.

Officer Riley nodded. "So whoever struck Mr. Norris must have done it sometime before seven o'clock, though we still don't know who it was."

Isabelle tensed, waiting for Mr. Hardy to mention Mr. Adair, but he said nothing. Had he changed his mind about the young man?

Officer Riley turned to Arminda Truelock. "And as to your question, madam, Miss Wilder is not off the hook just yet. She might not have been in London to do the deed, but she still could have poisoned the wine in advance, here on the island."

Mr. Booker argued, "Any number of people might have done so once the bottles were in the pantry in the London house."

The officer ran a frustrated hand over his face. "Which puts us back where we started."

"There is another possibility. . . ." Mr. Booker said.

He told Officer Riley about Mr. Hardy's gunshot wound

and the late-night visitors who had struck him and left the island by boat.

The officer's eyebrows rose and his mouth quirked in skepticism. "I don't suppose this phantom assailant has a name?"

"Enos Redknap."

The officer stilled, smirk fading. "Enos Redknap?"

"Have you heard of him?"

"Every officer in London has heard of him. There's a hefty reward offered for his capture. Are you sure you aren't laying the blame at his door simply to spare your lovely Miss Wilder?"

"He is telling the truth." Isabelle told the officer about Mr. Redknap's interest in using Belle Island, her refusal, and his promise to return. She did not mention Evan's role in their initial meeting.

The officer shook his head. "Well, miss. I would not wish such a dangerous enemy on anyone."

He considered, then rose. "I would be remiss not to at least search the house while I'm here with a warrant." He turned to Mr. Hardy. "But first, sir, I am glad to see you alive and well. Anything you can tell me about your assailant? Do you think the shooting was related to Norris's death?"

Hardy nodded. "I believe Enos Redknap tried to kill me. Probably killed Percival too. I'll see him hang if it's the last thing I do."

Officer Riley gestured to the hall. "Why don't you tell me all about it while I search the house?"

Hardy nodded, and the two men walked from the room.

Mr. Booker and Isabelle shared a concerned look, then followed them while the others quietly dispersed.

Officer Riley focused on the wine cellar as Benjamin and Mr. Hardy had done. Isabelle held her breath as he searched, waiting for him to come upon the poison as Benjamin had, and for her ordeal to begin all over again. But he found nothing, and neither Benjamin nor Mr. Hardy mentioned the poison. She wondered why.

"Any more bottles of orange wine?" Riley asked, looking around the cellar and surveying the bins.

With a nervous glance at the lawyers, she said, "I am afraid not."

"No?"

"No. I drank some, and then I . . ."

Mr. Booker spoke up. "We decided to pour out the rest, as a precaution, so no one else would be hurt. If that was wrong, you can blame me."

"I see." Riley looked from her to the lawyer standing nearby. "Oh yes, I do."

They walked back to the drawing room, where the officer heaved a long-suffering sigh. "Well, apparently I return to London empty-handed a second time, which will not please the magistrate. But at least I can report on this new development with Redknap. If I can catch him, the magistrate will be a happy man, and I a rich one. But don't imagine I am through with you lot. After all, there is still the matter of who struck Mr. Norris."

Christopher Adair stepped into the room, face pale but resolved. "I did."

Officer Riley took a statement from Mr. Adair, but Benjamin argued that since the coroner's report confirmed his blow was not what killed Mr. Norris, and since the young man had acted in self-defense, that he should not be hauled off like a murderer.

In the end, Riley reluctantly agreed to leave without Adair but warned the young man that he would face consequences for his actions, at least a battery charge and perhaps even manslaughter. Benjamin doubted a jury would convict him of a manslaughter charge, assuming Adair had a good lawyer and the services of a skilled barrister. Time would tell.

After Officer Riley left, Isabelle went to lie down to recover from her ordeal, and Benjamin and Mr. Hardy retreated to the study for a private word.

"Are you all right, sir?" Benjamin asked. "Feeling ill or weak?"

"Not too bad. Why?"

"You were rather quiet during all that. And you were shot, after all."

Robert Hardy shrugged, though he did indeed look tired.

Benjamin persisted, "I was surprised you did not jump at the chance to mention the poison we found or to reveal Adair's actions."

Hardy replied evenly, "Riley found no poison during his search."

Benjamin wondered why. It was of course possible Miss Wilder had removed it when she'd removed the remaining wine bottles. But Ben didn't like to think she would.

Hardy continued. "Besides, many people keep rat poison in their cellars. As you said, it doesn't necessarily mean anything. And after her performance today when being forced to the bridge—"

"You think it was an act?"

The older man pursed his lips. "At first I thought it might be, but a gentlewoman of her character and breeding, acting in such an undignified manner . . . ?" Hardy shook his head. "Can you imagine my Cordelia behaving in such a fashion? No. Not if she could help it.

"Miss Wilder may suffer from some sort of hysteria, but I don't see her as a killer. Not anymore. And clearly you do not." His eyes glinted knowingly. "You're quite besotted with her—I think."

"If I were, you would disapprove."

"Perhaps. But it is quite natural. She is a beauty and a lady."

Shifting awkwardly, Benjamin asked, "And Adair?"

Hardy waved a hand. "He is barely more than a boy. I took him aside and advised him it would go better for him if he came forward himself. Apparently, he heeded my advice. A surprise—the young so rarely do."

Remembering how stunned Mr. Hardy had been to learn someone had struck his friend, Benjamin was all the more impressed by the merciful gesture. "That was good of you, sir."

"I might have done the same in his place had Percival pointed a gun at me."

Hardy sighed and stared out the window. When he spoke again, his tone had changed, almost as if talking to himself. "A man doesn't deserve to have his entire life ruined—or ended—because of the irrational actions of another."

Benjamin studied his mentor's profile, intrigued by this change of heart. What had prompted it? He'd thought his mentor was set against Miss Wilder and disliked the young man. Had he been wrong? Misjudged Mr. Hardy's intent?

After Mr. Hardy returned to his room to rest, Benjamin found himself thinking of his father again. Had he been unjust in his conclusions and criticisms of the man—misjudged him too?

Benjamin thought back. When he'd first gone to work for the law firm as a temperamental youth, he had secretly liked hearing Mr. Hardy's thinly veiled criticisms of his father's profession. But when Mr. Hardy had murmured some sly comment about patent medicines or equated apothecaries to quacks, a retort would sometimes arise in Benjamin's mind. *"Not my father, sir. He would never do anything harmful to his patients."* But his rebuttals, left unvoiced, were eventually silenced in his mind as well.

Ben again recalled Mr. Hardy praising him for charting his own course in life. But now he wondered . . . Had he charted his own course, or followed wherever Robert Hardy led?

Because the truth was, with years and maturity, Benjamin had come to realize his father was far more than a shopkeeper or peddler of patent medicines, despite Mr. Hardy's jokes. He knew the people in their neighborhood admired and depended on his father to treat their ailments and care for their children.

How many Christmases had Benjamin been home, sitting over the Christmas goose with Reuben and their parents, when a knock sounded at the door and old Betty came and whispered her master's help was needed? He might have groaned and risen begrudgingly with a longing look at the mince pie and pudding yet to come, but he *had* gone. Mamma had helped him on with his greatcoat, kissed his cheek, and assured him they would save a big piece of each for his return. When Reuben grew older, he had often gone along. But not Benjamin.

How much time with his father he had missed, and how unfair of him to belittle his profession because he wasn't as adept at it as he and Reuben were. He had some apologizing to do, Ben realized. This Christmas, he promised himself, would be one of peace and joy with his family. *Lord, let it be so.*

That night, Benjamin read in bed, determined to finish *The Notorious Highwayman.*

As Joe had told him, the charming highwayman, perhaps grown a bit too cocksure of himself, held up the same gentleman's chaise a second time.

Ordering all to "Stand and deliver," he disarmed the guard and took the ladies' jewels while the dandy just sat there, impotent and humiliated once more, or so it seemed.

Growing impatient, the highwayman prodded him with the muzzle of his gun, urging, "Come, my little friend, before a brace of balls makes the sun shine through your belly."

"Wh-what do you w-want?" the dandy faltered.

"Your purse, fool, your purse."

"I have tucked it away."

"Well, draw it out, man, and be quick. I haven't got all day."

And the dandy opened his secret compartment and drew out not a purse but a flintlock pistol, and with it shot the highwayman straight through the heart.

Suddenly Benjamin sat up straight, book forgotten. *Secret compartment . . . ?*

Why had he not thought of it before? It was exactly because of the prevalence of highway robberies a few decades earlier that carriage makers began building concealed compartments into their carriages to protect valuables.

He recalled coming across a faded document in Mr. Wilder's files, an invoice for a traveling chariot from a Windsor carriage maker, detailing the size and custom specifications. Might they have included just such a compartment? He decided to investigate that possibility at his first opportunity.

twenty-three

The next day dawned grey and rainy, which perfectly suited Isabelle's mood.

She sat in her father's study, facing their former coachman—the man who had driven her parents to their deaths. Mr. Booker stood beside her. He had agreed to join her without question. But secretly, she needed his strength more than any legal advice.

Mr. Grant stood before her, hat in gnarled hands, balding head bowed.

"I'm sorry, miss. Awful sorry. If I could go back an' do different, I would. If I coulda lost my life in their place, I would."

Isabelle took a deep breath, steeling herself. "I know you feel badly, Mr. Grant. I will try to forgive you, but it will be difficult. I don't want to add to your pain, but learning you were inebriated that night has added to mine. It was not an unforeseeable, unavoidable accident as I have thought all these years, but a preventable one caused by an incapacitated driver."

He grimaced. "I thought I could manage it. Almost did. But that mail coach come outta nowhere, its lamps not lit. The driver were runnin' behind and let the tapers run low 'stead 'a stoppin' to replace 'em. I should 'ave noticed the coach sooner. Perhaps I would 'ave, had my head been clearer. Don't know. How many times I've sifted through those few seconds . . . wonderin' if I could 'ave avoided it somehow."

He slowly shook his head, bending his hat brim. "I know it's my fault, at least mostly. Not tryin' to shift blame. But it's hard to live with."

"That I can well imagine."

"I'm awful sorry," he repeated.

"I am too."

He hesitated, then looked up at her beseechingly. "If ye want to take me to the magistrate, I'll go willing-like. I've not had a drop to drink since that night, and I've given up drivin'. Only drove to London because Teddy said it would help ye. I'd do anything to help ye, if I could. If there was any way I could make up for what I did, for what I cost ye. But there ain't, I fear."

"No, I'm afraid not."

She glanced at Benjamin. "I will talk to my lawyer. I doubt there is anything to be gained by pressing for charges at this point, but I shall let you know. Good day."

He nodded, murmuring "Miss," and turned toward the door.

Mr. Booker called after him. "May I ask one question before you go?"

The old man turned back.

"Miss Wilder believes her father wrote a new will before setting out on that journey. Do you happen to know anything about that?"

The grizzled head nodded. "Aye. Asked me and the groom to sign it, Mr. Wilder did. He meant to deliver it to the lawyers after we met the ship at the London docks. Sadly, that never happened." He looked down at his hands.

Isabelle was glad for this confirmation, though it still didn't explain where the document was now.

Mr. Booker said, "That will has never been found."

Mr. Grant looked up in surprise. "No? That's odd. I'm afraid I don't know anything else about it."

"Well, thank you anyway."

The man slunk from the room, head bowed, the picture of shame and defeat.

When they were alone, Isabelle sighed and looked up at Benjamin. "I suppose you think I was too hard on him."

"You were honest. It will take time to get over this new blow."

"Yes, well, thank you for being here."

Benjamin considered the situation. "I think it would be very difficult to get a conviction on the elder Grant after so many years, and without any witnesses except his own confession, but if you want to pursue it, I . . ."

"I don't think so. He has punished himself enough. Served ten years of self-torment and self-inflicted exile."

Benjamin nodded. "And his son? You could charge the doctor with abduction."

She looked thoughtfully out the rain-streaked window to the river beyond. Something wasn't right. . . . With a frown she rose and moved closer, leaning nearer the glass. The water level had risen.

Forcing her thoughts back to the topic at hand, she inhaled deeply, then made her decision. "No formal charges, I don't think. Dr. Grant believed he was doing something 'for my own good' and did return me safely, as he said. But he had to know it was wrong. One doesn't act so secretive and sneaky otherwise."

"So what will you do?"

She turned from the window. "Leave that to me."

Isabelle wrote a note to Dr. Grant, asking him to meet with her. Jacob delivered it to the physician's office and returned wet through for his efforts.

"Thank you, Jacob. Sorry to send you out in the rain. Why don't you go down to the kitchen, ask Mrs. Philpotts for a cup of chocolate, and sit near the fire. You'll be warm and dry soon enough."

"Yes, miss. Thank you. Sounds a treat."

In the meantime, Isabelle kept returning to the window to look out at the river. The rain shower continued—normal for spring, she reminded herself, but the water was definitely rising.

Carlota joined her there, wringing her hands.

Isabelle sought to reassure her. "The river rises every few years, Lotty. Don't worry."

Carlota shook her head. "Jacob saw old Mr. Colebrook in the village. His joints are warning him something fierce. There's a storm coming, he says, the likes of which we've not seen in years."

"Willy Colebrook likes to be dramatic, Lotty. He's exaggerating."

As if to contradict her, the wind began to blow, bending the trees and chasing leaves across the ground. Ominous grey clouds gathered, churning the sky, and the former shower became a cascade. She repeated the same reassurance to herself, hearing her father's voice as she did so. *"The river rises every few years, Isabelle. Don't worry."*

Even so, she shivered.

A couple of hours later, Isabelle received her old friend in her father's study, the desk between them to shield her heart and trembling hands.

Theodore Grant stood before her, damp top hat in pale fingers, auburn head bowed. She was struck by the similarities between this and the recent, awkward scene with his father.

"I am sorry, Isabelle."

"Sorry it didn't work, or sorry you were caught?"

He flinched. "Both. I really did think I could help you."

"Fix me, I think you mean. Change me. Like one of your patients with a chronic illness or addiction. I am the patient with a mental disorder you were certain you could cure in time."

He looked up, green eyes wide. "Of course I wanted to help you. I care for you, Isabelle. You know I do. As a friend, and possibly as . . . more."

She bit the inside of her cheek, clamping down her emotions. Then she said, "*Possibly* being the salient word. I used to wonder what you were waiting for. Arminda, Rose, even Lotty, asked me why you didn't propose. Why a man with your ability and ambition was apparently content to stay here and practice in tiny Riverton, having to stitch wounds and lance goiters and everything else that needs doing, instead of moving to Edinburgh to join a large, prestigious practice.

"Arminda suggested that perhaps you thought you were not good enough, not yet established enough to marry. But as the years passed, that excuse grew rather spindly. Rose, ever the romantic, said you were not sure of my affections, if only I would show myself willing, make some grand romantic gesture, then you would be spurred to act. Only Carlota doubted your affection for me."

She slowly shook her head. "Another answer lingered in the back of my mind, but I didn't want to believe it. We were friends. We were fond of one another. Even . . . loved one another, I thought. But the truth was there all along. It wasn't that you thought you were not good enough for me, but that

I was not good enough, not *whole* enough, for you. You were waiting not to further establish your practice but to cure me. You would not marry me as I was—imperfect, trapped by my fears, and evidence of your failure to heal a patient."

He spread his hands. "Is that so wrong—to want to cure you, to want to not be limited to this island for the rest of my life? Yes, I am ambitious. I want to practice elsewhere. But I want to take you with me, as my wife. So I waited. Hoped. Tried. But patience, understanding, and encouragement had no effect, so—"

"So you took matters into your own hands. Devised a new experiment, like on one of your caged mice. Yes, I see. Well, your experiment failed."

"Isabelle, I still think we—"

She raised a palm. "No. There is no 'we' without trust."

She rose and faced him squarely. "I think it is time, Dr. Grant. Time for you to accept that partnership in Edinburgh. Time for you to take all of your frustrated ambition and modern methods somewhere far away, where they might be better appreciated. I won't press for charges unless you return."

For a moment he stood there, studying her face for any crack in her resolve, biting his lip as he waited.

She did not move a muscle.

Then his shoulders slumped, and he nodded. "More than fair."

He reached toward her but then let his hand fall back to his side without touching her. "Well. Good-bye, Isabelle."

"Good-bye, Dr. Grant," she coolly replied, but her disillusioned, battered heart silently cried, *Good-bye, Teddy, my oldest friend, confidant, and companion. How lonely I shall be without you.*

She listened to his receding footfalls, then stepped to the

window. From there, she watched him walk away through the rain, over the bridge, and out of her life.

Isabelle retreated to her room to collect herself. Carlota was there, again standing at the window.

The water had risen to the top of the bank, the current moving fast, the color a malevolent brackish grey. The wind continued to howl, blowing the rain sideways.

Carlota said, "I've never seen it like this before. The current seems almost . . . angry and carrying along so much flotsam."

Concern increasing, Isabelle decided to talk to Abel, who was always a voice of calm reason—when he spoke at all. Knowing an umbrella would be useless in such gusts, Isabelle donned her brother's long storm coat instead and went outside. The water was beginning to creep up the lawn. Farther out, the usual fishing boats and eel skiffs were absent. No netmakers sat on the opposite shore. Even the ducks and grebes had flown elsewhere, looking for shelter. In the paddock, she saw the London carriage horses jigging and tossing their heads, uneasy in the storm.

She found her groundsman with the sheep, trying to soothe the restless, bawling ewes.

"They don't like this weather, and neither do I," Abel said. "Time to take them inland. Sir John's steward won't mind, not with it raining hatchets and hammers."

Isabelle nodded. "Can you bring the horses into the stables first? Get them to settle down? We may need them to pull the chaise later."

"I shall try. Maybe Evan can help me." He looked around to no avail and then started to the paddock on his own, just as Mr. Grant appeared, collar turned up, water dripping from his hat brim.

He sent her a pained look, then quickly averted his gaze. "I can help with the horses."

Isabelle hesitated, then stifled her refusal. Silas Grant was famously good with horses, and Abel and the sheepdog would have their work cut out for them trying to herd the panicked sheep over the bridge.

"Very well." She knew the man was desperate to make amends, but even so the words *thank you* stuck in her throat.

Mr. Grant calmed the carriage horses enough to put leads on them and led them into the relative safety of the stables.

Safe for how long?

As soon as Benjamin was free, he retrieved the file and read the old invoice for a custom-built traveling chariot more closely. The special features included a rooftop imperial—which was a storage space over the roof, like a large, built-in valise—and inside the chariot, velvet upholstery and a concealed security compartment. Had Abel Curtis known of this compartment and looked there already? Probably. Such features were fairly common, he supposed, though he did not know from personal experience as no one in his family had ever owned such a fine carriage.

Studying the diagram once more, he decided to go outside for another look.

Dashing through the rain with a lantern a few minutes later, he passed Mr. Grant on the path and was surprised to find Miss Wilder just leaving the stables, the carriage horses in stalls behind her.

Something in his expression must have caught her attention, for she asked, "What is it?"

"Probably nothing," he replied, not wanting to raise her hopes, or his.

Even so, she followed him back inside.

He explained, "The traveling chariot had a hidden compartment. I thought I'd try to find it, just in case." He glanced over at her. "Are you sure you want to see it again?"

"No." She continued to follow him anyway.

Benjamin led the way to the last stall and hung the lantern on a hook. As he removed the tarpaulins, she held back, hovering outside the gate.

"I didn't think it would affect me so, not after all this time." She swallowed. "I was wrong."

He pulled open the carriage door again and searched for the concealed compartment. Running his hand beneath the bench, his fingers found a small latch. He pulled and pushed and felt it release, but the drawer did not open. "I'll need a crowbar or something."

"There are tools in the tack room."

She led the way and opened the door. He selected a few metal tools and carried them back to the carriage. The first was too thick, but the second file slipped into the groove, and he was able to pry open the drawer.

"Anything?"

"Yes. Not sure what though." Using his fingernails, he peeled up a corner of the lining and extracted the drawer's contents— folded paper. It could be anything, he reminded himself. He carried it to the lantern for better light.

She followed him. "What is it?"

Benjamin looked over the page, scanning the handwriting that had become familiar after reviewing so many pages of correspondence in Mr. Wilder's office. Holding his breath, he turned the page over. Was it signed? Dated?

Exultation filled him.

"His last will and testament. He still bequeaths the estate

to be managed through the trust with Mr. Norris as trustee, but only until you reached your majority, at which point, you and Rose, through Grace, become heirs outright and the trust is terminated."

"Yes!" She raised her hands in victory, then threw them around his neck in an exuberant embrace.

He reacted without thinking, his arms encircling her waist, drawing her close. For a moment, they stood like that, Benjamin's heart pounding, breathing in the sweet smell of her hair and relishing the narrowness of her waist.

She glanced up at him, and he sank deep into her beautiful blue eyes, tempted to kiss her.

He leaned closer, but then Miss Wilder seemed to recall her surroundings . . . or her companion . . . and stepped back with an awkward little laugh. "Sorry."

"Don't be."

Her tongue darted over her lips. "Is it legal?"

Kissing you? he thought. *It should be.* Then he cleared his throat. "I think so. It is signed by your father and witnessed by Silas Grant and a . . ." He squinted to read the scrawled signature. "Will Tompkins?"

"He was a groom here."

"Just as Mr. Grant said." Benjamin read further, then stated, "With this document, we should be able to revoke the trust or at least establish you as the sole trustee."

"Thank God."

"Yes. And thank your father. Well, I had better show this to Mr. Hardy. But we'll talk later, all right?"

"Yes, of course." She smiled tremulously and left the stable before him.

He covered the chariot and walked out after her, his heart still thumping, which had little to do with the excitement of the find.

Returning to the house, he found Mr. Hardy in the study and showed him the newer will.

The more seasoned attorney reviewed the hurriedly composed lines, the somewhat scrawled handwriting, and barely legible signatures.

He knit his brow. "I don't know, Ben. I am not certain this will stand up in court. Especially when compared to the entire, professionally drafted document. After all, Miss Wilder was only twenty when her father wrote this, and he was clearly rushed and harried and perhaps not thinking clearly. It is possible we can convince a judge, of course, but I would not want you to raise Miss Wilder's hopes prematurely."

Ben wondered fleetingly if Mr. Hardy had changed his mind about wanting to serve as trustee. Either way, his mentor's caution deflated Ben's exhilaration. Yet he hesitated to tell Miss Wilder of Mr. Hardy's concerns. He had liked seeing her so happy, especially after the sad losses of the family pet and her oldest friend, not to mention worries about Redknap and the flood. He had also liked the warm admiration shining in her eyes when she'd embraced him and thanked him for finding it. Would it really all be for nothing? He hoped not.

How ironic, Isabelle thought, to finally find the newer will naming her mistress of the estate, just when she was in danger of losing it to a flood.

The rain continued to fall, the water to rise, and Isabelle to pace. She, Carlota, and the housemaids had already carried as many family heirlooms as they could from the ground floor to the higher floors. Just in case. But surely the water wouldn't reach the house.

Looking for comfort and wisdom, Isabelle pulled out her

memorabilia box, opened her father's New Testament and Psalms, and skimmed through its well-worn pages. Why had she not done so before? Three verses in the Psalms leapt out at her.

God is our refuge and strength, a very present help in trouble. Therefore will not we fear, though the earth be removed, and though the mountains be carried into the midst of the sea. Though the waters roar and be troubled.

The words seemed to carry equal parts comfort and warning. Troubled waters, indeed.

She turned next to the New Testament. Where was that verse Mr. Booker's mother so often quoted when anxiety struck . . . ? Flipping pages, she finally reached Paul's letter to the Philippians and drew in a breath of surprise. There it was, in the fourth chapter. Underlined in ink by her own father. There all the time.

Be careful for nothing; but in every thing by prayer and supplication with thanksgiving let your requests be made known unto God. And the peace of God, which passeth all understanding, shall keep your hearts and minds through Christ Jesus.

"Thank you . . ." Isabelle whispered, and she prayed to her heavenly Father for the first time in far too long.

Later, she went down to the kitchen to gather the midday meal for the weavers. There, she heard old Roy Howton and Mrs. Philpotts debating the likely causes of the flood: heavy snow in the winter, late melt, changes in the tide, rain . . . perhaps all of the above.

Noticing her, Mrs. Philpotts said, "I already sent Jacob down with the hamper, miss. You shouldn't be going out in this."

"That was kind of you both, though I would not have minded." In fact, Isabelle could remain indoors no longer. Again slipping into her brother's storm coat, she went outside and walked around the island in the rain, surveying the encroaching water.

When she reached the weaving shed, she saw Mr. Linton inside lifting tools and supplies to higher shelves. Around the room, the weavers were still trying to work, though their nervous glances at the ever-nearing water showed they were struggling to concentrate. Isabelle couldn't blame them.

Mr. Linton approached her and lowered his voice. "Told you we should have built it on higher pilings."

"Yes, you did. But it's too late for reproaches about the past. What do we do now?"

"Get all the completed baskets out of here and the boathouse before they're ruined."

"Can't willow withstand water?"

"Not foul floodwaters. They'll be moldering and rank if they sit in that muck. Unsellable."

Dread filled Isabelle at the thought. "We have orders for those baskets. And we will need the revenue to pay next year's cutters."

He nodded. "All the more reason to get them out of here."

"Abel has yet to return from herding the sheep inland, but Jacob and Roy could help, and the weavers, if they are able."

"I'll help too," Mr. Booker said, striding around a large puddle to join them. He was wearing a familiar oilcloth coat.

Seeing her studying it, he said apologetically, "I assume it's your father's. I asked if there was an oilskin I could borrow and this is what Adair's valet found. I hope you don't mind."

"Not at all. I am glad to see you . . . in it."

Silas Grant rode up in the wagon. How strange to see their old coachman with reins in his hands once more. Disapproval swept over her, but she decided this was not the time to refuse anyone's help.

Mr. Linton called, "Let's form a line."

As the weavers moved into place, Isabelle saw the expectant Jenny and her mother and said kindly, "You go on home, Jenny, and you too, Mrs. Winkfield."

"Nothing doing. We want to help."

The weavers, along with Mr. Booker, Jacob, and Roy Howton, formed a line between the shed and the wagon. Evan Curtis and Carlota soon joined them, wading into the ankle-deep water.

Isabelle noticed Mr. Christie, the blind basket-maker, hesitating near the stacks of precious baskets in the shed.

"Mr. Christie . . . perhaps you had better make your way to higher ground?" Isabelle suggested. "Joe would escort you, I'm sure."

"While all of our work is washed away? No, thank you, Miss Wilder. I will stay and help. I am not an invalid."

Isabelle felt her cheeks heat. "Of course not, I didn't mean to imply you were, but—"

"Right here, Mr. Christie," Evan called. "We could use another man in line."

Joe led him to a place between Roy and Evan, and Mr. Christie extended his capable hands to Roy, accepted the large woven hamper handed to him, swiveled, and placed it into Evan's hands as quickly and efficiently as anyone there.

After a few minutes, Isabelle saw Rose and Mr. Adair making their way gingerly toward them, huddled together under a futile umbrella. They skirted the lake that had formerly been the path, her niece's eyes wide in concern. "Aunt Belle, do you need more help?"

Mr. Adair looked from the muddy water to his polished boots with a pinched expression. "Looks dangerous, my love."

Isabelle took pity on the young dandy. "Perhaps you two had better go and pack. Might be wise to be ready to leave. Just in case."

"Surely you don't think the water will reach the house."

"I didn't think it would reach this shed, and I was wrong. The ground is lower here, but I don't want to take any more risks."

"Come, my dear." Mr. Adair took Rose's arm and turned her back. "We shall help O'Toole and Manvers pack our things."

"Rose?" Isabelle called after her. "Warn everyone in the house to be ready to leave if the water continues to rise."

"I will."

"Mrs. Philpotts is packing up the silver and will alert the kitchen staff and housemaids. But Mr. Hardy may not realize what's going on."

"I'll find him and make sure he knows."

"Thank you." Isabelle turned back to the task at hand.

She surveyed the human chain, and her chest expanded with fondness and gratitude. The baskets her family of weavers had so carefully crafted were now being conveyed to safety by several people dear to her, including, she realized, Mr. Booker.

Her gaze rested on him and her heart thumped. He had removed his outer coats and worked in waistcoat and shirt-sleeves. Again and again he hefted a stack of baskets or a large hamper into the wagon. His hair fell over his forehead and his face glistened with sweat. He had never looked more handsome.

-◦❦ CHAPTER ❦◦-
twenty-four

Two hours later the baskets had been loaded, and Mr. Grant had driven them to the Faringdons' barn for safekeeping. Their work party broke up, Jacob and Carlota returning to the house, and the weavers and tenants leaving for their own homes—Roy Howton leading Mr. Christie, while Evan Curtis disappeared over the bridge with the weavers. She was surprised he would leave his father . . . and Lotty, at such a time and briefly wondered what he was doing, but soon more pressing concerns crowded out the thought.

Mr. Booker remained nearby, gathering his discarded coats and wrestling them on again. When the wagon returned, Isabelle was surprised to see Abel at the reins instead of Mr. Grant.

As Abel neared, he explained, "Silas stopped to secure a room at the inn for the Howtons. Roy's missus is poorly, as you know, and the tenant cottages are close to the water."

She swallowed hard at the thought and made do with a nod.

"He said he'd also make sure the boat was secured so it doesn't float away like so many have already."

"Good idea." Mr. Grant was certainly determined to help her. A bud of gratitude, of forgiveness, sprouted in her heart.

Abel hesitated, puckering his brow uncertainly. He sent an uneasy glance toward Mr. Booker and lowered his voice. "And I thought you should know, miss. I don't know what Evan is up to, but I saw him calling to some men in a sailing barge—that Redknap fellow among them. They were trying to dock at Riverton, but the pier is under water."

Isabelle's pulse accelerated, and she and Mr. Booker exchanged raised-brow looks. So . . . Enos Redknap and his crew were still nearby. Why was Evan hailing them? She hoped he was urging them to leave.

After Abel moved on with the wagon, Mr. Booker went indoors, saying he was going to warn Mr. Hardy. Isabelle lingered outside, surveying the rising water. She watched the menacing flow with trepidation and saw the flotsam both Abel and Lotty had mentioned: branches and rowboats driven loose from their moorings and there, a bloated sheep. *Ugh*. Her stomach twisted at the sight.

Realizing the tenant cottages might be in danger, Mr. Truelock came over to offer Mr. Christie the spare room in the vicarage for as long as needed.

Isabelle thanked him and returned to the house. Venturing belowstairs, she found Mrs. Philpotts in a panic, she and the kitchen maids scurrying about with mops and buckets. "Water in the cellar and coming into the larder. Kitchen's next."

Oh no . . . Isabelle was torn. Did she set the servants to work on setting up barricades and bailing water, or did she send them to higher ground?

She thought again of what her father had once told her, describing a terrible flood years before, when he and his parents had been trapped in the house as the water drew closer and closer to the doors.

But the water was already in the house . . . at least below-stairs. Did that mean this flood was even worse? What now? She could not bear the thought of damage to her beloved home, but she would not put anyone else in harm's way.

"Mrs. Philpotts, please instruct the staff to gather their important possessions and go to their families' homes or, if they haven't somewhere else to go, to the inn in Riverton until the flood passes."

"Are you sure, miss?"

"Yes. Hurry."

"And what will you do?" the older woman asked, concern deepening the lines on her face.

"Don't worry about me. This is only a precaution. The house has withstood many storms and floods over the years and will withstand this one as well, no doubt. But just in case, make sure everyone gets out." Isabelle looked around the kitchen for her puppy. "Have you seen Ollie?"

"Not in some time, miss. And what about our guests?"

"Mr. Booker went to find Mr. Hardy, but I'll make sure everyone knows."

Going upstairs, she stopped at the bedchambers one by one.

She found Mr. Adair scolding his valet for careless packing while at the same time urging him to hurry. In Rose's room, capable Miss O'Toole latched the final valise.

"Where is Rose?" Isabelle asked.

"Said she was going to look for the dog."

"Good. Well, it looks like you're almost ready to depart. Thank you, O'Toole. Don't forget to pack her mother's jewelry. Just in case."

She turned to go, but O'Toole blurted, "I doubt I shall ever see you again, miss."

Isabelle started and turned back. Was the woman predicting her demise? "Of course you will."

"I don't know. . . . After my mistress marries, I fear she will want a more skilled lady's maid, or the Adairs will engage some fashionable French woman, and I"—her voice hitched—"I shall be dismissed."

Compassion swelling in her breast, Isabelle stepped nearer and squeezed the woman's hand. "My dear Miss O'Toole, Rose depends on you and has never said a word to me about letting you go. But you will always have a place here with me, should the need arise."

"Really?" The woman's thin face brightened. "Thank you, Miss Wilder. That eases my mind."

Isabelle went next to Mr. Booker's room. The door was open, but there was no sign of the man. Mr. Hardy's room was empty too. From the end of the passage, she heard footsteps ascending stairs. She followed them up one level but found only the servants quickly packing their belongings. She heard a door slam and more footsteps. Someone had gone to the roof. Not Mr. Booker, she knew. Maybe Mr. Hardy went to gain a better view of the flood surrounding them. Not a bad idea. Isabelle saw the young scullery maid struggling to carry her trunk and hurried to help her. Perhaps later she would go up there as well.

Looking for Mr. Hardy, Benjamin stopped first in the study. Mr. Hardy's leather brief bag sat open on the desk, papers piled on either side. He'd been there, apparently packing in haste to leave, but where was he now? Benjamin guessed he had gone to his room to find something or to begin packing there too.

Glancing at the papers, Benjamin was surprised to notice several documents related to the Wilder estate piled within the bag, including the newer will Benjamin had found. His stomach dropped. An odd suspicion prickled over him, but he reasoned with himself. Mr. Hardy was only taking it for safekeeping, in case Benjamin forgot to pack it.

Beneath these papers, a corner of what appeared to be a letter protruded, catching his eye. He bent to look closer and saw feminine handwriting and part of a St. James's Square address. Curiosity overcoming concerns of privacy, he slid the letter out and saw that it was addressed to *Mr. Percival Norris.* Benjamin had seen Miss Wilder's handwriting often enough since coming here to recognize it—on invoices and correspondence related to the basketmaking business left on the same desk.

Dread gathering at the corners of his mind, Benjamin unfolded the letter, planning to read only enough to assure himself his suspicions were wrong . . . only to find they were terribly right.

Dear Mr. Norris,

I was very unhappy with your recent visit and your presumption in bringing a stranger to look over the island with a view to letting out part of our property. And by "our" property, I mean mine and Rose's. It is not your property to do with as you like. As trustee, you are only its steward, not its owner. Forgive me for writing so bluntly and perhaps rudely. I have never raised the issue before, never felt compelled to remind you that though we are distantly related, you are not, in reality, our uncle or other such close kin. Yes, you have been granted some authority by my father, but with the intention you would facilitate his wishes for the estate and his heirs. He would never have approved of this latest scheme of yours.

Leasing part of the island to a boatbuilder would have been bad enough, disrupting the osier growing and the basketmaking industry we have started here. But after you left, I discovered that among my retainers is one who was acquainted with your Mr. Redknap in the past and knew him not as a boatbuilder or reputable man of business, but as a man with criminal connections who is not at all to be trusted.

Perhaps I should give you the benefit of the doubt that you were ignorant of the man's reputation and dealings. It is possible that he hoodwinked and manipulated you as he has so many others, according to my friend. But I wonder. For I have grown increasingly concerned about your management of estate funds and some of the invest-ments you have entered into on our behalf.

Recently, I received a letter from a banker (an old friend of Father's), who informed me that your latest venture failed at a significant loss. What you do with the stipend you receive as trustee is your own affair, but it is time to put an end to such risky investments with estate funds before we find ourselves bankrupt!

At all events, you told me to reconsider Mr. Redknap's offer, urged me not to make a rash decision, because as a "sheltered, naïve female" I did not know what was best for me and the island. I disagree. I have thought it over, and I do not grant permission to lease any land to Mr. Redknap or to anyone else. And if you attempt to override my decision, insist that your authority as trustee usurps mine, then I will have no choice but to take steps to replace you as trustee, as perhaps I should have done years ago.

I do not mean to sound ungrateful. After my parents died, you were helpful to me, and later to Rose, but in the intervening years you have progressively overstepped the bounds of your authority, controlling more and more of our lives and financial resources, and ignored or even gone directly against my father's expressed wishes. This cannot go on.

I am an educated, accomplished woman of thirty years. I am capable of managing my own affairs and providing any guidance Rose should need until she marries. I am also capable of convincing a judge of this fact if need be.

Most sincerely,
Miss Isabelle Wilder

Benjamin was stunned, but there was no mistaking it. This was the angry letter Miss Wilder had written to Percival Norris, the letter Mr. Hardy told him Percival had destroyed. His mentor's explanation echoed in Benjamin's mind: *"He read parts aloud to me, then in his anger wadded it up and tossed it onto the fire."*

Yet here it was, smooth and whole.

Robert Hardy had lied to him.

What else had he done?

Suddenly other moments and incongruous details began shooting through his brain like lightning strikes, one after another. Mr. Hardy smelling of citrus in the public house, which Benjamin had put down to a new shaving tonic or brand of tobacco. The old, stained gloves he'd worn that day. The stilted way he'd reacted when they first heard Mr. Norris was dead, compared to the very real surprise he'd shown when they learned he'd been struck. Then sending Benjamin away from the scene of the crime and trying so hard to shift the blame to Miss Wilder or Captain Curtis—anyone. Finally showing up here with papers and . . . poison? Had Hardy placed that poison in the cellar himself, determined to prove the wine had been poisoned on the island at any cost?

Another thought went through his mind. Had the house-maid's death been an unforeseen second murder, or had Hardy some reason to think Mary Williams might have seen *him* in the house that day, fiddling with the bottles in the butler's pantry, so he made sure she was done away with? Benjamin shuddered and shook his head. Surely not. He could believe Mr. Hardy might hide an incriminating letter. But the rest? No.

Even as he told himself his imagination was getting the better of him, long ago whispers he'd heard returned to him, about Hardy's father being a charlatan who cared more about profits than patients, who'd supposedly developed a popular elixir that left children addicted to opium but him rich enough to buy a country house on a lake.

Benjamin had always attributed the rumors to mean-spirited gossip, reasoning that, even if there was a hint of truth to them, the claims were against Mr. Hardy senior, not Robert Hardy himself—who'd wisely not followed his father's footsteps. Surely he could not be blamed for the sins of the father.

But then again, as Ben's Welsh grandmother used to say, "The *afal* does not fall far from the tree."

No. There must be some other explanation.

Folding the letter and newer will within a piece of sturdy parchment, he tucked them into his inside coat pocket and strode to Mr. Hardy's bedchamber. He found it empty, except for a valise waiting near the door. In the passage, he encountered

Adair's valet, hurrying past with two valises and a hatbox, and asked him if he had seen Mr. Hardy.

"Yes, sir. Saw him go upstairs. Said he wanted to look at the river from the roof."

Benjamin groaned. Did it have to be the roof? He forced his feet up the stairs and pushed open the door.

Robert Hardy stood at the low balustrade, the Wilders' field glasses to his eyes, aimed toward the southern tip of the island. The rain had stopped—a lull in the storm, though the skies were still grey and the air heavy with the promise of more rain to come.

Hardy glanced over, then fitted his eyes to the glasses once more, returning his gaze to the river. "Did Miss Wilder describe Redknap's sailing barge as having red-brown sails?" The anxiety in the older man's voice gave Benjamin pause.

Without answering, Benjamin looked out and saw a dark vessel rocking in the choppy water. Was Hardy worried Enos Redknap planned to take another shot at him? Had Captain Curtis been right when he'd said that, with Percival dead, Redknap had moved on to squeezing Percival's associates? Is that why Hardy had taken the newer will—to destroy it and guarantee his position as successor trustee, so he could deliver the island to Redknap after Percival failed to do so?

When Benjamin remained silent, Mr. Hardy lowered the glasses and turned to him again, his look of irritation transforming into something else as he studied his protégé's face. Awareness. A *knowing*.

Benjamin took a shaky breath, his chest tight. "Why did you do it?"

"Do what?"

"I read Miss Wilder's letter to Percival, the one you said he'd destroyed."

Hardy glared at him. "Why were you poking about my personal property?"

"It isn't yours."

Hardy shrugged. "So I wasn't eager to have my firm's name blemished by sharing the contents of that letter. That isn't a crime."

"No? You lied to me."

Hardy huffed. "Yes, Ben, I lied to you. Welcome to the real world of adults. Sometimes we lie when we must. For the greater good."

Remaining near the door, Benjamin recalled Hardy's long-ago advice once again. *"State what you suspect as fact with confidence, and nine times out of ten times people will believe you in possession of the evidence and respond accordingly."*

Emboldened by it, Benjamin said, "Percival's reckless actions were threatening your way of life, your reputation, and you could not stand by and do nothing."

Hardy frowned. "What are you talking about?"

"I think you know, sir. And . . . so do I."

Ben made the mistake of glancing over the parapet and felt the world spin, but then he forced himself to hold his mentor's gaze. Not to back down, not even to blink. If he was wrong, he'd be cut loose. Unemployed. If he was right? It would be even worse.

Hardy hesitated, perhaps weighing his options. Then his expression tightened into grim resolve. "Percival was determined to destroy himself, and me with him. I have a daughter to think of. A grandchild. A well-known firm. I could not let him ruin everything I had worked so hard for—my reputation, my livelihood.

"I tried reason. Pointed out all the ways he was endangering not only himself and the Wilder fortune but also me and my family. I lent him money, helped him avoid the shame of bankruptcy. But he would not stop. Always one more deal, one more investment that could not fail, but always did."

Hardy shook his head. "When a pair of ruffians came to my house while my daughter was visiting, I knew I had to do something. There was no point in going after one moneylender or smuggler, for Percy would always find another, or they would find him. It was *him* I had to stop."

Hardy sighed. "I had thought we were friends. It is why I allowed him to retire quietly from the firm, instead of bringing his misdeeds to light."

Surprise flashed though Benjamin. "He was already involved in illegal dealings while a full-time partner for the firm?"

"Yes. Small infractions at first. Questionable business dealings that were not unequivocally illegal. A master of the loophole was Percy. I had thought I was doing him a favor by not revealing his wrongdoings. But now I see that left unchecked, his deeds only worsened."

"Why did you not go after him legally?"

"You know why. A big scandal like that would destroy the firm's standing and the confidence of future clients. Not only would my reputation suffer but so would that of everyone linked to the firm, including you and my own daughter."

An apologetic smile creased his face. "I admit to you that at first I was drawn into a few of Percival's schemes, his claims of easy money. Invested some of my own savings. Guilt by association would be bad enough, but he threatened to bring me down with him if he faced any legal repercussions. He had receipts and my signature on documents that I would never have signed had I not trusted him so implicitly—at least until I learned not to. I'm ashamed to confess it to you. I know you think . . . thought . . . very highly of me at one time. And now I have let you down."

"But to kill a man? Your friend?"

"As I saw it, he destroyed himself. I would not let him destroy you and Mr. Hunt and Cordelia too."

"And yourself."

"Yes! That's just it. It was self-defense. But I had to be careful to not tip my hand. I didn't want Percival to make good on his threat to send evidence against me to the newspapers or Bow Street. So we remained on friendly terms while I awaited my chance and planned the best course. I figured if luck was with me, the servants would think their master had finally drunk himself to death. It's what we all thought would kill him eventually, if some cutthroat didn't do so first."

Robert Hardy shook his head. "Imagine my surprise when we arrived and learned he'd been struck a blow. I could not account for the scene. Percival with a gun in his hand and a gash to the temple—one I had not delivered. My first thought was that a vengeful moneylender had paid a call. I did not know whether that turn of events was good news or bad. The blow deflected suspicion of poisoning—until you pointed out the signs—but it also dashed my hope that the death would be attributed to natural causes."

"You poisoned those bottles yourself and then tried to pin the blame on Miss Wilder!"

Hardy shook his head. "I didn't let myself into the house that day with the intention of laying blame at Miss Wilder's door, but when the only two bottles I found in the butler's pantry were Belle Island wine, what else was I to do? He didn't care for wine, but I also knew he would drink almost anything if desperate enough. So I did what I came for and left."

"That's why you seemed so distracted and uneasy when we met that night at the Queen's Head."

"Was I? I thought I hid it better than that. Or at least, that you attributed my less than jovial mood to your own recent failure."

"I did think that, yes, at the time."

"You think too much, Benjamin. Always have. If you had kept quiet about what you suspected, that overworked coroner-brother of yours might not have noticed any symptoms of poisoning. Not on a man who regularly poisoned himself with too much drink. But you can't resist saying aloud every thought that comes into your head."

Benjamin's hands were damp against the door behind him. His mind whirling, he forced himself to focus on Hardy's face alone. The face of the man who had once been a trusted mentor. But no more.

"That's why you sent me here." Ben's prideful words to his father came back to sicken him. *"Mr. Hardy has confidence in me, even if you don't."* What a fool he'd been.

"Yes, I wanted you off the scent. I didn't like the way you were looking at every jot and tittle. I feared you might find something in Percy's office that implicated me. Something a medical man wouldn't notice but a fellow lawyer might. I wanted to go through his papers alone, to find Miss Wilder's letter and any other incriminating evidence. And there was the legitimate mystery of the blow to the head to investigate. Considering the heated arguments between Percy and Miss Wilder, Miss Lawrence, and Mr. Adair, I honestly thought it very likely one of them might have struck him down, not realizing the man was already poisoned."

"Did you intend to kill Mary Williams too?"

"No." The first sign of remorse sagged his features. "That I did not foresee. When I later looked into the pantry and found it bare, I thought perhaps Percy had drunk both bottles, though it was strange that no one knew where the empty bottles were. If the second bottle had still been there, I would have disposed of it safely. It's not my fault the greedy housemaid stole it for herself. Considering the looks she was giving me that night when she said she'd overheard Percy arguing with some man, I thought she might be hinting she had heard something or perhaps had even seen me leaving the house."

"I believe she was looking at Mr. Adair."

"May have been. Those two argued as well. Either way, it was perhaps a fortunate turn of events that she should not be around to testify against me."

Benjamin could not believe what he was hearing.

Mr. Hardy drew a long inhale and slowly shook his head.

"Benjamin, Benjamin, why must you always interfere? Things had been going so well. I had decided to stop trying to implicate Miss Wilder—that's why I borrowed your key and removed the rat poison from the cellar and didn't mention it to Officer Riley. Isabelle is still reasonably young and has many years ahead of her, as, of course, do Miss Lawrence and Adair. I am not a heartless man. In fact I had begun feeling a little guilty about all the angst and danger I was exposing them to. Riley was getting nowhere and never once looked in my direction. I was in the clear. If there was no risk of my being a suspect, then I was willing to let the rest lie."

"I did notice your apparent change of heart over the last few days with Adair and even Miss Wilder."

Hardy nodded. "There, you see? But you would go and spoil things. Have you any proof? That letter proves nothing against me."

Do I have any solid proof? Benjamin asked himself. *No.*

Robert Hardy's eyes glinted as if reading his mind. "That's what I thought."

Again he sighed. "Ah, Benjamin. If only you were my son-in-law, then I know you wouldn't turn against me like this.

Surely you won't make your accusations public without sufficient evidence?"

Everything in Ben wanted to get off that roof. But if he ran into the house, Hardy would follow, drawing the gun no doubt in his pocket and endangering others. So he swallowed the mounting nausea and asked, "And if I do?"

"The theory I'll put forward is that Miss Wilder poisoned the wine, then instructed Miss Lawrence to serve it to Percival and Mr. Adair to strike him, to make sure the deed was done."

"She did not do so."

"So she says. But one cannot trust the word of a woman in her mental state. Look, I know you are fond of her, so I will recommend a genteel, private asylum rather than prison or hanging."

"I won't let you do that, sir."

"Unfortunately, you won't be here to stop me."

Benjamin sent the man a nervous glance. "And where will I be?"

The older man's mouth and eyes turned down in apology. Robert Hardy looked truly remorseful. "As much as it hurts me to say, I am very much afraid that you suffered another bout of vertigo while high on the roof of the Wilders' house." He patted the parapet. "This really ought to be taller to keep a dizzy person from falling off."

Benjamin's stomach dropped, and he began to perspire profusely. "Do you really think people will believe that?"

"Yes, I will make sure they do." Sadness creased the older man's countenance. "It's not what I want, Ben. You have been like a son to me, the son I never had. But if you turn against me, threaten me, what choice do I have?"

Benjamin shook his head, heart thumping. "I am not your son. My father is Thomas Booker, who would never hurt anyone for personal gain. A man more worthy of respect than I realized or than you will ever be."

Another flash of pain crossed Hardy's face. "Will you give me your word you will say nothing of my involvement in any of this?"

"How can I promise that? I have no desire to hurt you, but you can't ask me to stay silent while an innocent person takes the blame for a murder you committed."

Hardy frowned. "How bad you make it sound."

"It *is* bad. Have you no conscience?"

"Can't afford one. Percy stole that from me as well."

Benjamin shook his head, disbelief and betrayal washing over him anew. To think he had taken this man's side over his father's time and time again. Held him in higher esteem. Distanced himself from a good man, in hopes of winning the approval of this man. A self-centered, unrepentant killer.

Another ill-advised glance toward the balustrade sent a bolt of nerves through his body like an electric shock. Blood pounding in his ears, Benjamin tried to think of a way to talk Hardy out of his plan. He stammered, "I . . . I thought you cared for me. I looked up to you as my mentor all these years."

"I did care for you, Ben—I do. I hate having to do this." He drew the gun from his pocket and beckoned Benjamin away from the door. "Come here. If you have a compromise to offer me, I am willing to listen."

Did Hardy think he would keep his secret, be complicit in his crime to save his own skin? Would he? Benjamin took one shaky step forward, then another and another. Through the balusters, he glimpsed the veranda far below and felt the earth shift beneath him. *Steady* . . . Could he overpower the older man, stunned and dizzy as he was? Unlikely.

The door creaked open behind them. From the corner of his eye he saw Isabelle peek out. *No.*

"Mr. Booker . . . ?"

She glanced at Mr. Hardy, who had, he noticed, hidden the gun behind his back.

"Go back inside, Miss Wilder," Benjamin commanded. "Mr. Hardy and I are having a . . . disagreement. Nothing to concern you." He did not want to give Hardy any cause to kill Miss Wilder too. Now that he'd told Benjamin all, he supposed Hardy felt he had no choice but to guarantee his silence one way or another. But he didn't want the same threat to extend to Isabelle.

"Are you . . . sure you're all right out here?"

"Yes. Leave us. Don't interfere." His voice sounded sharp in his own ears, but at least it was effective. The door slammed shut behind her.

Mr. Hardy shook his head, a sardonic gleam in his eye. "Now you've gone and hurt her feelings, Ben. You don't fool me, you know. Trying to protect the pretty woman again. I warned you it would be your downfall."

Downfall. Fall . . . His pulse raced. Nausea soured his mouth. He sent another nervous glance to the hard and unforgiving paving stones below. If he landed on his head, he would probably die. He would be injured no matter what.

He saw a flash of movement from the corner of his eye as Hardy charged headfirst like a bull. The sharp impact to his chest knocked the wind from Benjamin's lungs. His feet came out from under him, and the world spun. As he toppled over the rail, he looked wildly about, flailed, reached. He caught the edge of one of the stone balusters and held on for dear life, fingers grappling for purchase, rough stone scraping the skin from his palms.

Would Hardy pry his fingers loose? But the man must have thought he'd fallen all the way over or was he worried he'd been seen pushing him, for he disappeared into the house. *Dear God, please don't let him hurt anyone else.*

Benjamin's hands shook. He was going to fall. The wet baluster began slipping from his grip. But hopefully this way, stretched out to his full six feet—and landing feetfirst, not headfirst—he would survive the impact.

Suddenly a voice called to him from below. "Mr. Booker! Oh, merciful heaven. Be careful!"

He risked a glance over his shoulder. There was Isabelle. So much for scaring her off. She'd dragged over the large cushion from the veranda sofa and folded it double.

"It's all I could think of."

He tried to remember what his father had taught him. How to fall to minimize injury.

God help me. . . .

Fingers releasing, body falling, air rushing, he hit the cushion and rolled. Even so, with his weight and velocity, the cushion felt like concrete. His ankle buckled, his backside hit hard, and something like a sledgehammer struck his shin. Palms scraping the paving stones, he rolled to a stop.

"Oh! Mr. Booker! Please be all right."

He opened his eyes and found her kneeling beside him. His legs throbbed, his hands burned, his spine felt out of place, but her beautiful eyes were on him, so wide, so blue, so full of concern for him. The pain faded.

"Are you all right?"

"I'll live."

"Thank God." Isabelle leaned near and whispered, "I was so afraid."

Her gaze locked with his, then shifted to his mouth. Benjamin's heart beat hard in anticipation. She lowered her head and . . .

Footsteps sounded on the paving stones. Miss Wilder pulled back, and he barely resisted the urge to reach out and draw her near again.

Evan Curtis appeared, without a gun this time. He frowned at the sight of the two of them crumpled on the veranda. "What's happened?"

"Mr. Hardy pushed him off the roof."

"What the . . . ?" Curtis muttered a curse, then turned and sprinted away. In pursuit? Benjamin was not sure.

He returned his gaze to Isabelle. "Thank you for thinking so quickly. I'm sorry I snapped at you."

She took his hand. "I was insulted for all of two seconds before I realized how out of character it was for you. I knew something was wrong."

"Very wrong. Mr. Hardy killed Percival. And tried to kill me to keep his secret."

She nodded, expression tight. "I overheard some of what he said but never dreamed he'd try to kill you too." She looked around. "Where is he now?"

Benjamin grimaced and levered himself up into a sitting position. "I don't know, but we'd better find out." With her help, he struggled to his feet. When he put weight on his right side, his ankle screamed a rebuke.

"You shouldn't walk on that. It may be broken."

He gritted his teeth. "I'll worry about that later. Let's block the bridge so he doesn't escape."

"Does he still have his gun?"

"Good point. You go into the house."

"What good would that do? You block the bridge, and I will fetch the Curtises and their guns. Hopefully Evan has already gone for his."

"Knew you were clever. But be careful. If you see Hardy, steer clear."

She nodded. "And if he points his gun at you?"

"I don't know, but I have to try to stop him. I shall pray for your safety." He pressed her hand, leaned near, and kissed her cheek. "Please return the favor."

Isabelle looked into Benjamin Booker's handsome face, her hand in his, her cheek still warm from his kiss, her stomach fluttering. Would she pray? She had not prayed much in recent years, but her heart was changing. And for this man . . . ? She nodded. "I will."

Turning, she followed the veranda around the side of the house, a prayer already on her lips. *Please, God, keep him safe. Help us. . . .*

Movement caught her eye. She looked over and saw Mr. Hardy running toward the boathouse, carrying a bag. She called over her shoulder, "Benjamin, look! There he is!"

Mr. Booker limped toward her, wincing in pain with each stride. Leaning heavily on the rail for support, he struggled down the veranda steps. She followed.

At that moment, Evan Curtis ran back into view, rifle in hand. He raised the barrel to aim. With a loud report, the bullet hit the boathouse over Hardy's head, splinters of wood flying.

"Stop!" Curtis called. "That's your only warning!"

Pulling the handgun from his pocket, Mr. Hardy spun wildly around and lunged behind a tree.

Rose came hurrying over from the paddock, a wriggling Ollie in arms. "Found him!"

Isabelle's throat tightened. She opened her mouth to shout a warning as Rose neared Hardy, but he reached out and grabbed her.

Isabelle cried out. The pup squirmed loose and jumped to the ground.

Hardy held Rose in front of himself like a shield, arm braced around her shoulders, pistol in his free hand.

"Don't shoot!" he yelled, backing toward the boathouse.

"Evan, be careful," Isabelle called, hurrying to his side.

Evan hesitated, then lowered the rifle, cursing under his breath.

Mr. Adair ran from the house, no doubt drawn by the gunshot. Seeing his intended trapped by an armed man, he panicked, yanking the rifle from Curtis and swinging it in their direction.

Isabelle grabbed his arm. "Don't—you might hit Rose."

Adair grimaced and lowered the gun. "What is the madman doing?"

"Trying to escape."

"Then let him, as long as he lets Rose go."

Mr. Booker lurched forward, favoring his injured leg. Isabelle caught up with him.

"Go back," he said. "Stay safe."

"Not this time." She lifted his arm over her shoulder and supported him as he hobbled down the path. "What are we going to do?"

"I don't know."

Curtis and Adair followed. As the four of them moved toward the front of the boathouse, Isabelle saw its lower level and the pier were submerged beneath the floodwaters. Their old fishing boat had been tied to a tree on higher ground upstream to keep it from floating away. Mr. Grant's work, she knew.

Hardy tossed his bag into the stern, then half pushed, half carried Rose into the bow, untied the rope, and leapt in after her.

"Hurry," Isabelle said. "We have to stop them."

Adair frowned. "How?"

"I don't know, but if he takes her to Taplow, we won't be able to catch them."

"Is that the only boat?" Adair asked.

"Yes."

Evan looked around as if for answers. "He's risking both of their lives. That small boat isn't safe in such conditions."

"Mr. Hardy, don't!" Isabelle shouted. "It's too dangerous!"

Struggling to row against the turbulent current, he either didn't hear her or ignored her.

Rose looked terrified. Isabelle called to her, "Rose! Hang on!"

The small craft moved away from the shore . . . two feet, three feet, four.

The girl she loved like a daughter was moving away from the island, from safety, from her, and Isabelle was utterly powerless to help her. Fear for Rose gripped her heart like invisible hands trying to tear it in two.

A flash of movement from above jerked Isabelle out of her frozen state. She swung her gaze to the upper story of the boat-house and the open loft door. From out of its shadowy mouth, Silas Grant ran, launching himself toward the boat.

Hardy turned as Grant hurtled toward him, arms out-stretched. Hardy fired his gun with a metallic *crack*. For a moment, the former coachman seemed to float in the air sus-pended. Then he barreled into Hardy, knocking him from the stern and toppling both men into the water.

Rose shrieked as the boat lurched to the side, threatening to spill her overboard as well. She grabbed the gunwales and held on tight.

Isabelle sucked in a panicked breath, clutching a hand to her chest and crying out, "She can't swim!"

The boat righted, and Rose sat looking wildly around, clearly unsure what to do.

Isabelle searched the water, fearing any second Hardy would surface and, in his desperation to haul himself back into the boat, either capsize the craft or succeed in reboarding, which would be almost as bad.

The current continued to push the small boat farther downriver. Inexperienced as she was, Rose would never be able to fight the swirling flood to make her way back. "Row, Rose!" Isabelle called. "Row to Riverton! To shore!"

She turned to Mr. Adair. "Christopher, go and help her land the boat. Stay with her in case Hardy comes back."

"Right." He ran off to do so.

Beside her, Evan and Benjamin searched the surface of the river. Benjamin stripped down to his shirt-sleeves, trousers, and braces, then bent and began yanking off his shoes, a groan of pain escaping as he did so.

Isabelle turned to him. "You don't swim."

"I know, but I can't stand here and do nothing. Curtis?"

Evan Curtis ran a helpless hand over his face. "I can't swim either."

Dr. Grant came loping around the house, medical bag in hand. "What's wrong? I heard gunshots. Adair shouted something about Mr. Hardy as I passed him."

Isabelle had thought she would never see him again after their falling-out, but she wasn't sorry to see him now. She pointed to the boat. "He forced Rose to go with him at gunpoint. Your father jumped in after them and knocked Hardy into the water."

The doctor's gaze snapped to the river. "Where are they?"

"Neither has surfaced, that we've seen." Isabelle swallowed a lump of remorse. "Your father may have been shot."

Teddy dropped his bag, pulled off his shoes and coat, and ripped off his waistcoat, sending buttons flying. "Where did he go down?"

Isabelle gestured in front of the boathouse. "Right there, but with the current . . . ?"

They hurried downriver toward the southern tip of the island, scanning the water as they went. A flash of movement caught her eye. Near shore, a man's hand gripped an overhanging willow branch. Mr. Grant's head broke the surface gasping for air.

Isabelle pointed, shouting, "There!"

The current pulled the branch from his grasp, and he went under. Teddy ran toward the spot and dove in. He swam a few yards, then disappeared beneath the water.

Benjamin stepped forward to follow him, but Isabelle grabbed his arm. "No. Teddy can swim, and so can his father. If he is . . . able. We don't need anyone else going down. Keep an eye out for Hardy."

Benjamin nodded, Isabelle's firm commands breaking through his panicked confusion. He scanned the surface again, pulse racing, ankle throbbing. If Hardy didn't come up soon, he wouldn't at all.

Benjamin searched the Riverton shoreline, then looked toward Taplow. There, a head broke the surface before disappearing again. He watched closely, and seconds later the same head surfaced again briefly.

Relief and disappointment wrestled within him. Had Hardy drowned, Benjamin would have grieved his loss—the loss of the man he thought he had known—but this ordeal would be over. Benjamin could tell Hardy's beloved Cordelia that her father had drowned. Perhaps he would not have to reveal what he had done. Or at least . . . not everything. No humiliating trial. No imprisonment. No transportation or hanging to suffer through, to further damage the reputation of the firm, to disillusion his friends and family and scar his daughter forever. But now?

Movement in the water nearby interrupted his thoughts. Dr. Grant resurfaced with a ragged inhale that was part desperate breath, part moan. He gripped his father across the chest with one arm and was struggling to stay afloat. He stroked and kicked, eventually managing to draw near the island's point.

Despite the pain in his ankle, Benjamin walked into the flood-waters toward them, the water rising to his waist. Captain Curtis followed his lead. Seeing them, the doctor renewed his efforts in their direction. Benjamin stepped in as far as he dared, reaching toward Mr. Grant, whose eyes remained closed through it all. Behind him, Captain Curtis grabbed hold of Ben's braces to keep him from being swept away.

He gripped the old man's arm and relieved the weary doctor of his burden. Together he and Curtis hauled the unresponsive Mr. Grant to shore and hoisted him onto dry ground. Dr. Grant emerged after them, panting and dropping to his knees beside his father.

He felt for a pulse. "He's still alive but barely."

He pulled away his father's shirt, revealing an angry hole, most of the blood washed away and barely flowing.

Isabelle carried over the discarded medical bag and knelt beside them, her voice thick with emotion. "Mr. Grant, thank you for saving Rose. I should have forgiven you before now. I do forgive you. Do you hear me? I forgive you."

The old man's eyelids fluttered open. He looked up at her. Understanding flickered in his gaze, and then he squeezed his eyes shut in apparent relief. A moment later, he breathed his last.

The physician's professional façade fell away, and the grieving son laid his hand, then his head on his father's chest and sobbed.

Benjamin felt the pain of it through his very soul. *Father, forgive me.*

Captain Curtis squeezed Dr. Grant's shoulder, and Isabelle said softly, "Do you remember telling me your father would do anything to help me? He did. He gave his life to save Rose. I owe him a great debt."

Theodore Grant shook his and whispered, "No. But at least he finally paid his."

Benjamin turned his face away, giving the old friends privacy for their grief, feeling guilty and out of place, and somehow responsible. He should have guessed earlier, should have sent Hardy away.

If Hardy survived, Benjamin would be obligated to pursue him, physically and legally—to make known his wrongdoings, or at least his poisoning of Percival Norris. But could he prove it? Hardy would certainly disavow the confession he'd made on the roof, call it a work of wishful fiction, claim Benjamin was determined to redeem his own reputation and save another beautiful, scheming female. It would not go well.

Through a renewed deluge of rain, Ben's gaze traced the river once more. A sailing barge now lurched in the floodwaters. Men leaned over the side, hauling Hardy on board. Enos Redknap's men? Benjamin shivered. Robert Hardy might end up drowned yet.

twenty-five

Hindered by the pouring rain, Dr. Grant examined Ben's bruised shin and swollen ankle, declaring the latter sprained and possibly fractured. He wrapped it securely to help support it until Ben could consult a surgeon, then returned his attention to his father, covering the man's lifeless body with his discarded coat.

Benjamin limped into the house to pack up the papers Mr. Hardy had left behind in his haste to flee. He added the newer will to his case as well, thankful for God's nudging or whatever impulse had caused him to tuck it along with the letter into his coat pocket. Otherwise it might be in Hardy's possession right now, or lost to the swollen river. Then Ben went back outside, adding his case to the others being loaded onto the estate wagon.

Shortly thereafter, the undertaker's cart bearing Silas Grant's body splashed through the rising water and rumbled over the bridge. Dr. Grant sat on the back, head hung low.

When the estate wagon was finally loaded, Abel Curtis lifted the reins and urged the horse to walk on. Mrs. Philpotts sat on the bench beside him, holding the puppy. Jacob, Carlota, and a young maid sat in the back among the trunks and cases.

Miss O'Toole and Manvers, he knew, had already ridden in the chaise with the elderly tenants to the inn, to wait with Rose and Mr. Adair for the weather to clear so they could start back to London.

But for the present, the rain continued to fall. The water was now mere inches from the bridge deck and showed no signs of abating.

On the veranda, Ben saw Captain Curtis talking earnestly to Isabelle. Asking her to leave with him, he guessed. Ben longed to interrupt, to plead his own case and hopes, whether Booker men were any good at expressing their feelings or not. But before he could, Isabelle adamantly shook her head. Curtis pressed her hand and turned away, slinging a knapsack over his back. As he passed Benjamin, he said, "It's up to you, counselor. She won't heed me. Then again, she never did."

The captain descended into the floodwaters, striding heedlessly through the murky flow in his tall Hessian boots. He still carried his gun, Benjamin noticed, perhaps anticipating the return of Mr. Hardy or the sailing barge.

Ben called after him, "By the way, what did you say to Redknap's men on the barge? Your father mentioned you hailed them."

Curtis turned back. "I simply passed along Hardy's message. You remember. He said, 'I believe Enos Redknap tried to kill me. Probably killed Percival too. I'll see him hang if it's the last thing I do.'" The captain smirked. "Enos seemed to find the words most . . . interesting."

Ben raised his chin with understanding. "Ah. And what will you do now? Not return to your former way of life, I hope."

"No. I plan to take up the study of birds."

"Birds?" Ben echoed in surprise.

"Yes. I have been observing a rare and beautiful Spanish

songbird and am determined to learn all I can about her, perhaps even win her regard."

"I see. Well, all the best to you both."

With a grin, Curtis continued over the bridge.

Benjamin splashed up the veranda steps to join Isabelle near the front door. She held her father's old field glasses to her eyes and surveyed the village beyond. But even with a naked eye, Benjamin could see that the river had breached its banks there as well, covering the River Road and climbing toward the shops and homes.

"Mrs. Winkfield's garden is already underwater," she said. "Poor thing will be devastated. All her beautiful flowers and the vegetables she practically lives on—gone. And the water is nearing the courtyard of the inn too. I hope Rose and Christopher and everyone else who went there for shelter will be all right."

"They will be. You know you can trust Mrs. Philpotts to make arrangements to move everyone farther inland if Riverton itself is threatened."

"True . . ."

"Time to go now, Isabelle. You don't want to be trapped here."

She lowered the glasses and gave a choked little laugh. "I do, actually. Have I not been so these last ten years?"

"This is different. You are risking your life. And mine."

"Yours?" she asked, brows raised high.

"I am not leaving without you. Do I have to carry you?"

She huffed. "Good luck with that. Teddy and his laudanum have already left. And you saw what happened when the officer tried to force me to leave."

"Very well, I won't try to force you, but I do beseech you most . . . ardently. I will go with you. Rose is already on the other side. Your friends and neighbors are waiting to welcome you. Your tenants and workers need you, Isabelle. You are the mistress of Belle Island. Riverton's main employer and benefactor to dozens of people."

"They will survive without me."

"Will they? How will Jenny and Mrs. Winkfield, Joe and the Joneses, Abel and the Howtons get on without you? And what about Rose? You are her last living relative. And what about me?"

"What about you?" she retorted. "You came here to discover Percival's murderer and you did. End of story."

He slowly shook his head. "I hope that isn't true. I hope our story is just beginning. I realize we have only known one another for, can it be less than a fortnight? But I . . . I have come to care for you, Isabelle Wilder. A great deal."

She stared at him, mouth ajar and eyes wide, clearly astonished. "Oh, Benjamin . . ." she breathed, expression softening.

Touched to hear his Christian name on her lips, he stepped closer, pressing his advantage. "Just come with me as far as the bridge. It's not yet submerged. Just that far." He extended his palm to her. "Hold my hand. Please."

Her eyes, round and troubled, held his. She reached out and took his hand.

He led her down the steps into the cold water, which felt good on his swollen ankle. "Hold tight."

Sloshing through knee-high water, Benjamin reached the bridge and stepped onto the first plank. He turned back to her, their hands still clasped. "Will you take one step onto the bridge, Isabelle? Join me here?"

In his peripheral vision, Benjamin noticed something ominously large looming toward him. He looked upriver and saw a wooden pier with metal railings rushing at him. It slammed into the bridge, shaking its foundations and shuddering along its length like a whip snapped by a giant's hand.

The bridge lurched, and Benjamin's hip slammed into the railing. He almost fell over it but released Isabelle and gripped the rail tight.

Isabelle cried out, "Benjamin! Be careful. Come back."

He shook his head and reached toward her once more. "The bridge held. Take my hand, Isabelle. Come with me. To safety."

"Safety? Here is safety. The island is where I am safe."

"Not anymore."

Isabelle's chest squeezed tight, and her legs trembled. Every fiber of her being wanted to remain where she was, on the island. Yet she could not deny it would be wise to seek higher ground, or that she was drawn to the man reaching toward her.

She looked longingly back to the house. The water had reached the veranda and was still rising. Repairs would be needed to the house as well as the tenant cottages. And the weaving shed would need to be rebuilt on taller pilings. But what if she wasn't here to do so?

Perhaps she might go up to the higher floors and wait out the flood on her own. The kitchen would be inaccessible and all the food in the larder spoiled, but she would not starve to death, assuming the water receded in a few days or a week. How long could one live without food and fresh water? She supposed, if desperate, she could drink water directly from the Thames instead of their spring, but recalling all the flotsam in the river presently, her stomach soured at the thought.

Even so, the island had been her refuge for years. It would shelter her even now. Would it not?

Phrases she'd read in her father's Bible washed over her. *"God is our refuge and strength, a very present help in trouble.*

Therefore will not we fear . . . though the waters roar and be troubled."

She looked past Benjamin across the bridge. In her panicked state, the span seemed to constrict and stretch out in a dizzying illusion. She felt breathless and light-headed, damp through from the water and perspiration. The flood roared in her ears, blocking out every other sound but Benjamin's appealing baritone voice.

"You can do it, Isabelle. I know you can. I will help you."

Isabelle swallowed. She reminded herself that Rose was about to marry a man who had no interest in living on the island. If Isabelle was not there, how long would it be until he convinced Rose to sell Belle Island to someone else, to a boatyard or even a smuggler like Mr. Redknap?

Isabelle shook her head. She had to stay alive and make sure that didn't happen. She reached for the railing.

Anxiety rose up in her so strong she could barely breathe. She searched her mind for Mrs. Booker's exhortation and found it in her heart. *"Don't be anxious but pray instead. . . ."*

Please, Lord, Isabelle silently pleaded. *Please help me.*

She took a step onto the bridge. A step of faith. But a long narrowboat, unmanned and floundering, came straight toward them, wheeling sideways in the turbulent current. Isabelle screamed.

Slam. A cannon blast erupted in her ears, a shuddering collision knocking her off her feet. Benjamin's arms flew out and caught her before she could fall headlong into the swirling water. The world was spinning, shifting, floating . . . ? *Oh my heaven.*

The bridge had been knocked from its foundations and now floated free.

Isabelle clutched Benjamin with one hand and the railing with the other. She could hardly believe it. After all these years, she was on the dreaded bridge at the worse possible moment. So much for safety.

She whipped her head around and watched in shock as her island whirled away from her.

Then she looked the other way toward Riverton as they rushed past the churchyard, the floodwaters climbing its stone wall. She blinked at the startling sight and felt her world spin again. Isabelle suddenly had a better understanding of what Mr. Booker must suffer with his vertigo, to be standing on something that should be solid and still but was instead moving beneath one's feet.

She looked up into his face, wondering how this wild ride was affecting him. She noticed him gripping the railing hard, expression tense. She prayed he would not become dizzy or incapacitated. Not when their lives were at risk! But he met her gaze with strength and reassurance and held her closer.

Benjamin's words echoed through her mind: *"I hope our story is just beginning. . . . I have come to care for you, Isabelle Wilder. A great deal."*

But was their story about to end in violent death?

Ahead, Isabelle saw an obstacle in their way—the ruins of someone's old boathouse, lodged in a logjammed inlet.

"Benjamin!" she warned, then tensed, anticipating impact. The bridge that had become their life raft collided with the boathouse. They came to a sudden, jarring halt, and Benjamin lost his grip on her. Half the bridge ripped away.

Isabelle shrieked, falling toward the menacing current, but Benjamin's hand shot out and caught her once again. One arm clutching the railing, he bracketed his other arm around her waist, drawing her close, her back to his chest.

"Th-thank you," Isabelle breathed.

A loop of rope landed on the bridge near their feet. *What in the world?*

"Grab hold!" Evan Curtis shouted from Riverton's shore. "Tie it to the rail!"

Snagging her hand, Benjamin bent to grab the rope. Behind them, the old boathouse shifted and groaned, wood splintering as the powerful current tried to push it out of its way. Any second, it would give, and they would be swept away with it. Already the beleaguered bridge was falling apart, section by section. How long would it hold them afloat?

There, on the shore, she saw them. Rose and Mr. Adair watching anxiously. Carlota and Mrs. Philpotts waiting with blankets. Jenny with her arm around young Joe. Arminda and her father, hands clasped in prayer. Abel and Jacob steadying two harnessed horses, the rope tied between them.

Benjamin looked at the sagging railing but hesitated. Instead he looped the rope around them both and pulled it tight.

With a reverberating *crack*, the boathouse came loose and lurched away. The bridge jerked to the side. One end rose, sending the other end down into the water, pulling the remaining section of bridge out from under them. The rope binding her to Benjamin dug deep, pressing against her chest and under her arms. For a moment they were held aloft. Then they hit the surface together. Going under, blind and suffocating, Isabelle was sure she had breathed her last. She had left the island—what else had she expected? The curse was real and would continue with her.

Yet something in her rebelled at the thought. *That is superstition. God holds my fate in His hand. God alone.*

Might He allow her to die as He had the rest of her family? He might. But what happened to her was up to Him. And either way, she wanted to live. *Oh God, forgive my many sins. Save my soul for Jesus' sake. . . .*

The tension on the rope tightened as the horses waged battle with the current and their combined weight. She felt Benjamin beating the water with his hands and kicking with his feet, desperate to reach the surface. Desperate for air.

Suddenly, their heads broke the surface. Isabelle gasped, sucking in a watery breath and choking. She heard Benjamin sputter and cough behind her and praised God he was alive.

On land, Abel and Jacob urged the horses up the rise, and the animals strained in their harnesses, pulling them from the water. Benjamin's arm came around her again, holding her close, easing the raw sting of the rope against her wet clothing. She knew she would be bruised, but better bruised and alive than dead.

They reached solid ground at last. Lying there in the mud, Benjamin's arm around her, she closed her eyes in blessed relief.

Voices swarmed, caring and familiar.

"Make way for the horses. Clear a path."

"We have blankets and hot tea."

"Where's Dr. Grant?"

Rose's voice. "Aunt Belle? I'm here."

"Thank God you're safe, Miss Wilder."

Thank God indeed.

CHAPTER
twenty-six

Isabelle had crossed the river and come out on the other side. She had survived the ordeal. And how long would she live now that she had left her island? Only God knew, but she planned to live each day, each month, each year He gave her to the fullest.

Though always aware of the taut cord binding her to Belle Island, she spent time in London with Rose while the floodwaters lingered and the legalities related to recent deaths were resolved.

Rose decided to forgive Christopher Adair and stood by him through his court case. The experience seemed to mature Adair appreciably. To everyone's relief, he was acquitted in the end, thanks to some excellent legal work by Benjamin and the skilled barrister he engaged, along with the testimony of his coroner-brother, who declared with renewed resolve that a blow delivered in self-defense by slight, boyish Adair would not have proved fatal to anyone.

Armed with her father's most recent will, Benjamin and Mr. Hunt—a competent solicitor—appealed to the Court of Chancery for the disillusion of the Wilder trust, returning control of the estate to Isabelle and Rose.

After sorting through all of the papers, bills, investments, and accounts Percival had left behind, they discovered that, while he himself was on the verge of bankruptcy, the financial condition of the Wilder estate was not as bleak as he—likely planning to pocket more money for himself—had led Isabelle to believe. So she would have sufficient funds for repairs as well as a new bridge and workshop.

Although he had not seen Hardy since the man boarded Red-knap's boat, Mr. Booker had felt duty-bound to inform Officer Riley that Robert Hardy had confessed to poisoning Percival Norris. Out of a remnant of loyalty, however, he refrained from mentioning the shove off the roof. Isabelle had overheard part of their rooftop conversation but not enough to fully corroborate Benjamin's testimony. Because no one else had heard the whole of Hardy's confession, and they had little other proof, Benjamin doubted a jury would convict him.

But the marine police, who had long pursued Enos Redknap and his band of smugglers, intercepted his sailing barge with Hardy onboard. Redknap's men, in a bid for lesser charges, agreed to give evidence against their leader. They also told officials that Robert Hardy had, under Redknap's threatening persuasion, confessed to killing his former partner and had also agreed to use his position as successor trustee to secure the use of Belle Island for Redknap and his crew if they let him live.

With this evidence, along with statements from Mr. Booker and Isabelle, the courts indicted Robert Hardy for "feloniously killing and slaying" Percival Norris. He was taken to Newgate Prison to be held until trial. Enos Redknap, indicted for grand larceny, violent theft, tax offenses, and more, was held there too.

Before the trial date, Robert Hardy was killed in prison. Poisoned. Whether by Enos Redknap himself or a bribed guard was unclear. Either way, Redknap soon met his fate on the scaffold, unrepentant.

On an especially hot summer afternoon, Mr. Booker came to St. James's Square to tell Isabelle the news of Mr. Hardy's death in person. She had seen him from time to time since returning to Town, but their conversations had been limited primarily to legal matters.

Isabelle listened to his account, then said, "I am sorry, Mr. Booker. I know you cared for Mr. Hardy, despite his recent crimes."

"I did. Thank you. You may think it wrong of me, but I am oddly relieved. Not for my sake, but for his. For a man like him, months of his name being vilified in the newspapers, everyone dissecting the scandal and his trial, followed by a public execution . . ."

He shook his head, a grimace on his handsome face. "If he had to die, better to die quickly and with as little rumor-mongering as possible. This way, his daughter can put it behind her far sooner and try to go on with her life, which I know he would have wanted."

Isabelle was not sure a loving daughter would agree but understood the sentiment.

For a moment Mr. Booker held her gaze and seemed about to say something more, but he quickly shifted his attention to his brief bag and asked some question about the estate.

She believed the sentiments he'd expressed on Belle Island had been sincere at the time. But his warm, romantic words—about caring for her and hoping their story was just beginning—had been spoken in the midst of danger. After the danger passed, had he begun to regret them? As he had said, they had known each other less than a fortnight. And nothing in his surprising declaration could have been construed as an offer of marriage.

He had not committed himself. They were both free—free to go back to their relationship as lawyer and client, apparently. She felt bereft at the thought.

Suppressing a sigh, Isabelle answered his question, and he moved on to explaining the revised terms of Rose and Adair's marriage settlement. She considered hinting about their own relationship, but now that he was back in his beloved London, he'd likely decided that a future between them would be fraught with insurmountable obstacles. She had been relieved to spend time with Rose in London without paralyzing fear but had no desire to live there long-term. Belle Island was her home.

Sometimes she still shook her head in disbelief that Teddy had thought he could convince her to move to Edinburgh. Did Mr. Booker know her better? Had he realized it would be futile to ask her to live in London? If so, he was right. Isabelle sadly shook her head at the realization. As much as she admired Benjamin Booker, she probably would turn down such an offer.

So she accepted his retreat without pressing him. Nor did he raise any objection a few weeks later when she mentioned her plans to return to the island soon, having received a promising report from Arminda about the receding floodwaters. Perhaps it was for the best, she told herself. It would cause less heartache for all involved if she departed quickly. But her conscience smote her for the lie. Her heart ached already.

Leaving Rose in the care of Miss O'Toole and the Adairs, Isabelle returned to Belle Island by hired boat. She contracted builders to begin construction of a new bridge and workshop without delay, and then spent the rest of the summer and much of autumn overseeing those projects as well as working on repairs to the house and tenant cottages. A stonemason was able to repair the statue of the woman feeding swans. Despite her scars, she was still beautiful.

It was lonelier on the island without Teddy and Lotty, and without a bridge to connect her to Arminda and the other villagers who'd become such an important part of her life.

Carlota and Evan had married not long after the flood. The two had moved to Bristol, where he found work and she began singing again, but they promised to visit as soon as they could.

With Theodore Grant gone to Scotland, Riverton was without a doctor, and villagers had to travel to Maidenhead for medical care when the need arose. The empty office in Riverton was being advertised at a good rate, and Isabelle hoped to soon find another physician—or at least a surgeon or apothecary—willing to move to the area.

While the new bridge was being built, a resourceful Joe asked permission to use her old boat, which had been left in Riverton and damaged in the flood. With her blessing, he had it repaired using the wages he'd earned weaving baskets and started a ferry service to bring people to and from the island. He told Isabelle he'd read about such ferries in a book. She patted his shoulder and told him how proud of him she was, assuring him Mr. Booker would be impressed too when he heard about it. Isabelle wasn't certain she would be seeing much of Mr. Booker in the future, at least socially, but he was still her lawyer after all.

After allowing some time for the news of his trial and acquittal to die down, Mr. Adair and Rose finally named a new date for their wedding that had been postponed due to legal uncertainties. Her niece's every letter contained hints of Christopher's deepening character and love, and Isabelle began to believe the young couple would have a happy life together. They planned to marry just after Christmas. So in early December,

Isabelle returned to London to help her niece prepare for the big day.

On a mild December afternoon, Benjamin went to see his parents. For months, he had been so busy preparing cases for court that he had only been able to steal away from the office for brief visits. But now he had a whole afternoon free. He would not, in fact, be spending his days in the offices of Norris, Hardy, and Hunt for much longer. Mr. Hunt, as the last remaining principal, announced plans to dissolve the firm in the wake of recent events, though he had asked Benjamin to enter into a new partnership with him.

Ben hailed a hackney coach to take him as far as Westminster Abbey, then walked the rest of the way, enjoying the cool, crisp, sunny day. Fastening the buttons of his greatcoat against the breeze, he walked by St. Margaret's Workhouse and the Grey Coat Hospital School, and then followed Rochester Row past a tobacconist, butcher's shop, printer, and bookseller.

When he reached his boyhood home on Willow Street, he pushed open the apothecary shop door to familiar smells and the sound of the bell ringing in his arrival. He warmly greeted his mother and father, and the three exchanged news. Then, longing to be out-of-doors after so much time spent poring over law books, Benjamin volunteered to work in their physic garden, which raised his parents' eyebrows but no objections.

In the small plot behind the shop, warmed by afternoon sunshine absorbed by the garden's stone walls, Benjamin culled the last of the year's harvest and prepared the garden for winter, cutting back plants, and raking up the rows of spent stalks and wilted fronds to add to the compost heap. He gathered the few useful seedpods and roots he'd found into a basket and carried it inside. The basket reminded him of Isabelle, of course. Then again, most things did.

Inside the shop, he found his father handing a paper-wrapped parcel to a customer. The stocky man of about his own age turned at his entrance, revealing a stained apron.

The man's square face lit up. "Well, if it isn't Benny Booker. Haven't seen you in years."

Benjamin hesitated. "I am sorry, do I know you?"

"Don't remember me? Davey Paulson. A too-frequent patient of your father's. Always getting into some scrape or other as a lad. One time, I managed to cut off part of my finger with a cleaver."

Recognition dawned. "That I do remember. I am glad to see you well. A nasty injury, as I recall."

"No lasting damage." He lifted his hands, showing all ten digits. "You and Mr. Booker did a first-rate job saving the finger. My parents always said so."

Benjamin shook his head. "I did nothing."

"That's not how I remember it," Davey said. He laughed. "Then again, I *had* lost a great deal of blood."

Benjamin glanced at the butcher's blood-stained apron, the awful memory returning. "Still in the family business, I see."

"That I am. I have taken over the shop for my pa. Perhaps you heard?"

"I had not. Congratulations."

Davey nodded, his face cheerful if weary. "Well, I am no lawyer, but the missus and I do all right. Or we will, once we get our youngest over this colic. None of us have slept through the night all week." He lifted the parcel, thanked Mr. Booker, and took his leave.

As the door shut behind him, his father's parting smile faded. Gazing vaguely into memory, he said, "I'll never forget how we struggled to stop the bleeding. I was so afraid I'd fail and he would end up losing his finger or even his life."

Benjamin looked at him in surprise. "I didn't know you were afraid. You hid it well." Although his angry frustration with Benjamin at the time had been plain enough.

His father shrugged. "Doesn't do to show fear. Not to a patient and certainly not to his frantic parents."

Benjamin hesitated. Should he broach the long-avoided subject? He took a deep breath and said, "I've always regretted how I failed you that day, running off as I did. Truth is, I was terrified. Afraid he would die, and it would be my fault. I tried to put pressure on the wound as you said, but my hands were shaking so hard, I could not."

His father nodded, then frowned. "I handled things poorly, I know, snapping at you like that in my panic. Wasn't your fault. A boy your own age, a severed appendage, and so much blood . . . It is no wonder you were shaken by it."

Benjamin crossed his arms and managed a sheepish smile. "After that, I did everything I could to avoid being asked to assist again."

His father regarded him with interest. "Is that why? I wondered. It was about the same time you began complaining of dizziness. I admit I sometimes thought it was an excuse to get out of work."

"No, sir. In fact, vertigo still plagues me now and again, at the most inconvenient times."

"Then forgive me for doubting you."

"Happily. And I hope you will forgive me. You were right about Mr. Hardy. I'm sorry I did not heed your warnings . . . and for so much more."

"It's all forgiven. All in the past."

His father considered, then said, "I hope you give me grandchildren one day so I can have a second chance to do better. And if you experience the challenges of raising adolescents yourself, you may be more understanding."

He grinned wryly, and Benjamin returned the gesture. He wondered if he would ever have the chance to be a father. He hoped so too.

His father added, "In the meantime, we shall have to try harder to find a remedy to help you."

"Thank you, sir."

But somehow, Benjamin felt better already.

Later, he sat with his mother in the family's private quarters behind the shop—kitchen on this floor, sitting room and bed-chambers above. Together they lingered over cups of tea and savory rosemary scones.

His father was busy in his surgery with a patient. Benjamin was glad they were reconciled but also grateful for some time alone with his mother, for a chance to finally unburden his soul to the kind woman who knew him so well.

He had previously given his parents a brief account of what had transpired on Belle Island as it related to Mr. Norris and Mr. Hardy. Now his mother listened in patient silence as he described everything else that had happened, though he said nothing outright about his feelings for Isabelle.

When he finished, his mother studied his face and said, "You love this Miss Wilder, don't you?"

Benjamin looked at her in surprise. How had he given himself away?

He faltered, "I . . . do care for her, yes. Though I suppose that is foolish to say, after so short an acquaintance."

She spread expressive hands. "A brief time span, perhaps, but what an eventful one! You two have been through so much: working together, learning to trust one another, facing danger

371

and almost losing your lives. I'd say you know each other better than many couples who have been acquainted far longer. Does she admire you too?"

Looking away from his mother's probing gaze, he fiddled with a stray rosemary needle among the crumbs on his plate. "Even if she did, I have little to offer her."

"What are you talking about? Mr. Hunt has offered you a new partnership."

"True, but I live here in London in a small apartment while Miss Wilder lives on Belle Island. You should see the place, Mamma. It's beautiful."

His mother tilted her head to one side. "Perhaps I shall see it one day. But right now, I am more interested in your Miss Wilder."

"She is not *my* Miss Wilder," Benjamin replied, feeling his neck heat.

His mother sent him a knowing grin. "Maybe not yet."

Ben looked down into his teacup but saw only Isabelle's face. "She is pretty and intelligent and capable. She cares about people. Not only her family but her tenants and neighbors, especially those less fortunate. She is everything a gentlewoman should be, with no airs or vanity. She is a real lady, Mamma. I am not good enough for her."

She pressed his hand. "Don't make that decision for her. That is for her to say. Where is she now?"

"She has recently returned to Town."

When Benjamin had delivered the final copy of the new marriage settlement to Mr. Adair, the young man mentioned Miss Wilder's arrival with apparent pleasure. Benjamin had been surprised to hear it. To come to London after literally being swept off the island was one thing, but to return by her own volition? He was impressed anew by Isabelle's courage. Though to his mother he said only, "She is here helping her niece prepare for her upcoming wedding."

"Will we get to meet her?"

"Oh, I don't know about that, Mamma. I would not get your hopes up."

She smiled. "Too late."

twenty-seven

Isabelle thanked God that she was able to be with her niece in London, to help with plans and preparations and soon to attend the wedding itself, when she had long feared she would be unable to do so. She was even growing fond of Mr. Adair.

Isabelle had not seen Mr. Booker since her return. Now that the court cases were behind them, there had been no reason for him to call. She missed him but did not allow herself to dwell on her disappointment. She wanted nothing to dampen Rose's happiness.

Together they selected wedding clothes for Rose, including gowns and other finery. Their shopping trips to warehouses, dressmakers, and milliners took them to several areas of London Isabelle was less familiar with. Thankfully the new coachman and groom were resourceful fellows.

Seated with her niece in their carriage, amid stacks of parcels and bandboxes, Isabelle looked out at landmarks and street names as they passed. When she saw the Grey Coat Hospital, she said, "Do you know . . . Mr. Booker mentioned his parents live near here."

"Oh?" Rose looked out with interest. "Shall we stop and see his father's shop?"

"On what pretense?" Isabelle asked.

"Need we a pretense?"

"Well, I would not want Mr. Booker to hear we came poking around."

"He would be glad you showed an interest in his family. I know I am. Besides, I am all out of, em, liquorice lozenges."

Isabelle raised an eyebrow. "Liquorice?"

"Purely for medicinal purposes, I assure you." Rose sniffed daintily. "I feel a slight cold coming on."

"I see." Knowing her niece was hoaxing her—and fond of liquorice—she did not worry. Rose looked perfectly healthy to her. And she supposed it would do no harm to stop by. An apothecary shop was open to everyone, after all.

A smart rap to the roof with her umbrella brought the carriage to a stop. She instructed the groom to take them to Booker's apothecary shop next. The young man stopped to ask a passerby the way, then directed the coachman down Rochester Row to Willow Street.

Reaching the address, the two women alighted, Rose all eagerness, and Isabelle feeling unaccountably nervous.

The many-paned bowed window looked freshly painted and in good repair. As they approached, Isabelle read the rather new-looking sign with interest:

Thomas Booker
Surgeon-Apothecary
Member of the Royal College of Surgeons
Patients Seen in Office or at Home
Proprietary and Patent Medicines Sold

For a few moments they stood at the window, peering at the display of colorful jars and ready-made remedies. Isabelle's nerves tingled with anticipation. Should they do this, or was it too forward of her? What would she say to his father?

When Isabelle hesitated, Rose pushed open the door and vigorously gestured her inside. Taking a deep breath, Isabelle complied.

The shop bell jingled, and strong aromas greeted her, exotic and earthy. She looked up and noticed the source—strings of herbs hanging in bunches from the ceiling beams.

Isabelle glanced around the orderly premises with approval. Shelves of neatly arranged pottery jars lined two walls. Below these were rows of small, knobbed drawers. A tidy counter held pill tiles, mortars and pestles, scales, and other tools of the trade. To the right was a closed door marked *Surgery*. To the rear, a discreet unmarked door—to the family's private quarters, she guessed.

That door opened and her stomach lurched. She steeled herself to meet his stern father . . . but instead, Benjamin Booker himself stepped out. She stifled a gasp. He looked as stunned to see her, and her cheeks instantly heated. Oh, why had she allowed Rose to persuade her to come inside?

For a moment he stood speechless, then quickly recovered. "Miss Wilder. Miss Lawrence. Welcome. What a pleasant surprise. Mr. Adair mentioned your return. How goes your time in London?"

She answered mechanically, all the while longing to know what was passing in his mind and if there was any chance he still cared for her.

He politely congratulated Rose on her upcoming wedding.

Rose smiled. "Thank you. We are so grateful for all you've done for us."

"You are very welcome."

Not only had Mr. Adair agreed to the new marriage settlement he had drawn up, but his parents were so appreciative of Benjamin's legal work on behalf of their son that they'd recommended him to their many acquaintances.

Rose added, "I do hope you will come to our wedding?"

"I would be honored. Thank you."

He tucked his hands behind his back and rocked awkwardly on his heels. "So . . . what brings you here? I hope you are not poorly. Surely there are apothecaries nearer St. James's."

Isabelle faltered, "No, we simply . . . That is, we did not expect to see you here. I thought you would be in the law office today or we would not have intruded."

He lifted one brow, a touch of vulnerable humor in his eyes. "No? I am sorry to hear it. For I am happy to see you. I had intended to pay a call on you tomorrow."

"Oh, well, I . . . Good." She looked away from his too-direct gaze.

A woman in her midfifties stepped out from the same door. His mother, she guessed, noticing the similar dark eyes and wavy hair.

Seeing her, Benjamin said, "Will you allow me to introduce my mother to your acquaintance?"

"Of course."

"Miss Wilder, Miss Lawrence, please allow me to present Mrs. Booker."

Isabelle and Rose curtsied, then Isabelle impulsively advanced, hand extended. "I am so happy to meet you, Mrs. Booker. Your son has spoken so highly of you."

"Has he indeed? I am all astonishment." Her intelligent eyes glinted playfully, and she looked from one to the other with a warm, slightly crooked smile.

"And I can return the compliment," Mrs. Booker added, "as he was just praising you in my hearing."

Isabelle knew not what to say to that, but Rose was not so shy. "Was he indeed?"

Benjamin looked down, embarrassed. "Mamma . . ."

"Do tell, Mrs. Booker!" Rose urged, sending Benjamin a teasing grin.

Mrs. Booker gestured to the door behind her. "Come up to our humble sitting room, ladies, and I shall tell all."

Benjamin groaned. "I am doomed."

"Yes, my dear, you are," his mother said with a wink, thoroughly pleased with herself. She linked arms with Isabelle and led the way.

Isabelle thought his mother delightful and liked her immediately. Before they departed that day, Mrs. Booker extracted a promise from Isabelle to join them for Christmas dinner. Knowing Rose would be busy with the Adairs, Isabelle agreed.

She knew it was probably foolish to spend time with Benjamin and his family. It would be wiser to guard her heart. He had been offered a partnership here in London, and she was going home to Belle Island after the wedding. But she could not resist savoring this time with him and planned to store away sweet memories for lonely nights to come.

On Christmas, Isabelle returned and met the rest of the Booker family. His father was somewhat serious and reserved, but he made an effort to be polite and to include her in conversation, asking well-thought-out questions about her home and family. His brother, Reuben, joined them for dinner too. She instantly saw the resemblance between the two. Both tall and lanky with dark wavy hair. But for her part, she thought Benjamin far more handsome.

At first, Reuben struck her as rather proud and aloof, but as the evening progressed, he warmed to her and became more talkative. The two brothers roasted one another a bit, as brothers will do, but amid the teasing and barbs, she saw mutual admiration and fondness between them. It made her miss her own brother and sister. And she wondered what it would be like to become a member of such a family.

After dinner, Benjamin escorted her home and said he would see her at the wedding. But he said little else, leaving Isabelle to wonder what he was thinking.

On the appointed day, Mr. Booker, as good as his word, showed up at the church to witness the solemnization of Rose and Christopher's marriage. He looked handsome and masculine in a new blue tailcoat, his hair freshly cut.

After the service, he came to the house in St. James's Square for the wedding breakfast. He wished the bride and groom happy, then approached Isabelle. He bowed over her hand and said in a low voice, "You are to be congratulated as well, Miss Wilder. I know you hoped this wedding would take place on Belle Island or at least in Riverton, but it was beautiful, even here in London. Best of all, you are here to share Rose's joy, as you've long wished." He added with a lopsided grin, "Does it make me sound ancient to say that I am proud of you?"

Isabelle felt tears prick her eyes but blinked them back. She pressed his hand and smiled at him. "Thank you."

He took his leave shortly after that. Isabelle was sad to see him go but too busy greeting guests and making sure they had plenty to eat and drink to try to prevent him. And really, she told herself, why delay the inevitable?

After the celebration was over and Rose and Mr. Adair set

out on their wedding trip, Isabelle returned to Belle Island. She again made her home there but planned to return to London to visit Rose now and again after the couple settled down to live in St. James's Square. Perhaps she might see Mr. Booker and his family on occasion as well.

In the meantime, she kept herself busy overseeing the few remaining repairs, answering questions that arose, and watching the progress and eventual completion of the new workshop and bridge with satisfaction.

That March, against all dire predictions about the osier beds after such a flood, they had an excellent harvest.

With the coming of spring, new life returned to Belle Island, and Isabelle Wilder was filled with hope for the future.

CHAPTER
twenty-eight

On a spring day, the words again echoed through Benjamin's mind, *Go to Belle Island, and quickly. . . .* But this time, the voice urging him was his own. His mission was far different. The desire to travel there more sincere. The anticipation sweeter.

Once more, Benjamin Booker found himself bounced, jostled, and thoroughly shaken on the coach journey into Berkshire. Thankfully, he was now armed with ginger lozenges for his stomach and a tonic of cowslip, blessed thistle, and feverfew his father had decocted for his vertigo. He'd also given Benjamin a strong dose of encouragement for what he was about to do.

As the miles passed, Benjamin popped another ginger lozenge into his mouth and recalled with fondness the Christmas Isabelle had spent with his family. Even proud Reuben had seemed to approve of her, and his parents certainly did. In her turn, Isabelle had joined in the family conversations and good-natured teasing with warmth and ease. It was the happiest Christmas of his memory.

Arriving at Maidenhead's Bear Inn, Benjamin hired a driver—the same young man with his rickety gig who had delivered him to Belle Island on his first visit almost a year ago. If Ben wasn't so eager to see Isabelle again, he probably would have walked the few miles instead.

Finally, they reached the outskirts of Riverton. The hamlet curved around the riverbank, like a gently angled arm, beckoning him closer. What an inviting picture it made on this sunny spring day, with its jumble of shops and cottages brightened by flowerpots and blooming gardens. The river, he saw, had returned to its banks and flowed peacefully past, as though in apology for its former violence. The ducks and swans had returned, the fishermen and netmakers. And so had he.

Benjamin surveyed the new arched bridge spanning the sparkling water and thought it a marked improvement over the old one.

"Set me down here, if you would," Benjamin told the driver, foot tapping against the floorboards. Now that he was close, his heart beat uncomfortably hard.

He paid the driver and turned to look at the island. No fog shrouded it this time. He savored the sight of the green lawn and budding trees, and the tall stone manor house swathed in flowering vines.

Movement caught his eye. Across the bridge, a figure appeared—a familiar female figure in a long red coat, a deep bonnet framing her lovely face. Seeing him, Isabelle waved, a welcoming smile splitting her mouth.

Walking over the bridge, Benjamin took stock of its solid strength. On the other side, Isabelle hesitated when she reached the bridge but then stepped up and started across.

When he'd first come to Belle Island, out of his element and already longing for the comforts of London, some inner sense or God's Spirit had told him his life would never be the same again. It turned out to be true. He thanked God for all that had transpired since he'd become acquainted with this place . . . and with this woman.

They met in the middle of the arched structure. "The new bridge turned out well," he said.

"Thank you. I think so too." She hesitated. "I hope some new legal tangle has not arisen. You did not explain when you wrote."

He swallowed. "No, I . . . Miss Wilder, Isabelle, I have come to ask you a question."

"Oh?" She blinked, a dozen emotions crossing her countenance.

"How would you feel about marrying a country lawyer?"

Her mouth twitched with humor. "That depends. Do I know him?"

"Not as well as I would like." Eager to bridge the space between them, he stepped nearer and took her hands in his.

She stared up at him, wonder and hope and questions written on her face. "What about the partnership with Mr. Hunt?"

"I thanked him but turned it down. An attorney in Maidenhead has also expressed interest. Or I may practice on my own, in Riverton."

"But you love London."

He shook his head, his gaze traveling over her brow, her cheeks, her lips. "I like London. I love you."

For a few heartbeats, she simply stared at him. Then she rose on tiptoes and kissed him warmly on the lips. She pulled back, smiling up at him, her eyes brimming with tears. "Then my answer is yes."

Sweet pleasure filled him, and he felt his heart crack open, like the clicking of a lock. He cupped the sides of her face and leaned near, pressing his lips to hers softly, then angling his head to deepen the kiss. Finally he straightened and pulled her close, savoring her nearness and her answer and her touch.

A warm flush spread over him, as though he'd sipped orange wine. He felt light-headed, even a little dizzy, but this time vertigo had nothing to do with it.

Two months later, the banns had been read, the ring purchased, and the wedding breakfast planned. Rose and Mr. Adair arrived early to help with preparations.

The nuptials would not take place in London, nor in the chapel in the Wilder house. They had amicably agreed to marry in St. Raymond's in Riverton. The Bookers were happy to travel to Berkshire, and the small family chapel was not large enough for the many local friends and neighbors who wished to celebrate with them. They would, however, host the wedding breakfast on Belle Island.

The happily anticipated day finally arrived. A fine, sunny summer morning.

Rose, as Isabelle's attendant, had chosen an elegant dress of ivory satin for the occasion, and Miss O'Toole wove flowers into her hair. Isabelle wore a new gown of palest blue silk and a veiled cap. O'Toole offered to curl and arrange her hair as well for the special day, and Isabelle gratefully accepted. She missed Lotty but was glad she and Evan were happily married.

Someone knocked on the bedchamber door and poked her head into the room. "Are old friends welcome?"

Seeing Carlota's mischievous smile, Isabelle gasped in delight. "Definitely!"

She rose and embraced her. "What a happy surprise."

"I could not miss my chance to see you as a bride at last. I hoped to arrive earlier to help you dress, but ooh la la, your hair is perfection already. Miss O'Toole, you are a genius!"

The elderly matron grinned and blushed like a schoolgirl.

"May I help with your veil, and perhaps a bit of rouge?" Carlota asked. "For old times' sake?"

Isabelle pressed her hand. "Of course."

Carlota deftly applied a touch of rouge to Isabelle's lips and cheeks, then helped pin the veil to the cap and arranged it on her head just so.

She stepped back and surveyed her handiwork. "*Novia bonita*," she concluded. "Now, the bride is ready for her wedding day . . . and night." She winked, and Isabelle found herself grinning and blushing more than O'Toole.

Promising to see her after the ceremony, Carlota slipped out to rejoin Evan and walk with him to the church.

When they were both dressed and ready, Rose took Isabelle's hands and beamed at her in affection and pleasure. "Lotty is right. How beautiful you are, Aunt Belle."

"As are you!" Isabelle touched her face. "I have never seen you look lovelier. You are absolutely glowing."

"Thank you. That is as it should be." Rose's eyes sparkled. "For I am expecting a child. It's early days yet, but is that not good news?"

Isabelle's heart squeezed, and she drew in a long breath. "Very good news."

She embraced her beloved niece and whispered, "Your mother and father would be so proud of you."

When she released her, tears brightened Rose's eyes. "I miss them, but I am ever so thankful to have you."

Isabelle kissed her cheek. "My sentiments exactly."

Together, she and Rose walked from the house toward the bridge, arm in arm. Reaching it, Isabelle hesitated, as she always did. But today, her pulse pounded not from fear but from excitement as she anticipated the ceremony, the marriage, and the life to come.

Rose studied her profile and asked tentatively, "All right?"

"Yes. Better than all right." Isabelle smiled and the two walked on, the new bridge reassuringly solid beneath their feet.

She recalled again the cherished memory of happily crossing the old bridge with her loved ones to attend Grace's wedding at the village church, surrounded by friends and neighbors, and afterward welcoming everyone back to Belle Island for a joy-filled wedding breakfast. For so long Isabelle had hoped to relive that memory. And now she would. The bride in her dream had changed, but the reality was even better than she'd imagined.

When they arrived at the church, there was Benjamin, handsome in a dark suit of clothes and snowy white cravat. He stared in wonder as she joined him at the altar, love and admiration shining in his deep brown eyes. Isabelle had never felt prettier or more cherished.

The service was warmly officiated by Mr. Truelock, who had known Isabelle all her life. His daughter, Arminda, played the new organ, filling the church with music along with friends and loved ones.

After the ceremony, Isabelle and Benjamin walked back over the new bridge together, hand in hand. There on the veranda, near the place they had first met, the new-wed couple shared a lingering kiss while they awaited the others.

The guests—led by village girls holding a large arch of flowers and ribbons—began the procession over the bridge, eager for the festive banquet being held on the veranda of the Wilder house. There, a generous buffet meal awaited, prepared by Mrs. Philpotts and the kitchen maids, including a large bride cake decorated with sugar icing and flowers.

Then came the servants and tenants who'd attended the wedding, Mr. Linton and the weavers, the Faringdons, and many other friends and neighbors. And finally came three couples arm in arm—Rose and Mr. Adair, Evan and Lotty, and Mr. and Mrs. Booker—followed by Reuben Booker, Mr. Hunt, and the Truelocks bringing up the rear. Isabelle was delighted to see Mr. Christie offer Arminda his arm. The vicar's daughter lay her gloved hand on his with a dimpled smile.

What pleasure to see so many dear, happy faces walk over to Belle Island to join the celebration. Yes, Isabelle wished her parents, brother, and sister might have lived to see this day, but she refused to let their absence spoil her joy. God had given her a new family in the Bookers as well as her staff and tenants.

Although they were surrounded by dozens of people, Benjamin could not keep his eyes from one person in particular. His bride. His Isabelle. She had never looked more beautiful, and he had never been happier or more thankful.

They sat side by side among those feasting together at long tables set up on the veranda, but Benjamin had little appetite for food. He felt full already, his heart, his stomach, his life. He ate a few bites of this and that without really tasting anything, stopping often to acknowledge a well-wisher or accept congratulations, or to squeeze Isabelle's hand.

After they had eaten, he and Isabelle rose and crossed the veranda together to speak to his parents.

Benjamin leaned down and kissed his mother's plump cheek. "We are so pleased you are here with us. Thank you for coming."

She beamed her ready, crooked smile, eyes warm. "We would not have missed it for the world."

His father rose and awkwardly patted Benjamin's shoulder, the most affection he recalled receiving from him in years, and for a moment, he could not speak over the emotion clogging his throat.

"Congratulations, son," his father said, then he turned to Isabelle and pressed her hand. "Welcome to the family, my dear."

Isabelle smiled from one to the other. "Thank you. I could not be happier about that."

His father looked around at the grand house and idyllic island setting. "So this is your new home. . . . I can see why you like it here." He returned his gaze to Benjamin and said, "A country lawyer, ay?" He nodded his approval. "It suits you."

"Thank you, sir."

Isabelle said, "You know, there is a medical office for let in the village. If you ever decide to leave London, you would be more than welcome to move your practice here."

Mrs. Booker and her husband exchanged looks of surprise and interest. She said, "That is very kind of you, my dear."

"We shall give it some thought," he added.

Then Mrs. Booker asked, "Will you be taking a wedding trip?"

"Yes." Benjamin pressed Isabelle's fingers and looked into her eyes. "A short one."

They were planning to travel to the south coast to spend a few romantic days in Weymouth. They would start small, until Isabelle's comfort with travel increased.

The island remained the place she most wanted to be, and he guessed Isabelle would always be a homebody.

Anxiety still visited her from time to time, but she no longer let it trap her. He was proud of her for taking small steps—first London, and soon Weymouth. But deep down he knew that after any journey, her favorite sight to see would always be the bridge to Belle Island. And now it was his as well.

Author's Note

I hope you enjoyed your visit to Belle Island. Some eighty islands (up to one hundred eighty, if you count all the smaller islets, aits, and eyots) dot the River Thames (pronounced *temz*) as it follows its serpentine course from its source in the idyllic Cotswolds eastward for over two hundred miles, passing many picturesque villages and eventually bisecting London before flowing out into the North Sea. I enjoyed researching several of these tiny, fascinating places with intriguing names like Eel Pie Island, Pharaoh's Island, Magna Carta Island, Monkey Island, Frog Mill Ait, and many more.

Some of these islands have fine homes on them, others are uninhabited. Some are reachable by bridge, others only by boat. Some are susceptible to flooding, and many have colorful histories.

Belle Island is a fictional place, but it is something of a composite of the islands I researched. Physically, it resembles Ray Mill Island near Maidenhead, Berkshire, which I've had the pleasure of visiting a few times. Named after the Ray family, who once operated a flour mill there, the island is now a public park with lovely gardens and wooded paths. While there, my husband and I watched boats passing through adjacent Boulter's Lock and walked around the island's scenic shoreline. Later we sat on a bench, watching families picnicking on the grounds and regal swans and playful ducks frolicking on the water.

We noticed a memorial plaque on the bench in honor of a man named Roy Francis Howton with the description "He loved this island." This inspired the name of the old gardener and his wife in the novel. If you would like to read more about these islands yourself, I would recommend the book *Eyots and Aits: Islands of the River Thames* by Miranda Vickers.

I also enjoyed learning a little about willow basketry but confess to not being an expert in the least (assuming you don't count teaching basket weaving to 4-H campers while in college), so I hope aficionados will forgive any errors. My husband and I did enjoy visiting the Museum of English Rural Life in Reading and perusing their collection of baskets and other fine displays, which helped with my research.

Speaking of research, the opening courtroom scene is based loosely on an actual trial transcript from the Old Bailey, though the names have been changed. While reading about London watermen and lightermen, I ran across the name Enos Redknap, a man with likely smuggling connections, and thought the name ideal for this book. But beyond that, my character of Enos Redknap is fictional. The real Enos was prosecuted for stealing coal on the Thames in 1815, but he absconded to avoid capture.

Now for some acknowledgments.

I would like to thank my husband, who travels with me, tirelessly taking research photographs, and who also listened to many audiobook mysteries with me for inspiration while writing this book.

Thanks also goes to author friends Becky Wade, Katie Ganshert, Jody Hedlund, Karen Witemeyer, and Courtney Walsh, who helped brainstorm ideas for the novel on a retreat in Branson.

I am indebted to my first reader, Cari Weber, for her valuable input; my agent, Wendy Lawton; and my editors, Karen Schurrer and Raela Schoenherr, along with everyone else at Bethany House who helped hone and promote this book.

Gratitude also goes to Anna Paulson and Josie Kawlewski for help with research into Bow Street runners and legal procedures of the day. Anna also reviewed the manuscript and gave me valuable ideas, as did my dear writing friend Michelle Griep. You are both so talented.

I would also like to express my appreciation to attorney and Jane Austen scholar James Nagle for reviewing the legal aspects of this novel for me. Thanks, Jim. Any remaining errors are mine.

Finally, I would like to thank you for reading this book. I appreciate you. If you would like to make my day, please write a review online, but remember please, no spoilers!

DISCUSSION

Questions

1. How did the book's opening epigraphs (quotes) relate to later happenings in the book?

2. This novel is set in a time before the establishment of a centralized police force as we know it today. What did you learn about criminal justice in early nineteenth-century England that surprised you?

3. Did you find the book's island setting appealing? How so?

4. How did loss and grief affect Isabelle? How have you dealt with similar losses in your own life?

5. Benjamin has grown up believing his father preferred his older brother and still feels lesser in his parents' view. Is this a struggle you can relate to? If you are a parent, have your children ever accused you of preferential treatment of a sibling?

6. Isabelle's fears keep her trapped on the island (becoming what we might today call agoraphobic), and

Benjamin suffers from vertigo. Did you appreciate reading about characters with these issues? Have you known anyone who struggles with something similar? How has modern medicine offered solutions not available two hundred years ago?

7. What was your reaction when Dr. Theodore Grant's actions came to light? Do you think he should have faced harsher consequences, or were you satisfied with the outcome?

8. Isabelle struggles to forgive Mr. Grant, and Benjamin carries a similar resentment against his father. Have you ever been in a similar situation? What are the benefits of forgiving someone who has caused you pain?

9. How early did you figure out the identity of the killer? Did you like the mystery element of this novel?

10. Isabelle's worries render her unable to trust God with the lives of those she loves. Can you relate to this at all? How easy or difficult is it for you to "not be anxious about anything, but in every situation, by prayer and petition, with thanksgiving, present your requests to God" (Philippians 4:6 NIV)?

Julie Klassen loves all things Jane—*Jane Eyre* and Jane Austen. Her books have sold over a million copies, and she is a three-time recipient of the Christy Award for Historical Romance. *The Secret of Pembrooke Park* was honored with the Minnesota Book Award for Genre Fiction. Julie has also won the Midwest Book Award and Christian Retailing's BEST Award, and has been a finalist in the RITA and Carol Awards. A graduate of the University of Illinois, Julie worked in publishing for sixteen years and now writes full-time. Julie and her husband have two sons and live in a suburb of St. Paul, Minnesota. For more information, you can follow her on Facebook or visit www.julie klassen.com.

Sign Up for Julie's Newsletter!

Keep up to date with Julie's news on book releases and events by signing up for her email list at julieklassen.com.

Also from Julie Klassen

Visit the idyllic English village of Ivy Hill, where friendships thrive, romance blossoms, and mysteries await. As the villagers of Ivy Hill search for answers about the past and hope for the future, might they find love along the way?

TALES FROM IVY HILL: *The Innkeeper of Ivy Hill, The Ladies of Ivy Cottage, The Bride of Ivy Green*